THE REMORSEFUL DAY
&
THE WENCH IS DEAD

The Inspector Morse Novels

LAST BUS TO WOODSTOCK
LAST SEEN WEARING
THE SILENT WORLD OF NICHOLAS QUINN
SERVICE OF ALL THE DEAD
THE DEAD OF JERICHO
THE RIDDLE OF THE THIRD MILE
THE SECRET OF ANNEXE 3
THE JEWEL THAT WAS OURS
THE WAY THROUGH THE WOODS
THE DAUGHTERS OF CAIN
DEATH IS NOW MY NEIGHBOUR

Also available in Pan Books

MORSE'S GREATEST MYSTERY AND OTHER STORIES
THE FIRST INSPECTOR MORSE OMNIBUS
THE SECOND INSPECTOR MORSE OMNIBUS
THE THIRD INSPECTOR MORSE OMNIBUS
THE FOURTH INSPECTOR MORSE OMNIBUS

COLIN DEXTER

THE REMORSEFUL DAY & THE WENCH IS DEAD

PAN BOOKS

The Remorseful Day first published 1999 by Macmillan
First published 2000 by Pan Books
The Wench is Dead first published 1989 by Macmillan.
First published 1990 by Pan Books

This omnibus edition published 2004 by Pan Books
an imprint of Pan Macmillan Ltd
Pan Macmillan, 20 New Wharf Road, London N1 9RR
Basingstoke and Oxford
Associated companies throughout the world
www.panmacmillan.com

ISBN 0 330 43253 2

1 3 5 7 9 8 6 4 2

A CIP catalogue record for this book is available from the British Library.

Typeset by SetSystems Ltd, Saffron Walden, Essex
Printed and bound in Great Britain by
Mackays of Chatham plc, Chatham,Kent

THE REMORSEFUL DAY

For

George, Hilary, Maria, and Beverley

(Please note the Oxford comma)

Acknowledgements

My special thanks are due, imprimis to Terry Benczik from New Jersey, for sending me so many apposite quotations; to Cyndi Cook from Hawaii, for singing to me as I wrote these chapters; to Allison Dexter, for sharing with me her expertise on coronary care; to Eddie Andrews, one of my former pupils, for initiating me (at last!) into some of the mysteries of the SOCOs; and to Chris Burt, producer of so many Morse episodes on TV, for his constant support and encouragement.

The author and publishers wish to thank the following who have kindly given permission for use of copyright materials:

Extracts from *More Poems* XLI, *More Poems* XVI and *A Shropshire Lad* by A. E. Housman are reproduced by permission of The Society of Authors as the literary representative of the Estate of A. E. Housman.

Extract from *On the Dole in Darlington* by David Mackenzie reproduced by permission of the author.

Extract from translation of *An Die Musik* by Basil Swift reproduced by permission of the author.

Ensanguining the skies
How heavily it dies
  Into the west away;
Past touch and sight and sound
Not further to be found
How hopeless under ground
  Falls the remorseful day.

(A. E. Housman,
More Poems, XVI)

When I wrote my 1997 letter I thought I had little to look forward to in 1998, but it turns out that I was stupidly optimistic

(David Mackenzie,
On the Dole in Darlington)

PROLEGOMENON

As o'er me now thou lean'st thy breast,
With launder'd bodice crisply pressed,
Lief I'd prolong my grievous ill –
Wert thou my guardian angel still
(Edmund Raikes, 1537–65,
The Nurse)

'SO I OFTEN hook my foot over the side of the mattress.'

'You *what*?'

'Sort of anchors me to my side of the bed.'

'Double bed?'

'Not unknown is it, for a married couple? People can share the same bed but not the same thoughts – old Chinese saying.'

'Still makes me jealous.'

'Idiot!'

'Everybody gets a bit jealous sometimes.'

'Not everybody.'

'Not you, nurse?'

'I've just learned not to show it, that's all. And it's none of your business in any case.'

'Sorry.'

'How I hate men who say "sorry"!'

'I promise not to say it again, miss.'

'And will you promise me something else? To

be a bit more honest with yourself – and with me?'

'Scout's honour!'

'I can't believe you were ever in the Scouts.'

'Well, no, but . . .'

'Shall I test you?'

'Test me?'

'Would you like me to jump into bed with you *now*?'

'Yes!'

'You're quick on the buzzer.'

'Next question?'

'Do you think *I'd* like to jump into bed with *you*?'

'I'd like to think so.'

'What about the other patients?'

'You could draw the curtains.'

'What excuse . . . ?'

'You could always take my blood pressure.'

'*Again?*'

'Why not?'

'We know all about your blood pressure. High – very high – especially when I'm around.'

'It's those black stockings of yours.'

'You're a stocking-tops man!'

'Nice word, isn't it – stocking-tops?'

'If only you weren't stuck in this bloody ward!'

'I can always discharge myself.'

'Not a wise move, good sir – not in your case.'

'What time are you off duty?'

'Half-eight.'

'What'll you do then?'

'Off home. I'm expecting a phone call.'

'You're trying to make me jealous again.'

'After that, I suppose I'll just poke the thingummy, you know, around the four channels.'

'Five, now.'

'We don't get the new one.'

'What about Sky?'

'In *our* village, satellite dishes are most *definitely* discouraged.'

'You could always take a video home.'

'No need. We've got lots of videos. You should see some of them – you know, the sex ones.'

'You watch that sort of thing?'

'When I'm in the mood.'

'When's that?'

'Most of the time.'

'And even if you aren't in the mood?'

'Oh yes! They soon turn anybody on. Haven't you seen some of these Amsterdam videos? All sorts of bizarre things they get up to.'

'I haven't seen them, no.'

'Would you like to?'

'I'm not quite sure I would, no.'

'Not even if you watched them with me?'

'Please, nurse, am I allowed to change my mind?'

'We could arrange a joint viewing.'

'How – how bizarre's bizarre?'

'Well, in one of 'em there's this woman – about my age – lovely figure – wrists tied to the top of the four-poster bed – ankles tied to the bottom . . .'

'Go on.'

'Well, there's these two young studs – one black, one white – '

'No racial discrimination, then?'

' – and they just take turns, you know.'

'Raping her . . .'

'You're so *naive*, aren't you? She wouldn't have *been* in the bloody video, would she, if she didn't want to be? There *are* some people like her, you know. The only real sexual thrill they get is from some sort of submission – you know, that sort of thing.'

'Odd sort of women!'

'Odd? Unusual, perhaps, but . . .'

'How come you know so much about this?'

'When we were in Amsterdam, they invited me to do some porno-filming. Frank didn't mind. They made a pretty good offer.'

'So you negotiated a fee?'

'Hold on! I only said this particular woman was *about* my age – '

' – and had a lovely figure.'

'Would you like to see if it *was* me?'

'One condition.'

'What's that?'

'If I come, you mustn't hook your foot over the side of the mattress.'

'Not much danger of that.'

'Stay with me a bit longer!'

'No. You're not my only patient, and some of these poor devils'll be here long after *you've* gone.'

'Will you come and give me a chaste little kiss before you go off duty?'

'No. I'm shooting straight back to Lower Swinstead. I told you: I'm expecting a phone call.'

'From . . . your husband?'

'You must be kidding! Frank's in Switzerland for a few days. He's far too mean to call me from there – even on the cheap rates.'

'Another man in your life?'

'Jesus! You don't take me for a dyke, do you?'

'You're an amazing girl.'

'Girl? I'll be forty-eight this Thursday.'

'Can I take you out? Make a birthday fuss of you?'

'No chance. According to your notes, you're going to be in at least till the end of the week.'

'You know, in a way, I wish I *could* stay in. Indefinitely.'

'Well, I promise one thing: as soon as you're out, I'll be in touch.'

'Please! If you can.'

'And you'll come and see me?'

'If you invite me.'

'I'm inviting you now.'

Chapter One

You holy Art, when all my hope is shaken,
And through life's raging tempest I am drawn,
You make my heart with warmest love to waken,
As if into a better world reborn

(From *An Die Musik*, translated by Basil Swift)

Apart (of course) from Wagner, apart from Mozart's compositions for the clarinet, Schubert was one of the select composers who could occasionally transport him to the frontier of tears. And it was Schubert's turn in the early evening of Wednesday, 15 July 1998, when – *The Archers* over – a bedroom-slippered Chief Inspector Morse was to be found in his North Oxford bachelor flat, sitting at his ease in Zion and listening to a Lieder recital on Radio 3, an amply filled tumbler of pale Glenfiddich beside him. And why not? He was on a few days' furlough that had so far proved quite unexpectedly pleasurable.

Morse had never enrolled in the itchy-footed regiment of truly adventurous souls, feeling (as he did) little temptation to explore the remoter corners even of his native land; and this, principally, because he could now imagine few if any places closer to his heart than Oxford – the city which, though not his natural mother, had for so many years performed the duties of a loving foster-parent. As for foreign travel, long faded were his boyhood dreams that roamed the sands round Samarkand; and a lifelong pterophobia still precluded any airline bookings to Bayreuth, Salzburg, Vienna – the trio of cities he sometimes thought he ought to see.

Vienna . . .

The city Schubert had so rarely left; the city in which he'd gained so little recognition; where he'd died of typhoid fever – only thirty-one.

Not much of an innings, was it – thirty-one?

Morse leaned back, listened, and looked semi-contentedly through the french window. In *The Ballad of Reading Gaol*, Oscar Wilde had spoken of that little tent of blue that prisoners call the sky; and Morse now contemplated that little tent of green that owners of North Oxford flats are wont to call the garden. Flowers had always meant something to Morse, even from his schooldays. Yet in truth it was more the nomenclature of the several species, and their context in the works of the great poets, that had compelled his imagination: fast-fading violets, the globèd peonies, the fields of asphodel . . . Indeed Morse was fully aware of the etymology and the mythological associations of the asphodel, although quite certainly he would never have recognized one of its kind had it flashed across a Technicolor screen.

It was still true though: as men grew older (so Morse told himself) the delights of the natural world grew ever more important. Not just the flowers, either. What about the birds?

Morse had reached the conclusion that if he were to be reincarnated (a prospect which seemed to him most blessedly remote) he would register as a part-time Quaker, and devote a sizeable quota of his leisure hours to ornithology. This latter decision was consequent upon his realization, however late in the day, that life would be significantly impoverished should the birds no longer sing. And it was for this reason that, the previous week, he had taken out a year's subscription to *Birdwatching*; taken out a copy of the RSPB's *Birdwatchers' Guide* from the Summertown Library; and purchased a second-hand pair of 8/50mm binoculars (£9.90) that he'd spotted in the window of the Oxfam Shop just down the Banbury Road. And to complete his programme he had called in at the Summertown Pet Store and taken home a small wired cylinder packed with peanuts – a cylinder now suspended from a branch overhanging his garden. From *the* branch overhanging his garden.

He reached for the binoculars now and focused on an interesting specimen pecking away at the grass below the peanuts: a small bird, with a greyish crown, dark-brown bars across the dingy russet of its back, and paler underparts. As he watched, he sought earnestly to memorize this remarkable bird's characteristics, so as to be able to match its variegated plumage against the appropriate illustration in the *Guide*.

Plenty of time for that though.

He leaned back once more and rejoiced in the radiant warmth of Schwarzkopf's voice, following the

English text that lay open on his lap: 'You holy Art, when all my hope is shaken . . .'

When, too, a few moments later, his mood of pleasurable melancholy was shaken by three confident bursts on a front-door bell that to several of his neighbours sounded considerably over-decibelled, even for the hard-of-hearing.

Chapter Two

When Napoleon's eagle eye flashed down the list of officers proposed for promotion, he was wont to scribble in the margin against any particular name: 'Is he *lucky*, though?'

(Felix Kirkmarkham, *The Genius of Napoleon*)

'Not disturbing you?'

Morse made no direct reply, but his resigned look would have been sufficiently eloquent for most people.

Most people.

He opened the door widely – perforce needed so to do – in order to accommodate his unexpected visitor within the comparatively narrow entrance.

'I *am* disturbing you.'

'No, no! It's just that . . .'

'Look, matey!' (Chief Superintendent Strange cocked an ear towards the lounge.) 'I don't give a dam if I'm disturbing *you*; pity about disturbing old Schubert, though.'

For the dozenth time in their acquaintance, Morse found himself quietly re-appraising the man who first beached and then readjusted his vast bulk in an armchair, with a series of expiratory grunts.

Morse had long known better than to ask Strange whether he wanted a drink, alcoholic or non-alcoholic.

If Strange wanted a drink, of either variety, he would ask for it, immediately and unambiguously. But Morse did allow himself one question:

'You know you just said you didn't give a dam. Do you know how you spell "dam"?'

'You spell it "d – a – m". Tiny Indian coin – that's what a dam is. Surely you knew that?'

For the thirteenth time in their acquaintance . . .

'Is that a single malt you're drinking there, Morse?'

It was only after Morse had filled, then refilled, his visitor's glass that Strange came to the point of his evening call.

'The papers – even the tabloids – have been doing me proud. You read *The Times* yesterday?'

'I never read *The Times.*'

'What? The bloody paper's there – there! – on the coffee table.'

'Just for the Crossword – and the Letters page.'

'You don't read the obituaries?'

'Well, perhaps just a glance sometimes.'

'To see if you're there?'

'To see if some of them are younger than me.'

'I don't follow you.'

'If they *are* younger, so a statistician once told me, I've got a slightly better chance of living on beyond the norm.'

'Mm.' Strange nodded vaguely. 'You frightened of death?'

'A bit.'

Strange suddenly picked up his second half-full

tumbler of Scotch and tossed it back at a draught like a visitor downing an initiatory vodka at the Russian Embassy.

'What about the telly, Morse? Did you watch *News-room South-East* last night?'

'I've got a TV – video as well. But I don't seem to get round to watching anything and I can't work the video very well.'

'Really? And how do you expect to understand what's going on in the great big world out there? You're supposed to *know* what's going on. You're a police officer, Morse!'

'I listen to the wireless—'

'*Wireless?* Where've you got to in life, matey? "Radio" – that's what they've been calling it these last thirty years.'

It was Morse's turn to nod vaguely as Strange continued:

'Good job I got *this* done for you, then.'

Sorry, sir. Perhaps I am a bit behind the times – as well as *The Times*.

But Morse gave no voice to these latter thoughts as he slowly read the photocopied article that Strange had handed to him.

Morse always read slowly.

MURDER POLICE SEEK ANONYMOUS CALLER

A MAN HAS rung the police anonymously with information that could help identify the killer of Mrs Yvonne Harrison who was found handcuffed and battered to death a year ago.

Detectives yesterday appealed for the caller to make contact again. No clear motive has ever been established for the murder of the 48-year-old nurse who was alone in her home in the Oxfordshire village of Lower Swinstead when her killer broke in through a ground-floor window.

Detective Chief Superintendent Strange of Thames Valley CID said that a man had rung twice: "We are very anxious to hear from this caller again as soon as possible. He can contact us in the strictest confidence. We don't believe the calls are a hoax and we don't believe the caller himself is the killer. But we think that he can give us more information to substantially further our enquiries into this brutal murder."

At the time of the murder Mrs Harrison's husband Frank was in London where he works for the Swiss Helvetia Bank. Their son Simon works at the Daedalus Press in Oxford; their daughter Sarah is a junior consultant in the Diabetes Centre at the Radcliffe Infirmary in Oxford.

Had Morse's eyes narrowed slightly as he read the last few lines? If they had, he made no reference to whatever might have puzzled or interested him there.

'I trust it wasn't you who split the infinitive, sir?'

'You never suspected that, surely? We're all used to sloppy reporting, aren't we?'

Morse nodded as he handed back the photocopied article.

'No! Keep it, Morse – I've got the original.'

'Very kind of you, sir, but . . .'

'But it interested you, perhaps?'

'Only the bit at the end, about the Radcliffe.'

'Why's that?'

'Well, as you know, I was in there myself – after I was diagnosed.'

'Christ! You make it sound as if you're the only one who's ever been bloody diagnosed!'

Morse held his peace, for his memory needed no jogging: Strange himself had been a patient in the selfsame Radcliffe Infirmary a year or so before his own hospitalization. No one had known much about Strange's troubles. There had been hushed rumours about 'endocrinological dysfunction'; but not everyone at Police HQ was happy about spelling or pronouncing or identifying such a polysyllabic ailment.

'You know why I brought that cutting, Morse?'

'No! And to be honest with you, I don't much care. I'm on furlough, you know that. The quack tells me I'm run down – blood sugar far too high – blood pressure far too high. Says I need to have a quiet little rest-cure and try to forget the great big world out there, as you call it.'

'Some of us can't forget it though, can we?' Strange spoke the words very softly, and Morse got to his feet and turned off the CD player.

'Not one of your greatest triumphs that case, was it?'

'One of the few – very few, Morse – I got no-bloody-where with. And it wasn't exactly mine, either, as you know. But it was my responsibility, that's all. Still is.'

'What's all this got to do with me?'

Strange further expanded his Gargantuan girth as he further expounded:

'I thought, you know, with the wife . . . and all that . . . I thought it'd help to stay in the Force another year. But . . .'

Morse nodded sympathetically. Strange's wife had died very suddenly a year previously, victim of a coronary thrombosis which should surely never have afflicted one so slim, so cautious, so physically fit. She'd been an unlovely woman, Mrs Strange – outwardly timid and inwardly bullying; yet a woman to whom by all accounts Strange had been deeply attached. Friends had spoken of a 'tight' marriage; and most agreed that the widower would have been wholly lost on his own, at least for some while, had he jacked things in (as he'd intended) the previous September. And in the end he'd been persuaded to reconsider his position – and to continue for a further year. But he'd been uneasy back at HQ: a sort of supernumerary Super, feeling like a retired schoolmaster returning to a Common Room. A mistake. Morse knew it. Strange knew it.

'I still don't see what it's got to do with me, sir.'

'I want the case re-opened – not that it's ever been closed, of course. It worries me, you see. We should have got further than we did.'

'I still—'

'I'd like you to look at the case again. If anyone can crack it, *you* can. Know why? Because you're just plain bloody lucky, Morse, that's why! *And I want this case solved.*'

Chapter Three

Which of you shall have a friend and shall go unto him at midnight and say unto him, Friend, lend me three loaves. And he from within shall answer and say, Trouble me not: the door is now shut; I cannot rise and give thee. I say unto you, though he will not rise and give him, because he is his friend, yet because of his importunity he will rise and give him as many as he needeth

(*St Luke*, ch. XI, vv. 5–8)

Lucky?

Morse had always believed that luck played a bigger part in life than was acknowledged by many people – certainly by those distinguished personages who saw their personal merit as the only cause of their appropriate eminence. Yet as he looked back over his own life and career Morse had never considered his own lot a particularly lucky one, not at least in what folk referred to as the affairs of the heart. Strange may have had a point though, for without doubt his record with the Thames Valley CID was the envy of most of his colleagues – his success-rate the result, as Morse analysed the matter, of all sorts of factors: a curious combination of hard thinking, hard drinking (the two, for Morse, being synonymous), hard work (usually undertaken by Sergeant Lewis), and, yes, a sprinkling here and there of good fortune. The Romans had poured their libations not only to Jupiter and Venus and their associate deities in the Pantheon; but also to Fortuna, the goddess of good luck.

Lucky, then?

Well, a bit.

It was high time Morse said something:

'Why the Lower Swinstead murder? What's wrong with the Hampton Poyle murder, the Cowley murder . . . ?'

'Nothing to do with me, either of 'em.'

'That's the only reason then? Just to leave a clean slate behind you?'

For a few moments Strange appeared uncomfortable: 'It's partly that, yes, but . . .'

'The Chief Constable wouldn't look at any new investigation – not a serious investigation.'

'Not unless we had some new evidence.'

'Which in our case, as the poet said, we have not got.'

'This fellow that rang – '

'No end of people ring. We both know that, sir.'

' – rang twice. He knows something. I'm sure of it.'

'Did you speak to him yourself?'

'No. He spoke to the girl on the switchboard. Didn't want to be put through to anybody, he said. Just wanted to leave a message.'

'For you?'

'Yes.'

'A "he", you say?'

'Not much doubt about that.'

'Surely from the recordings . . . ?'

'We can't record every crazy sod who rings up and asks what the bloody time is, you know that!'

'Not much to go on.'

'*Twice*, Morse? The first time on the anniversary of the murder? Come off it! We've got a moral duty to re-open the case. Can't you understand that?'

Morse shook his head. 'Two anonymous phone calls? Just isn't worth the candle.'

And suddenly – why was this? – Strange seemed at ease again as he sank back even further in his chair:

'You're right, of course you are. The case wouldn't be worth re-opening – *unless*' (Strange paused for effect, his voice now affable and bland) 'unless our caller – identity cloaked in anonymity, Morse – had presented us with some . . . some new *evidence. And*, after my appeal, my nationally reported appeal, we're going to get some more! I'm not just thinking of another telephone call from our friend either, though I'm hopeful about that. I'm thinking of information from members of the public, people who thought the case was forgotten, people whose memories have had a jog, people who were a bit reluctant, a bit afraid, to come forward earlier on.'

'It happens,' conceded Morse.

The armchair creaked as Strange leaned forward once more, smiling semi-benignly, and holding out his empty tumbler: 'Lovely!'

After refilling the glasses, Morse asked the obvious question:

'Tell me this, sir. You had two DIs on the case originally – '

'Three.'

' – several DSs, God knows how many DCs and PCs and WPCs—'

'No such thing now. All the women are PCs – no sex discrimination these days. By the way, you were never guilty of sexual harassment, were you?'

'Seldom. The other way round, if anything.'

Strange grinned as he sipped his Scotch. 'Go on!'

'As I say, you had all those people on the case. They studied it. They lived with it. They—'

'Got nowhere with it.'

'Perhaps it wasn't altogether their fault. We're never going to solve everything. It's taken these mathematicians over three hundred years to solve Fermat's Last Theorem.'

'Mm.' Strange waggled his tumbler in front of him, holding it up towards the light, like a judge at the Beer Festival at Olympia.

'Just like the colour of my urine specimens at the Radcliffe.'

'Tastes better, though.'

'Listen. I'm not a crossword wizard like you. Sometimes I can't even finish the *Mirror* coffee-break thing. But I know one thing for sure. If you get stuck over a clue – '

'As occasionally even the best of us do.'

' – there's only one way to solve it. You go away, you leave it, you forget it, you think of the teenage Brigitte Bardot, and then you go back to it and – Eureka! It's like trying to remember a name: the more you think about it the more the bloody thing sinks below the horizon. But once you forget about it, once you come to it a second time, fresh—'

'I've never come to it a *first* time, apart from those early couple of days – you know that. I was on another case! And not particularly in the pink either, was I? Not all that long out of hospital myself.'

'Morse! I've *got* to re-open this case. You know why.'

'Try someone else!'

'I want you to think about it.'

'Look.' A note of exasperation had crept into Morse's voice. 'I'm on furlough – I'm tired – I'm sleeping badly – I drink too much – I'm beholden to no one – I've no relatives left – I can't see all that much purpose in life – '

'You'll have me in tears in a minute.'

'I'm only trying to say one thing, sir. Count me out!'

'You won't even *think* about it?'

'No.'

'You do realize that I don't *need* to plead with you about this? I don't want to pull rank on you, Morse, but just remember that I *can*. All right?'

'Try someone else, sir, as I say.'

'OK. Forget what I just said. Let's put it this way. It's a favour I'm asking, Morse – a personal favour.'

'What makes you think I'll still be here?'

'What's that supposed to mean?'

But Morse, it appeared, was barely listening as he stared out of the window on to his little patch of greenery where a small bird with a grey crown and darkish-brown bars across its back had settled beneath the diminishing column of peanuts.

'Look!' (He handed the binoculars to Strange.) 'Few nuts – and some of these rare species decide to take up special residence. I shall have to check up on the plumage but . . .'

Strange had already focused the binoculars with, as it seemed to Morse, a practised familiarity.

'Know anything about bird-watching, sir?'

'More than you, I shouldn't wonder.'

'Beautiful little fellow, isn't he?'

'She!'

'Pardon?'

'Immature female of the species.'

'*What* species?'

'*Passer domesticus,* Morse. Can't you recognize a bloody house-sparrow when you see one?'

For the fourteenth time Morse found himself re-appraising the quirkily contradictory character that was Chief Superintendent Strange.

'And you'll at least *think* about things? You can promise me that, surely?'

Morse nodded weakly.

And Strange smiled comfortably. 'I'm glad about that. And you'll be pleased about one thing. You'll have Sergeant Lewis along with you. I . . . did have a word with him, just before I came here, and he's—'

'You mean you've already . . .'

Strange flicked a stubby finger against his empty, expensive, cut-glass tumbler: 'A little celebration, perhaps?'

Chapter Four

He and the sombre, silent Spirit met –
They knew each other both for good and ill;
Such was their power, that neither could forget
His former friend and future foe; but still
There was a high, immortal, proud regret
In either's eye, as if 'twere less their will
Than destiny to make the eternal years
Their date of war, and their 'Champ Clos' the spheres
(Byron, *The Vision of Judgment*, XXXII)

It is possible for persons to be friendly towards each other without being friends. It is also possible for persons to be friends without being friendly towards each other. The relationship between Morse and Strange had always been in the latter category.

'Read through this as well!' Strange's tone was semi-peremptory as he thrust a folded sheet of ruled A4 across at Morse, in the process knocking his glass on to the parquet flooring. Where it broke into many pieces.

'Ah! Sorry about that!'

Morse rose reluctantly to fetch brush and pan from the kitchen.

'Could have been worse, though,' continued Strange. 'Could have been full, eh?'

As Morse carefully swept up the slivers of the cut-glass tumbler – originally one of a set of six (now three) which his mother had left him – he experienced an irrational anger and hatred wholly disproportionate to the small accident which had occurred. But he counted up to twenty; and was gradually feeling better, even as Strange extolled the bargain he'd seen in the Covered Market recently: glasses for only 50p apiece.

'Better not have any more Scotch, I suppose.'

'Not if you're driving, sir.'

'Which I'm bloody *not*. I'm being driven. And if I may say so, it's a bit rich expecting me to take lessons in drink-driving from you! But you're right, we've had enough.'

A further count, though this time only to ten, prolonged Morse's invariably slow reading of the two handwritten paragraphs, and he said nothing as he finally put the sheet aside.

It was Strange who spoke:

'Perhaps, you know, on second thoughts, we might, er . . . anither wee dram?'

'Not for me, sir.'

'That was meant to be the "royal we", Morse.'

Morse decided that a U-turn was merely a rational readjustment of a previously mistaken course, and he obliged accordingly – for both of them, with Strange's measure poured into one of the cheap-looking wine glasses he'd bought a few weeks earlier from the Covered Market, for only 50p apiece.

'Is this' (Morse pointed to the paper) 'what our dutiful duty-sergeant transcribed from the phone calls?'

'Well, not quite, no.' (Strange seemed curiously hesitant.) 'That's what *I* wrote down, as far as I – we – could fix the exact words. Very difficult business when you get things second-hand, garbled—'

Morse interrupted. 'No problem, surely? We *do* record everything that comes into HQ.'

'Not so easy as that. Some of these recordings are poor-quality reception; and when, you know, when somebody's speaking quietly, muffled sort of voice . . .'

Morse smiled thinly as he looked directly across at his superior officer. 'What you're telling me is that the recording equipment packed up, and there's no trace.'

'Anything mechanical packs up occasionally.'

'*Both* occasions?'

'Both occasions.'

'So all you've got to rely on is the duty-sergeant.'

'Right.'

'Atkinson, was that?'

'Er, yes.'

'Isn't he the one who's been taken off active duties?'

'Er, yes.'

'Because he's become half-deaf, I heard.'

'It's not a *joke*, Morse! Terrible affliction, deafness.'

'Would you like me to have a word with him myself?' For some reason Morse's smile was broader now.

'I've already, er . . .'

'Were you at home, sir, when this anonymous caller rang you?'

Strange shifted uncomfortably in the chair, finally nodding slowly.

'I thought you were ex-directory, sir.'

'You thought right.'

'How did he know your number then?'

''Ow the 'ell do I know!'

'The only people who'd know would be your close friends, family . . . ?'

'And people at HQ,' added Strange.

'What are you suggesting?'

'Well, for starters . . . have *you* got my telephone number?'

Morse walked out into the entrance hall and returned with a white-plastic telephone index, on which he pressed the letter 'S', then pushed the list of names and numbers there under the half-lenses now perched on Strange's nose.

'Not changed, has it?'

'Got an extra "five" in front of it. But you'd know that, wouldn't you?' The eyes over the top of the lenses looked shrewdly and steadily up at Morse.

'Yes. It's just the same with my number.'

'Do you think I should get a tap on my phone?'

'Wouldn't do any harm, if he rings again.'

'*When* he rings again.'

'Hoaxer! Sure to be.'

'Well-informed hoaxer, then.' Strange pointed to the paper still on the arm of Morse's chair. 'A bit in the know, wouldn't you say? Someone on the inside, perhaps? You couldn't have found one or two things referred to there in any of the press reports. Only the police'd know.'

'And the murderer,' added Morse.

'And the murderer,' repeated Strange.

Morse looked down once more at the notes Strange had made in his appropriately outsized, spidery handwriting:

Call One

That Lower Swinstead woman – nickers up and down like a yo-yo – a lot of paying clients and a few non-paying clients like me. Got nowhere much with the case did you – incompetant lot. For starters you wondered if it was one of the locals, didn't you? Then for the main course you wasted most of your time with the husband. Then you didn't have any sweet because you'd run out of money. Am I right? Idiots, the lot of you. No! Don't interrupt!
(Line suddenly dead.)

Call Two

Now *don't* interrupt this time, see? Don't say a dicky-bird! Like I said, that woman had more pricks than a second-hand dart-board, mine included, but it's not me who had anything to do with it. Want a clue? There's somebody coming out of the clammer in a fortnight – listen! He's one of your locals, isn't he? See what I mean? You cocked it all up before and you're lucky bastards to have another chance.
(Line suddenly dead.)

Morse looked up to find himself the object of Strange's steady gaze.

'It's incompet*ent*, sir, with an "e".'

'Thank you very much!'

'And most people put a "k" on "knickers".'

Strange smiled grimly. 'And Yvonne Harrison put an embargo on knickers, however you spell 'em!'

He struggled to his feet. 'My office Monday morning – first thing!'

'Eight o'clock?'

'Nine-thirty?'

'Nine-thirty.'

'Now get back to your Schubert – though I'm surprised you weren't listening to Wagner. Just the job, *The Ring*, for a long holiday, you know. Especially the Solti recording.'

Morse watched his visitor waddling somewhat unsteadily towards the police car parked confidently in the 'Resident's Only' parking area. (Yes! Morse had mentioned the apostrophe to the Chairman of the Residents' Welfare Committee.)

He closed the front door and for a few moments stood there motionless, acknowledging with a series of almost imperceptible nods the simple truth about the latest encounter between two men who knew each other well, both for good and ill:

Game, Set, Match, to Strange.

Or was it?

For there was something about what he had just learned, something he had not yet even begun to analyse, that was perplexing him slightly.

The following Sunday was a pleasant summer's day; and along with three-quarters of the population of

Hampshire, Morse decided to go down to Bournemouth. It took him over an hour to park the Jaguar; and it was a further half-hour before he reached the seafront where car-loads and bus-loads of formidable families were negotiating rights to a couple of square metres of Lebensraum. But moving away from the ice-cream emporia, Morse found progressively fewer and fewer day-trippers as he walked towards the further reaches of the shore-line. He'd always told himself he enjoyed the changing moods of Homer's deep-sounding sea. And he did so now.

Soon, he found himself standing alongside the slowly lapping water, debating with himself whether the tide was just coming in or just going out, and staring down at the glass-like circular configuration of a jellyfish.

'Is it dead?'

Until she spoke, Morse had been unaware of the auburn-haired young woman who now stood beside him, almost wearing a bikini.

'I don't know. But in the absence of anything better to do, I'm going to stand here till the tide comes in and find out.'

'But the tide's going *out*, surely?'

Morse nodded somewhat wistfully. 'You may be right.'

'Poor jellyfish!'

'Mm!' Morse looked down again at the apparently doomed, transparent creature at his feet: 'How very sad to be a jellyfish!'

He'd sounded a comparatively interesting man, and

the woman would have liked to stay there awhile. But she forced herself to forget the intensely blue eyes which momentarily had held her own; and walked away without a further word, for she felt a sudden, slight suspicion concerning the sanity of the man who stood there staring at the ground.

Chapter Five

In the country of the blind, the one-eyed man is King
(Afghan proverb)

It was on Tuesday the 14th, the day *before* Strange's visit to Morse, that Lewis had presented himself at the Chief Superintendent's office in Thames Valley Police HQ, in punctual obedience to the internal phone call.

'Something for you, Lewis. Remember the Lower Swinstead murder?'

'Well, vaguely, yes. And I've seen the bits in the paper, you know, about the calls. I was never really on the case myself though. We were on another—'

'Well, you're on it now – from next Monday morning, that is – once Morse gets back from Bermuda.'

'He hasn't left Oxford, has he?'

'*Joke,* Lewis.' Strange beamed with bonhomie, settling his chin into his others.

'The Chief Inspector's agreed?'

'Not much option, had he? And you enjoy working with the old sod. I know you do.'

'Not always.'

'Well, he always enjoys working with *you.*'

A strangely gratified Lewis made no reply.

'So?'

'Well, if it's OK with Morse . . .'

'Which it is.'

'I'll give him a ring.'

'No, you won't. He's tired, isn't he? Needs a rest. Give him a bit of time to himself – you know, crosswords, booze . . .'

'Wagner, sir. Don't forget his precious Wagner. He's just bought *another* recording of that *Ring Cycle* stuff, so he told me.'

'Which recording's that?'

'Conductor called "Sholty", I think.'

'Mm . . .' Strange pointed to three bulging green box-files stacked on the side of his desk. 'Little bit of reading there. All right? Chance for you to get a few moves ahead of Morse.'

Lewis got to his feet, picked up the files, and held them awkwardly in front of him, his chin clamping the top one firm.

'I've never been even *one* move in front of him, sir.'

'No? Don't you under-estimate yourself, Lewis! Let others do it for you.'

Lewis managed a good-natured grin. 'Not many people manage to get a move ahead of Morse.'

'Oh, really? Just a minute! Let me hold the door for you . . . And you're not quite right about what you just said, you know. There *are* one or two people who just occasionally manage it.'

'Perhaps you're right, sir. I've just not met one of 'em, that's all.'

'You have though,' said Strange quietly.

Lewis's eyes turned quizzically as he manoeuvred his triple burden through the door.

That same evening, Lewis had just finished his eggs and chips, had trawled the last slice of brown bread across the residual HP sauce, and was swallowing the last mouthful of full-cream cold milk, when he heard the call from above:

'Dad? Da – ad?'

Lewis looked down at the (presumably problematical) first sentence of his son's A-level French Prose Composition: 'Another bottle of this excellent wine, waiter!'

'Easy enough, that, isn't it?'

'What gender's "bottle"?'

'How am I supposed to know? What do you think I bought you that dictionary for?'

'Left it at school, didn't I!'

'So?'

'So you mean you don't know?'

'You're brighter than I thought, son.'

'Can't you guess?'

'Either masculine or feminine, sure to be.'

'That's *great.*'

'Feminine, say? So it's, er, "*Garçon! Une autre bouteille de cette—*"'

'No! You're useless, Dad! If you say "*Une autre bouteille*", you mean a *different* bottle of wine.'

'Oh.'

'You say "*Encore une bouteille de*" whatever it is.'

'Why do you ever ask me to help you?'

'Agh! Forget it! Like I say, you're bloody useless.'

Lewis had never himself read *Little Dorrit*, and unlike Morse would not have known the soothing secret of counting up to however-many. And in truth he felt angry and belittled as he walked silently down the stairs, picked up the box-files from the table in the entrance hall, walked past the living room, where Mrs Lewis sat deeply submerged in a TV soap, and settled himself down at the kitchen table, where he began to acquaint himself with the strangely assorted members of the Harrison family – wife, husband, daughter, son – four of the principal players in the Lower Swinstead case.

He concentrated as well as he could, in spite of those cruel words still echoing in his brain. And after a while he found himself progressively engaged in the earlier, more grievous agonies of other people: of Frank, the husband; of Sarah, the daughter; of Simon, the son; and of Yvonne, the mother, who had been murdered so brutally in the Cotswold village of Lower Swinstead, Oxon.

Chapter Six

The English country gentleman galloping after a fox
– the unspeakable in full pursuit of the uneatable
(Oscar Wilde)

At first he'd felt some reluctance about an immediate interview with her. But finally he decided that earlier rather than later was probably best; and in tones considerably less peremptory than those in which Strange had summoned Lewis three days earlier, he called her to his office at 4.30 p.m.

At which time she stood silent and still for a few seconds at the door before knocking softly, feeling like a schoolgirl outside the headmistress's study.

'Come in!'

She entered and sat, as directed, in the chair opposite him, across the desk.

Professor Turner was a fair-complexioned, mild-mannered medic, in his early sixties – the internationally renowned chief-guru of the Radcliffe Infirmary's Diabetes Centre in Oxford.

'You wanted to see me, sir?'

Yes, he wanted to see her; but he also wanted to put her rather more at ease.

'Look, we're probably going to be together at lots of do's these next few months – years, perhaps – so, please, let's forget this "Sir" business, shall we? Please call me "Robert".'

Sarah Harrison, a slimly attractive, brown-eyed brunette in her late twenties, felt her shoulder muscles relax a little.

Not for long.

'I've sat in with you once or twice, haven't I?'

'Three times.'

'And I think you're going to be good, going to be up to it, you know what I mean?'

'Thank you.'

'But you're not quite good enough yet.'

'I'd hoped I was improving.'

'Certainly. But you're still strangely naive, I'm sorry to say. You seem to believe everything your patients tell you!'

'There's not much else to go on, is there?'

'Oh, but there is! There's a certain healthy and necessary scepticism; and then there's experience. You'll soon realize all this. What I'm saying is that you might as well learn it now rather than later.'

'Is there anything particular . . . ?'

'Things, plural. I'm thinking of what they tell you about their blood-sugar records, about their sexual competence, about their diet, about their alcohol-intake. You see, the only thing they can't fool you about is their *weight*.'

'And their blood pressure.'

Turner smiled gently at his pupil. 'I haven't got *quite* as much faith as you in our measurements of blood pressure.'

'But they don't all of them make their answers up.'

'Not *all* of them, no. It's just that we all like to pretend a bit. We all tend to say we're fine, even if we're feeling lousy. Don't we?'

'I suppose so.'

'And *our* main job' (Turner spoke with a quiet authority) 'is to give *information* – and to exert some sort of *influence* – about the way our patients cope with what, as you know, is potentially a very serious illness.'

Sarah said nothing. Just sat there. A little humiliated.

And he continued: 'There are a good many patients here who are professional liars. Some of them I've known for years, and they've known me. We tell each other lies, all right. But it doesn't matter – because we *know* we're telling each other lies . . . Anyway, that's enough about that.' (Turner looked down at her folder.) 'I see you've got Mr David Mackenzie on your list next Monday. I'll sit in with you on him. I think he did once tell me his date of birth correctly, but he makes everything else up as he goes along. You'll enjoy him!'

Again Sarah said nothing. And she was preparing to leave when Turner changed the subject abruptly, and in an unexpected direction.

Or *was* it unexpected?

'I couldn't help seeing the articles in the newspapers . . . and the department was talking about them.'

Sarah nodded.

'Would it mean a lot to you if they found who murdered your mother?'

'What do *you* think?' The tone of her voice bordered almost on the insolent, but Turner interpreted her reply tolerantly, for it was (he knew) hardly the most intelligent question he'd ever formulated.

'Let's just wish them better luck,' he said.

'Better brains, too!'

'Perhaps they'll put Morse on to it this time.'

Sarah's eyes locked steadily on his.

'Morse?'

'You don't know him?'

'No.'

'Heard of him, perhaps?' Turner's eyes grew suddenly shrewd on hers, and she hesitated before answering:

'Didn't my mother mention she'd nursed him somewhere?'

'Would you like to meet him, next time he comes in?'

'Pardon?'

'You didn't know he was diabetic?'

'We've got an awful lot of diabetics here.'

'Not too many like him, thank the Lord! Four hefty injections a day, and he informs me that he's devised a carefully calibrated dosage that exactly counterbalances his considerable daily intake of alcohol. And when I say considerable . . . Quite a dab hand, too, is Morse, at extrapolating his blood-sugar readings – backwards!'

'Isn't he worried about . . . about what he's doing to himself?'

'Why not ask him? I'll put him on your list.'

'Only if you promise to come along to monitor me.'

'With *you* around? Oh, no! Morse wouldn't like that.'

'How old is he?'

'Too old for you.'

'Single.'

'Gracious, yes! Far too independent a spirit for marriage . . . Anyway, have a good weekend! Anything exciting on?'

'Important, perhaps, rather than exciting. We've got a meeting up at Hook Norton tomorrow at the Pear Tree Inn. We're organizing another Countryside March.'

'That's the "rural pursuits" thing, isn't it? Fox-hunting—'

'Among other things.'

'The "toffs and the serfs".'

Sarah shook her head with annoyance. 'That's just the sort of comment we get from the urban chattering-classes!'

'Sorry!' Turner held up his right hand in surrender. 'You're quite right. I know next to nothing about fox-hunting, and I'm sure there must be things to be said in favour of it. But – please! – don't go and tell Morse about them. We just happened to be talking about fox-hunting the last time he was here – it was in the news – and I can't help remembering what he said.'

'Which was?' she asked coldly.

'First, he said he'd never thought much of the argument that the fox enjoys being chased and being pulled to little pieces by the hounds.'

'Does he think the chickens enjoy being pulled to little pieces by the fox?'

'Second, that the sort of people who hunt do considerably more harm to themselves than they do to the animals they hunt. He said they run a big risk of brutalizing themselves . . . dehumanizing themselves.'

The two of them, master and pupil, looked at each other over the desk for an awkward while; and the Professor of Diabetes Studies thought he may have seen a flash of something approaching fury in the dark-brown eyes of his probationary consultant.

It was the latter who spoke first:

'Mind if I say something?'

'Of course not.'

'I'm surprised, that's all. I fully, *almost* fully, accept your criticisms of my professional manner and my strategy with patients. But from what you've just said *you* sometimes seem to talk to your patients about other things than diabetes.'

'Touché.'

'But you're right . . . Robert. I've been getting too chatty, I realize that. And I promise that when I see Mr Morse I'll try very hard, as you suggest, to instil some sort of disciplined regimen into his daily life.'

Turner said nothing in reply. It was a good thing for her to have the last word: she'd feel so much better when she came to think back on the interview. As she would, he knew that. Many times. But he allowed himself a few quietly spoken words after the door had closed behind her:

'Oh Lady in Pink – Oh lovely Lady in Pink! There is very, very little chance of a disciplined regimen in Morse's life.'

Chapter Seven

Whoever could possibly confuse 'Traffic Lights' and 'Driving Licence'? *You* could! Just stand in front of your mirror tonight and mouth those two phrases silently to yourself

(Lynne Dubin, *The Limitations of Lip-reading*)

Disabilities, like many sad concomitants of life, are often cloaked in euphemism. Thus it is that the 'blind' and the 'impotent' and the 'deaf' are happily no longer amongst us. Instead, in their respective clinics, we know our fellow out-patients as those affected by impaired vision; as victims of chronic erectile dysfunction; as citizens with a serious hearing-impediment. The individual members of such groups, however, know perfectly well what their troubles are. And in the latter category, they tend to prefer the monosyllabic 'deaf', although they realize that there are varying degrees of deafness; realize that some are very deaf indeed.

Like Simon Harrison.

He had been a six-year-old (it was 1978) attending a village school in Gloucestershire when an inexplicably localized outbreak of meningitis had given cause for most serious concern in the immediate vicinity. And in particular to two families there: to the Palmer family in High Street, whose only daughter had tragically died; and to the Harrison family in Church Lane, whose son had slowly recovered in hospital after three weeks of intensive care, but with irreversible long-term deafness: twenty-five per cent residual hearing in the left ear; and almost nothing in the right.

Thereafter, for Simon, social and academic progress had been seriously curtailed and compromised: like an athlete being timed for the hundred-metres sprint over sand-dunes wearing army boots; like a pupil, with thick wadges of cotton-wool in each ear, seeking to follow instructions vouchsafed by a tutor from behind a thickly panelled door.

Oh God! Being deaf was such a dispiriting business.

But Simon was a fighter, and he'd tried hard to make the best of things. Tried so hard to master the skills of lip-reading; to learn the complementary language of 'signing' with movements of fingers and hands; to present a wholly bogus facial expression of comprehension in the company of others; above all, to come to terms with the fact that silence, for those who are deaf, is not merely an absence of noise, but is a wholly *passive* silence, in which the potential vibrancy of active silence can never again be appreciated. Deafness is not the brief pregnant silence on the radio when the listener awaits the Greenwich time-signal; deafness is a radio-set that is defunct, its batteries dead and non-renewable.

Few people in Simon's life had understood such things; and in his early teens, when the audiographical readings had begun to dip even more alarmingly, fewer and fewer people had been overly sympathetic.

Except his mother, perhaps.

And the reason for such lack of interest in the boy had not been difficult to fathom. He was an unattractive, skinny-limbed lad, with rather protuberant ears, and a whiny, nasal manner of enunciating his words, as though his disability were not so much one of hearing as one of speaking.

Yet it would be an exaggeration to portray the young Harrison as a hapless adolescent, so often mishearing, so often misunderstood. His school fellows were not a gang of unmitigated bullies; nor were his teachers an uncaring crew. No. It was just that no one seemed to like him much; certainly no one seemed to love him. Except his mother, perhaps.

But Simon did have some residual hearing, as we have seen; and the powerful hearing-aids he wore were themselves far more valuable than any sympathy the world could ever offer. And when, after many a struggle, he left school with two A-level certificates (a C in English and a D in History) he very soon had a job.

Still had a job.

In the early 1990s, Oxfordshire's potential facilities for business and industry had attracted many leading national and international companies. During those years, the county could boast the largest concentration of printing and publishing companies outside the metropolis; and it was to one of these, the Daedalus Press in North Oxford, that on leaving school Simon had applied for the post of apprentice proofreader. And had been successful, principally (let it be admitted) because of the employers' legal obligation to appoint a small percentage of semi-disabled applicants. Yet the 'apprentice' appellation was very soon to be deleted from Simon's job description, for he was proving to be surprisingly and encouragingly competent: accurate, careful, neat – a fair combination of qualities required in a proof-reader. And with any luck (so it was thought) experience would gradually bring with it that needful extra dimension of tedious pedanticism.

On the morning of Friday, 17 July, he found on his desk a photocopied extract from some unspecified tabloid which some unspecified colleague had left, and which he read through with keen attention; then read through a second time, with less interest in its content, it appeared, than in its form, since his proof-reading pen applied itself at five points in the article.

NEW CLUE TO OLD MURDER

Information received by Thames Valley Police seems likely to prompt renewed enquireis into the bizzarre murder of Mrs Yvonne Harrison just over a year ago.

Residents of the small hamlet of Lower Swinstead in Oxfordshire are bracing themselves for further statements and a fresh upsurge of media interest in the ghastley murder of their former neighbour

Tom Biffen, landlord of the Maidens Arms, remains philosophical however 'You can't blame people, can you? Exactly the same as Jack the Ripper. Nobody knows who he was. That's why he's so interesting. Same with who done Mrs Harrison in. Nobody knows who he was. Or she was.'

Its difficult to disagree. Would we still be reading about the Ripper if we knew who it was who murdered and mutilated a succession of prostitutes in the East End of London in the 1870s? As it is, his idetnity remains unknown, just like that of Yvonne's murderer.

The villagers themselves are less than forthcoming, and seem dubious about any new breakthrough in the case. 'Let's just wish the police a bit better luck this time round,' says Mrs May Kennedy, who runs the surprisingly well-stocked village shop.

And so say all of us. All of us, that is, except the murderer.

Chief Inspector Morse had not as yet encountered Simon Harrison; but he would have been reasonably impressed by the proof-reader's competence. Only reasonably, of course, since he himself was a man who somewhere, somehow, had acquired the aforementioned dimension of 'tedious pedanticism', and would have made three further amendments. *And*, of course, would have corrected that gross anachronism, since historical accuracy had engaged him from the age of ten, when he had taken it upon himself to memorize the sequence of the American presidents, and the dates of the kings and queens of England.

Chapter Eight

Bankers are just like anybody else,
Except richer

(Ogden Nash,
I'm a Stranger Here Myself)

The London offices of the Swiss Helvetia Bank are tucked away discreetly just behind Sloane Square. The brass plaque pin-pointing visitors to these premises, albeit highly polished, is perhaps disproportionately small. Yet in truth the Bank has little need to impress its potential clients. On the contrary. Such clients have every need to impress the Bank.

Just after 4 p.m. on Friday, 17 July, a smartly suited man in his late forties waved farewell to the uniformed guard at the security desk and walked out into the sunshine of a glorious summer's day. Traffic was already heavy; but that was of no concern to Frank Harrison, one of six Portfolio and Investment Managers of SHB (London). His company flat was only a few minutes' walk away in Pavilion Road.

Earlier in the day he'd been very much what they paid him so handsomely for being – shrewd, superior, trustworthy – when his secretary had poured coffee for a small, grey-haired man and for his larger, much younger, cosmetically exquisite wife.

'You realize that SHB deals principally with portfolio

investments of, well, let's say, over a million dollars? Is that, er . . .?'

The self-made citizen from South Carolina nodded. 'I think you can feel assured, sir, that we shall be able to meet that figure – ah! – *fairly* easily, shan't we, honey?'

He'd taken his wife's heavily diamonded left hand in his own and smiled, smiled rather sweetly, as Harrison thought.

And he himself had smiled, too – rather sweetly, as he hoped – as mentally he calculated the likely commission from his latest client.

Almost managed a smile again now, as he stopped outside Sloane Square Underground Station and bought a copy of the *Evening Standard*, flicking through the sheets, almost immediately finding the only item that appeared to interest him, then swiftly scanning the brief article before depositing the paper in the nearest litter bin. Had he been at all interested in horse-racing, he might have noticed that Carolina Cutie was running in the 4.30 at Kempton Park. But it had been many years since he had placed a bet with any bookie – instead now spending many hours of each working day studying on his office's computer-screens the odds displayed from the London, New York, and Tokyo stock exchanges.

Considerably safer.

And recently he'd been rather lucky in the management of his clients' investments.

And the bonuses were good.

He let himself into his flat, tapped in the numbers

on the burglar alarm, and walked into the kitchen, where he poured himself a large gin with a good deal of ice and very little tonic. But he'd never had any drinking problem himself. Unlike his wife. His murdered wife.

Lauren had promised to be along about 6 p.m., and she'd never been late. He would call a taxi . . . well, perhaps they'd spend an hour or so between the sheets first, although (if truth were told) he was not quite so keenly aware of her sexual magnetism as he had been a few months earlier. Passion was coming off the boil. It usually happened. On both sides, too. It had happened with Yvonne, with whom he'd scaled the heights of sexual ecstasy, especially in the first few months of their marriage. Yet even during those kingfisher days he had been intermittently unfaithful to her; had woken with heart-aching guilt in the small hours of so many worryful nights – until, that is, he had discovered what he *had* discovered about her; and until he had fallen in love with a woman who was living so invitingly close to him in Lower Swinstead.

The front-door bell rang at 5.50 p.m. Ten minutes early. Good sign! He felt sexually ready for her now; tossed back the last mouthful of his second gin; and went to greet her.

'You're in the paper again!' she blurted, almost accusingly, brandishing the relevant page of the *Evening Standard* in front of his face after the door was closed behind them.

'Really?'

For the second time Harrison looked down at the

headline, NEW CLUE TO OLD MURDER; and pretended to read the article through.

'Well?' she asked.

'Well, what?'

'What have you got to tell me?'

'I'm going to take you out for a meal and then I'm going to take you upstairs to bed – or maybe the other way round.'

'I didn't mean that. You know I didn't.'

'What are you talking about?'

'I want you to tell me what *happened*. You've never spoken about it, have you? Not to me. And I want to know!' Her upper lip was suddenly tremulous. 'So before we do anything else, you'd better—'

'Better what?' He snapped the words and his voice seemed that of a different man. 'Listen, my sweetheart! The day you tell me what to do, that's the day we finish, OK? And if you don't get that message loud and clear' (paradoxically the voice had dropped to a whisper) 'you'd better bugger off and forget we ever met.'

There were no tears in her eyes as she replied: 'I can't do that, Frank. But there's one thing I *can* do: I'm going, as you so delicately put it, to bugger off!'

In full control of herself she turned the catch on the Yale lock, and the door closed quietly behind her.

Chapter Nine

He looked at me with eyes I thought
I was not like to find
(A. E. Housman,
More Poems, XLI)

It had been the previous day, Thursday, when after collecting her boss's mail Barbara Dean had walked along the corridor, white blouse as ever perfectly pressed, flicking through the eleven envelopes held in her left hand. And looking with particular attention (again!) at the one addressed with a scarlet felt-pen, in outsize capital letters, to:

STRANGE (SUPER!)
POLICE
KIDLINGTON
OXFORD

The execution of this lettering gave her the impression of its being neither the work of a particularly educated nor of a particularly uneducated correspondent. Yet the lower-case legend along the top-left of the envelope – 'Private and Confidencial' (*sic*) – would perhaps suggest the latter. Whatever the case though, the envelope was always going to be *noticed* – by whomsoever. It was like someone entering a lucky-dip postal competition with multicoloured sketches adorning the periphery of the envelope; or like a lover mailing off a vastly outsize Valentine.

What would her boss make of it?

Barbara had been working at Police HQ for almost six years now, and had enjoyed her time there – especially these past three years working as the personal secretary of Chief Superintendent Strange; and she was very sad that he would be leaving at the end of the summer. 'Strange by name and strange by nature' – that's what she often said when friends had asked about him: an oddly contradictory man, that was for sure. He was a heavyweight, in every sense of the word; yet there were times when he handled things with a lightness of touch which was as pleasing as it was unexpected. His was the reputation of a blunt, no-nonsense copper who had not been born with quite the IQ of an Aristotle or an Isaac Newton; yet (in Barbara's experience) he could on occasion exhibit a remarkably compassionate insight into personal problems, including her own. All right (yes!) he was a big, blundering, awkward teddy-bear of a man: a bit (a lot?) hen-pecked at home – until recently of course; a man much respected, if not particularly liked, by his fellow officers; and (from Barbara's point of view) a man who had never, hardly ever, sought to take the slightest advantage of her . . . well, of her womanhood. Just that once, perhaps?

It had been at the height of the summer heat-wave of 1995. One day when she had been wearing the skimpiest outfit the Force could ever officially tolerate, she had seen in Strange's eyes what she thought (and almost hoped?) were the signs of some mild, erotic fantasy.

'You look very desirable, my girl!'

That's all he'd said.

Was that what people meant by 'sexual harassment'?

Not that she'd mentioned it to anyone; but the phrase was much in the headlines that long, hot summer, and she'd heard some of the girls talking in the canteen about it.

'*I* could do with a bi' o' that sexual harássment!' confessed Sharon, the latest and youngest tyro in the typing pool.

That was the occasion when one of the senior CID officers seated at the far end of the table had got to his feet, drained his coffee, and come across to lay a gentle hand on Sharon's sun-tanned shoulder.

'You mean sexual hárassment, I think. As you know, we usually exercise the recessive accent in English; and much as I admire our American friends, we shouldn't let them prostitute our pronunciation, young lady!'

He had spoken quietly but a little cruelly; and the uncomprehending Sharon was visibly hurt.

'Pompous prick! Who the hell does he think he is?' she'd asked when he was gone.

So Barbara told her.

Not that she knew him personally, although his blue eyes invariably smiled into hers, a little wearily sometimes but ever interestedly, whenever the two of them passed each other in the corridors; and when she sometimes fancied that he looked at her as though he knew what she was thinking.

God forbid!

It was not of Morse, though, but of Strange that she was thinking that morning when she tapped the customary twice on his office door and entered. Sometimes, when he sat there behind his desk – tie slightly askew, a light shower of dandruff over the shoulders of his jacket, hairs growing a little too prominently from his ears and from his nostrils, white shirt rather less than white and less than smoothly ironed – it was then, yes, that she wished to mother him. She – Barbara! – less than half his age.

That he'd never had such a complicated effect on other women, she felt completely convinced.

Well, no; not *completely* convinced . . .

Chapter Ten

He was a self-made man who owed his lack of success to nobody

(Joseph Heller, *Catch-22*)

'Probably some nutter!' growled Strange as he slipped a paper-knife inside the top of the envelope, and unfolded the single, thin sheet of paper contained therein. And for a while frowned mightily; then smiled.

'Have a look at that, Babs!' he said proudly, making as if to hand the sheet across the desk. 'May well be what we've been waiting for – from my appeal, you know.'

'Won't there be some fingerprints on it?' she asked tentatively.

'Ah!'

'You can *get* fingerprints from paper?'

'Get almost anything from anything these days,' mumbled Strange. 'And what with DNA, forensics, psychological profiling – soon be no need for us detectives any more!'

But in truth he appeared a little abashed as he held the top of the sheet between his thumb and forefinger and leaned forward over the desk; and Barbara Dean leaned forward herself, and read the undated letter, typed on a patently antiquated machine through a red/black ribbon long past its operative sell-by date, with each keyed character unpredictably produced in either colour.

```
   You got it right when you said the
calls wsan't from the person that done it
because that wsa me, see! I made them
calls. But you got it wrong when you
didn't look a bit longer in the village,
Mister Strange. So you want some help so
there's a fellow due out of Bullingdon
Friday next week 24th OK. WATCH HIM
CAREFULLY!
   The Ringer.
   PS You can buy me a pint of Bass in the
Maidens if you recognize me.
```

'Bit illiterate?' suggested Strange.

'I wonder if he really is,' said Barbara, replacing her spectacles in their case.

'You should wear 'em more often. You've got just the face for specs, you know. Hasn't anyone ever told you that?'

No one ever had, and Barbara hoped she wasn't blushing.

'Thank you.'

'Well?'

'I'm not in the Crime Squad, sir.'

'But you don't think he'd last long in the typing-pool?'

'You fairly sure it's a "he"?'

'Sounds like it to me.'

Barbara nodded.

'Not much of a typist, like I say.'

'Spelling's OK – "recognize", and so on.'

'Can't spell "was".'

'That's not really spelling though, is it? You sometimes get typists who are sort of dyslexic with some words. They try to type "was", say, and they hit the "s" before the "a". Do things like that regularly but they don't seem to notice.'

'Ah!'

'Grammar's not so hot, I agree. Probably good enough to pass GCSE, I suppose, sir.'

'Does anyone ever *fail* GCSE?'

'Could do with a bit more punctuation too, couldn't it?'

'Dunno. Not as much as Morse'd put in.'

'Who do you think "The Ringer" is?'

'Ringer? One who rings, isn't it? Chap who's been ringing us up, like as not.'

'Does the postmark help?'

'Oxford. Not that that means anything. It could have been posted anywhere in our patch of the Cotswolds . . . Carterton! Yes. That's where they take the collections and do the sorting before bringing everything to Oxford.'

'Scores of villages though, sir.'

'Go and fetch Sergeant Dixon!'

'Know where he is?'

'Give you three guesses.'

'In the canteen?'

'In the canteen.'

'Eating a doughnut?'

'Doughnuts, plural.'

It was like some of the responses she'd learned so well from the Litany.

'I'll go and find him.'

'And send him straight to me.'

'The Lord be with you.'

'And with thy spirit.'

'You *do* go to church, sir!'

'Only for funerals.'

Sergeant Dixon was not so corpulent as Chief Superintendent Strange. But there was not all that much in it; and the pair of them would have made uncomfortable co-passengers in economy-class seating on an airline. Plenty of room, though, as Dixon drove out alone to Carterton in a marked police car. He'd arranged a meeting with the manager of the sorting office there. A manageress, as it happened, who quickly and competently answered his questions about the system operating in West Oxfordshire.

Yes, since the Burford office had been closed, Carterton had assumed postal responsibility for a pretty wide area. Dixon was handed a printed list of the Oxon districts now covered; was informed how many postmen were involved; where the collection points were, and how frequently the boxes were emptied; how and when the accumulated bags of mail were brought back to Carterton, and how they were there duly sorted and categorized – but not franked – before being sent on to Oxford.

'Any way a particular letter can be traced to a particular post-box?'

'No, none.'

'Traced to a particular village?'

'No.'

Dixon was not an officer of any great intellectual capacity; indeed Morse had once cruelly described him as 'the lowest-watt bulb in the Thames Valley Force'. He had only five years to go before retirement, and he knew that his recent elevation to the rank of sergeant was as high as he could ever hope to climb. Not too bad, though, for a man who had been given little encouragement either from home or from school: if he'd made something of himself he'd made something of himself *himself*, as he'd once put things. Not the most elegant of sentences. But 'elegance' had never been a word associated with Sergeant Dixon.

And yet, as he looked down at his outsize black boots, buffed and bulled, he was thinking as hard as he'd thought for many a moon. He was fully aware of the importance of his present enquiries, and he felt gratified to have been given the job. How good it would be if he could impress his superiors – something (he knew) he'd seldom done in his heretofore somewhat nondescript career.

So he took his time as he sat in that small postal office; took his time as he wrote down a few words in his black notebook; then another few words; then asked another question; then another . . .

When finally he drove back to Oxford, Sergeant Dixon was feeling rather pleased with himself.

That letter-cum-envelope was still exercising Strange's mind to its limits; but there seemed no cause for excitement. In late morning he had driven down to the Fingerprint Department at St Aldate's in Oxford – only to learn that there was little prospect of further enlightenment. The faint, over-smeared prints offered no hope: the envelope itself must have been handled by the original correspondent, by the collecting postman, by the sorter, by the delivering postman, by a member of the HQ post department, by Strange's secretary, by Strange himself – and probably by a few extra intermediary persons to boot. How many fingers there, pray?

Forget it?

Forget it!

Handwriting? Only those red-felt capitals on the cover. Was it worth getting in some under-employed graphologist to estimate the correspondent's potential criminality? To seek possible signs of his (?) childhood neglect, parental abuse, sexual perversion, drugs . . . ?

Forget it?

Forget it!

The typewriter? God! How many typewriters were there to be found in Oxfordshire? In any case, Strange held the view that in the early years of the new millennium the streets of the UK's major cities would be lined with past-sell-by-date typewriters and VDUs and computers and the rest. And how was he to find an obviously *ancient* typewriter for God's sake, one with a tired and overworked ribbon of red and black? He might as well try to trace the animal-inventory from the Ark.

Forget it?

Forget it!

What Strange needed now was new ideas.

What Strange needed now was Morse to be around.

Chapter Eleven

Take notice, lords, he has a loyal breast,
For you have seen him open 't. Read o'er this;
And after, this: and then to breakfast with
What appetite you have

(Shakespeare, *Henry VIII*)

Detective Sergeant Lewis of the Thames Valley CID kept himself pretty fit – very fit, really – in spite of a diet clogged daily with cholesterol. Quite simply, he had long held the view that some things went with other things. He had often heard, for example, that caviare was best washed down with iced champagne, although in truth his personal experience had occurred somewhat lower down the culinary ladder – with fried eggs necessarily complemented with chips and HP sauce; and (at breakfast time) with bacon, buttered mushrooms, well-grilled tomatoes, and soft fried bread. And, indeed, such was the breakfast that Mrs Lewis had prepared at 7.15 a.m. on Monday, 20 July 1998.

It will be of no surprise therefore for the reader to learn that Sergeant Lewis felt pleasingly replete when, just before 8 a.m., he drove from Headington down the Ring Road to the Cutteslowe roundabout, where he turned north up to Police HQ at Kidlington. No problems. All the traffic was going the other way, down to Oxford City.

He was looking forward to the day.

He'd known that working with Morse was never going to be easy, but he couldn't disguise the fact that his own service in the CID had been enriched immeasurably because of his close association, over so many years now, with his curmudgeonly, miserly, oddly vulnerable chief.

And now? There was the prospect of another case: a big, fat, juicy puzzle – like the first page of an Agatha Christie novel.

Most conscientiously therefore (after Strange had spoken to him) Lewis had read through as much of the archive material as he could profitably assimilate; and as he drove along that bright summer's morning he had a reasonably clear picture of the facts of the case, and of the hitherto ineffectual glosses put upon those facts by the CID's former investigating officers.

From the very start (as Lewis learned) several theories, including of course burglary, had been entertained, although none of such theories had made anywhere near complete sense. There had been no observable signs of any struggle, for example. And although Yvonne Harrison was found naked, handcuffed, and gagged, she had apparently not been raped or tortured. In addition, it appeared most unlikely that she had been forcibly stripped of the clothes she'd been wearing, since the skimpy lace bra, the equally skimpy lace knickers, the black blouse, and the minimal white skirt, were found neatly folded beside her bed.

Had she been lying there completely unclothed when some intruder had disturbed her? Surely it was an unusually early hour for her to be a-bed; and if she *had* been abed then, and if she had heard the front-door bell, or heard something, it seemed quite improbable that she would have confronted any burglar or (unknown?) caller without first putting something on to cover a body fully acknowledged to be beautiful. Such considerations had led the police to speculate on the likelihood of the murderer being well known to Mrs Harrison; and indeed to speculate on the possibility of the murderer living in the immediate and very circumscribed vicinity, and of being rather *too* well known to Mrs Harrison. Her husband was away from home a good deal, and few of the (strangely unco-operative?) villagers would have been too surprised, it seemed, if his wife conveniently forgot her marriage vows occasionally. In fact it had not been difficult to guess that most of the villagers, though loth to be signatories to any specific allegations, were fairly strongly in favour of some sort of 'lover-theory'. Yet although the Harrisons often appeared more than merely geographically distanced, no evidence was found of likely divorce proceedings.

Once Mr Frank Harrison, with a very solid (if very unusual) alibi, had been eliminated from the enquiries, painstakingly strenuous investigations had produced (as one of the final reports admitted) no sustainable line of positive enquiry . . .

As he pulled off right, into Thames Valley Police HQ, Lewis was smiling quietly to himself. Morse would very soon have established some 'sustainable line of positive enquiry'. Even if it was a wrong line.

So what?
Morse was very often wrong – at the start.
So what?
Morse was almost always right – at the finish.

Chapter Twelve

Yet ev'n these bones from insult to protect
Some frail memorial still erected nigh,
With uncouth rhimes and shapeless sculpture deck'd,
Implores the passing tribute of a sigh
(Thomas Gray, *Elegy Written in a Country Churchyard*)

THE FOLLOWING IS an extract from *The Times*, Monday 20 July 1998:

A VILLAGE MURDER

TWO PSYCHICS AND a hypnotist have already been involved in the case. It has caught the attention of the *Still a Mystery* series on ITV, although it has yet to be promoted to the Premier Division of such classical unsolved cases as the disappearance of Lord Lucan, the fate of the racehorse Shergar, or the quest for the Holy Grail itself.

Although the murder of Yvonne Harrison has long been out of the immediate headlines, we are led to believe that the box-files concerning the case, stacked on the shelves at Thames Valley Police HQ, are definitely not accumulating layer upon layer of undisturbed dust. After all it is only just over a year since the body of Mrs Harrison was discovered in the bedroom of her Grade-II-listed Georgian house, set in four acres of wooded ground in the Cotswold village of Lower Swinstead. The home, 'The Windhovers', was sold for £350,000 fairly soon after the murder, and the family have long since left the quiet leafy village – all except Yvonne, of course, who is buried in the small, neatly mown churchyard of St Mary's, where, in the form of a Christian cross, a low, wooden stake is the only memorial to the body reposing beneath it:

Perhaps, when the ground is sufficiently settled, the murdered woman will have some worthier monument. But for the present the grave shows little if any sign of tender loving care, and flowers no longer adorn this semi-neglected spot.

Yvonne Harrison, a fully qualified nurse, had resumed work in Oxford after her two children had left home, and on the evening of her murder had returned to an empty house, her husband Frank, as normally during the week, spending his time in his London apartment. 'The Windhovers' had been broken into a few years earlier, when TV sets, video-equipment, radios, a computer, and sundry electrical items had been stolen. As a result, the Harrisons had installed a fairly sophisticated burglar alarm, with 'panic-buttons' in the main bedroom and beside the main entrance door; had enlisted in the local Neighbourhood Watch group; and had acquired a Rottweiler puppy, christened Rodney, who had subsequently displayed a healthier taste for Walkers Crisps than for any unwelcome visitors, and who had sadly been run over a few months previously.

With the smashed rear window, the burglary theory was at first the favourite, although there was no apparent theft of several readily displayed items of silverware and non-too-subtly concealed pieces of jewellery. What was far more obvious to those who entered the house later that night was a body – the body of Yvonne Harrison, lying on the bed in the main bedroom: naked, handcuffed, and gagged. And dead.

What immediately caught public interest was the fact that the man who discovered the body was none other than the murdered woman's husband.

A somewhat delayed post-mortem established that Yvonne Harrison had probably been murdered by some sort of 'tubular metal rod' two or three hours before her body was discovered at 11.20 p.m., and fairly certainly not after 9.30 p.m. Independent evidence corroborated the pathologist's findings. A local builder, Mr John Barron, had rung Mrs Harrison at 9 p.m. – on the dot, as instructed. But he had heard only the 'engaged' signal. At about 9.30 p.m. he had rung again; but although he had persisted there had been no reply. The phone was quite certainly ringing at the other end. Either the Ansaphone had not been activated . . . or else the lady of the house was not alive to take the call.

Another call however had been made more successfully that evening. An extraordinarily puzzling call. At just after 9 p.m. Yvonne's husband picked up his phone in Pavilion Road, London, to hear a man's voice informing him that his wife was in trouble and that he ought to get out there immediately. Normally he would have driven home post-haste in his BMW. But with the car in for repairs, he took a taxi to Paddington where he caught the 9.48 train to Oxford, arriving at 10.50, where he took another taxi for the ten-mile journey out to Lower Swinstead.

Late-night traffic was thin, and when Mr Patrick Flynn braked his Radio Taxi outside 'The Windhovers' at 11.20 p.m. he saw a village mansion ablaze with lights turned on in almost every room, and the burglar-alarm box emitting sharp blue flashes and a continuous ringing. The front door stood open . . . and the rest is history.

Or it **was** history until a fortnight ago, when two anonymous phone calls were received at Thames Valley Police HQ, where it is the view of Chief Superintendent Strange that promising new lines of enquiry may soon be opened.

It is surely universally to be hoped that the identity of Yvonne Harrison's murderer will finally be revealed; and that on some more permanent memorial in St Mary's churchyard the name of the murdered woman will be spelt correctly.

Chapter Thirteen

Ponderanda sunt testimonia, non numeranda
(All testimonies aggregate
Not by their number, but their weight)
(Latin proverb)

Most of the Thames Valley Police personnel were ever wont to pounce quickly upon any newspaper clipping concerning their competence, or alleged lack of competence. And that morning Lewis had been almost immediately apprised of the article in *The Times* – which he'd read and assimilated swiftly; far more swiftly (he suspected) than Morse would read it when he took it along at 8.30 a.m. The Chief was a notoriously slow reader, except of crossword clues.

Lewis remembered the case well enough; certainly remembered the frustration and disappointment that many of his CID colleagues had felt when lead after lead had appeared to peter out. Yes, he'd often experienced frustration himself, but seldom any prolonged disappointment; for which he was grateful – profoundly grateful – to Morse.

Most usually (Lewis knew it well) a murder investigation revolved around corroborated suspicion. A clue was pursued; a suspect targeted; an alibi checked; a motive weighed in the balances; a response to questioning interpreted as surly, cocky, devious, frightened

. . . It was all cumulative – that was the word! – a series of pieces in the jigsaw that seemed to form a coherent pattern sufficiently convincing for a formal charge to be brought; for a dossier to be sent to the DPP; for a period of remand, further questioning, sometimes further evidence, with nothing cropping up in the interim to vitiate the central police hypothesis: that in all probability the arrested suspect was guilty as hell.

That was the usual pattern.

Not with Morse though.

For some reason Morse often shunned the standard heap-of-evidence approach. In fact Lewis had seldom if ever observed him, through distaste or idleness perhaps, riffle through any heap of dutifully transcribed statements, claiming (as Morse did) that since he could seldom remember what he'd been doing himself the previous evening, he found it difficult to give much credence to people who claimed to recall anything from a week last Wednesday – unless, of course, it was watching *Coronation Street* or listening to *The Archers*, or some similar regularly timetabled ritual.

No, Morse seldom worked that way.

The opposite, more often than not.

With most prime suspects, if female, youngish, and even moderately attractive, Morse normally managed to fall in love, sometimes only for a brief term, yet sometimes throughout Michaelmas and Hilary and Trinity. Towards some other prime suspects, if men, Morse occasionally appeared surprisingly sympathetic, especially if he suspected that the quality of their lives had hardly been enhanced by getting hitched to some potential tart who had temporarily managed to camouflage her basic bitchiness . . .

Lewis had a quick look at the *Mirror*, drained his coffee, and looked at his watch: 8.25 a.m. Time he got moving.

As he walked out of the canteen, he (literally) bumped into the stout figure of Sergeant Dixon – 'Dixon-delighting-in-doughnuts' as Homer would have dubbed him.

'You see the thing on the Lower Swinstead thing?' (Variety was not a feature of Dixon's vocabulary.)

Lewis nodded, and Dixon continued:

'I was with him on that for a while. Poor ol' Strange. He thought he knew who done it, but he couldn't prove it, could he? Poor ol' Strange. Like I say, I was with him on that thing.'

Lewis nodded again; then climbed the stairs, wondering how that Monday morning would turn out – knowing how Morse hated holidays; how little he normally enjoyed the company of others; how very much he enjoyed a very regular allotment of alcohol; how he avoided almost all forms of physical exercise. And knowing such things, Lewis realized that in all probability he would fairly soon be driving Morse out to the muzak-free pub at Thrupp where a couple of pints of real ale would leave the Chief marginally mellower and where a couple of orange juices would leave the chauffeur (him!) unexcitedly unintoxicated.

Chapter Fourteen

The man who says to one, go, and he goeth, and to another, come, and he cometh, has, in most cases, more sense of restraint and difficulty than the man who obeys him

(John Ruskin, *The Stones of Venice*)

Lewis knocked deferentially on Morse's door before entering.

'Welcome home, sir! Nice break?'

'No!'

'You don't sound very—'

'Sh!'

So Lewis sat down obediently in the chair opposite, as his chief contemplated the last clue: 'Stiff examination (7)' A – T – P – Y; then immediately wrote in the answer, and consulted his wristwatch.

'Not bad, Lewis. Ten and a half minutes. Still it's usually a bit easier on Mondays.'

'Well done.'

'Have you done it, by the way?'

'Pardon?'

'That *is* a copy of today's *Times* you've got with you?'

'They showed it to me in the canteen—'

'Does Mrs Lewis know that the first place you head for after breakfast is the canteen?'

'Only for a coffee.'

'Not a crime, I suppose.'

'It's this article, sir – about the Harrison case.'

'So?'

'So you're not interested?'

'No!'

'But we're supposed to be re-opening the case, sir – you and me.'

'You and *I*, Lewis. And we are not.'

'But the Super said you'd agreed.'

'*When* am I supposed to have agreed?'

'Last week – Tuesday.'

'Last week – Wednesday! He came to see me on *Wednesday*.'

'You mean . . . he hadn't seen you *before* he saw me?'

'You're bright as a button this morning, Lewis.'

'But you must have agreed, surely?'

'In a way.'

'So what's biting you?'

Morse's blue eyes flashed across the desk. 'I'd had too much Scotch, that's what! I'd been trying to enjoy myself. I was on a week's furlough, remember?'

'But why start the week off in such a foul mood?'

'Why *not*, pray?'

'I don't know. It's just that, you know – another case for us to solve perhaps? Gives you a good feeling, that.'

Morse nodded reluctantly.

'So why agree to it, if you've no stomach for it?'

Morse looked down at the threadbare carpet – a carpet stopping regularly six inches from the skirting boards. 'I'll tell you why. Strange's carpet goes right up to the wall – you've noticed that? So if you ever get up to Super status, which I very much doubt, you just make sure you get a carpet that covers the whole floor – and a personal parking space while you're at it!'

'At least you've got your name on the door.'

'Remember that fellow in Holy Writ, Lewis? "I also am a man set under authority." I'm just like him – *under* authority. Strange doesn't *ask* me to do something: he tells me.'

'You could always have said no.'

'Stop sermonizing me! That case stinks of duplicity and corruption: the family, the locals, the police – shifty and thrifty with the truth, the whole bloody lot of them.'

'You sound as if you know quite a bit about it already.'

'Why shouldn't I? About a local murder like that? I do occasionally pick up a few things from my fellow officers, all right? And if you remember I *was* on the case right at the beginning, if only for a very short while. And why was that? Because we were on *another* case. Were we not?'

Lewis nodded. 'Another murder case.'

'Murder's always been our business.'

'So why—?'

'Because the case is old and tired, that's why.'

'Who'll take it on if we don't?'

'They'll find another pair of idiots.'

'So you're going to tell the Super . . .?'

'I've already *told* you. Give it a rest!'

'Why are you so sharp about it all?'

'Because I'm like the case, Lewis. I'm old and tired myself.'

The ringing of the telephone on Morse's desk cut across the tetchy stichomythia.

'Morse?'

'Sir?'

'You ready?'

'Half-past nine, you said.'

'So what?'

'It's only—'

'So what?'

'Shall I bring Sergeant Lewis along?'

'Please yourself.'

The phone was dead.

'That was Strange.'

'I could hear.'

'I'd like you to come along. All right with you?'

Lewis nodded. 'I'm a man under authority too.'

'*Lew*-is! Quote it accurately: "a man *set* under authority".'

'Sorry!'

But Morse was continuing with the text, as if the well-remembered words brought some momentary respite to his peevishness: '"Having under me soldiers, and I say unto one, Go and he goeth; and to another, Come and he cometh".'

'Lewis cometh,' said Lewis quietly.

Chapter Fifteen

I have received no more than one or two letters in my life that were worth the postage

(Henry Thoreau)

'C'M IN! C'M IN!'

It was 8.45 a.m.

'Ah! Morse. Lewis.'

Perhaps, in all good faith, Strange had intended to sound brisk rather than brusque; yet, judging from Morse's silence as he sat down, the Chief Superintendent had not effected a particularly good start. He contrived to beam expansively at his two subordinates, and especially at Morse.

'What does "The Ringer" mean to you?'

'Story by Edgar Wallace. I read it in my youth.'

Morse had spoken in clipped, formal tones; and Lewis, with a millimetre rise of the eyebrows, glanced quickly at his impassive face.

Something was wrong.

'What about you, Sergeant? You ever read Edgar Wallace?'

'Me?' Lewis grinned weakly. 'No, sir. I was a *Beano*-boy myself.'

'Anything else, Morse?'

'A campanologist?'

'Could be.'

Morse sat silently on.

'Anything else?'

'It's a horse that's raced under the name of a different horse – a practice, so they tell me, occasionally employed by unscrupulous owners.'

'How does it work?'

Morse shook his head. 'I've seldom donated any money to the bookmakers.'

'Or anyone else for that matter.'

Morse sat silently on.

'Anything else?'

'I can think of nothing else.'

'Well, let me tell *you* something. In Oz, it's what you call the quickest fellow in a sheep-shearing competition. What about that?'

'Useful thing to know, sir.'

'What about a "dead ringer"?'

'Somebody almost identical with somebody else.'

'Good! You're coming on nicely, Morse.'

'No, I'm not. I've stopped.'

Strange shook his massive head and smiled bleakly. 'You're an odd sod. You never seem to see anything that's staring you in the face. You have to look round half a dozen corners first, when all you've really got to do is to look straight up the bloody street in front of you!'

Lewis, as he sat beside his chief, knew that such a criticism was marginally undeserved; and he would have wished to set the record aright. But he didn't, or couldn't. As for Morse, he seemed quietly unconcerned about the situation: in fact (or was Lewis misunderstanding things?) even a little pleased.

'What about this, then?' Suddenly, confidently, Strange thrust the letter across the desk; and after what seemed to both the other men an unnecessarily prolonged perusal, the slow-reading Morse handed it back. Without comment.

'Well?'

'"The Ringer", you mean? You think it's the fellow who decided to ring you—'

'Ring me *twice*!'

'It's a possibility.'

'Where do you think it was posted?'

'Dunno. You'll have to show me the envelope.'

'Guess!'

'You're expecting me to say Lower Swinstead.'

'No. Just waiting for your answer.'

'Lower Swinstead.'

'Explain *that*, then!' Strange produced a white envelope on which, above the lurid red capitals, the pewter-gold first-class stamp was cancelled with a circular franking:

'All right,' conceded Morse. 'I'll try another guess. What about Oxford?'

'Hm! What about the writing on the envelope?'

'Probably an A-level examiner using up one of his red pens. His scripts were sending him bananas and he happened to see your invitation in one of the newspapers. He just wondered why it was only the candidates who were allowed to make things up, so he decided to have a go for himself. He's a nutter, sir. A harmless nutter. We always get them – you know that.'

'Oh, thank you, Morse!'

'No fingerprints, sir?' asked Lewis diffidently.

'Ah, no. No fingerprints. Good question, though!'

'Best forget it, then,' counselled Morse.

'Rea-lly?' Strange allowed the disyllable to linger ominously. 'When I was a lad, Morse, I once wrote off an entry for a Walt Disney competition and I drew a picture of Mickey Mouse on the front of the envelope.'

'Did you win?'

'No, I didn't. But let me just tell you one thing, matey: I'd like to bet you that somebody noticed it! That's the whole point, isn't it?'

'You've lost me, sir.'

Strange leaned back expansively. 'When I asked Sergeant Dixon where *he* thought the letter was posted, he agreed with you: Lower Swinstead. And when I showed him the postmark he said it might *still* have been posted there, because he knew that some of the letters from that part of the Cotswolds were brought to Oxford for franking. So he went out and did a bit of leg-work, and he traced the fellow who did the collections last week; and the postman remembered the envelope! There'd only been three letters that day in the box, and he'd noticed one of 'em in particular. Not surprising, eh? So Dixon decided to test things, just for his own satisfaction. He addressed an envelope to himself and posted it at Lower Swinstead.'

Strange now produced a white unopened envelope and passed it across the desk. It was addressed in red Biro to Sergeant Dixon at Police HQ Kidlington, the pewter-gold first-class stamp cancelled with the same circular franking:

Strange paused for effect. 'Perhaps you ought to start eating doughnuts, Morse.'

'They won't let me have any sugar these days, sir.'

'There's no sugar in beer, you're saying?'

Lewis was expecting some semi-flippant, semi-prepared answer from his chief – something about balancing his intake of alcohol with his intake of insulin. But Morse said nothing; just sat there staring at the intricate design upon the carpet.

'One of these days, perhaps,' persisted Strange quietly, 'you might revise your opinion of Dixon.'

'Why not put him in charge of the case? If you're still determined—'

'Steady on, Morse! That's enough of that. Just remember who you're talking to. And I'll tell you exactly why I'm not putting that idiot Dixon in charge. Because I've already put somebody else in charge – you and Lewis! Remember?'

'Lewis maybe, sir, but I can't do it.'

Feeling most uncomfortable during these exchanges, Lewis watched the colour rise in Strange's cheeks as several times his mouth opened and closed like that of a stranded goldfish.

'You do realize you've got little say in this matter, Chief Inspector? I am *not* pleading with you to undertake an investigation for Thames Valley CID. What I *am* doing, as your superior officer, is telling you that you've been assigned to a particular duty. That's all. And that's enough.'

'No. It's not enough.'

For several minutes the conversation continued in similar vein before Strange delivered his diktat:

'I see . . . Well, in that case . . . you give me no option, do you? I shall have to report this interview to the Chief Constable. And you know what that'll mean.'

Morse rose slowly to his feet, signalling Lewis to do the same. 'I don't think you're going to report this interview to the Chief Constable or to the Assistant Chief Constable or to anyone else, for that matter, are you, Superintendent Strange?'

Chapter Sixteen

The vilest deeds like poison weeds
Bloom well in prison-air,
It is only what is good in Man
That wastes and withers there:
Pale Anguish keeps the heavy gate,
And the warder is Despair
(Oscar Wilde,
The Ballad of Reading Gaol)

UNTIL COMPARATIVELY RECENTLY, Harry Repp had associated the word 'porridge' chiefly with the title of the TV comedy series and not with oatmeal stirred in boiling water. For as long as he could remember, his breakfasts had consisted of Corn Flakes covered successively (as his beer-gut had ballooned) with full, semi-skimmed, and finally the thinly insipid fully skimmed varieties of milk. It was his common-law wife, Debbie, who'd insisted: 'You keep pouring booze into your belly every night and it's low-fat milk for breakfast! Understood?' So there'd been little choice, had there? Until almost a year ago, when he had come to realize that the TV title was wholly appropriate, with porridge (occasionally ill-stirred in luke-warm water) providing the basic breakfast diet for prison inmates.

Normally Repp would have accepted the proffered dollop of porridge; but he asked only for two sausages and a spoonful of baked beans as he and his co-prisoners from A Wing stood queuing at the food counter at 8 a.m. He had read that prisoners in the condemned cell were always given the breakfast of their choice; but he felt he could himself have eaten little in such circumstances – with the twin spectres of death and terror so very close behind him. And even now, back in his cell, he managed only one mouthful of beans before pushing his plate away from him. He felt agitated and apprehensive, although he found it difficult to account for such emotions. After all, he wasn't awaiting the Governor and the flunkey from the Home Office and the Prison Chaplain . . . and the Hangman. Far from it. It was that day, Friday 24 July, that was set for his release from HM Prison, Bullingdon.

At 8.35 a.m., still in his prison clothing, he heard steps outside the cell, heard his name called, and was on his feet immediately, picking up the carrier bag in which he'd already placed his personal belongings: a battered-looking radio, a few letters still in their grubby envelopes, and a 'sexy-western' paperback that had clearly commanded regular re-reading. 'Let's hope we don't meet again, mate!' one of the prison officers had volunteered as the double doors were unlocked and Repp was escorted for the last time from the spur of A Wing.

At 8.50 a.m., after changing into his personal civvies, he was admitted into a bench-lined holding-cell, where another prisoner, a thin sallow-faced man in his forties, was already seated. Their exchange of conversation was brief and unmemorable:

'Not much more o' this shit, mate.'

'No,' said Repp.

At 9.05 a.m. his name was again called, and he was taken along to a reception desk where one of the Principal Officers took him through the forms pertaining to his release: identity check, behaviour and health records, details of destination and accommodation. It seemed to Repp somewhat reminiscent of a check-in at Heathrow or Gatwick. Except that this, as he kept reminding himself, wasn't a check-in at all. It was a check-out.

He signed his name to several documents without bothering too much what they were. But before signing one form he was asked to read some relevant words aloud: 'I understand that I am not allowed to possess or have anything to do with firearms or ammunition of any description . . .' It didn't matter anyway. In all probability there'd be no need to use the gun; and apart from himself only Debbie knew its whereabouts.

Almost finished now.

He took possession of an order issued under the Criminal Justice Act re Supervision in the Community, specifying the Oxford Probation Service in Park End Street as the office to which he was required to report regularly. Then he completed the Discharge Certificate itself, with a series of initials against Travel Warrant (Bullingdon to Oxford), Personal Property (as itemized), Personal Cash (£24.50), Discharge Grant (£45), Discharge Clothing (offered but not issued). And, finally, one further full signature, dated and countersigned by the Principal Officer, underneath the unambiguous assertion: I HAVE NO OUTSTANDING COMPLAINTS. And indeed Harry Repp had nothing much to complain about. At least, not about Bullingdon – except perhaps that any residual good in him had wasted and had withered there.

He was escorted across the prison yard to the main gates, where he reported to the Senior Officer, citing his full name and prison number to be checked against the Discharge List. And that was it. The heavy gates were opened, and Harry Repp stepped out of prison. A free man.

He looked at his wristwatch, repeatedly glancing around him as if he might be expecting someone to meet him. But there seemed to be no one. According to the bus timetable they'd given him, there would be a wait of ten minutes or so; and he walked slowly down the paved path which led from the Central Reception Area to the road. There he turned and looked back at the high concreted walls, lightish beige with perhaps a hint of some pinkish coloration, lamp-posts stationed at regular intervals in front of them, sturdily vertical until, at their tops, they leaned towards the prison, like guardsmen inclining their heads around a catafalque.

Harry Repp turned his back on the prison for the last time, and walked more briskly towards the bus stop and towards freedom.

Chapter Seventeen

What is it that roareth thus?
Can it be a Motor Bus?
All this noise and hideous hum
Indicat Motorem Bum
(A. D. Godley)

SEATED AT THE front window of the Central Reception Area, Sergeant Lewis had been a vigilant observer of the final events recorded in the previous chapter, immediately ducking down when the newly released man had turned to look back at the prison complex. Needlessly so, for the two men were quite unknown to each other.

This was hardly the trickiest assignment he'd ever been given, Lewis knew that; and in truth he could see little justification for the trouble being taken. Except in Superintendent Strange's (not usually fanciful) imagination, there seemed only a tenuous connection between the Harrison murder and Harry Repp – the latter sentenced to fifteen months' imprisonment, and now released early on parole on grounds of exemplary behaviour. And in any case, Strange's instructions (not Morse's) had been vague in the extreme: 'Keep an eye on him, see where he goes, who he meets, and, er, generally, you know . . . well, no need to tell an experienced officer like you.'

And yet (Lewis considered the point afresh) had Strange's motivation been *all* that fanciful? Repp was known to have been active in the vicinity at the relevant period, and had in fact been under limited police surveillance for some time, although not of course on the night of the murder. And then there was the letter to Strange – a letter which, whilst pointing a finger only vaguely at the general locality of Lower Swinstead, had quite specifically pointed towards the man now being released from prison.

As Repp walked away Lewis got to his feet and shook hands with the prison officer who had communicated to him as much as anyone at Bullingdon was ever likely to know about the man just released: aged 37; height 5′ 10″; weight 13 stone 4 pounds; hair dark-brown, balding; complexion medium; tattoo (naval design) covering left forearm; sentenced for the receipt and sale of stolen goods; at the time of arrest cohabiting with Debbie Richardson, of 15 Chaucer Lane, Burford.

After driving the unmarked police car from the crowded staff car park, Lewis stopped on the main road, moving round the car as he slowly checked his tyre pressures, all the while keeping watch on the bus stop, only fifty yards away, where two men, Repp and a slimmer ferrety-looking fellow, stood waiting; from where Lewis could hear so very clearly the frequently vociferated plaints from the ferret: 'Where the fuckin' 'ell's the fuckin' bus got to?'

In fact, the fuckin' bus was well on its way; and a few minutes later the two men boarded a virtually empty bus, and uncommunicatively took their separate seats.

Lewis moved smoothly into gear and followed discreetly, not at all unhappy when another (rather posh) car interposed itself between him and the bus. (Another posh car behind him, for that matter.) Any minor worry that Repp might unexpectedly get off at some stage between Bullingdon and Bicester was taking care of itself very nicely, since the bus made no stop whatsoever until reaching the Bure Place bus station in Bicester, where the ferret straightaway alighted (and straightaway disappeared); and where Repp, the immediate quarry, walked up the line of bus shelters to the 27 OXFORD (Direct) bay, promptly boarding the bus already standing there.

Repp was not the only one who had done his homework on the Bicester–Oxford timetable. For Lewis, knowing there would be a full ten-minute wait before departure, and leaving his car in the capacious car park opposite, walked quickly through the short passageway to Sheep Street, passing the public toilets on his left, where at Forbuoys Newsagent's he bought the *Mirror*. Even if there was a bit of a queue, so what? He would rather enjoy not following but chasing the 27 to Oxford. But the bus was still there, filling up quite quickly, as he got back into his car.

After the implementation of the Beeching Report of the mid-sixties, passengers between Oxford and Bicester had perforce to use their own cars. But the former railway line had now been re-opened; and the deregulated bus companies were trying their best, and sometimes succeeding, in tempting passengers back to public transport. There were no traffic jams on the rail; and a newly designated bus lane from Kidlington gave a comparatively fast-track entry into Oxford. So perhaps (Lewis pondered the matter) it was hardly surprising that Repp had not been picked up at Bullingdon by a friend, or by a relative, or by his common-law wife. Yet it would surely have been so much easier, quicker, more convenient that way?

At 10.10 a.m. the 27 pulled out of the bus station and headed towards Oxford, in due course crossing over the M40 junction and making appropriately good speed along the A34, before turning off through Kidlington and then over the A40 down towards Oxford City Centre.

And again Lewis was fortunate, for no one had got off the bus along the route until the upper reaches of the Banbury Road.

Easy!

Driving at a safe and courteous distance behind the bus, Lewis had ample opportunity for reflecting once more on the slightly disturbing developments of the previous few days . . .

Morse had been as good as his word that Monday morning, when the latter part of their audience with Strange had turned almost inexplicably bitter. No, Morse could not agree to any involvement in the re-opening of the Harrison enquiries. Yes, Morse realized ('Fully, sir!') the possible implications of his non-compliance with the decision of a superior officer. Yet oddly enough, it had been Strange who had seemed the more unsure of himself during those final exchanges; and Lewis had found himself puzzled, and suspecting that there were certain aspects of the case of which he himself was wholly unaware.

Could it be . . . ?

Could it be perhaps . . . ?

Could it be perhaps that Morse had some reason for keeping his head above the turbid waters still swirling around the unsolved murder of Yvonne Harrison? Some *personal* reason, say? Some connection with the major participants in the case? Some connection (Lewis was thinking the unthinkable) with *the* major participant: with the murdered woman herself? For there must be *some* reason . . .

Some reason, too, for Morse's (virtually unprecedented) absence from HQ on those two following days, the Tuesday and the Wednesday? To be fair, he had rung Lewis (at home) early on the Tuesday morning, saying that he was feeling unwell, and in truth *sounding* unwell. He'd be grateful, he'd said, if Lewis could apologize to all concerned; perhaps for the following day as well. Lewis had rung Morse that Tuesday evening, but there was no answer; had rung again on the Wednesday evening – again with no answer.

Was Morse ill?

Not all that ill, anyway, because he'd appeared on the Thursday morning at his usual, comparatively early hour. And said nothing about his absence. Or about his row with Strange. Or about his health, for that matter. But Morse seldom mentioned his health . . .

Just below the Cutteslowe roundabout, the bus stopped and four passengers alighted – but not Repp.

At the Martyrs' Memorial, the majority of the passengers alighted – but not Repp.

At the Gloucester Green terminus, the last few passengers alighted – but not Repp.

The 27 bus was now empty.

CHAPTER EIGHTEEN

Any fool can tell the truth; but it requires a man of some sense to know how to lie well

(Samuel Butler)

LEWIS KNEW WHAT HE must do as soon as he saw Morse's maroon Jaguar parked in its wonted place.

'Still feeling better, sir?'

'Better than what?'

'Can you spare a minute?'

'Si' down!'

Seated opposite, in his own wonted place, Lewis said his piece.

'You're in a bit of a mess,' said Morse, at the end of the sorry story.

'That's not much help, is it?'

'Remember the Sherlock Holmes story, *Case of Identity*? A fellow gets in one side of a hansom cab, and gets out through the opposite side.'

'Doors on buses are always on the *same* side.'

'Really?'

'You never go on a bus.'

'But you weren't watching *either* side. You were queuing for coffee.'

'Buying a paper.'

'Listen!' Morse looked and sounded strained and

weary. 'I thought you were asking for my advice. Do you want to hear it?'

There was a brief silence before Morse continued: 'It's not really a question of your own competence or incompetence – probably the latter, I'm afraid. The main concern is what's happened to your man, Repp. Agreed?'

Lewis nodded joylessly.

'Well, the situation's fairly simple. You just lost contact with him in the middle of things, that's all. No great shakes, is it? He's fine, believe me! Absolutely fine. At this very second he's probably got his bottom on the top sheet with that common-law missus of his. She picked him up somewhere – that's for certain. Most of these people released from the nick have somebody to pick 'em up.'

'Except she doesn't drive a car.'

'All right. She arranged for somebody *else* to pick him up.'

'Why did he ask for a travel warrant, then?'

Morse looked less than happy. 'He got on the bus at Bicester and while he was sitting there somebody saw him and tapped on the window and offered him a lift to Oxford or wherever he was going – and we know where that is, don't we? *Home.* Which is exactly where he is now, you can put your bank balance on that! It's a racing certainty. And if you don't believe me, go and see for yourself!'

Lewis considered what he had just heard. 'It must have been somebody unexpected, sir. Like I say, he'd asked for a warrant.'

'You're right, yes. Well, partly right. Either unexpected – or not really expected . . . Perhaps not really welcome, either,' added Morse slowly, a weak smile playing on his lips as though for the first time that morning his brain was possibly engaged in some serious thinking.

'You reckon that's what happened?'

'Lewis! *Something* happened, didn't it? If you think your man decided to dematerialize, you've been watching too many space videos.'

'I don't watch—'

'Look! Remember what I've always told you when we've been on a case together – unlike this one! There's always, without exception, some wholly explicable, wholly logical causation for any chain of events, in any situation. In this case, you've just got to ask yourself where the link broke, then how it broke, then why it broke – and nothing in that sequence of events is going to be anything but simple and commonplace.'

Lewis looked the troubled man he was. 'I just can't see how . . .'

Morse's question was quietly spoken. 'You remember that car, the one you said somehow squeezed in between you and the bus from Bullingdon?'

Lewis looked across the desk in pained surprise. 'You don't think . . .'

'What do you remember about it?'

'Dark colour – black, I think – pretty recent Reg – one person in it – man, I think – pretty sure it was a man.'

'Not very observant – '

'I was looking at the *bus* all the time, for God's sake!'

' – and not much help, if you want the truth.'

No, it wasn't, Lewis knew that. 'What do I tell the Super, though?'

'If I were you? I certainly wouldn't tell him the truth. Not a very wise thing, you know, going through life telling nothing but the truth. So in this case, I'd tell him I'd followed the bus to Bicester, then followed the bus to Oxford, then seen Repp get off outside The Randolph, get picked up there in a car, and get driven off in the general direction of Chaucer Lane, Burford. Easy!'

Uneasy, however, was Lewis's minimal nod.

'But I'm *not* you, Lewis, am I? I'm a very accomplished liar myself, but I've never rated you too highly in that department.'

A puzzled look suddenly came over Lewis's brow. 'How come you know where Repp lives?'

'Great man Chaucer, born in 1343, it's thought—'

'You're not answering my question!'

'I know a lot of things, Lewis – far more than you think.'

'You've still not told me what I'm supposed to say to the Super.'

'Cut your losses and tell him the truth.'

'He'll tear me apart.'

'You may well be surprised.'

But, as he rose to his feet, Lewis appeared far from convinced.

'Well, I suppose I'd better—'

'Hold your horses!' (Morse looked at his wrist-watch.) 'It may just be that I can help you.'

Lewis's eyebrows lifted a little as Morse continued:

'*You* promise to buy me a couple of drinks, and *I'll* promise to give you a big, fat juicy clue.'

'If you say so, sir.'

'Off we go then.'

'What's this big, fat—?'

'I'll give you the Registration Number of the car that you followed from Bullingdon to Bicester! Bargain, is it?'

Lewis's eyebrows lifted a lot. 'No kidding?'

Morse rechecked his wristwatch. 'First things first, though. They've already been open five minutes.'

Chapter Nineteen

It's good to hope; it's the waiting that spoils it
(Yiddish proverb)

With increasing impatience and with incipient disquiet, lighting one cigarette from another, drinking cup after cup of instant coffee, Deborah Richardson had been watching from the front-room window, on and off from 10.30 a.m., on and off from 11.30 a.m., and virtually on and on from midday and thereafter – at first with that curiously pleasing *expectation* of happy events which Jane Austen would have swapped for happiness itself. Not that Debbie had ever read Jane Austen. Heard of her, though, most recently from that elderly Oxford don (well, wasn't fifty-eight elderly?) with whom she'd spent the night at the Cotswold Hotel in Burford . . .

It wasn't that she was keenly anticipating any renewal of sexual congress with her newly liberated partner. Although she felt gratified that physically he'd always been so demanding of her, it had often occurred to her that he was probably enjoying the sex more for its own sake than because he was having it with *her*. And perhaps that was why only occasionally did she experience that 'intercrural effusion' of which she'd read in one of the women's magazines . . .

Nor was she looking forward to the regular resumption of cooking and washing and ironing that had monopolized her time in the years prior to his arrest . . .

Nor – she ought to be honest with herself! – was she at all anxious to witness his eating habits again, especially at breakfast, when he would regularly offer some trite and ill-informed commentary on whatever article he was reading in the *Sun*, and openly displaying thereby a semi-masticated mouthful of whatever . . .

And – oh, most definitely! – she would never never ever tolerate again the demands his erstwhile criminal dealings had made upon the space, *her* space, in the quite unpleasantly appointed little semi he'd bought three years earlier at rock-bottom price during the slump in the housing market. After which, at almost any given time, every conceivable square foot of space had been jam-packed with crates of gin and whisky, cartons of cigarettes, car radios, video recorders, cameras, computers, and Hi-Fi equipment. No! There'd have to be an end to all that stolen-property lark; and surely (now!) there'd be little further risk of Harry himself taking part in any of the actual burglaries. For he *had* taken part occasionally, Debbie knew that, although the police hadn't seemed to know, or perhaps just couldn't find sufficient evidence to prosecute. Certainly Harry had never asked for any further offences to be taken into consideration. He'd made only the one plea in mitigation of his sentence: he might have known the possible provenance of the miscellaneous merchandise he'd acquired; *might* have known, if only he'd asked – but he'd just never asked.

He was in business, that was all. He knew a few clients who wanted to buy things at less than market price. Who didn't? 'Just like yer duty-frees, innit? Everybody's always looking round for a bargain, officer' . . .

So?

So why was she still standing there at the window, staring up and down the quiet road? The answer was simple: she just wanted a man *around* the place. Without Harry she felt isolated, lonely, unshared. She'd lost her man; and there was no man there to talk to, to talk to others about, to grumble at, to argue with, even to walk out on – because you couldn't walk out on a man who wasn't there to start with, now could you?

Where was he? What had happened? . . .

Not that her grass-widowhood had been entirely minus men. There'd been that nice little affair with the young plasterer who'd come in to patch up a crack in the kitchen wall. And that civilized little liaison with the Oxford don (so undemanding, so appreciative) she'd met in a Burford pub. But in each case, and on every occasion, she'd been so very, very careful . . .

Only once had she had *that* dreadful worry, after buying a Home Pregnancy Kit from Boots, when she'd just had to tell Harry, and when he'd been surprisingly sympathetic. If they did have a kid, it'd be good for him (him!) to have a mum *and* a dad. Yeah! He'd hated both his mum and his dad – but he'd hated his mum *less*, and it was proper to have a choice. Something else too: you know, when the poor little bugger went to school and one of the other kids said what's your name or what's your dad do – well, it was probably old-fashioned to think like that but, yeah!, better to have two of them, two parents. So she ought to change her name to his, but no need for any of all that nuptial stuff! Just for the kid's sake, mind – nothing to do with any social worker!

But she'd be 'Debbie Repp', then; and that would be too close to 'demirep' (a word she'd met in the 'intercrural' article), which she'd looked up in the biggest dictionary she could find in the Burford Public Library: 'a person, esp. a woman, of dubious and libidinous disposition'. Her name, she'd decided, would henceforth remain 'Richardson'. And in any case the subsequent messy miscarriage had settled *that* domestic crisis.

At 12.50 p.m. she left her vigil for the kitchen, where she felt the neck of the champagne bottle, standing beside two glasses on the table there. Inappropriately *chambré* she decided (another recent addition to her vocabulary), and she put it back in the fridge. Not Premier Division stuff: £8.99 from the supermarket, although in truth she'd begrudged even that. Money! God, how important that was in life! They had enough money – what's more, money temporarily held in her own name. But that was Harry's money, and she would never dare to touch more of it than the reasonably generous allowance he'd authorized.

She'd taken some occasional office-cleaning jobs in Burford, usually from 6 p.m. to 8 p.m. But £4.75 per hour was hardly the rate of remuneration to support any reasonable lifestyle; certainly not the style she'd begun to get accustomed to with Harry. So did she find herself *almost* hoping that he might pick up again on some of those very shady but very profitable activities?

No! No! No!

At 1.15 p.m. she rang Bullingdon Prison, learning that Harry Repp had left on schedule that morning with a bus warrant for Oxford. Nothing further they could tell her: no longer their responsibility, was he? She could ring the Probation Office in Oxford – that might have been his first port-of-call. Which number she was about to dial when she noticed a car pulling up outside – an R-Reg., dark blue, expensive-looking model; and a man she'd never seen before getting out of it, and walking towards her up the narrow, amateurishly cemented front-path.

Chapter Twenty

Then said the Jews unto him, Thou art not yet fifty years old, and hast thou seen Abraham? Jesus said unto them, Verily, verily, I say unto you, Before Abraham was, I am

(*St John*, ch. VIII, vv. 57–58)

Already, an hour or so before driving out to see Debbie Richardson, it had been an unusual morning for Sergeant Lewis.

Morse had insisted on buying the second round in the Woodstock Arms, albeit one consisting only of one pint of Morrell's Best Bitter for himself, since as yet Lewis was only halfway down his obligatory orange juice.

Unusual? Yes. And quite certainly surprising.

'Do you really mean it – about the car number, sir?'

'Just be patient!'

'What do you think I *am* being?'

'You say the car was darkish, newish, toppish range?'

'Like I said, I was really concentrating on the bus.'

'Be more *specific,* man! Go for it. Back your hunches!'

'All right: black; R-reg; twenty thou.'

'That's better.'

Lewis smiled dubiously. 'Thank you.'

'And how many people in that car of yours? One? Two? Three?'

'Certainly one, sir.'

'We'll make a detective of you yet,' mumbled Morse, leaning forward as he buried his nose in the froth.

'Could've been two, I suppose. I can't really remember but . . . you know, it was a bit like one of those cars going off on a family holiday, you know what I mean?'

'No.'

'Well, you know—'

'For Christ's sake stop saying "you know"!'

'Well, you've got things packed everywhere, haven't you? Not just cases and things but nappies, bedding, towels, boots, wellingtons, thermoses, carrier bags – all piled up so you can hardly see out of the back window.'

'What sort of bags?'

Lewis was trying hard to re-visualize the scene, and fortunately Morse had picked on the one thing that finally jogged his fading memory. Bags! Yes, there'd been bags in the back of that car: bags you could stick all sorts of things inside. And suddenly the picture had grown clearer:

'Black bags!'

'You think he was off to the rubbish dump?'

'Could've been. "Waste Reception Area", by the way, sir.'

'Where's the biggest rubbish dump in Oxfordshire?'

'Or in Oxford, perhaps?' Lewis's face had brightened. 'Redbridge. People go there from all over the county – straight down the A34 – then turn off—' But Lewis stopped. 'Forget it, sir. From Bullingdon you'd turn on to the A41, and then straight on to the A34. You wouldn't go into Bicester at all.'

'And you're quite sure the car went into Bicester?'

'That's one thing I am sure about.'

'If only you'd concentrated on that car, Lewis, and forgotten all about the bus!'

'I just don't understand why you're so interested in the car. Repp was on the *bus.*'

'So you keep saying,' said Morse quietly. 'But you're not right, are you? Repp *wasn't* on the bus.'

'Not when he got to Oxford, no.'

'You lost him. You might as well face it.'

Lewis drained his orange juice. 'Yep! I agree. I lost him. And that's exactly why I need a bit of help.'

'Like the number of that car, you mean?'

'I think you're having me on about that.'

'Oh no. And if you think it'll help . . .'

Morse took out his pen and pushed his empty glass across the table: 'Your round! And pass me your notebook.'

A minute later, Lewis stared down at Morse's small, neat handwriting:

R456 LJB

And incredulity vied with amazement in his face as Morse continued quietly: 'You know, you weren't your usual sharp self this morning, were you? You failed to observe the car in *front* of you – and you failed to observe the car *behind* you.'

'You – you don't mean . . .?'

'I do mean, yes. *I* was right behind you this morning. But being the law-abiding citizen I am, I instructed my driver to keep an appropriately safe distance from the vehicle in front.'

'I just don't believe this. I just don't understand.'

'Easy, really. I thought it wouldn't be a bad idea to keep an eye on our Mr Repp, just like Strange did. So I rang up the prison Governor, an old friend of mine, and told him what I was intending to do; and he said there was no need because he'd had a call from Strange setting up *your* surveillance. So I just told him to forget it – told him we'd got some crossed wires – came out in an unmarked car, like you did – parked in the visitors' area – listened to Mahler's Eighth – and watched and waited. *And* took a flask of coffee – yes, *coffee*, Lewis – and the rest is history.'

'You're having me on!'

'Oh no! How the hell do you think I could give you that car number unless I'd *seen* the bloody thing? You don't think I'm psychic or something, do you?'

Lewis reflected on this extraordinary new development. Then slowly formulated his thoughts aloud. 'You saw the car in front of me. You saw who was in it and what was in it – '

'Black plastic bags, yes. You were right.'

' – and you saw the Registration Number.'

'Only just. You know, I'll have to see an optician soon.'

'You told me off for saying "you know",' snapped Lewis.

Morse curled his right hand lovingly round his beer glass. 'Sometimes, you don't fully appreciate my help, you know.'

Lewis let it go. 'And you knew the car went into Bicester, to the bus station. You knew it all the time.'

'Yes.'

'So when I went to get a paper you saw Repp get out of the bus and get into the car. But you didn't tell *me* – oh no! You just left me to go on a wild goose chase after the bus. Well, thank you *very* much.'

For a while Morse was silent. Then: 'How many times have I been to the Gents this morning?'

'Twice since you've been here.'

'Six times in all, Lewis! And the reason for such embarrassingly frequent retirements is not any lack of bladder-control. It's those diuretic pills they've put me on.'

The light slowly dawned; and Sergeant Lewis suddenly looked a happy man. 'The thermos, sir? Three cups of coffee in that, say?'

Morse nodded. Not a happy man.

'So when you got to Bicester bus station you were dying for a leak and you saw the Gents' loo there, and when you came out – the car was gone. Right?'

Reluctantly Morse nodded once more. 'And we followed you, you and the bus, back to Oxford.'

A gleeful Lewis looked as if he'd won the Lottery.

'You really should have kept your eyes on that car, sir!'

'You mean the black R-reg Peugeot, Lewis? You were right, by the way: £19,950 licensed and on the road, so they inform me. Not far off, were you?'

'And the owner?'

'Some insurance-broker in Gerrard's Cross reported it missing two days ago.'

Chapter Twenty-One

BURMA (Be Undressed Ready My Angel)
(An acronym frequently printed on the backs of envelopes posted to sweethearts by servicemen about to go on leave, or by prisoners about to be released)

Unlike the (equally unknown) man who had called upon her the previous evening, he held up his ID for several seconds in front of her face, like a conjurer holding up a playing card towards an audience.

But she didn't really look at it; didn't even notice his name. He seemed a decent, honest-looking sort of fellow – not one of those spooky pseuds who occasionally sought her company. And she was hardly too bothered if he *wasn't* one of those decent, honest-looking sort of fellows.

'Deborah Richardson?' (He sounded rather shy.)

'Yes.'

'Sergeant Lewis, Thames Valley CID.'

'He's not here, yet. It *was* Harry you wanted?'

'Can I come in?'

'Be my guest!'

As she sat opposite him at the Formica-topped table, Lewis saw a woman in her mid-thirties, of medium build, with short blonde hair, and wearing a white dress, polka-dotted in a gaudy green, that reached halfway down (or was it halfway up?) a pair of thighs now comfortably crossed in that uncomfortable kitchen. She was not by any standards a beautiful woman; certainly not a pretty one. Yet Lewis had little doubt that many men, including Morse perhaps, would have called her quietly (or loudly) attractive.

She lit a cigarette and smiled rather nervously, the pleasingly regular teeth unpleasingly coated with nicotine.

'He's OK, isn't he?'

'I'm sure he is, yes.'

'It's just – well, I was expectin' him a bit before now.'

'You didn't arrange to meet him at the prison?'

'No. We've got a car, in the garage, but I never got on too well with drivin'.'

'Perhaps one of his mates . . .?'

'Dunno, really. Expect so. He just said he'd be here as soon as he could.'

'He might have rung you.'

'Havin' a few beers, I should think. Only natural, innit? The champagne's back in the fridge anyway.'

Lewis looked at his watch, surprised how quickly the latter part of the morning had sped by. 'Only half-past one.'

'So? So why have you called then, Sergeant?'

Lewis played his less than promising hand with some care. 'It's just that we've received some . . . information, unconfirmed information, that Harry might have . . . well, there might be some slight connection between him and the murder of Mrs Harrison.'

'Harry never had nothin' to do with that murder!'

'You obviously remember the case.'

'Course I do! Everybody does. Biggest thing ever happened round here.'

'So as far as you know Harry had nothing—'

'You reckon I'd be tellin' you if he *had*?'

'But you say he hadn't?'

'Course he hadn't!'

'You see, all I'm saying is that Harry's a burglar – '

'*Was* a burglar.'

' – and there was some evidence that there could have been a burglary that night that might have gone a bit wrong perhaps.'

'What? Her lyin' on the bed there with her legs wide open? Funny bloody burglary!'

'How did you know that? How she was found?'

'Come off it! How the hell do any of us know anythin'? Common knowledge, wasn't it? Common gossip, anyway.'

'Where did you hear it?'

'Pub, I should think.'

'Maiden's Arms?'

'Shouldn't be surprised. Everybody talks about everythin' there. The landlord, 'specially. Still, that's what landlords—'

'Is he still there?'

'Tom? Oh, yes. Tom Biffen. Keeps about the best pint of bitter in Oxfordshire, so Harry said.' (Lewis made a mental note, for Morse would be interested.)

'You know him fairly well, the landlord?'

She lit another cigarette, her eyes widening as she leaned forward a little. '*Fairly* well, yes, Sergeant.'

Lewis changed tack. 'You saw Harry pretty regularly while he was inside?'

'Once a week, usually.'

'How did you get there?'

'Friends, mostly.'

'Awkward place to get to.'

'Yep.'

'When did you last see him?'

'Week ago.'

'What did you take him?'

'Bit o' cake. Few cigs. No booze, no drugs – nothin' like that. You can't get away with much there.'

'Can you get away with *anything* there?'

She leaned forward again and smiled as she drew deeply on her cigarette. 'Perhaps I could have done if I'd tried.'

'Could he give *you* anything? To take out?'

'Well, nothin' he shouldn't. Just as strict about that as the other way round. We all sat at tables, you know, and they were watchin' us all the time – all the screws. You'd be lucky to get away with anythin'.'

But Lewis knew that it was all a little too pat, this easy interchange. Things got in, and things got out – every prison was the same; and everybody knew it. Including this woman. And for the first time Lewis sensed that Strange was probably right: that the letter received by Thames Valley Police had been written by Harry Repp at Bullingdon Prison, handed to one of his visitors, and posted somewhere outside – at Lower Swinstead, say.

For whatever reason.

But as yet Lewis couldn't identify such a reason.

'*Did* Harry ever ask you to take anything out of prison?'

'Come off it! What'd he got in there to take *out*?'

'Letters perhaps?' suggested Lewis quietly.

'If he'd forgotten some address. Not often, though.'

'To some of his old cronies?'

'Crooks, you mean?'

'That's what I'm asking you, I suppose.'

'Few letters, yes. He didn't want them people in there lookin' through everythin' he wrote. Nobody would.'

'So you occasionally took one away?'

'Not difficult, was it? Just slip it in your handbag.'

'What was the last one you took out?'

'Can't remember.'

'I think you can.' Lewis was surprised with the firm tone of his own voice.

'No, I can't. Just told you, didn't I?' (Yet another cigarette.)

'Please don't lie to me. You see, I *know* you posted a letter at Lower Swinstead. Harry'd asked you to post it there because he thought – he was wrong as it turned out – that it would be postmarked from there.'

For the first time in the interview, Debbie Richardson seemed unsure of herself, and Lewis pressed home his perceptible advantages.

'How did you get to Lower Swinstead, by the way?'

'Only three or four miles—'

'You walked?'

'No, I drove—' She stopped herself. But the words, in Homeric phrase, had escaped the barrier of her teeth.

'Didn't you say you couldn't drive?'

'Lied to you, didn't I?'

'Why? Why lie to me?'

'I get used to it, that's why.' She leaned forward across the table. And Lewis saw for certain what he had already suspected for semi-certain – that she wore no bra beneath her dress; probably no knickers, either.

'How often do you go to the pub there, the Maiden's Arms?'

'Often as I can.'

'Not in the car, I hope?'

'Sometimes get a lift there – you know, if somebody rings.'

'When were you there last?'

'When I posted the letter.'

'Open all day, is it?'

'What's all this quizzin' about?'

'Just that my boss'll be interested, that's all.'

'You're all alike, you bloody coppers!'

It seemed a strange reply, and Lewis looked puzzled.

'Pardon?'

'What you just asked me – about the pub bein' open all day. Exactly what the other fellow asked.'

'What other fellow?'

'Can't remember his name. So what? Can't remember yours, come to that.'

'When was this?'

'Last night. Asked me out for a drink, didn't he? I reckon he fancied me a little bit. But I was already—'

'From the *police*, you say?'

'That's what he said.'

'You didn't check?'

Debbie Richardson shrugged her shoulders. 'Nice he was – sort o' well educated. Know what I mean?'

'You can't recall his name?'

'No, sorry. Tell you one thing though, Sergeant, er . . .'

'Lewis.'

'Had a lovely car, he did. Been nice it would – ridin' round in that. A Jag – maroon-coloured Jag.'

Chapter Twenty-Two

> . . . a mountain range of Rubbish, like an old volcano, and its geological foundation was Dust. Coal-dust, vegetable-dust, bone-dust, crockery-dust, rough dust, and sifted dust – all manner of Dust in the accumulated Rubbish
>
> (Dickens, *Our Mutual Friend*)

'NOT FOR SCRAP, is she?' Stan Cox nodded towards the Jag parked in the no-parking area outside his office window in the Redbridge Waste Disposal Centre.

'Getting on a bit,' conceded Morse, 'like all of us. You know, windscreen wipers packing up, gear-box starting to jam, no heat . . .'

'Sounds a bit like the missus!'

'Pardon?'

'Joke, sir.'

'Ah, yes.' Morse's smile was even weaker than the witticism as he looked round the cramped office, his eyes catching a girlie calendar in the corner, from which a provocatively bare-breasted bimbo, with short blonde hair, stared back at him.

'Nice, ain't she!'

Morse nodded. 'Past her sell-by date, though. She's the May girl.'

'Remember the ol' song, sir – "From May to September"?'

'You just like having her around.'

It was Cox's turn to nod: 'Drives me mad, she does. Keeps me sane at the same time though, if you follows me meaning.'

Morse wasn't at all sure that he did, but he was conscious that he'd drunk too much beer that lunch-time; that he should never have driven himself out to Redbridge; that what he'd earlier seen as a clear-cut outline had now grown blurred around the periphery. In the pub, with Lewis, he'd felt convinced he could see a cause, a sequence, a structure, to the crime.

Perhaps two crimes now.

It was the same old tantalizing challenge to puzzles that had faced him ever since he was a boy. It was the certain knowledge that something *had* happened in the past – happened in an ordered, logical, very specific way. And the challenge had been, and still was, to gather the disparate elements of the puzzle together and to try to reconstruct that 'very specific way'.

Not too successfully now, though. For here, at Red-bridge, there seemed a great gulf fixed between the fanciful hypothesis he'd so recently formulated, and the humdrum reality of a rubbish dump.

Is that what Cox was trying to say?

'How d'you mean? Keeps you sane?'

'Well, it's not exactly your Botanical Gardens here, is it? Just all the filth and useless stuff people want shut of. So there's not much good to look at, 'cept her, bless her heart! Pearl in a pigsty – that's what she is.'

'Why don't you write her a fan-letter?'

'Think she'd read it?'

'No.'

'So what can we do for you, Chief?'

Morse told him, making most of it up as he went along.

And when he'd finished, Cox nodded. 'No problem. We'd better just let the County Authorities know.'

'Already done,' lied Morse. And refusing a cup of coffee, he left the office and walked unaccompanied around the site, only a few hundred yards from the southern stretch of Oxford's Ring Road, thinking about the things he'd learned from Cox . . .

'Do you reckon,' he'd asked, 'you could dispose of a body here, in one of your, er . . . ?'

'Only in one of the compactor bins – that'd be the best bet. You'll be able to see for yourself, though. The others are a bit too open, really.'

'Black bag, say? Put a body in it? Just chuck it in?'

'You'd need a big bag.'

'Well, let's say we've got a big bag.'

'Heavy things, bodies. Ten, twelve stone, say? You couldn't just . . . well, unless you had two people, I suppose.'

'Or cut the body in half, perhaps.'

'Mm. Still a bit awkward, wouldn't you think? Unless it were stiff, of course.'

'Yes . . .'

'*Was* it stiff, this body of yours?'

'Er, no. No, I don't think it was.'

'Or unless it was a pretty small body. *Was* it small, this body of yours?'

'Er, no. No. I don't think it was.'

'Well, as I say . . .'

'How would *you* get rid of a body here?'

'Well, if it were a littl'un, like I said, I'd go for a compactor bin. They got ramps that go back and forrard reg'lar like, and everything soon gets pushed through into the back o' the bin. Doubt anybody'd notice it really – not *this* end, anyway.'

'There's *another* end?'

'Sutton Courtenay, yes, out near Didcot. The bins get driven out there, to the landfill-site. Somebody might notice summat there, I suppose.'

'Funny, isn't it? Dustmen always seem to notice some things, don't they?'

'You mean our Waste Disposal Operatives.'

'They refused to take my little bag of grass cuttings last week.'

'Ah, now you're talking business, sir.'

'Put a human head in the bottom of the bag though – '

' – and you'd probably get away with it? Right! But I shouldn't try your grass cuttings again, Inspector.'

As he walked around, Morse was impressed by the layout and the management of the large area designated there to the various categories of Oxford's disposable debris: car batteries; can bank; engine-oil cans; paper bank; clothing bank; tools; bottles (green, brown, white); bulky items; scrap metal; fridges and freezers; garden waste (green); garden waste (other) . . .

Only the vast 'Bulky Items' bins seemed to offer any scope so far; and even there a body would have lain uncomfortably and conspicuously amid the jagged edges of broken tables, awkwardly angled cupboards, tilted mattresses.

Then Morse stood still for many minutes inspecting what he'd been waiting to see: the compactor bins – twelve of them in a row. Each bin (Morse attempted a none-too-scientific analysis) was a 12-ton, 6 ft. × 20 ft., white-bodied metal container, a broad green stripe painted horizontally along its middle, with a grilled covering at the receiving end which customers could easily lift before depositing their car-booted detritus there; and where a ramp was ever moving forward and back, forward and back, and pushing the divers deposits from the bin's mouth through into some unseen, unsavoury interior. On the side of each bin were 'start/stop' and 'red/green' buttons and switches which appeared to control the complex operation; and even as Morse watched, a site-workman came alongside, somehow interpreting the evidence and (presumably?) deciding whether any particular bin was sufficiently stuffed to get lifted on to one of the great lorries lumbering around, and to get carted off to – where was it? – Sutton Courtenay.

Morse tackled the young pony-tailed operative as he was tapping one of the bins, rather like a man tapping the upturned hull of some stricken submarine to see if there were any signs of life.

'How long's it take to fill one of these things?'

'Depends. Holidays and weekends? Pretty quick – only a day, sometimes. Usually though? Two, three days. Depends, like I said.'

'How many bins have gone today?'

'Two? No, three, I think.'

'You didn't, er, notice anything unusual about ... about anything?'

'What sort o' thing, mate?'

'Forget it, son! And, by the way, I wasn't aware I *was* one of your mates.'

'An' I wasn't aware you was me fuckin' father, neither!' spat the spotty-faced youth, as an outsmarted Morse walked unhappily away.

It had not been a particularly productive afternoon. Morse hadn't even had the nous to bring his little bag of grass cuttings along, to be tossed, with full official blessing, into the garden waste (green) depository.

Back in Cox's office Morse was (for him) comparatively generous with his gratitude for the help he'd been provided with. And before leaving, he took a last look at the month of May's lascivious self-offering to all who looked and longed and lusted after her. People like Stanley Cox; like Cox's fellow Waste Disposal Operatives; like Chief Inspector Morse, who stood in front of her again and thought she reminded him of another woman – a woman he'd met so very recently.

Reminded him of Debbie Richardson.

Chapter Twenty-Three

A novel, like a beggar, should always be kept 'moving on'. Nobody knew this better than Fielding, whose novels, like most good ones, are full of inns

(Augustine Birrell, *The Office of Literature*)

It was still only 2.30 p.m. that same day when Lewis pulled into the small car park of the Maiden's Arms, a low-roofed building of Cotswold stone which was Lower Swinstead's only public house. A notice beside the entrance announced the opening hours for Friday as 12 noon–3 p.m., 6.30–11 p.m.

At a table by the sole window of the small bar sat two aged villagers drinking beer from straight pint glasses, smoking Woodbines, and playing cribbage. Only one other customer: a pale-faced, ear-pierced, greasy-haired youth, who stood feeding coin after coin into an unresponsive fruit machine. When Lewis asked for the landlord, the man behind the bar introduced himself as no less a personage.

'What can I get you, sir?'

Lewis showed his ID. 'Can we talk?'

Tom Biffen was a square of a man, small of stature and wide of body, his weather-beaten features framed with a grizzly beard, a pair of humorous eyes, and a single ear-ring in the left lobe. A dark-blue T-shirt paraded 'The Maidens Arms' across a deep chest.

Lewis came to the point without preamble: 'You know a woman called Deborah – Deborah Richardson?'

'Debbie? Oh yeah. Everybody knows Debbie.' He spoke with a West Country burr, and clearly neither of the card-players was hard-of-hearing, for had Lewis had occasion to turn round at that moment he would have noted a half-smiling nod of agreement on each of their faces.

Lewis continued: 'Her partner's been released from prison this morning. You know Harry Repp?'

'Harry? Oh yeah! Everybody knows Harry.' (The fingers of the card-players froze momentarily, and each had stopped smiling.)

'He's not been in this morning?'

'I'd've seen him if he had, wouldn't I?'

'It's just that he's not been home yet, that's all. And we want to make sure he's OK.'

'Having a noggin or two somewhere, I shouldn't wonder. That's what I'd be doing.'

'How long have you been landlord here?'

'Let's see now . . .'

'Seven year come September, Biff,' came an answer from behind.

'Thank you, Bert!' Biff turned his attention back to Lewis as he held a proprietorially polished glass up to the light like a radiographer examining an X-ray. 'You're going to ask me about the murder – I know that. There's been things in the papers, and we're all interested. Can't pretend we're not. Biggest thing ever happened round here.'

'Lots of rumours, weren't there? You know, about Mrs Harrison. Having a bit on the side, perhaps?'

'Well, it weren't me! And Alf and Bert here, they're both a bit past it now.'

('Speak for yourself!' – from one of the septuagenarians.)

'Did she ever come in here with any men?'

Biff shook his head indeterminately: 'Simon, the boy? Only occasionally though. Deaf, see! I 'spect it was a bit dull for him – not being able to hear the sparkling repartee of my regulars, like Alf and Bert here.'

('Used to drink Coca-Cola – ' from Alf, or was it Bert?)

'What about the daughter?'

'Sarah? Nice pair o' legs, Sarah.'

('Not the only nice pair o' things!' – *sotto voce* from behind.)

'With a boyfriend in tow, was it?'

'Sometimes.'

'With her mum?'

'Nah! Wouldn't have wanted *her* around, would she?'

'Why not?'

'Well . . . attractive, wasn't she, Sarah? It was her mum had the real sex-appeal, though. Could have had most fellahs round here, if they'd had a jar or two.'

('Even if they hadn't!' – from Bert, or was it Alf?)

'Did you ever come up with any names?'

'Names? Nah! Like I said . . .'

'Must have been rumours though?'

'Never heard any meself.' Biff looked over Lewis's shoulder: 'You ever hear any rumours, lads?'

'Not me,' said Bert.

'Nor me,' said Alf.

Lewis felt certain that all three of them were lying. And, according to the report, the police on the original enquiry had felt very much the same: that the villagers were quite willing to hint that Yvonne Harrison had not exactly been the high priestess of marital fidelity; but that when it came to naming names, they'd decided to clamp up. En bloc.

'Drink on the house, sir?'

Lewis declined, and bade his farewell, nodding to the card-players as he walked to the door, where he stopped and turned back towards the landlord, pointing to the T-shirt:

'Shouldn't there be an apostrophe before the "s"?'

Biff grinned. 'Funny you should say that. Fellow in here last night asked me exactly the same thing!'

Lewis walked slowly round to the car park, noting the plaque on the side-wall:

Parking strictly for customers.
Other vehicles will be clamped.
Release fee £25

Need more than that, thought Lewis, to un-clamp a small community which was so clearly still maintaining its conspiracy of silence.

But Lewis was wrong.

As he took out his car-keys, he saw the youth who had just been feeding the fruits of his labours into the fruit machine. Waiting for him. Beside the car.

'Police, aincha?'

'Yes?'

'You was asking about things in there.'

'I'm always asking about things.'

'Just that somebody else was asking them same sort o' questions, see? Couldn't help hearing, could I? And this fellah – he was asking *me* a few things. About Mrs Harrison. About if I'd ever seen her with any fellah in the pub. But I couldn't quite remember. Not at the time.'

'You remember now, though?'

'Right on the nail, copper. Told me to give 'im a buzz if I suddenly remembered something. Said, you know, it might be worthwhile like.'

'Why didn't you ring him?'

'That's just it, though. I'd seen her with the fellah that *asked* me, see? Same bleedin fellah!'

'You mean . . . it was *him* you'd seen with Mrs Harrison?'

'Right on the nail, copper.'

'What did he look like, this fellow?'

'Well, sort of . . . I can't really . . .'

'He gave you his name?'

'No. Gave me 'is phone number though, like I said.'

The youth produced a circular beer-mat from his pocket.

Lewis looked down at a telephone number written above the red *Bass* triangle, written in the small, neat hand he knew so well: the personal ex-directory telephone number of Chief Inspector Morse.

Chapter Twenty-Four

In many an Oxfordshire Ale-house the horseshoe is hung upside-down, in the form that is of an Arch or an Omega. This age-old custom (I have been convincingly informed) is not to allow the Luck to run out but to prevent the Devil building up a nest therein.

(D. Small, *A Most Complete Guide to the Hostelries of the Cotswolds*)

As he stood amid the wilderness of waste, a High Viz jacket over his summer shirt and a red safety helmet on his head, Chief Inspector Morse realized that he had miscalculated rather badly. But he'd had to check it up.

It had always been the same with him. Whenever as a young boy reading under his bedside lamp he'd come across an unfamiliar word, he'd known with certainty that he could never look forward to sleep until he'd traced the newcomer's credentials and etymology in *Chambers' Dictionary*, the book that stood alongside *The Family Doctor* (1910), *A Pictorial History of the Great War*, and *The Life of Captain Cook*, on the single short shelf that comprised his parents' library.

His father (sadly, almost tragically) had been a clandestine gambler. And Morse was fully aware that this time he himself had put his money on a rank outsider: the possibility that someone had murdered Harry Repp; had disposed of his body in the Redbridge Waste Disposal Centre; had disposed of this hypothetical body in a particular part of that Centre – specifically in one of the compactor bins perhaps: further, that the said and equally hypothetical bin had been, was being, or was about to be, driven out in a hypothetical black bag to Sutton Courtenay. And, above all, that somebody might have *observed* such a hypothetical deposit. Ridiculous! William Hill or Ladbrokes would probably have offered odds of 1,000,000–1 against any such eventuality.

On impulse Morse had driven down the A34, thence along the A4130, to the land-fill site on the outskirts of Sutton Courtenay. Where, after a series of telephone calls from the temporary (permanent) Portakabins, the management had finally acknowledged the *bona fides* of their dubious visitor.

It was in a Land-rover that (finally) Morse had been driven out to the tipping area, where virtually continuous convoys of lorries from the whole of Oxfordshire were raising the telescopic legs of container-cargoes to some 45 degrees as they began to tip their loads; moving forward in disjunctive jerks as they ensured the contents were fully discharged, and leaving behind a distinctive trail of their own particular type of rubbish. As a rather dispirited Morse watched these operations, he imagined that perhaps when viewed from some hovering helicopter each truck would seem like an artist's brush, with the trail of the gradually extending rubbish like a stroke of variegated paint being smeared across the canvas of the landscape. But Morse accepted the more prosaic truth of the situation immediately: the truck drivers themselves would very seldom, if ever, have occasion to notice, let alone to examine, the contents of the loads they were emptying.

He voiced his thoughts. 'If a driver dumped a body . . . well, he wouldn't really know much about it, would he?'

Colin Rice, the site manager, hesitated awhile before replying – not because he had the slightest doubt about the answer to this question, but because he felt reluctant immediately to disappoint his somewhat melancholic inquisitor.

'No.'

'How many of those compactor bins do you get from Redbridge every day?'

'Depends.'

'Today?'

'Four or five? I could check.'

'No. No need.'

Morse watched as the yellow-painted BOMAG tractors were once again setting about their dismal business, the metal teeth of their giant wheels compacting the recently deposited mounds; and then, with a fair-weather frontage reminiscent of a snowplough, pushing forward the levelled rubbish towards its burial ground.

For the moment Morse said nothing more, suddenly

and strangely aware that, if he half-closed his eyes, the piles of refuse around him could almost appear like some wondrously woven multi-coloured quilt, black and white mostly, but interspersed with vivid little patches of blue and red and yellow.

It was Rice who spoke: 'If anybody'd see anything it'd be those chaps on the levellers. They're looking forward at all the rubbish, see? Your normal truck driver, he's not even looking backwards at it.'

'You wouldn't be able to pin-point the place where any lorry-loads from Redbridge . . . ?'

The site manager shook his head. 'No chance.'

'If you had enough personnel though?'

'How many?'

'Five or six?'

'Five or six hundred, you mean?'

Morse decided to quit the unequal struggle. He kicked a hole in one of the black plastic bags at his feet, and briefly surveyed the nauseating mixture of spaghetti and tomatoes that oozed therefrom, like the innards of a road-squashed rabbit.

'If you'd like to stay?' suggested Rice, without enthusiasm. 'You never know. We had a load of brand-new cameras dumped here once.'

'I've never had a camera myself,' admitted Morse. 'I just hope you appropriated one for yourself.'

Rice smiled, forgivingly. 'You don't really know much about the rules in a place like this, do you, sir?'

Morse lifted his eyes from the ground towards the

giant cooling-towers of Didcot Power Station which stood sentinel on the immediate landscape, only a few hundred yards away.

'No, I don't,' he said quietly.

As he drove back along the A34 into Oxford, Morse doubted he'd expressed adequate thanks to Greenways Waste Management. He was (he acknowledged the fact) never a man renowned for voicing much gratitude. He'd even dismissed, and that cursorily, Rice's thoughtful offer of issuing a memo to everyone working either permanently or temporarily on the site, acquainting them with the situation.

But Morse felt unable to feel too self-critical, because he knew there *was* no 'situation'. And he repeated to himself this recently corroborated conviction as he turned on the car radio, and listened again to the slow movement of Bruckner's Seventh.

When later that same afternoon Lewis arrived back at Kidlington HQ, he felt more pleased, more excited, and (yes!) more confident in himself than he'd been for a long, long while. In almost all previous cases he'd usually reached first base only to find that Morse was already sprinting off to second base; and so on, and so on, all round the baseball pitch. So now he decided to do a little sprinting for himself.

First, he rang Redbridge – only to discover that Morse had already visited the site.

Second, he rang Sutton Courtenay – only to discover that Morse had already visited the site, and where he'd pronounced that any search of said site was quite certainly foredoomed to failure.

So Lewis had coolly countermanded these instructions.

It was as if he – Lewis – was taking charge of the case.

Well, he was, wasn't he?'

CHAPTER TWENTY-FIVE

Sometimes it is that searchers spot
The kind of thing they'd rather not
(Lessing, *Nathan der Weise*)

DURING 'JAMMIE' JARNOLD'S twenty-two years' service on the Sutton Courtenay site, he'd seen most things. Not everything. For example, he'd never caught a glimpse of that sack of notes the Metropolitan Police were certain had been deposited in one of the trucks on that long train which arrived in the early hours of each morning from Brentford, via a branchline from Didcot, with its thousands of tons of the capital's refuse. Four hundred and fifty thousand pounds, they'd said, in fivers and tenners. Yes, Jammie had kept his eyes wide open on that occasion; had occasionally climbed down from his cab to prod anything that seemed even minimally promising.

If, on balance, it was a steady old job, it was also a job that was unmemorable and predictably monotonous. For this reason, neither Jammie nor his colleagues in the team of BOMAC tractor-operators had dismissed as so much negligible bumf the single Xeroxed sheet which had been handed out that Saturday morning, both to permanent on-site personnel and to every dumper-truck driver entering the site from the far quarters of Oxfordshire.

> **MEMO FROM SITE MANAGER**
>
> Thames Valley Police have advised of the possibility of a human body, probably bagged, being recently conveyed from the Redbridge Centre in Oxford. Everyone is asked to be extra vigilant and to report anything unusual (or usual, provided its a body).

(Morse himself would have been pleased to write such a succinct note – though inserting, of course, an apostrophe in the humorous parenthesis.)

Just after the start of the shift, a colleague shouted across at Jammie, waving a copy of the memo.

'Better keep your eyes open!'

'What's the reward?'

'Night with Sophia Loren in the Savoy.'

'Bit young for me.'

'I still reckon you'll keep your eyes open.'

'Yeah! I reckon.'

'Like looking for a needle in an 'aystack though.'

'Like finding a shadow in the black-out, as me ol' mum used to say.'

'I like that, Jammie. Sort o' poetic, like.'

Jarnold braked his tractor at 10.05 a.m. and jumped down from his cab on to the semi-levelled, semi-compacted mound of recently deposited rubbish. It was not that the specific item he'd spotted was unusual in any way. In fact, any pair of shoes was a very common sight: thousands of pairs were ever to be observed on every part of the site, worn down, worn out, worn beyond any possible repair. But there were unusual aspects about this particular pair of shoes. For a start, they looked comparatively new and were clearly of good quality; then, they were the only objects sticking out of a large black bag; what's more, they seemed strangely reluctant to drop *out* of that large black bag, as if (perhaps?) they might be attached, permanently, to something *inside* that large black bag.

Jarnold shouted over to a colleague.

'Come over 'ere a sec!'

But already he had half-torn one side of the plastic.

'Christ!'

He turned away to vomit full-throatedly over a piece of conveniently positioned carpeting.

Had he been dining with Miss Loren at the Savoy, this would have caused considerable consternation. Not here, though. Not at the land-fill site at Sutton Courtenay in Oxfordshire.

Chapter Twenty-Six

UNDERGRADUATE:	But you're blowing up the wrong tyre, sir. It's the back one that's flat.
DON:	Goodness me! You mean the two of them are not connected?

(Freshman seeking to assist his tutor outside Trinity College, Oxford)

MORSE (FOR SOME REASON) was in that Saturday morning when Lewis knocked on his office door just after ten.

'Spare a few minutes, sir?'

'C'm in! I've finished the crossword.'

'How long?'

'Let's just say the brain is deteriorating.'

'Thirty thousand brain-cells a day we lose after thirty, so you told me once.'

Morse nodded morosely. 'I just thought I was the exception, that's all. Si' down!'

Lewis did so, and took a deep breath. 'I've been following you, sir.'

Morse looked across at his sergeant uncomprehendingly.

'You were at Debbie Richardson's house – before me; you were at the Maiden's Arms – before me; you were at Bullingdon – before me; you were at Redbridge – before me; you were out at Sutton Courtenay – before me. You've been one move ahead of me all the time.'

'Only *one*?'

'Why couldn't you just *tell* me?'

'Tell you what?' asked Morse. 'And don't forget that time when it was *me* following *you*: from Bullingdon. At exactly the distance recommended in the Highway Code.'

'Which is?'

'Next question?'

'You will be taking on the case, won't you?'

'Next question?'

'Why not?'

'Pass.'

'You're getting people's backs up here, you know that?'

'Nothing new about that.'

'But surely—?'

'Listen!' Unblinking blue eyes glared across the desk. 'I am not taking on the Harrison case.'

'I was just hoping you'd help me, that's all.'

'Yes?'

'Well, do you mind me asking you if . . . if you've got any personal interest in all of this?'

'Nil.' If there had been a quick flicker of unease in Morse's eyes, it was as quickly gone.

'But you know a lot about it, don't you? So you must have some idea about what happened on the night she was murdered?'

'Ideas – plural.'

'There was a logical sequence of events, as you would say.'

'There was a concatenation of events, yes, with each link of the chain causally connected to its predecessor.'

'What do you think happened that night?'

'Not much argument about that, is there?'

'You'd agree with this, then?' Lewis produced a sheet of A4 on which he had typed a timetable for the day of the murder:

7 a.m.–1 p.m.	Yvonne on early shift at JR2 Ward 7C
1.15–2 p.m.	Lunches in staff canteen
2.15–4 p.m. (?)	Drives down to Oxford shopping at M&S and Austin Reed
4.00(?)–4.30 p.m.	Drives home avoiding main traffic exodus
6–7 p.m.	Evening meal of mushroom omelette
9.00 p.m.	Local builder rings – number engaged or phone off hook
9.10 p.m.	Frank H gets phone call and catches 21.48 Paddington to Oxford train
9.30 p.m.	Builder rings again – ringing-tone but no reply
11.00 p.m.	F H gets taxi to Lower Swinstead
11.20 p.m.	Discovers wife naked, gagged, handcuffed and dead

Morse glanced at the sheet in perfunctory fashion.

'You ought to use the Oxford comma more.'

'Pardon?'

'The presumption was – is – that somewhere between nine and half-past . . .'

'Pathologist's report seemed to confirm that.'

'Would I had your faith in pathologists!'

'Not just that though, is it? The whole thing hangs together. Pretty well everything there's confirmed: statements from the hospital; receipts from the two shops; post-mortem details on the meal; phone calls checked out—'

'Nonsense! The builder? First time the number's engaged? Second time nobody answers? How the hell do you check that?'

'You can't check absolutely everything—'

'What about the husband? Odd sort of call, wasn't it? Drop whatever you're doing and get here double-quick! So who was it who rang him?'

'That's what I'm asking you, sir.'

'His number couldn't have been too well known. He was renting a flat, wasn't he?'

'Still is.'

'But somebody knew it – and rang him. Did we check the phone records of the suspects?'

'What suspects?'

'The two children?'

'They *weren't* suspects. And if they were, why shouldn't they ring their dad occasionally?'

'How did he pay for his train journey?'

'No credit-card record – must have paid cash. *And*

for the taxi ride. Anyway, he'd got the best alibi of anybody: taxi driver remembers the time exactly. He was just listening to the 11 o'clock news-headlines.'

'Was the train a bit late that night? If it's the one I sometimes catch, it's due in at 22.53.'

'Too late to find out, sir.'

'Rubbish! Too difficult, possibly. But they keep all these times of arrivals: they make statistical tables out of 'em, for heaven's sake.'

'Must've been on time, surely?'

'What? Seven minutes for somebody in one helluva rush? From Platform 2 to the taxi-rank? It'd only take a geriatric like me a couple of minutes.'

'Perhaps there was a queue.'

'*Was* there a queue?'

'Dunno. Perhaps he nipped into the snack-bar.'

'Closed.'

'I don't quite see what you're getting at.'

'What is essential, Lewis, is usually invisible to the outward eye.'

'Which doesn't help *me* much, does it?'

'All right. Get back to your facts.'

'She was burgled. At some point that evening the back patio window was smashed in from the outside and somebody was after something. The TV was unplugged – '

'But not taken.'

' – so he was probably disturbed. He must have thought the place was empty. Probably none of the lights would have been on – not then anyway. Midsummer, wasn't it? Sunset was about a quarter-past nine –

I looked it up.' (Morse nodded approvingly.) 'I know some people always leave one or two lights on anyway when they go out—'

'But she *didn't* go out.'

'No. So as I say the burglar must have thought the coast was clear, and must have been prepared for the alarm to ring – it's quite a way to the next house – while he grabbed a few of the valuables, smartish like.'

'The alarm was ringing when Harrison got there, wasn't it? Twenty-past eleven.'

Lewis nodded. 'Two hours or so after she was murdered.'

'And the alarm would cut out automatically after twenty minutes' ringing?'

'Yes.'

'So?'

'I dunno, sir. But it seems we didn't discount the theory that the murderer might have set it off himself.'

'You mean two hours *later*?'

'I don't know what I mean.'

'Pretty little puzzle.'

'You're not trying to help me, are you? You've usually got some theory or other of your own.'

Morse smiled amiably. 'The obvious one. Mrs H surprised a burglar and the burglar panicked and murdered her. Or perhaps . . .' (the smile had faded) '. . . perhaps she was entertaining one of her lovers that night and things went wrong – things went sadly wrong. That's all I've got to offer: the burglar theory and the lover theory. What else is there?'

'Maybe a bit of both, sir? Say she was in bed with

some fellow when she heard the window being smashed in and . . .'

'Could well be.'

'You see, she'd *not* had sex that night, sir – certainly not been raped or tortured or physically assaulted. Clothes all neatly folded by the side of the bed.'

'Couldn't the murderer have folded them? Doesn't take me long to fold a pair of pyjamas.'

Lewis shook his head slowly. 'Naked, gagged, handcuffed . . .'

'Yes,' agreed Morse. 'Don't forget the handcuffs.'

'Not much good remembering them, either.'

'No. I recall they were, er, not to be found later on.'

'But all the proper procedures were gone through. Left on her wrists till the PM, and the path people did all the usual checks – blood, fibres, hairs. Couldn't come up with anything though, could they? *And* they checked them for prints – job they'd normally leave to the SOCOs. Bit of a muddle, by the sound of it. Probably that's how they came to be lost.'

'Temporarily misplaced, Lewis.'

'Not the only things that went missing, were they? There was a file of personal letters . . .'

'I doubt they'd ever have been much help.'

'We still didn't do a very good job.'

'Bloody awful job.'

'If only we knew who rang Frank Harrison in London that night!'

'One of his children, the builder, the burglar, the lover, the candlestick-maker? I'm like you: I don't know. But unlike you I'm not concerned with the case.'

Lewis looked shrewdly into Morse's face. 'You're *interested* though, I think.'

Morse got to his feet. 'Just give me a lift down to Oddbins. I'm out of Glenfiddich.'

The phone rang as they were leaving.

'Morse?' (Strange's unmistakable voice.)

'Sir?'

'Listen to this!'

'Not me, sir. It just so happens that Sergeant Lewis—'

'MORSE!' But the receiver had already been transferred; and although aware of the explosions at the other end of the line, Morse walked out into the corridor and along to the Gentlemen's loo.

On his return, the telephone conversation had concluded.

'They've found a body. Out at Sutton Courtenay.'

'Just like I said.'

'No, sir. Not just like you said. *You* told the people there not to worry any more. It was *me* who told them to keep looking.'

'Well done! You were right and I was wrong. I *thought* Repp was due for his come-uppance, and probably he thought so too. But I just didn't follow it through. That letter he wrote from prison was a cry for help in a way, asking us to keep a protective eye on him. Which we did, of course. Or rather which we didn't.'

Suddenly he gave his chest a vigorous massage with his right hand.

'OK, sir?'

'Bit of indigestion.'

'You sure?'

'They've found the body, you say?'

'Half an hour ago.'

'You'd better get off then.'

'Will you come along?'

'Certainly not. I'm not worried about him any longer. He was a cheap crook, a part-time burglar, a nasty piece of work – should have been rumbled years ago. Good riddance, Harry Repp!'

Chapter Twenty-Seven

In the afternoon they came unto a land
In which it seemèd always afternoon,
All round the coast the languid air did swoon,
Breathing like one that hath a weary dream
(Tennyson, *The Lotos-eaters*)

After an excited, if somewhat dispirited, Lewis had dropped him off at Oddbins, Morse picked up two bottles of single-malt Glenfiddich ('£4 Off When Two Are Purchased'); then walked further down the Summertown shops to Boots, where he bought two large boxes of Alka-Seltzer (sixty tablets in all) and two packets of extra-strength BiSoDoL (sixty tablets in all), reckoning that such additional medicaments might keep him comparatively fit for a further fortnight. But in truth his acid-indigestion and heartburn were getting even worse. All right, it was a family affliction; but it gave little comfort to know that father and paternal grandfather had both endured agonies from hiatus hernia – a condition not desperately serious perhaps, but certainly far more painful than it sounded. The cure – so simple! – had been repeatedly advocated by his GP: 'Just pack up the booze!' And indeed Morse had occasionally followed such advice for a couple of days or so; only to assume, upon the temporary disappearance of the symptoms, that a permanent cure had been effected; and that a resumption of his erstwhile modus vivendi was thenceforth justified.

He would try again soon.

Not today, though.

He walked down South Parade to the Woodstock Road, turned right, and soon found himself at the Woodstock Arms, where the landlord rightly prided himself on a particularly fine pint of Morrell's Bitter – of which Morse took liberal advantage that early Saturday lunchtime. The printed menu and the chalked-up specials on the board were strong temptations to many a man. But not to Morse. These past two decades he had almost invariably taken his lunchtime calories in liquid form; and he did so now. Most of the habitués he knew by sight, if not by name; but after a few perfunctory nods he settled himself in a corner of the wall-seating, and thought of many things . . .

Instinctively (or so he told himself) he'd known that Harry Repp was doomed to die from the moment he'd left Bullingdon. Harry had known too much. Harry had been a bit-player – a bit more than a bit-player in the drama that had been enacted on the evening Yvonne Harrison was murdered. But Harry had decided to remain silent. And the reason for such silence was probably the reason for many a silence – money. Someone had ensured that Harry's discreet silence had been profitably rewarded. On his release Harry had probably decided that the goose could soon be persuaded to change the golden eggs from medium to large. But he'd miscalculated: something had happened – probably there'd been some communication during the last few weeks of his imprisonment – that had cast a cloud of fear over his impending release; justifiable fear, since he now lay stiff and cold amidst the trash and the filth of Sutton Courtenay.

It seemed a predictable outcome though far from an inevitable one, and Morse felt no real cause for any self-recrimination. Lewis would go along there – was probably there already; would join the SOCOs and supervise the necessary procedures; would draw a few tentative, temporary conclusions; would report to Strange; and all in all would probably do as good a job as any other member of the Thames Valley CID in seeking the motive for Repp's murder.

He ordered himself a third pint, conscious that the world seemed a considerably kindlier place than heretofore. He even found himself listening to the topics of conversation around him: darts, bar-billiards, Aunt Sally, push-penny . . . and perhaps (he thought) his own life might have been marginally enriched by such innocent divertissements.

Perhaps not, though.

Leaving the Woodstock Arms, he slowly walked the few hundred yards north to Squitchey Lane, where he turned right towards his bachelor flat.

No messages on the Ansafone; no letters or notes pushed through the letter-box. A free afternoon! – for which, in his believing days, he would have given thanks to the Almighty. His dark-blue Oxford University diary was beside the phone, and he looked through the following week's engagements. Not much there either, really: just that diabetes review at the Radcliffe

Infirmary at 9 a.m. on Monday. Only an hour or so that; but the imminent appointment disturbed him slightly. He had promised his consultant, and promised himself, that he would present a faithful record of his blood-sugar measurements over the previous fortnight. But he had failed to do so, and there was little he could now do to remedy the situation except to take half a dozen such measurements in the remaining interval of thirty-six hours and to extrapolate backwards therefrom, in order to present a neatly tabulated series of satisfactory readings. He'd done it before and he would do it again.

Kein Problem.

He half-filled a tumbler with Glenfiddich, then topped it up with commensurate tap-water. Such dilution (a recent innovation) would, as Morse knew, mark him out in the eyes of many a Scot as a sacrilegious Sassenach. But according to his GP, the liver preferred things that way; and Morse's liver (according to the same source) was in need of a bit of tender loving care, along with his heart, kidneys, stomach, pancreas, lungs.

Lungs . . .

Well, at least he'd finally managed to pack up smoking, a filthy habit, as he now recognized; but one which had given him almost as much pleasure as any other vice in life. And he knew that were he privy to the date and time of an early Judgement Day (the following Monday, say) he would set off immediately to the nearest newsagent's to buy in a store of cigarettes. And he almost did so now, as if he could already hear the trumpets sounding on the other side.

In the living room, he selected Bruno Walter's early recording of *Die Walküre*, with Lauritz Melchior and Lotte Lehmann singing the rôles of Siegmund and Sieglinde. Wonderful! So Morse turned the volume-control to maximum as he listened to the anagnorisis at the end of Act I, and heard neither of the telephone calls made to his ex-directory number that afternoon, conscious only that he was falling deliciously asleep as the benighted brother and sister rushed off into the forest to beget Siegfried . . .

It was coming up to 2.45 p.m. when Morse jerked abruptly awake, disappointed that his semi-erotic dream was prematurely terminated: a dream of a woman seated intimately close to him – a dream of Debbie Richardson, with legs provocatively crossed, the texture of the cheap black stockings tautly stretched along her upper thighs.

Wonderful!

But even as she'd leaned towards him, he'd voiced his deep anxiety: 'Aren't you frightened someone will come in?'

'No one'll come in. Harry won't be comin' back. Ever. I'll get you another drink. Just – stay – where – you – are.'

So Morse had stayed where he was, awaiting her return with impatience, and with an empty glass beside him. And when he awoke, he was still sitting there alone, awaiting her return with impatience, and with an empty glass beside him.

Wagner had long since run his course, and finally Morse got to his feet and turned off the CD player. He felt tired, hot, thirsty – and a sharp pain in his chest betokened another bout of indigestion. In the bathroom, he cleaned his teeth and dropped three Alka-Seltzer tablets into a glass of water; then he filled up the wash-basin and thrice dipped his head into the cold water. The tablets had fizzed and dissolved and he downed the dosage at a single draught. Thence to his bedroom, where he took his blood-sugar level: 24.8 – almost off the scale. His own fault, since he'd forgotten to inject himself at lunchtime – making up for it now, though, with an extra four units of Actrapid insulin. Just to be on the safe side. Back in the bathroom, he drank two further glasses of cold water, acknowledging how surprisingly pleasing was its taste, since water had seldom figured prominently in his drinking habits. Finally he decided that a couple of Paracetamol would be appropriate. So he shook out the tablets on to his palm; shook out three in fact – and decided to take the three. Just to be on the safe side.

Suddenly he was feeling much better, his faith in this curious combination of assorted medicaments seemingly justified once more. Suddenly, too, he decided to follow his consultant's somewhat despairing exhortation to take a bit of exercise occasionally. Why not? It was a warm and gentle summer's day.

In the small entrance hall, he noticed the figure '2' on the window of his Ansafone. Pressing 'Play' he listened to the first message:

Morse? Janet! Ten-past one Saturday afternoon. Good news! I hope to be back in Oxford on the 14th. So you'll be able to take me somewhere? To bed perhaps? Give me a ring – soon. Bye!

Any semi-remembrance of Debbie Richardson was lingering no longer, and Morse smiled happily to himself. He would ring immediately. But the second message had followed without a pause, and he was destined not to ring Sister McQueen that afternoon.

Instead he dialled HQ and finally got through to the young PC who had driven him out to Bullingdon the previous morning in an unmarked police car.

'Get the same car, Kershaw – nice, comfy seats – and pick me up from home *quam celerrime.*'

'Pardon?'

'Smartish!'

'Sir, I was just going off duty when you rang and I've—'

'Make it five minutes!'

Deeply puzzled, Morse walked back into the sitting-room where he sat in the black-leather armchair; and where his right hand reached for whisky once more as mentally he rehearsed that second, quite extraordinary message on the Ansafone:

Sir? Lewis here – half-past one, nearly – I'm out at Sutton Courtenay. Please come along as soon as you can – for my sake if nobody else's. I think you should get here before we move the body. You see, sir, it isn't the body of Harry Repp.

Chapter Twenty-Eight

Alas, poor Yorick! – I knew him, Horatio
(Shakespeare, *Hamlet*)

It was just after 4 p.m. that same Saturday afternoon when Morse and Lewis finally sat down together in the requisitioned office of the site manager.

'Straightaway I knew it wasn't him, sir, when I saw his arms. Harry Repp had this tattoo: all twisted chains and anchors, you know – a sort of . . .' Lewis undulated his hands vertically, as if tracing a woman's willowy figure.

'Convoluted involvement,' suggested Morse gently.

'Well, this fellow's not got any, has he? Anyway he's much smaller, only – what? – five-four, five-five. Doesn't weigh much either – eight, nine stone? No more.'

Morse nodded. 'And he's got different coloured hair, and he's got a port-wine stain on his neck, and he's not wearing Repp's clothes, and his shoes are three sizes smaller—'

'All right. I wasn't expecting the Queen's Medal!'

At which Eddie Andrews, the 2i/c senior SOCO, knocked on the door and entered the office, at once uncertain whether to address himself to Morse or to Lewis. He decided on the former:

'Safe, I reckon, to move him now? Dr Hobson says there's not much else she can do here.'

Morse shrugged. 'You'd better ask Sergeant Lewis. He's in charge.'

And Lewis rose to the occasion. 'Yes, move him. Thank you.'

As he was about to leave, Andrews noticed the TV set.

'Mind if I just see how Northants are getting on in the cricket?'

'Important to you, is it?' queried Morse mildly.

Andrews was digitally discovering Sport (Cricket) on Ceefax when the office door burst open to admit a florid-faced Chief Superintendent Strange, an officer resolutely determined to retain the appellation 'Chief', whatever most of his collateral colleagues in the Force were doing.

'You've ruined my afternoon's golf, Lewis! You know that?'

Surprisingly, the words were spoken with little sign of animus. But before Lewis could respond in any way, Strange was addressing Morse in considerably sharper tones:

'And how exactly do *you* come to be here?'

'Same as you really, sir. Ruined my day, too. I was just indulging in a little Egyptian PT – '

'After indulging in a lot of Scottish whisky by the smell of it!'

' – when Lewis here rang and asked me to come along. Well, he's been a faithful soul most of the time, so . . .'

'So you just came along as a sort of personal favour?'

'That's about it.' (Andrews sidled silently from the room.)

'Well let me tell you one thing, matey. You won't be staying *on* as a personal favour – is that clear? You'll be staying on because you're in charge of *this* case – because that's an *order*. You may have had some excuse as far as the Harrison case was concerned: I could just about understand that.' (Strange's voice had momentarily dropped to a semi-sympathetic register.) 'But you've no bloody excuse now. And if you decide to get on your high horse again and start arguing the toss with me, you'll be up before the Chief Constable first thing Monday morning!'

'The Chief's on furlough,' interposed a brave Lewis.

'Shut up, Lewis! And he'll have your guts for garters, Morse. So that's settled. All you've got to do is sober up and put your thinking-cap on.'

'I usually think better when—' But Morse's disquisition on his personal style of ratiocination was cut short by a further knock, with Dr Hobson's pretty head appearing round the door.

'Oh, sorry! It's just—'

'Come in!' growled Strange, his jowls still wobbling.

'Just thought I'd check. We've got him outside and Andrews says it's OK if—'

'Who *is* he?' asked Strange.

'Don't know. I had a tentative feel round his pockets. No wallet, though, no cards—'

'He's pretty easily recognizable though?'

'Oh, yes. His face is fine. It's his stomach that's all a gory mess where the knife or whatever it was went in.'

'At least we've got a good mug-shot of him then.'

'Probably identify him straightaway. I got this from his trouser-pocket.'

Strange looked down at a white 'Cardholder's Copy' receipt from Oddbins of Banbury Road, itemizing the purchase of a crate of Guinness, the number of the Visa credit card printed below in a faded indigo.

'There we are, Lewis! Shouldn't be too difficult, should it?' He handed over the receipt with an unconvincing smile. 'Unless you manage to lose *that*, of course.'

It was a hurtful dig. But the patient Lewis briefly examined the evidence himself, and sought to put a finger on the fairly obvious:

'Not much chance this afternoon, sir. Saturday? The banks'll all be shut.'

'What? For Christ's sake, man! We've put someone on the moon, remember? And you say we can't trace a credit-card number because it's a bloody *Saturday*! Is that what you're telling me?'

Morse had remained silent during these exchanges; and remained so now, his brain already galloping several furlongs ahead of the field. And Lewis, after such a withering rebuke, also remained silent, holding the receipt tightly, like a punter clutching a winning betting-slip. Only Strange, it appeared, was willing to break the awkward silence as he turned again to Dr Hobson.

'They're just carting him off, you say?'

'Yes.'

'Well, let us know – let Chief Inspector Morse know – what you come up with. Sooner the quicker. Understood?'

'Of course.'

The assembled personages rose to their feet; and matters at Sutton Courtenay were seemingly now at an end.

But not so; not quite.

It was Morse, at last, who made his brief though extraordinarily significant contribution to the afternoon's developments.

'Sir, I think you ought to have a look at him.'

'I don't like dead bodies any more than you do, Morse.'

'I know that, but . . .'

'But *what*?'

'. . . but you ought to have a look at him.' Morse spoke his words slowly and quietly. 'You see, I think it's quite possible that you'll recognize him.'

Frequently afterwards, in the post-Morse years, would Sergeant Lewis recall that afternoon at the fill-in site in Oxfordshire: when Chief Superintendent Strange had looked at the bloodless face of a murdered man; and when his erstwhile ruddy cheeks had paled to chalky white.

'Bloody 'ell! I knew him, Morse. I interviewed him twice in the Harrison murder enquiry.'

When the top brass had finally dispersed, Eddie

Andrews let himself back into the now deserted office, turned on the TV, found Sport (Cricket) on Ceefax and noted with quiet satisfaction that Northamptonshire were really doing rather well that day.

Chapter Twenty-Nine

CALIPH: And now how shall we employ the time of waiting for our deliverance?
JAFAR: I shall meditate upon the mutability of human affairs
MASRUR: And I shall sharpen my sword upon my thigh
HASSAN: And I shall study the pattern of this carpet
CALIPH: Hassan, I will join thee: Thou art a man of taste

(James Elroy Flecker, *Hassan*)

MOST PATIENTLY – NO, most impatiently – had PC Kershaw been waiting for his passenger to emerge from the closeted consultations. Like some starry-eyed teenager he had been looking forward so much to his first date with Susan Ho, a delightful, delicately featured Chinese girl, a researcher at Oxford's Criminological Department; and although he had been able to contact her after Morse's diktat, neither he nor she had been particularly pleased.

He opened the passenger door as Morse approached.

'It's all right, Kershaw. Sergeant Lewis'll be taking me back to Oxford.'

'You mean—?'

'I mean you can bugger off, yes.'

'Couldn't you have told me earlier, sir? I've been . . .'

But his voice trailed off as he found Morse's blue eyes looking straight at him; uncomprehending, cold.

Lewis was grinning wryly as he pushed the police car into first gear. 'You never treated even me as bad as that.'

'Cocky young sod! University graduate, God help us!'

'What's he doing with us?'

'Dunno. Learning how to make a cup o' tea, I shouldn't wonder.'

'Exactly where I started.'

'I hope he's better than you were.'

'Isn't it about time you told—'

'I just don't believe this!' said Morse as he picked up the single cassette that lay in the tray beside the gear-lever, inserted it into the player, and subsequently sank back into his seat with the look of a man sublimely satisfied with life.

'Just find out who usually drives this car, Lewis. He's a man after my own heart. I never realized we had such sensitivity in the Force. There's not much of it out there, you know.'

For a moment it seemed that Lewis was going to speak. But clearly he thought better of it; and as he drove way above the speed limit down the A34 to Oxford, he listened, with considerable enjoyment himself, to the Prelude to Wagner's *Parsifal*, convinced that Morse was soundly albeit unsnoringly asleep.

'Turn off here, Lewis.'

'Next exit's best, sir – avoid the city traffic that way.'

'Turn off *here*!'

So Lewis turned off there, driving sedately now, up the Abingdon Road, past Christ Church, straight over through Cornmarket and Magdalen Street, where (as bidden) he turned left at the lights by the Martyrs' Memorial and duly stopped (as bidden) on the double-yellows beneath the canopy of the Randolph, above which the Union Jack and the flag of the EC drooped languorously that late afternoon.

Lewis was still in brave mood. 'Like the Super said, don't you think you ought—'

'*Think*? That's exactly why I'm here – to think! I can't think unless I'm given the chance to think. You don't imagine I drink just for the *pleasure* of it, do you?'

Morse sat back with his pint of bitter and stared serenely at the Ashmolean Museum just opposite in Beaumont Street. 'If there's a bar anywhere in Britain with a better view than this . . .'

Lewis hesitated awhile over his orange juice. 'You ready to tell me how you knew it was Paddy Flynn?'

'I didn't really *know*. Just that I always wondered about him a bit. Key witness, agreed? Picked up Frank Harrison from the railway station, then parked outside the house just when the burglar alarm was ringing.'

Lewis nodded. 'Only person to give Harrison a convincing alibi.'

It was Morse's turn to nod. 'That's why Strange interviewed him.'

'Interviewed him twice.'

'Suspicious mind, that man's got!'

'But you're still not telling me how you guessed it was *him.*'

'Full of guesses, what we do, isn't it? After the first couple of days, I only read about the case at second hand – '

'Like me.'

' – but I remember thinking I'd have put an each-way bet on some of the outsiders in the race: the builder – he gave himself and several others an alibi; the landlord at the Maiden's Arms – he's got the testosterone level of a randy billy-goat; and then there was the taxi driver . . .'

'Why *him,* though?'

'Put yourself in his position. You pick up your fare outside the station and drive him out to Lower Swinstead; and there you're asked if you want to earn a bit – a lot – of extra money. You don't really have to do much at all. Fellow says he's going into the house – *his* house, anyway – and the burglar alarm is going to ring. All you've got to do is to say, if you're questioned about things, that you heard the alarm ringing while you were parked outside. Not too difficult? The alarm *was* ringing by then. And you're offered – what? I dunno – twenty or thirty quid, two or three hundred quid? But the key point is that Flynn never fully realized how vital his testimony was going to be.'

'Are you making it all up?'

'Yes! So allow me to continue making it all up. Flynn's got little idea of why he's getting such a bonus for doing virtually bugger-all. But then he starts to read a few press-reports; and unlike our boys he puts two and two together, and he smiles to himself because he knows the answer. And pretty soon he realizes he's sold himself stupidly cheap, and he decides he'll balance the books a bit better.'

'Are you saying what I think you're saying? He's been trying to blackmail Frank Harrison?'

Morse drained his pint. 'Not sure. But I'd like to bet that someone that night was more than ready to pay his way out of trouble.'

'Or her way.'

'Could be, yes.' Morse contemplated an empty glass. 'Is it your round or mine, by the way?'

'Yours.'

Morse consulted his wristwatch. 'Good gracious me! Time you drove me home. I need a shot of insulin, Lewis. You should've reminded me.'

'You still haven't told me why you thought it was Flynn,' complained Lewis as he drove north through the Summertown shopping area.

'Small man – that's why.'

'So's the landlord of the Maiden's Arms.'

'Ah, but Flynn was very fond of Guinness.'

'What the hell's *that* got to do with anything?'

'I forget. I'm, er, I'm getting muddled.'

Lewis pulled up outside Morse's flat.

'Anything . . . anything I can do for you, sir?'

'Certainly not. It's just that I'm beginning to feel exquisitely sleepy, that's all. The day's still comparatively young, I grant you. But don't ring me – not tonight – not unless anything dramatic happens.'

'You mean' (Lewis's heart rose within him) 'you mean you *are* going to take on the case?'

'Different ball-game, isn't it? As they say in Chicago or somewhere.'

'Shall I let the Super know?'

'I've already told him – when we were at the rubbish tip.'

Lewis shook his head in benign bewilderment as Morse made to get out of the car.

'And I'll take possession of this – just temporarily, of course. And if you can find out whose it is . . .'

He pocketed the *Parsifal* cassette and was walking towards his front door when Lewis wound down the car window.

'You can keep it as long as you like, sir. But let me have it back when you've finished with it. They said at Blackwell's it's the top recording – by a fellow called Napperbush.'

'You mean . . .?'

Lewis nodded happily.

'Thou art a man of taste.'

'I thought you'd be pleased, sir.'

'By the way, Lewis, we pronounce him "K-napper-t-s-busch",' amended the Chief Inspector, pedantically separating the consonantal clusters.

Chapter Thirty

Often would the deaf man know the answers had he but the faculty of hearing the questions. Likewise would the unimaginative man guess wisely at the answers had he but the wit of posing to himself the appropriate questions

(Viscount Mumbles, from *Essays on the Imagination*)

As Lewis drove up to HQ, one particular thought was troubling him – as it often had: the marked inferiority of his own mental processes compared with those of the man he had just left; the man who was doubtless now sleeping off the effects of what had been (even for Morse) a hyper-alcoholic afternoon. It wasn't that his own processes were necessarily all that much slower; just that they seemed always to leave the starting-blocks way after Morse had sprinted on ahead. Obviously (Lewis knew it!) innate intelligence was a big factor in everything: the speed of perception and understanding, the analysis of data, the linkage of things. But there was something else: the knack of *prospective* thinking, of looking ahead and asking oneself the right questions, as well as the wrong questions, about what was likely to happen in the future; and then of coming up with some answers, be they right or wrong.

So frequently in previous cases had Morse led him along, and by prompting the right questions evinced the right sort of answers. 'Socratic dialectic', Morse had called it, recounting how Socrates had managed to elicit from a totally untutored slave-boy the basic principles of plane geometry – just by asking the right questions.

So.

So, in his office that early evening, Lewis visualized himself seated opposite Morse – opposite Socrates, rather.

You've got to find the car, haven't you? The car that dumped the body? Where will you find it?

I don't know.

Where would you *have driven that car?*

I don't know. Anywhere, I suppose.

Isn't there blood everywhere? Blood all over your clothes?

Yes.

Haven't you got to change your clothes then?

Yes.

So you couldn't just leave the car anywhere, *could you? You couldn't walk too far all covered in blood?*

No.

So where would you go?

I'd go home, like as not.

Before, or after, you'd ditched the car?

Before, probably, although . . .

Go on!

Might be a bit risky. Neighbours would probably

notice the strange car. Might even notice the blood-stained clothes.

What's the alternative for you?

Well, get someone to meet me somewhere and bring me a full change of clothes.

Where would you meet?

Anywhere. How do I know. Except . . .

Go on!

If we met in a lay-by, say, I'd have to leave the car there, wouldn't I? I couldn't get back in and get the new clothes almost as blood-stained as the old. And the car would pretty certainly get reported almost immediately. So . . .

So?

So I'd have somebody to meet me. Friend? Wife, perhaps?

Where do you meet?

I don't know.

You do *know. You know the Chesterton story – I've often mentioned it.*

Remind me.

Where do you hide a leaf?

Ah, yes. In the forest.

Where do you hide a pebble?

On the shore.

Where do you hide a corpse?

On the battle-field.

And where do you hide a car?

In a car park.

Which car park?

I don't know.

The bigger the better?

Yes.

In Oxford?

Probably.

How many car parks are there in Oxford?

Dozens.

If you'd committed a murder near Oxford what would you want to do above all?

Get the hell out of the place.

How?

Drive away.

You haven't got a car now, have you?

Bus?

Where's the bus station?

Gloucester Green.

Isn't there a car park opposite?

Yes.

And you could catch a train?

Yes.

Isn't there a station car park opposite?

Yes . . .

As he drove down towards Oxford, Lewis felt pleased with himself, and just after he'd negotiated the Cutteslowe roundabout he was tempted to call in on Morse. But he put the temptation behind him. He felt fairly certain that the great man would be asleep.

And on this occasion he was right.

Instead, he decided to continue the Socratic dialogue, though this time installing *himself* as Chief

Inquisitor, and making the far bolder hypothesis that if only the blurred outlines of the anonymous murderer could be adjusted more sharply, it was Harry Repp who would come into focus.

Don't you think it would be easier, sir, for Debbie Richardson to take a change of clothes to *him*? Wouldn't it be dangerous for him to go out to Lower Swinstead?

I don't know, Lewis.

I asked you *two* questions.

I don't know. I don't know.

What do *you* think Harry Repp did?

I just don't know.

What about the car? Where's that? Come on! Back your hunch!

The car? Oh, I know where the car is, Lewis. It's parked at the back of Oxford Railway Station.

Chapter Thirty-One

His voice was angry: 'What time do you call *this*?'

She stood penitently on the doorstep: 'Sorry!'

'Where've you parked?' (It was the decade's commonest question in Oxford.)

'*Exactly.* I just couldn't find a parking space anywhere.'

(Terry Benczik, *Still Life with Absinthe*)

Lucky Lewis!

He was walking up the steps to the station when the automatic doors opened in front of him, and Sergeant Dick Evans of the British Transport Police came towards him. Old friends, they greeted each other with appropriate cordiality.

'Know anything about a stolen car – R456 LJB?'

'Parked here?'

'Dunno,' Lewis admitted.

'Well, not as far as I know. I've been in Reading all day, though. Just got back. Bob Mitchell'd know, perhaps. He's on duty here.'

'I'd better go and wake him up then.'

'He's not in the office. I looked in a couple of minutes ago – door's locked. Probably called out on some trouble somewhere. Saturday! Football yobbos and all that.'

'But it's not the football season,' protested Lewis.

'What's that got to do with it?'

'You straight off home?'

'Well, yes. It's getting late. If I can do anything to help an old mucker though . . . What's the trouble?'

Lewis told him; and the two men walked down the steps and across to the station car park.

It had been more than a year since Lewis had visited the station complex; and he was immediately surprised to find that the previously fairly extensive car-parking space had been drastically reduced: the northern section had been taken over by 'Another Prestigious Development' – a series of Victorian-style town-houses, built in attractive terra-cotta bricks, with white stuccoed lower storeys; 'spacious and luxurious' as the site-board guaranteed.

'Year or two back,' volunteered Evans, 'I'd've parked up there if I'd wanted to keep out of sight for a while. Used to be a bit dark and creepy late at night, if you got back late from Paddington on the milk float.'

Lewis nodded, but without comment. Late-night returns from concerts and operas in the capital had never figured large in the lifestyle of the Lewises. But now, in sunny daylight, the area seemed wholly benign, and still almost packed with cars marshalled there in semi-legitimate rows.

'What if you come,' asked Lewis, 'and you just can't find a space?'

'Not easy, is it? You can always try Gloucester Green' (Evans pointed vaguely across towards Hythe Bridge Street) 'or one of the side roads.'

The two sergeants walked together to the northern area of the park, away from the main road where, with any choice in the matter, any murderous villain (as well as Sergeant Evans) would surely have headed with an incriminating car. But things had changed. Parading the site, tall stanchions now stood there, topped with video-cameras and floodlights. No guarantee of complete security perhaps, but a sufficient deterrent for casual car thieves.

'You could still squeeze one or two more cars in?' suggested Lewis (himself a wizard at vehicular manoeuvring) pointing to a few square metres amid heaps of sand and piles of jagged half-bricks and broken tiles.

'Not if you're worried about your suspension.'

'Which he wasn't, Dick.'

'No sign of it though, is there?'

They walked systematically through the lines of cars down to the southern end of the car park, bounded by the Botley Road.

Again, nothing.

And the questions that had already worried Morse were worrying his sergeant now. *Was* there any sign of criminal activity here? Were they on some profitless pursuit of a questionable quarry?

Morse!

Top-of-the-head Morse!

Things just didn't happen like that.

At bottom, any police investigation was a matter of pretty firm facts; of accumulating such facts; and of aggregating them into a hard core of evidence, on which suspicion could be progressively corroborated, until an arrest could be made, a charge brought, a prosecution formulated, and finally a case heard in a court of law. That's how things happened.

A dispirited Lewis stood with Evans for only a few seconds longer before walking up to the exit-booth, where a red-and-white striped barrier was being intermittently raised as a few patrons returning early to Oxford inserted their parking-tokens, and where a uniformed Transport Policeman, clearly not at the peak of physical condition, came running towards them:

'What the 'ell are you doing here, Dick?'

'Just back from Reading, Bob. And what the 'ell's up with you? You know Sergeant Lewis here from HQ?'

Mitchell had regained some of his breath. 'HQ? Huh! That's exactly what's up. Chap who said he was from HQ. Rang about a car – said it was parked here at the station . . .'

Evans finished the sentence for him. 'But it wasn't.'

'No. But I thought I'd look around a bit. This chap'd sounded pretty positive, like. So I went over to Gloucester Green – and Bingo! Just behind the Irish pub there.'

'You've got this chap's number?' asked Lewis.

'In the office, yes. He said he couldn't get here himself. Said he was tired. Huh!'

'He must have given his name?'

'"Moss", I think it was. Look, I'll just . . .'

A temporarily rejuvenated Mitchell was bounding

up the station steps three at a time as Evans turned to Lewis:

'Reckon he misheard a bit.'

'Just a bit,' said Lewis, with quiet resignation.

Chapter Thirty-Two

Should any young or old officer experience incipient or actual signs of vomiting at the sight of some particularly harrowing scene of crime the said person should not necessarily attribute such nausea to some psychological vulnerability, but rather to the virtually universal reflex-reactions of the upper intestine

(*The SOCO Handbook*, Revised 1999)

Barry Edwards was another of the SOCO personnel called out that busy Saturday. In fact, simply because he lived only a short distance away along the Botley Road, he was the first of the team to arrive at the scene of the crime. A well-set, dark-haired man in his late twenties, he had a pair of diffident brown eyes that seemed to some of his colleagues strangely naive, as if he would ever be surprised by the scenes that would inevitably confront him in his new career.

His SOCO training had been completed only a few months previously, and now he was a fully fledged (civilian) officer, employed by the Thames Valley Police. Furthermore, thus far, he was enjoying his job. After leaving school, with a comparatively successful performance in the comparatively undemanding field of GCSE, he had worked as a supermarket shelf-filler, hospital porter, barman, and ironmonger's shop-assistant, before finally completing a police recruitment questionnaire and duly learning of the opportunities in his present profession. He had taken his chance; and he was enjoying his choice. He felt quite important sometimes, especially when he dealt off his own bat with some fairly minor affair, when (as he knew) he *was* important. And he'd looked forward to the time when he would be called out to a big job, to some major incident. Like murder. Like now – as he sensed immediately when he drove his van into the Gloucester Green Car Park. The full complement of the team would have been called in, and almost certainly he would witness, for the first time, the operation of those basic principles – preservation of the scene, continuity and non-contamination of evidence – which had guided his training in photography, fingerprinting, forensic labelling, and the meticulous procedure vital to all in-situ investigations.

Edwards had introduced himself immediately to the plain-clothed Sergeant Lewis, obviously the man in charge: yet perhaps only temporarily in charge, since (as Edwards guessed) it would only be a matter of time before some more senior-ranking officer would put in an appearance – just as he himself was awaiting Bill Flowers, the senior SOCO, a man who had seen everything in life. As he, Barry Edwards, hadn't. Not yet. For the moment, however, the appropriate procedure had been applied, with blue-and-white police ribbon cordoning off an area containing three cars, noses all to the wall: R 456 LJB; to its left, a grey H-Reg Citroën; to its right a dark-blue P-Reg Rover – the owner of the latter (just arrived) making a statement to one of two uniformed PCs summoned from the St Aldate's Station. No effort had as yet been made to disperse the growing band of curious onlookers who stood in silent, hopeful expectation of some gruesome discovery. Things were happening, though. Flowers arrived just before the other two SOCOs; and soon everything would be ready, once they got the word from someone. Doubtless the same someone awaited by Sergeant Lewis, the latter a man with 'under authority' written all over his honest and slightly worried features.

But there was a frustrating twenty-minute wait before the 'authority' put in his appearance, stepping from the back of a marked police car with a marked unsuppleness of limb, the slate-grey suit decidedly rumpled, the tell-tale crease around the waistband betokening an increase in girth over recent months. A white-haired man, of medium height, his face of a pale-olive colour, as if perhaps he had spent a holiday of less than uninterrupted sunshine in Torremolinos, or was suffering from incipient jaundice. But his voice was that of someone who demanded immediate attention – like another voice that Edwards once had known, that of his old Latin master.

Vox auctoritatis.

Lewis had approached the newcomer, and the two were in brief conversation before coming over to the others. Chief Inspector Morse (for such was he) appeared to recognize the other SOCOs, and nodded briefly as he was introduced to the youngest member of the team.

'Hello, Edwards!' He'd said nothing more, and Edwards gathered that the Chief Inspector was not a convert to the currently widespread practice of everyone addressing everyone – superiors, equals, and subordinates alike – by their Christian names. Yet he seemed a pleasant enough fellow, now surveying the scene with a keen if somewhat melancholy eye, while the SOCO team began to put on their green boilersuits and overboots.

'Anyone touched anything?'

'No more than we needed to, sir.' (It was Lewis who replied.)

Morse looked again at the car for some lingering while – the car he'd followed when Harry Repp had turned his back on Bullingdon. Then he lifted his eyes, and looked, again for some lingering while, at the pub sign of the Rosie O'Grady.

Bill Flowers was standing beside him.

'All yours!' pronounced Morse.

'Car's locked.'

'How do you know?'

'Door catches all in the locked position.'

Morse pressed a hand down on the nearside front handle.

'Don't—!' But Flowers checked his admonition in mid-voice.

'You're right. Any of your lads here ever a juvenile car thief?'

'I know somebody who was.'

'Where's he live?'

'Silverstone.'

Morse turned to Lewis. 'Give Johnson a ring.'

'Know his number?'

'Saturday afternoon? He'll be in the Summertown bookie's.'

'It's long gone afternoon, sir.'

'Ah!'

'There'll be a Local Directory in the pub.'

'You won't find him listed. They've cut his phone off.'

'So how—?'

'He'll be in the Dew Drop if he's won a few quid.'

'Perhaps he's not won a few quid.'

'He'll still be in the Dew Drop.'

'Do you know the number?'

'Get me a mobile!' snapped Morse.

Edwards watched as Morse turned his back on his colleagues, tapped out a number, and spoke *sotto voce* into the mouthpiece for a while, before blasting out *fortissimo*:

'Well, just tell him to get here on the bloody *bus* and get here bloody *quick*!'

Yet this order was not obeyed with either accuracy or immediacy, since there was a further twenty-minute wait before a rusting A-Reg Ford pulled up on the main road outside the Rosie O'Grady, whence emerged from the passenger seat a sparely built, non-descript man, in his late forties, a self-rolled cigarette dangling from a thin mouth that even from a few yards exuded the reek of strong, excessive alcohol.

'Mr Morse?'

The latter pointed to the car.

'Fee, is there?'

'Just open it, Malcolm!' (Edwards was surprised with the Christian-name address.)

The key-wizard made no further remonstration as he winched a bunch of skeleton-keys and bits of wire from his right-hand trouser-pocket. Then, turning his back on his expectant audience, he surveyed the problem synoptically. Like Capablanca contemplating his next move in the World Chess Championship.

'It's central-locking,' volunteered Flowers.

But Johnson said nothing, responding only for a semi-second with a look of contemptuous ingratitude.

As far as Edwards could make out, Morse had enjoyed that moment, since more than a semi-smile formed around his mouth when fifteen seconds later there was a quiet 'clunk' as the catches on the four doors sprang upwards in simultaneous freedom.

R456 LJB was open for inspection.

After pulling on a pair of green-latex gloves, Flowers now opened the two offside doors; and Morse glanced over the front seats, before contemplating for a good deal longer the darkly glutinous covering of blood that stained the seats and flooring in the back. With a softly spoken 'OK', he was walking away towards the Rosie O'Grady when Johnson tapped him on the shoulder.

'You mentioned expenses, Mr Morse?'

'I did. You're right.'

'Well, there's that taxi I came in – eight quid – two quid tip – ten quid – here and back. Twenny, I make that.'

'Since when's Snotty Joe been running a taxi business?'

'Well, you know, more a sort of . . . private hire, like.'

Morse felt in his pockets and pulled out a handful of coins. '85p, isn't it, the bus fare to St Giles'? And, you're right, you've got to get back.'

He handed Johnson two £1 coins. 'Keep the change. You can buy a copy of *The Times* to read on the ride back.'

'Wrong, aincha, Mr Morse! *Times* is 50p Sat'days.'

Unsmiling, Morse handed over a further 20p, and the pair parted without any further word. And Edwards, who had witnessed the brief scene, found himself wondering what exactly were the favours each had bestowed upon the other in the prosecution and pursuance of crime in North Oxford over recent years.

Morse was a few steps ahead of Lewis as he made his way to the pub entrance. 'We'd better leave 'em for half an hour or so. They won't want us breathing down their necks . . . By the way, you'd better lend me a fiver, Lewis. I've just parted with the only—'

Morse stopped. Turned round. Stepped back to the scene of the crime. Ordered Flowers to open the boot.

Not himself knowing the identity of the body he now saw curled up in foetal configuration there, young Edwards was to remember that particular moment with an oddly inappropriate sense of gratitude, for he saw the colour of Morse's cheeks fade by swiftly developing degrees from dingy yellow to sickly white, and watched as of a sudden the great man turned away and vomited violently over the recently renovated tarmac. It was like a fledgling actor appearing on stage with Sir John Gielgud and seeing *that* great man fluffing the friendliest of lines in rehearsal, and thereby giving some unexpected encouragement to the rest of the cast, all of them now less terrified of fluffing their own.

Chapter Thirty-Three

For the good are always the merry,
Save by an evil chance,
And the merry love the fiddle,
And the merry love to dance:

And when the folk there spy me,
They will all come up to me,
With 'Here is the fiddler of Dooney!'
And dance like a wave of the sea.
(W. B. Yeats,
The Fiddler of Dooney)

MORSE, AFTER DISAPPEARING into the Gents for several long minutes, now sat looking slightly more his wonted self as he sank his nose into the deep head on the Guinness.

'Just the stuff if you've got a foul taste in the throat!'

Giving his chief a little while to recover some measure of dignity, Lewis gazed around him. Everything was wooden there: the bar, the wall-settles, the floor, the table at which they sat – all good solid if somewhat battered wood, with any once-applied stain long since worn off. The walls and ceilings had originally been painted in yellow and orange, but now were coated over with the nicotine of countless cigarettes. The friezes of the walls were adorned with the dicta of several great Irishmen, their words attractively set in black-lettered Gaelic script. One in particular had already caught Lewis's eye:

Where is the use of calling it a lend
when I know I will never see it again?

Good question! But a question not so pressing as the one he now put to Morse:

'Was it a surprise to you?'

'Was *what* a surprise?'

'Finding Harry Repp's body in the boot?'

Morse nodded as he wiped away a white moustache.

'This morning I thought I had a fair idea about what we were dealing with. But now that I'm perfectly sure that I've none . . .' He pointed up at the wall to their right. 'Bit like Oscar Wilde, really.'

Lewis looked up at the words written there:

I was working on the proof of my poems all this morning and took out a comma. In the afternoon I put it back again.

For Lewis it was a sombre moment and he sipped his orange juice with little joy; even less joy as he saw the outline of Chief Superintendent Strange looming large in the doorway, then waddling awkwardly to their table, where he sat down, wiping his moistened brow with a vast handkerchief.

'Pretty kettle o' fish you've got us into now, Morse!'

Then, turning to Lewis: 'You in the chair?'

'Well—'

'Good! Good man! I'll have the same as the Chief Inspector here.'

'Pint, sir?'

'The *same* as the Chief Inspector – that's what I said, Sergeant.'

Lewis repaired to the bar once more and listened to the comparatively quiet background music that was as Irish as the pub was Irish, all flutes and fiddles, and wondered how long Morse would stick the noise before calling for a few less decibels.

After taking a deep draught, Strange turned to Morse. 'You do realize, don't you, that you and Lewis have dragged me away from the golf course twice!'

'I'd've thought you'd be glad, especially if you were losing.'

Strange grinned wryly. 'I don't often win these days, you're right.'

'None of us gets much better as we get older.'

'Only two things we can be sure of, Morse – death and taxes. Some US President said that.'

'Benjamin Franklin,' supplied Lewis, to whom each of the two senior officers turned with some surprise, though without enquiry into the provenance of such splendid knowledge.

'What do you make of all this?' continued Strange quietly.

Morse shook his head. 'You may have been having a lousy round of golf. I was having a lovely sleep myself.'

'That's no answer.'

'Dr Hobson'll be here soon.'

'Already here.'

'Nothing we can do till we get some reports, results of the post-mortems—'

'Somebody once told me the plural should be post-mortes.'

'Bloody pedant!'

'It was *you* actually, Morse.'

'Ah!'

'You've got a good team of SOCOs.'

Morse nodded. 'So we'll wait to hear about all the bits and bobs they'll be bagging up and labelling and sending off to forensics. And all the fingerprints they'll be taking from windows and side-mirrors and body-work and seat-belt buckles and cassettes and . . .' Morse had run out of potential surfaces.

'That's it!' Strange sounded somewhat heartened. 'All you've got to do is eliminate ninety-five per cent of the dabs, and then you've got your man.'

'Unless he was wearing gloves,' suggested Lewis.

'It's all tied up with that bloody Lower Swinstead business!' blurted out Strange.

'You're probably right,' said Morse.

'And don't forget the simplest answer is usually the correct answer! Spur o' the moment stuff, most homicides. You know that.'

'Perhaps so,' admitted Morse, beckoning the landlord over. 'Open all day?'

'All night too should you wish it, sorr.'

And yes, of course the police could make use of one of the bars for the evening; of course the police could make use of whatever the Rosie O'Grady had to offer: telephone, washing and toilet facilities, bar facilities . . .

'And perhaps . . . ?' The landlord pointed to the two empty glasses. 'On the house – the pleasure's all mine.'

'Well, perhaps, er . . .' said Strange.

'You're twisting my arm,' said Morse.

'Make it *three* pints of Guinness,' said Lewis.

Morse glanced across at his sergeant with a look of astonishment; the landlord departed; and Strange got down to business.

'Logistics, Morse. Let's talk logistics. How many men do you want?'

'If you gave me a hundred, I wouldn't know what to do with one of them – not yet.'

'Now come off it, matey! Couldn't you perhaps have a look at when and how and what and why your bloody corpses were doing? See their relatives, friends, enemies, wives, for God's sake?'

'Flynn hadn't got a wife,' interposed Lewis.

'*Repp* had!'

'No, sir,' corrected Lewis bravely. 'He'd got a partner—'

'Well go and see *her*!' snapped Strange.

'No,' said Morse. 'I'll go to see her myself.'

'Why's that?'

'I have my reasons.'

The landlord had returned with the drinks. 'As I said – on the house, gentlemen!'

Morse thanked him and made a request: 'You know this, er, music you're playing here – this Irish music . . . ?'

'Perhaps you'd like it . . . ?'

'Yes. If you could turn it up just a bit?'

Lewis glanced across at the Chief Inspector with a

look of astonishment; the landlord departed; and Strange leaned back with an expression of contentment. 'You know, Morse, I'm glad you said that. The missus . . . we had a couple of days in Cork and we did a bit of Irish dancing together . . . me and the missus . . . or I suppose you'd say the missus and me.'

'The missus and I, sir.'

But further grammatical preferences were curtailed by the arrival of Dr Laura Hobson.

'Everything all right, Doctor?' shouted Strange, above the background music that had suddenly lunged to the foreground.

'No, everything's all wrong! I can*not* cope with things as they are out there. I want the car moved out to the lab with the body kept in the boot. How on earth you think—?'

'Done!' Strange held up the great slab that was his right hand. 'Lewis will arrange it immediately, once he's finished his drink. Si' down, Doctor. Just give me a minute or two.' He sat back in his chair, beaming like a benign old uncle.

'Takes you back, Morse, doesn't it?'

'Remember the old poem, sir?

"When I play on my fiddle in Dooney,
Folk dance like a wave of the sea . . ."'

'Yes! Yes, I do,' said Strange gently.

And for a while Sergeant Lewis and Dr Hobson remained silent, as if they knew they should be treading softly; as if they might be treading on other people's dreams.

Chapter Thirty-Four

Sunt lacrimae rerum et mentem mortalia tangunt
(Always in life are there tears being shed for things,
and human suffering ever touches the heart)
(Virgil, *Aeneid*, I, l. 462)

As she opened the door, the recently re-applied blonde dye showed little or no trace of the hair's brunette inheritance.

'Oh, hullo.' The greeting was less than enthusiastic.

'May I come in?' asked Morse.

Apart from the minimal towel held in front of her body, she was naked: 'Just wait there a sec – I'll just . . .'

She re-closed the door and Morse stood, as she had bidden, on the threshold. Stood there for a couple of minutes. And when she re-opened the door and re-appeared, it puzzled him that in such a comparatively long time she had done little other than to exchange the white towel for an equally minimal white dressing gown.

They sat opposite each other in the kitchen.

'Drink?' she ventured.

'No. I've had a busy day on the drink.'

'That good or bad?'

'Bit of both.'

'Mind if I have one?'

'Can you wait? Just a minute?'

'It's about Harry, isn't it?'

'Yes.'

'He's dead, isn't he?'

'He's been murdered,' said Morse flatly.

Debbie Richardson leaned forward on her elbows, the long fingers with their crimson nails vertically veiling her features. Then after a while she got to her feet and turned to the sink, where she moulded her hands into a shallow receptacle under the cold tap.

As they had spoken at the kitchen table, Morse had observed (how otherwise?) that whatever else Debbie Richardson had done behind the closed front door she had certainly not been searching for a bra; and now, as she leaned forward and held her face in the water, he observed (how otherwise?) that she'd had no thought for any knickers either. A provocative prick-teaser, that was what she was. Morse knew it; had known it when they'd met that once before. But for the moment his mind was many furlongs from fornication . . .

He felt fairly sure that she'd been upstairs when he'd rung the bell, for the light had been on in the front bedroom with the night now drawing in. Yet she'd answered the door very quickly, almost immediately in fact. Whoever the caller was, had she wished to give the impression to someone that she'd been downstairs all the while? It seemed a bit odd. After all, he could well have been a Jehovah's Witness or an equally dreaded member of the Mormons or a charity-worker bearing an envelope. Quite certainly though she hadn't rushed down the stairs from a bath, since about her was none of that freshly scented aura of a woman recently risen from her toilet. Rather perhaps (although Morse was no connoisseur in such matters) it was the musky odour of sex that lingered around her.

Whilst she had stood silently at the sink, he had strained his ears as acutely as any astronomer waiting for the faintest bleep from outer space. But of any other presence in the house there had been no sound at all; no sight at all either, except for the two unwashed wine glasses that stood on the draining board, a heel-tap of red in each of them. And Morse guessed that Debbie Richardson would never have taken the slightest risk of Claret and intercourse that day with anyone – unless it were with Harry Repp. And it *couldn't* have been with Harry Repp . . . Yet she may well have been tempted, this flaunting, raunchy woman who now dried her face and turned back to Morse; could certainly have been tempted if one of her admirers had called that evening for whatever reason – and if she had already known that Harry Repp was dead.

Morse watched her almost disinterestedly as she returned to the table.

'Shall I pour you that drink now?' he asked.

'Only if you'll join me.'

Quite extraordinarily, Morse gave the impression that he was quite extraordinarily sober; and he poured their drinks – gin (hers), whisky (his) – with only a carefully camouflaged shake of the right hand.

Quietly, as gently as he could, he told her almost as much as he knew of what had happened that day; and of the help that immediately awaited her should she so need it: advice, comfort, counselling . . .

But she shook her head. She'd be better off with sleepin' pills than with all that stuff. She needed nothin' of that. She'd be copin' OK, given a chance. Independent, see? Never wanted to share any worryin' with anyone. Loner most of her life, she'd been; ever since she'd been a teenager . . .

A tear ran hurriedly down her right cheek, and Morse handed her a handkerchief he'd washed and ironed himself.

'We ought to ring your GP: it's the usual thing.'

She blew her nose noisily and wiped the moisture from her eyes. 'You go now. I'll be fine.'

'We'll need a statement from you soon.'

'Course.'

'You'll stay here . . .?'

Before she could reply the phone rang, and she moved into the hallway to answer it.

'Hello?'

. . .

'You've got the wrong number.'

. . .

'You've got the *wrong number.*'

Had she replaced the receiver with needless haste? Morse didn't know.

'Not one of those obscene calls?'

'No.'

'Best to be on the safe side, though.' Giving her no chance to obstruct his sudden move, Morse picked up the receiver, dialled 1471, and duly noted the number given.

She had said nothing during this brief interlude,

but now proceeded to give her views on one of the most recent developments in telephonic technology: 'It'll soon be a tricky ol' thing conductin' some illicit liaison over the phone.'

Morse smiled, feeling delight and surprise in such elegant vocabulary. 'As I was saying, you'll stay here?'

She looked at him unblinking, eye to eye. 'You could always call occasionally to make sure, Inspector.'

For some little while they stood together on the inner side of the front door.

'You know . . . It doesn't hit you for a start, does it? You just don't take it in. But it's true, isn't it? He's dead. Harry's *dead*.'

Morse nodded. 'You'll be all right, though. Like you said, you can cope. You're a tough girl.'

'Oh God! He kept talkin' and talkin' about gettin' in bed with me again. Been a long time for him – and for me.'

'I understand.'

'You really think you *do*?'

Her cheeks were dry now, unfurrowed by a single tear. Yet Morse knew that she probably understood as much as he did about those Virgilian 'tears of things'. And for that moment he felt a deep compassion, as with the gentlest touch he laid his right hand briefly on her shoulder, before walking slowly along that amateurishly concreted path that led towards the road.

Once in the car, Morse turned to Sergeant Dixon:

'Well?'

'Light went off upstairs soon as you rung the bell, sir.'

'Sure of that?'

'Gospel.'

'Anyone leave, do you think?'

'Must a' been out the back if they did.'

'What about the cars parked here?'

'I took a list, like you said. Mostly local residents. I've checked with HQ.'

'Mostly?'

'There was an old D-reg Volvo parked at the far end there. Not there any longer though.'

'*And?*'

Dixon grinned as happily as if he were contemplating a plate of doughnuts. 'Car owned by someone from Lower Swinstead. You'll never guess who. Landlord o' the Maiden's Arms!'

Morse, appearing to assimilate this new intelligence without undue surprise, handed over the telephone number of the (hitherto) untraced caller who had just rung Debbie Richardson; and could hear each end of the conversation perfectly clearly as Dixon spoke with HQ once more.

The call had been made from Lower Swinstead.

From the Maiden's Arms.

Chapter Thirty-Five

The trouble about always trying to preserve the health of the body is that it is so difficult to do without destroying the health of the mind

(G. K. Chesterton)

At 9.20 a.m. on Monday, 27 July, as he sat in the out-patients' lounge at the Oxford Diabetes Centre at the Radcliffe Infirmary, Morse reflected on the unco-ordinated, hectic enquiries which had occupied many of his colleagues for the whole of the previous day. He had himself made no contribution whatsoever to the accumulating data thus garnered, suffering as he was from one long horrendous hangover. Because of this, he had most solemnly abjured all alcohol for the rest of his life; and indeed had made a splendid start to such long-term abstinence until early evening, when his brain told him that he was never going to cope with the present case without recourse, in moderate quantities, to his faithful Glenfiddich.

Several key facts now seemed reasonably settled. Paddy Flynn had been knifed to death at around noon the previous Friday; Harry Repp had died in very similar fashion about two or three hours later. Flynn had probably died instantaneously. Repp had met a slower end, almost certainly dying from the outpouring of blood that so copiously had covered the earlier blood in the back of the car, and quite certainly had been dead when someone, somewhere, had lugged the messy corpse into the boot of the same car. No sign of any weapon; only blood blood blood. And, of course, prints galore – far too many of them – subimposed, imposed, and superimposed everywhere. The vehicle's owner had allowed his second wife and his three step-children regular access to his latest supercharged model, and fingerprint elimination was going to be a lengthy business. Even lengthier perhaps would be the analysis by boffins back at Forensics of the hairs and threads collected on the sticky strips the SOCOs had taped over every square centimetre of the vehicle's upholstery.

Yet in spite of so many potential leads, Morse felt dubious (as did Dr Hobson) about their actual value. Too many cooks could spoil the broth, and too many crooks could easily spoil an investigation. For the moment, it was a question of waiting.

As Morse was waiting in the waiting room now . . .

On the day before, the Sunday, Morse had woken up, literally and metaphorically, to the fact that he should have been keeping an accurate record of his blood-sugar levels for the previous month. Thus it was that he had taken four such readings that day: 12.2; 9.9; 22.6; 16.4. Although realizing that he could never hope for an average anywhere near the 4–5 range normal for non-diabetic people, he was nevertheless somewhat disturbed by his findings, and immediately halved that very high third reading to 11.3. Then he'd extrapolated backwards as intelligently as he could for the previous six days, with the result that a reasonably satisfactory set of readings, neatly tabulated in his small handwriting, was now folded inside his blue appointment-card.

He was ready.

He had finally managed to produce a 'specimen', although inaccuracy of aim had resulted in a puddle on the unisex-loo's floor; and the dreaded weighing-in was over.

And so was the waiting.

'Mr Morse?'

The white-coated, slimly attractive brunette led the way to a consulting room, her name, black lettering on a white card, on the door: DR SARAH HARRISON.

'You knew my mother a bit, I believe,' she said as she opened a buff-coloured folder.

Morse nodded, but made no comment.

A quarter of an hour later the medical side of matters was over. Morse had not attempted to be overly clever. Just short and reasonably honest in his replies.

'These readings – are they genuine?'

'Partly, yes.'

'You could lose a stone or two, you know.'

'I agree.'

'But you won't.'

'Probably not.'

'How's the drink going?'

'Rather too quickly.'

'It's *your* liver, you know.'

'Yes.'

'Any problems with sex?'

'I've always had problems with sex.'

'You know what I mean – sex-drive . . .?'

'I'm a bachelor.'

'What's that got to do with it?'

'Just that I lead a reasonably celibate life.'

'It *is* my job to *ask* these questions, you understand that.'

The dark-brown eyes were growing progressively less angry as she examined his feet, and then his eyes. She had in fact virtually finished with him when a nurse knocked and entered the room, explaining swiftly that an out-patient had just fainted in Reception; and since for the minute Dr Harrison was the only consultant there . . .

After she had left, Morse stepped quickly over to the desk and opened his own folder. On top lay a brief handwritten note:

> Don't be intimidated, Sarah! He's hugely economical with the truth, but he's really a softie at heart (I think).
> Robert (sic!)

And underneath it, a copy of a letter (Strictly Confidential) sent to the Summertown Health Centre and dated 18 May 1998.

Re Annual Review: E. Morse.

Dear Dr Roblin,

Haemoglobin A lc (as you'll see) is higher than we would like at 11.5%. I've instructed him to increase each of his four daily insulin doses by 2 units – up to 10, 6, 12, 36. In addition, his cholesterol level is getting rather worrying. It's pointless to ask him to cut his intake of alcohol, so please add to his prescribed medicines Atorvastatin 10 mg tablets nocte.

Eyes are remarkably good. Blood pressure is still too high. No problems with feet.

His general condition gives me no real cause for immediate anxiety, but I shall be glad if you can insist on a regular monthly review, at least for the rest of the year. I enclose the relevant clinical data.

Regards to your family.

With best wishes,
Professor R C Turner
Honorary Consultant Physician

P.S. He tells me he's stopped smoking! And he's certainly stopped listening to me.

Morse was sitting, slowly pulling on his socks, when Sarah Harrison returned.

'I'll tell you one thing: you've got quite nice feet.'

'I'm glad bits of me are OK.'

Whilst tying his shoelaces, Morse had missed the look of quick intelligence in the large brown eyes.

'Bit sneaky, wasn't it?' she held up the file.

Morse nodded. 'Don't worry, though. Professor Turner sent me a copy of that last letter.'

'Well, in that case, there's not really much more . . .' She got to her feet.

'Please!' Morse signalled to the chair, and obediently she sat down again. 'Why haven't you mentioned the murders, Doctor? They're all over the national papers.'

'I bought *six* of them yesterday, if you must know.'

'Your father? Your brother – Simon, isn't it? Do they know?'

'I've not seen Simon recently.'

'You could have phoned him.'

'Simon is *not* the sort of person you phone. He's deaf, *very* deaf – as you probably know anyway.'

'And your father?' repeated Morse.

'I . . . whether or not . . . Oddly enough I saw him last week. He came to stay with me for a couple of nights.'

'Which nights?'

'Wednesday and Thursday. He went back to London on Friday.'

'What time?'

'Is this the Inquisition?'

'It *is* my job to *ask* these questions, you understand that.'

'Touché! He caught the train – I'm not sure which one. He didn't bring the car – nowhere to park in Oxford, is there?'

'Why didn't you see him off?'

'I couldn't.'

'Were you working?'

'No. I'd arranged to have Thursday and Friday off myself. Like Dad, I'd a few days' holiday to make up.'

'So why not see him off?'

The eyes were fiery now. 'I'll tell you why. Because he took me out the previous night to Le Petit Blanc in Walton Street and we had a super meal *and* we had far too much booze – before, during, and after, all right? And I got as pissed as a tailed amphibian and tried to sleep things off with enough pills to frighten even you! And when I finally staggered downstairs – eleven? half-eleven? – I saw this note on the kitchen table: "Off back to London. Didn't want to wake you. Love Dad" – something like that.'

'Any time on the note?'

'Don't think so.'

'Have you kept it?'

'Course I've not kept it! Hardly a specimen of purple prose, was it?'

'Don't be cross with me,' said Morse gently as he got to his feet, and left the consulting room – with two blue cards for more immediate and urgent blood tests, and with instructions to fix up a further appointment for eight weeks' time.

After the door had closed behind him, Sarah dialled 9 for an outside line on the phone there; then called a number.

'Hullo? Hullo? Could you put me through to Simon Harrison, please?'

Chapter Thirty-Six

Dr Franklin shewed me that the flames of two candles joined give a much stronger light than both of them separate; as is made very evident by a person holding the two candles near his face, first separate, and then joined in one

(Joseph Priestley, *Optiks*)

As he sat awaiting his turn outside the cubicle reserved for blood-testing, Morse found himself wondering whether, wondering *how*, if at all, Sarah Harrison could have had any rôle to play in the appalling events of the weekend just passed. There *were* possibilities, of course (there were always possibilities in Morse's mind) and for a few minutes his brain accelerated sweetly and swiftly into that extra fifth gear. But stop a while! Strange had surely been right to remind him that the easiest answer was more often than not the correct one. What *was* the easiest answer, though? Lewis would know, of course; and it was at times like these that Morse needed Lewis's cautious 30 mph approach to life, if not to any stretch of road in front of him. Two heads were better than one, even though one of them was Lewis's. Yet what a cruel thought that was! And so unworthy . . .

'Mr Morse?'

A nurse led him behind the blood-letting curtain;

and as she wiped the inside of his right arm with a sterilizing swab of cotton wool before inserting a needle, Morse found himself thinking of Dr Sarah Harrison . . . wondering exactly what she was thinking (doing?) at that very moment.

'Hullo? Simon Harrison here.'

'Simon? Sarah! Are you hearing OK?'

'Where else? Course I'm here in the UK.'

'Are you *hearing* me all right?'

'Oh, sorry! Yes. Fantastic this new phone-system. You know that.'

'Are you on your own, Simon?' She was speaking softly.

'Yes. But you can never count on it, sis. You know that.'

'Now listen! I've only got a minute or so. I've just been talking to Chief Inspector Morse—'

'Who?'

'Morse! He's with the Thames Valley Police and he's just become one of my patients.'

'He wasn't on Mum's case.'

'Well, he's on *this* one.'

'So?'

'So we've got to be careful, Simon.'

'You told him Dad was here?'

'Had to! He'd have soon found out.'

'What's *wrong,* sis?'

'*Nothing*'s wrong. But I'm a bit frightened of him, and when he sees you—'

'Seizure? What? Say it again.'

'If he *sees* you, Simon, you did *not* come round last Wednesday. *You did not come*—'

'I *heard* you! I stayed at home and watched the telly. What was on, by the way?'

'Look it up in the *Radio Times*! And stop being—!'

A knock on the consulting-room door caused Sarah to replace the receiver hurriedly, almost hoping that another out-patient had passed out in Reception. But the knock was only a polite reminder that Dr Harrison's a.m. schedule was now running over half an hour late.

Yet even as the next out-patient was ushered in, Dr Sarah Harrison found herself wondering exactly what Chief Inspector Morse was thinking (doing?) at that very moment.

Turning right from the front entrance of the Radcliffe Infirmary, Morse began walking slowly down towards St Giles', noting that the time was 10.40 – twenty minutes before the pubs were due to open. Yet since drink was now definitely out for the duration, such an observation was of little moment.

The Oratory was on his right, a building he'd seldom paid attention to before, although he must have walked past it so many, many times. But apart from that wonderful line of cathedrals down the eastern side of England – Durham, York, Lincoln, Peterborough, Ely – the architecture of ecclesiastical edifices had never meant as much as they should have done to

Morse; and the reason why he now checked his step remains inexplicable.

He entered and looked around him: all surprisingly large and imposing, with a faint, seductive smell of incense, and statues of assorted saints around him, with tiers of candles lit beside their sandalled, holy feet.

A youngish woman had come in behind him, a Marks and Spencer carrier bag in her left hand. She dipped her right hand into the little font of blessed water there, then crossed herself and knelt in one of the rear pews. Morse envied her, for she looked so much at home there: looked as if she knew herself and her Lord so well, and was wholly familiar with all the trappings of prayer and the promises of forgiveness. She didn't stay long, and Morse guessed that the cause of her brief sojourn was probably the paucity of any sins worthy of confession. As she left, Morse could see some of the contents of the carrier bag: a Hovis loaf and a bottle of red plonk.

Bread and wine.

The door clicked to behind her, and Morse stepped over to meet St Anthony, wondering whence had sprung that oddly intrusive 'h'. According to the textual blurb at the base of the statue, this great and good man was clearly capable of performing quite incredible miracles for those who almost had sufficient faith. Morse picked up a candle from the box there and stuck it in an empty socket on the top row. At which point (it appeared) most worshippers would have prayed fervently for a miracle. But Morse wasn't at all sure what miracle he wanted. Nevertheless the elegant, elongated candle was of importance to him; and on some semi-irrational impulse he took a second candle and placed it beside the first. Together, side by side, they seemed to give a much stronger light than both of them separate.

A notice suggested an appropriate donation per candle, and Morse pushed a £1 coin into the slot in the wall behind St Anthony. Half of bitter. Then, remembering that he'd doubled his investment, the reluctant hagiolater pushed in a second £1 coin. A whole pint.

As he walked down to St Giles', the man who had virtually no faith in the Almighty and even less in miracles noted that the past few minutes had slipped by quickly. It was now just after 11 a.m.; and when he came in sight of the Bird and Baby on his right, he saw that the front door was open.

He went in.

Chapter Thirty-Seven

Careless talk costs lives

(Second World War slogan)

I think men who have a pierced ear are better prepared for marriage. They've experienced pain and bought jewelry

(Rita Rudner)

Five days after Morse had declined the free draw for a miracle at the Oratory, at noon, at Lower Swinstead, at the bar of the Maiden's Arms, Tom Biffen stood leaning forward on his tattooed arms. Very quiet so far for a Saturday. Just the two hardy perennials, horns already locked over their continuous cribbage; and the pale-faced, ear-pierced, greasy-haired youth already squaring up to the fruit machine.

It was twenty minutes later that the fourth customer arrived.

'Usual?'

The newcomer nodded and placed the requisite monies on the counter. The white van in the car park economically proclaimed the newcomer's profession: 'J. Barron, Builder'.

'Not out at Debbie's today, John?'

'What do you think? The day after the funeral?'

'No. Have you seen her since Harry . . .?'

'No. Well, I wouldn't have gone last weekend anyway, would I? Thought they'd like being on their own, like – you know, the day after they'd let him out and all that.'

'No.'

The youth was standing beside them, a £10-note folded lengthways between the index and middle fingers of his right hand.

'You're taking all me change,' complained Biffen as he exchanged the note for ten £1 coins from the till.

'You'll have bugger all left for the honeymoon,' ventured the builder; but the youth, unhearing or uncaring, had already walked back to what was perhaps the first great love of his life.

At the bar a few low-voiced confidences were being exchanged.

'When's the wedding, Biff?'

'Five weeks today.'

'Nice bit o' skirt?'

'Yeah. Dental receptionist down in Oxford somewhere.'

'Glad *one* of 'em's earning!' The builder half-turned towards the unremunerative machine. 'Nobody earns much of a living on them things.'

'Except the Company,' corrected the landlord.

'Except Tom Biffen,' corrected one of the cribbagers.

The landlord grunted.

Odd really. Most men in their latish seventies would ever have been susceptible to deafness, arthritis, baldness, sciatica, haemorrhoids, incontinence, impotence, cataracts, dementia, and all the rest. And perhaps (for all the landlord knew) the two old codgers suffered from every single one of them – except quite certainly the first.

Biffen lowered his voice: 'Did you get to the crematorium?'

'No. *Family*, wasn't it? I wasn't exactly a friend of the family.'

'I thought you builders and plumbers were friends of everybody, especially a strapping young fellow like you?'

'Young?'

But the landlord had a point. John Barron, tall and well built, with dark close-cropped hair and clean-cut features, certainly looked younger than his forty-one years; and what appeared a genuinely open smile appealed to all the local ladies – except his wife, who had been known occasionally to feel jealous.

'What exactly are you doing for Debbie?'

'In the back passage, off the kitchen – you know, the old coal-shed and the old loo. Knocking 'em into one so she can get her washing machine in – re-tiling the floor – re-plastering the walls – new electrical sockets – usual sort of thing.'

'Just at weekends?'

'Yeah, well . . .'

'Bit o' moonlighting? Cash payment?'

For a second or two Barron's mouth tightened distastefully, but he made no direct reply. 'I was hoping to finish it off before Harry was out.'

'Poor sod! Bet he was looking forward . . . you know. Attractive woman, our Debbie!'

'Yeah.' The builder took a deep draught of his bitter. 'Did you go – to the crem?'

'No. Like you said . . .'

'Have you seen her at all since . . . ?'

'No. Like you said . . .'

'The police've been round, they tell me.'

'Yeah. Came in – when was it? – Tuesday.'

'What'd they want?'

Doubtless the builder would have been enlightened immediately had not two further customers entered at that point: an elderly, back-packing, stoutly booted couple.

'Two glasses of orange juice, please!'

'Coming up, sir.'

'Beautiful little village you've got here. So quiet. So peaceful. "Far from the madding crowd" – you'll know the quotation?'

The landlord nodded unconvincingly as he passed over the drinks.

'And you serve meals as well!'

The couple walked over to the corner furthest from the fruit machine: she consulting the hostelry's menu; he plotting a possible p.m. itinerary from *Family Walks in the Cotswolds.*

'Quiet and peaceful!' mumbled the landlord, as one of the elders stepped forward with two empty straight glasses. Words were clearly superfluous.

'You were saying?' resumed the builder.

'Saying what?'

'About the police?'

'Ah, yes. That sergeant came in and asked some of us about Harry and Debbie.'

'But you hadn't seen either of them?'

'Right! But, I would've done, see – would've seen *her*, anyway, if it hadn't been for them – for the police. That Sat'day night I thought I'd just nip over and take 'em a bottle o' Shampers, like – give 'em both a bit of a celebration. Well, I'd just parked the car and I was just walking along when I saw this police car driving slowly round and the fellow inside making notes of Reg numbers by the look of it.'

'What'd you say?'

'Didn't say nothing, did I? Just waited till the coast was clear, then buggered off back here smartish. They'd seen the number, though. So not much point in . . .'

'Good story!'

'Bloody *true* story, mate!'

The builder finished his pint. 'Beer's in good nick, Biff.'

'Always in good nick!'

('Is it fuck!' came *sotto voce* from the region of the cribbage-board.)

'Summat else too,' continued the landlord as he pulled the builder a second pint. 'The police tell me there was a phone call for Debbie that Sat'day night – from the pay-phone here.'

'Could have been anybody.'

'Yeah.'

'Any ideas?'

'Sat'day nights? Come off it! Full up to the rafters, ain't we?'

The elderly lady now came to the bar and ordered gammon-and-pineapple with chips for two; and during this transaction the builder turned round and, with a fascination that is universal, watched the unequal struggle at the fruit machine.

From outside came the jingle of an ice-cream van – as happy a noise as any to the youngsters of Lower Swinstead that sunny lunchtime; almost as happy a noise as that clunk-clunk-clunk of coins falling into the winnings-tray of a fruit machine.

Conversation at the bar was temporarily suspended, since several noisy customers were now arriving, including three members of the highly unsuccessful Lower Swinstead Cricket Club. There was therefore a comparatively large audience for the seemingly endless music of the machine: clunk-clunk-clunk-clunk-clunk-clunk-clunk-clunk-clunk-clunk-clunk-clunk-clunk-clunk-clunk-clunk-clunk-clunk-clunk-clunk; and an even larger audience as the impassively faced youth pressed the 'Repeat' button – successfully – with a further twenty £1 coins duly clanking into the winnings-tray.

'Nearly enough for that honeymoon,' said the builder.

'Nonsense! He'll be putting it all back,' said one of the cricketers.

But he wasn't.

With a temporary lull in business, the landlord resumed the conversation. 'Business still pretty good, John?'

'Plenty o' work, yeah. Having to turn some things down.'

'What you got on at the minute?'

'Job in Burford in Sheep Street: bit o' roofing, bit o' pointing, bit o' painting.'

'High up, is it?'

'High enough. I'll need a coupla extensions on the ladder.'

Biffen screwed up his face and closed his eyes. 'You'd never get me up there.'

'You're OK, so long as things are firm.'

'Not if you get vertigo as bad as me.'

The coins bulged proudly in his trouser-pocket as the bride-groom designate walked out of the bar. Once in the passage that led to the toilets, he lifted the receiver from the pay-phone there, inserted 20p, and dialled a number.

But what he said, or to whom he spoke, not even the keen-eared elders could have known.

Chapter Thirty-Eight

All persons are puzzles until at last we find in some word or act the key to the man, to the woman; straightway all their past words and actions lie in light before us

(Emerson, *Journals*)

For much of the week Lewis had been working three-quarters of the way round the clock; but on Sunday, the day following the events described in the previous chapter, he felt refreshed after a good sleep and arrived at Kidlington Police HQ at 8.45 a.m. No sign of Morse. But that mattered little. It had been facts that were required. Not fancies. Not yet, anyway. And as he sat taking stock of the past week's activities, Lewis felt solidly satisfied – both with himself and with the performance of the personnel readily allocated to the case. There had been so much to cover . . .

Lewis had personally supervised the Monday and Tuesday enquiries into the activities of Paddy Flynn in the years, months, days – and morning – before his murder; and if the net result was perhaps somewhat disappointing, at least it had been thorough. Flynn had been living in an upstairs flat (converted a few years previously) in Morrell Avenue. He had been there for just over five months, paying £375 per calendar month for the privilege, and having virtually nothing to do with the tenant of the downstairs flat – a middle-aged accountant who, rain or shine, would walk each day down to St Clements, across Magdalen Bridge, and up the High to his firm's offices in King Alfred Street. He knew Flynn by sight, of course, but only exchanged words when occasionally they encountered each other in the narrow entrance hall. Of Flynn's lifestyle, he had no knowledge at all: no ideas about the activities in which his fellow-tenant might have been engaged. Well, just one little observation, perhaps, since not infrequently there was a car parked outside the semi – always a different car, and almost always gone the following morning. Lewis's notes had read: 'Has no knowledge of F's professional or leizure time activities'. But he'd consulted his dictionary, ever kept beside him, in case Morse decided to look at his notes, and quickly corrected the antepenultimate word.

By all accounts Flynn had led a pretty private, almost secretive life. He was quite frequently spotted in the local hostelries, quite frequently spotted in the local bookmakers, though never, apparently, the worse for excessive liquor or for excessive losses. His name figured nowhere in police records as even the pettiest of crooks, although he was mentioned in dispatches several times as the taxi driver who had picked up Frank Harrison from Oxford Railway Station on the night of Yvonne's murder. Radio Taxis had been his employer at the time; but he had been suspected of (possibly) fabricating fares for his own aggrandisement, and duly dismissed – without rancour, it appeared, and certainly without recourse to any industrial tribunal. Dismissed too, subsequently, by the proprietors of Maxim Removals, a firm of middle-distance hauliers, 'for attempted trickery with the tachometer'. (Lewis had spelled the last word correctly, having checked it earlier.) Since that time, five months previously, Flynn had reported regularly to the DSS office at the bottom of George Street. But lacking any testimonials to his competence and integrity, his attempts to secure further employment in any field of motor transport had been unsuccessful, his completed application forms seldom reaching even the slush-pile. It was all rather sad, as the woman regularly dealing with the Flynn file had testified.

He'd been thirty-two when, seven years earlier, he'd married Josie Newton, and duly fathered two daughters upon that lady – although (this the testimony of a brother in Belfast) the offspring had appeared so dissimilar in temperament, coloration, and mental ability, that there had been many doubts about their common paternity.

Josie Flynn had been unable or unwilling to offer much in the way of 'character-profiling' of her late husband (they'd never divorced); had scant interest in the manner of his murder; and, quite certainly, no interest in attending his 'last rites', whatever form these latter might take. Although he had treated her with ever-increasing indifference and contempt, he had never (she acknowledged it) abused her physically or sexually. In fact sex, even in the early months of their relationship, had never been a dominant factor in his life; nor, for that matter, had power or success or social acceptability or drink or even happiness. Just plain *money*. She'd not seen him for over two years; nor had her daughters – *she'd* seen to that. It was (again) all rather sad, according to Sergeant Dixon's report. Mr Paddy Flynn may not have been the ideal husband, but perhaps Ms Josephine Newton (now her preferred appellation) was hardly a paragon of rectitude in the marital relationship. 'Not exacly a saint herself?' as Dixon's handwritten addendum had suggested. And Lewis smiled to himself again, feeling a little superior.

It had been Lewis himself (no Morse beside him) who had visited Flynn's upstairs flat: smell of cigarette smoke everywhere; sheets on the single bed rather grubby; dirty cutlery and plates in the kitchen sink, but not too many of them; the top surface of the cooker in sore need of Mrs Lewis; soiled shirts, underpants, socks, handkerchiefs, in a neat pile behind the bathroom door; a minimal assemblage of trousers, jackets, shirts, underclothes, in a heavy wardrobe; a Corby trouser-press; eleven cans of Guinness in the otherwise sparsely stocked refrigerator; not a single book anywhere; two copies of the *Mirror* opened at the Racing pages; a TV set, but not even the statutory hard-core video; one CD, *Great Arias from Puccini*, but no CD player for Flynn to have gauged their magnitude; no pictures on the walls; no personal correspondence; and very little in the way of official communications, apart from Social Security forms: no sign of any bank account or credit facility.

Nothing much to go on.

And yet Lewis had sensed from the start that there was something missing. Sensed that he knew where that 'something missing' might well be.

And it was.

Most petty crooks had little in the way of imagination, having two or three favoured niches wherein to conceal their ill-gotten gains. And Paddy Flynn proved no exception. The small, brown-leather case was on the top shelf of the old mahogany wardrobe, tucked away on the far left, beneath a pair of faded-green blankets.

It took one DC just under twenty minutes to itemize the contents; a second DC just over thirty minutes to check the original itemization – a cache of legitimate bank-notes, in fifties, twenties, tens, and fives. The confirmed tally was £17,465 and Lewis knew that Morse would be interested.

And Morse, on being told, most decidedly *had* been interested.

A similarly painstaking review of Repp and Richardson had taken up the whole of the Wednesday. Little new had come to light except for the unexpected (?) discovery that an account with the Burford and Cheltenham Building Society showed a robust balance of £14,350 held in the name of Deborah Richardson, with regular monthly deposits (as was confidentially ascertained) always made in cash. Debbie Richardson had smilingly refused to answer Lewis's questions concerning the provenance of such comparatively substantial income, stating her belief that everybody – bishops, barmaids, presidents, prostitutes – all deserved some measure of privacy. Yes, Lewis had agreed; but he knew that Morse would be interested.

And Morse, on being told, most decidedly *had* been interested.

The Thursday and Friday had been taken up largely with a preliminary scrutiny and analysis of the scores of reports and statements taken from prison officers, bus drivers, rubbish-dump employees, car-park attendants, forensic boffins, and so on and so on – as well as from those members of the public who had responded to appeals for information. But so far there'd been little to show for the methodical police routine that Lewis had supervised. Vital, though! Criminal investigation was all about motives and relationships, about times and dates and alibis. It was all about building up a pattern from the pieces of a jigsaw. So many pieces, though. Some of them blue for the sky and the sea; some of them green and brown for the trees and the land; and sometimes, somewhere, one or two pieces of quirky coloration that seemed to fit in nowhere. And that, as Lewis knew, was where Morse would come in – as he invariably did. It was almost as if the Chief Inspector had the ability to cheat: to have sneaked some quick glimpse of the finished picture even before picking up the individual pieces.

Frequently when Lewis had seen him that week, Morse had been sitting in HQ, immobile and apparently immovable (apart from an hour or so over lunchtimes), occasionally and almost casually abstracting a page or two of a report, of a statement, of a letter, from one of the bulging box-files on his desk, YVONNE

HARRISON written large in black felt-tipped pen down each of the spines. Clearly (whatever else) Morse had come round to Strange's conviction that some causal connection between the cases had become overwhelmingly probable.

But that was no surprise to Lewis.

What had occasioned him puzzlement was the *number* of green box-files there, since he had himself earlier studied the same material when (he could swear it!) there had only been three.

Chapter Thirty-Nine

Q: Doctor, how many autopsies have you performed on dead people?

A: *All* of my autopsies are performed on dead people

(Reported in the *Massachusetts Lawyers' Journal*)

After (for him) an unprecedented early hour of retirement that same Sunday evening, at 9.30 p.m., Morse had awoken with a troublous headache. Assuming that the dawn was already breaking, he had confidently consulted his watch, to discover that it was still only 11.30 p.m. Thereafter he had woken up at regular ninety-minute intervals, in spite of equally regular doses of Alka-Seltzer and Paracetamol – his mind, even in the periods of intermittent slumber, riding the merry-go-round of disturbing dreams; his blood sugar ridiculously high; his feet suddenly hot and just as suddenly icy-cold; an indigestion pain that was occasionally excruciating.

Ovid (now almost becoming Morse's favourite Latin poet) had once begged the horses of the night to gallop slowly whenever some delightfully compliant mistress was lying beside him. But Morse had no such mistress beside him; and even if he had, he would still have wished those horses of the night to complete their course as quickly as they could possibly manage it.

He finally rose from the creased and crumpled sheets, and was shaving, just as rosy-fingered Dawn herself was rising over the Cutteslowe Council Estate.

At 6 a.m. he once more measured his blood-sugar level, now dipped dramatically from 24.4 at 1 a.m. to 2.8. Some decent breakfast was evidently required, and a lightly boiled egg with toast would fit the bill nicely. But Morse had no eggs; no slices of bread either. So, perforce, it had to be cereal. But Morse could find no milk, and there seemed no option but to resort to the solitary king-sized Mars bar which he always kept somewhere in the flat. For an emergency. *In rebus extremis*, like now. But he couldn't find it. Then – bless you St Anthony! – he discovered that the Co-op milkman had already called; and he had a great bowl of Corn Flakes, with a pleasingly cold pint of milk and several liberally heaped spoonsful of sugar. He felt wonderful.

Sometimes life was very good to him.

At 6.45 a.m. he considered (not too seriously) the possibility of walking up from his North Oxford flat to the A40 Ring Road, and thence down the gentle hill to Kidlington. About – what? – thirty-five to forty minutes to the HQ building. Not that he'd ever timed himself, for he'd never as yet attempted the walk.

Didn't attempt the walk that morning.

After administering his first insulin-dosage of the day, he drove up to Police HQ in the Jaguar.

Far quicker.

In his office, as he re-read the final findings of the two post-mortems (*sic*), Morse decided, as he usually did, that there was no point whatsoever in his trying to unjumble the physiological details of the lacerations inflicted on the visceral organs of each body. He had little interest in the stomach; had no stomach for the stomach. In fact he was more familiar with the nine-fold stomach of the bovine ilk (this because of cross-word puzzles) than with its mono-chambered human counterpart. Did it really matter much to know exactly how Messrs Flynn and Repp had met their ends? But yes, of course it did! If the technicalities pointed to a particular type of weapon; if the weapon could be accurately identified and then found; and if, finally, it could be traced to someone who was known to have had such a weapon and who had the opportunity of wielding it on the day of the murders . . .

Hold on though, Morse! Be fair! Amid a plethora of caveats, Dr Hobson *had* pointed to a fairly specific type of weapon, had she not? And he read again the paragraph headed 'Tentative Conclusions':

> The knife was quite probably not all that long, maybe no more than 6″–9″, since in each case the lacerations seem the result of forceful twisting, as if the murderer had gripped a handle that was short and firm, say perhaps not much more than 1″–1½″ in width. The knife-blade was fairly certainly short too (? 1½″), but very sharp, with its end shaped in triangular fashion (◺). It could have been something like a Stanley knife, the sort of thing commonly used in DIY household jobs, carpentry, building, that sort of thing.

Morse suddenly stopped reading, sat back in his chair, and placed his hands on his head, fingers interlinked, as he'd done so often at his teacher's bequest in his infant class. And what had been a faraway look in his eyes now gradually focused into an intense gaze as he considered the implications of the extraordinary idea which had suddenly occurred to him . . .

Very soon he was re-reading the whole report from Forensics, where almost all the earlier findings had been confirmed, although there remained much checking to be done. Prints of Flynn; prints of Repp; prints of the car-owner; and several other prints as yet to be identified. Doubtless some of these latter would turn out to be those of the car-owner's family. But (Morse read the last sentence of the report again): 'One set of fingerprints, repeated and fairly firm, may well prove to be of considerable interest'.

He leaned back again in his chair, pleasingly weary and really quite pleased with himself, because he knew whose fingerprints they were.

Oh yes!

Chapter Forty

Odd instances of strange coincidence are really not all that odd perhaps

(Queen Caroline's advocate, speaking in the House of Lords)

Morse jerked awake as Lewis entered the office just before 8 a.m., wondering where he was, what time it was, what day it was. Yet it had been a wonderful little sleep, the deep and dreamless sleep that Socrates anticipated after swallowing the hemlock.

'No crossword this morning, sir?'

'Shop wasn't open.'

'Why don't you pay a paper-boy?'

'Because, Lewis, a little occasional exercise . . .'

Lewis sat down. 'Do you mind if I ask you something?'

Morse pointed to the reports laid out on the desk. 'You've read these?'

Lewis nodded. 'But, like I say, I've got something to ask you.'

'And I've got something to *tell* you. Is that all right, Lewis?' The voice was suddenly harsh. 'You'll remember from all our times together how coincidence occurs in life far more frequently than anyone – except me – is prepared to accept. Coincidence isn't unusual at all. It's the norm. Just like those consecutive numbers cropping up in the National Lottery every week. But in this case the coincidence is even odder than usual.'

(Lewis raised his eyebrows a little.)

'Let's go back to Yvonne Harrison's murder. She was a woman with exceptional sex-drive; but she certainly wasn't just the deaf-and-dumb nymphomaniac with a bedroom just above the public bar that many a man has fantasized about. Oh, no. She was highly intelligent, highly desirable, like the woman in the Larkin poem with the 'lash-wide stare', who in turn was attracted by a variety of men. A lot of men. So many men that over the years she inevitably came across a few paying clients with kinky preferences. I doubt she ever went in for S and M, but it looks very likely that a bit of bondage was on her list of services, probably with a hefty surcharge. It's well known that some men only find sexual satisfaction with women who put on a show of being utterly submissive and powerless. It gives these men the only sense of real power they're ever likely to experience in life, because the object of their desire is lying there defenceless, unstruggling, sometimes unspeaking, too. Not uncommon, that, Lewis. And you can read all about it in Krafft-Ebing's case-studies . . .'

(Lewis's eyebrows rose significantly.)

'. . . although, as you know, I'm no great expert in such matters. In fact, come to think of it, I can't even remember whether he's got one or two "b"s in his name. But it means there's a pretty obvious explanation of two of the items that puzzled our previous colleagues: a pair of handcuffs, and a gag not all that tightly tied. The woman offering such a specialist service is never going to answer back, never going to scratch your eyes out – and Yvonne Harrison had just about the longest fingernails . . .'

(Lewis's eyebrows rose a lot.)

'On the night of the murder she had a client in bed with her, and if ever there was a *locus classicus* for what they call *coitus interruptus* this was it, because someone interrupted the proceedings. Or at the very least, someone saw them there in bed together.'

'Harry Repp?'

'Repp was certainly there at some point. But I think he kept his cool and kept his distance that night. I think he realized there could well be something in it for himself. He was right, too. Because what he saw that night – what he later kept from the police – was going to prove very profitable, as you discovered, Lewis. Five hundred pounds a month *from someone* just for exercising his professional skills as a burglar in staying well out of sight and keeping his eyes wide open. Exactly what he saw, we shan't know, shall we? Unless he told Debbie Richardson, which I doubt.'

'What do *you* think he saw?'

'Pretty obvious, isn't it?'

'You mean he saw who murdered Mrs Harrison?'

Morse nodded.

'And you think you know who . . . ?'

Morse nodded.

But Lewis shook his head. 'It's all so wishy-washy, what you've just said. I don't know where to start. *When* was she murdered? *Who* rang her husband? *Who* set off the burglar alarm? *Who* – ?'

'Lewis! We, remember, are investigating something else. But if any study of the first case facilitates the solving of the second? So be it! And it does, as you'll agree.'

'I will?'

Morse nodded again. 'Three people were coincidentally involved in a clever and profitable deception that night, each of them able and willing to throw his individual spanner into any reconstruction the CID could reasonably come up with. First, there was Flynn, our *corpus primum*, who told as many lies as anybody: both about the time he picked Frank Harrison up from Oxford Station, and about what he noticed – or more probably the person he saw – when he got to Lower Swinstead. Second, there was Repp, our *corpus secundum*, who told us no lies at all, but only because he told us nothing at all. Third . . .'

Morse hesitated, and Lewis looked across the desk expectantly.

'There's this third man of ours, and a man most unlikely to become our *corpus tertium*. Once Repp was out of jail, the three of them – Repp himself, Flynn, and this third man – they all arranged to meet together. They'd done pretty well so far out of their conspiracy of silence, and they were all keen on continuing to squeeze the milch-cow even drier. So they *did* meet – a meeting where things went tragically wrong. Greed . . . jealousy . . . personal antipathies . . . whatever! Two of them had an almighty row in the car in which they were travelling together. And one of them, probably in a lay-by somewhere, knifed one of the others: one of them knifed Flynn. And the remaining two disposed of the body neatly enough at Redbridge – the rubbish bags proving very handy, I should think. So any profits no longer needed to be split three ways. And now the talk between the two of them must have been all about a fifty-fifty share-out of the spoils, and how it could be effected. But somewhere in the discussion there was one further almighty row; and this time it was Repp who had his innards ripped open.'

'You know who this "third" man was, you're saying?'

'So do you. We mentioned him when you produced that admirable schema of yours for the night of Yvonne's murder.'

'You're saying there was somebody else there that night?'

'There was *always* somebody else, Lewis, wasn't there? The man in bed with Yvonne Harrison.'

'If you say so, sir.'

'You see, the major problem our lads had was the *timing* of the murder. Her body wasn't examined until several hours later, and all the pathological guesswork had to be married with the evidence gleaned at the time, or gleaned later. For example, with the fact that *someone* was in bed with Yvonne at some specific time that night, although nobody really tried to discover who that person was – until I did. For example, again, with the fact that *someone* had tried to ring her twice that night, at 9 p.m. when the line was engaged, and again half an hour later when the phone rang unanswered. And if you add all this together, you'll find that the person who sorely misled the police, the person who was in bed with her, and the person who murdered both Paddy Flynn and Harry Repp – *was one and the same man.*'

There fell a silence between the two of them, broken finally by Lewis. 'You're *sure* about all this?'

'Only ninety-five per cent sure.'

'We'd better get our skates on then.'

'Hold your horses! One or two things I'd like you to check first, just to make it one hundred per cent.'

'So we've got a little while?'

'Oh, yes. No danger of anyone murdering *him* – not today, anyway. So this afternoon'll be fine. Get out to Lower Swinstead – take someone with you, mind! – and bring him back here. OK?'

'Fine. Only one thing, sir. You forgot to tell me his name.'

'Did I? Well, you've guessed it anyway. He's got a little business out there, hasn't he? A little building business. "J. Barron, Builder", as it says on his van.'

Chapter Forty-One

But when he once attains the utmost round,
He then unto the ladder turns his back,
Looks in the clouds, scorning the base degrees
By which he did ascend

(Shakespeare, *Julius Caesar*)

TWENTY MILES WEST of Oxford, twenty miles east of Cheltenham, lies the little Cotswold town of Burford. It owes its architectural attractiveness to the wealth of the wool-merchants in the fifteenth and sixteenth centuries; and up until the end of the eighteenth century the small community there continued to thrive, especially the coaching inns which regularly served the E–W travel. But the town was no longer expanding, with the final blow delivered in 1812, when the main London road, which crossed the High Street (the present-day Sheep Street and Witney Street), was rerouted to the southern side of the town (the present-day A40). But Burford remains an enchanting place, as summer tourists will happily testify as they turn off at the A40 roundabout. Picturesque tea shops, craft shops, public houses – all built in the locally quarried, pale-honey-coloured limestone – line the steeply curving sweep of the High Street that leads to the bridge at the bottom of the hill, under which runs the River Windrush, with all the birds and the bright meadows and cornfields around Oxfordshire.

Mrs Patricia Bayley, aged seventy, had lived for only three years in Sheep Street (*vide supra*), a pleasingly peaceful, tree-lined road, first left as one descended the hill. The house-date, 1687, had been carved (now almost illegibly) in the greyish and pitted stone above the front door of the three-storeyed, mullion-windowed building. Her husband, a distinguished anthropologist from University College, Oxford, had died (aged sixty-seven) only two months after his retirement; and only four months after buying the Sheep Street property. Often, since then, she had considered leaving the house and buying one of the older-persons' flats that had been springing up for the last decade all over North Oxford, for her present house was unnecessarily extensive and inappropriate for her solitary needs. Yet the children and the grandchildren (especially the latter) loved to stay there with her and to find themselves lost amid the random rooms. Only one real problem: she'd have to do something about the windows. There could be no Council permission for replacement windows; but the casements were quite literally falling apart. And the whole of the exterior just had to be repainted, from the gutterings along the top to the front door at the bottom. Should she get it all done? Three weeks earlier she'd stood and surveyed the scene. Could she ever find anywhere else so pleasingly attractive as this?

No! She'd stay.

She'd consulted the Yellow Pages and found *Barron,*

J, Builder and Decorator; not so far away, either – at Lower Swinstead. She'd rung him and he'd called round to survey the job. He'd seemed a personable sort of fellow; and when he'd quoted a reasonable (if slightly steep) estimate for both the restructuring and the repainting, she'd accepted.

He'd promised to be with her at 7.30 a.m. on Monday 3 August. And it was precisely at that time that he knocked in civilized manner on the front door of 'Collingwood', again admiring as he did so the dripstone moulding above it.

Born in North Oxford, Mrs Bayley spoke her mind unapologetically: 'You look as if you've just come straight from the abattoir, Mr Barron!'

The builder (rather a handsome man, she thought) grinned wryly as he looked down at overalls bespattered with scarlet paint. 'Not my choice, Mrs B. I'm with *you*, all the way. If there's a better combination of colour than black and white and yellow, I don't know it.'

Mrs B felt gratified. 'Well, I'll let you get on then. I won't bother you – no one will bother you. It's all very quiet round here. Would you like some coffee later?'

'Tea, if you don't mind, Mrs B. Milk and two teaspoons of sugar, please. About ten? Smashing!'

From the ground-floor window she watched him as he removed the aluminium ladders from the top of the van, stood there for a few seconds looking up at the dormer window, then shaking out the first extension and, by means of a rope and pulley at the bottom, elongating the ladder to its fullest extent with a second, smaller extension. For a few seconds he stood there, holding the loftily assembled structure at right angles to the ground; then easing the pointed top of the third stage – most carefully, lovingly almost – into place against the casement of the dormer window some thirty feet above, before finally firming the bottom of the ladder on the compacted gravel of the pathway which divided the front of the houses there from the wide stretch of grass leading to the edge of Sheep Street, some four or five feet below.

For several minutes Mrs B stood by her front window on the ground floor, looking out a little anxiously to observe her builder's varied skills. Across the road, a solitary jogger in red trainers was running reasonably briskly past the Bay Tree Hotel, his tracksuit hood over his head, as if he were trying to work up a sweat; or just perhaps to keep his ears warm, since there was an unseasonal nip in the air that morning. Mrs B thought jogging a silly and dangerous way of keeping fit, though. She'd known the young North Oxford don who had written the hugely popular *Joys of Jogging*, and who had died aged twenty-seven, whilst on an early-morning not-so-joyful jog.

Jogging was a dangerous business.

Like climbing ladders.

And Mrs B's nerves could stand things no longer.

She would repair to the second-floor back-bedroom to continue with her quilting – as well as to quell the acute fear she felt for a man who (as she saw it) was risking his life at every second of his working day. But before doing so, she knew she had the moral duty to impart a few cautionary words of advice. And she opened the front door just as the builder was beginning his ascent, his left hand on a shoulder-high rung, his right hand grasping a narrowly serrated saw, a long chisel, and a red, short-handled Stanley knife.

'You *will* be careful, won't you? Please!'

The builder nodded, successively grasping each rung (each 'round' as the firemen say) at a point just above his shoulders as he climbed with measured step, professionally, confidently, to the top of the triple-length ladder. He'd always enjoyed being up high, ever since the vicar of St John the Baptist's in Burford had taken him and his fellow choirboys up to the top of the church. It was the first time in his young life he'd felt superior, felt powerful, as he traversed his way along the high places there with a strangely happy confidence, whilst the others inched their cautious way along the narrow ledges.

It was just the same now.

Once he had reached the top rung but three, he looked up and immediately decided he would be able to work at the top of the dormer without any trouble. Then he looked down, and saw that the ladder(s) beneath him, though sagging slightly in the middle (that was good), seemed perfectly straight and secure. Funny, really! Most people thought you were all right on heights just so long as you didn't look up or down. Rubbish! The only thing to avoid was looking laterally to left or right, when there really *was* the risk (at least for him) of losing all sense of the vertical and the horizontal. He dug his red Stanley knife into the upper lintel, then the lower sill; in each case, as he twisted the blade, finding the wooden texture crumble with ominous ease. Not surprising though, really, for he'd noticed the date above the door. He secured the top of the ladder to the gutterings – his normal practice – and began work.

At the appointed hour Mrs B boiled the kettle in the second-floor front (as her husband had called it); squeezed a Typhoo bag with the kitchen tongs; and stirred in two heaped spoonsful of sugar. Then, with the steaming cup and two digestive biscuits on a circular tray, she was about to make her way downstairs when something quite extraordinary flashed across her vision: she saw a pair of oblique parallel lines passing almost in slow motion across the oblong frame of the second-floor window. So sharply was that momentary configuration imprinted upon her retina that she was able to describe it so very precisely later that same afternoon; was able to recall that ear-splitting, skin-tingling shriek of terror as the man whose skull was about to be smashed to pieces fell headfirst on to the compacted pathway below, so very few yards from her own front door.

'Dead,' the senior paramedic had told her quietly, six minutes only after her panic-stricken call on 999. Incontrovertibly dead.

For the next hour or so Mrs Bayley wept almost uncontrollably. Partly from shock. Partly, too, from guilt, because (as she repeatedly reminded herself) it was *her* fault that he'd appeared upon the scene in the first place. She'd found his name among the local builders and house-renovators listed alphabetically in the Telephone Directory. In the Yellow Pages, in fact. Exactly where Sergeant Lewis, also, had discovered the address of J. Barron, Builder, together with a telephone number in Lower Swinstead.

Chapter Forty-Two

And what is the use of a book without pictures or conversations?

(Lewis Carroll, *Alice in Wonderland*)

HAD HE BEEN left to himself, had he been without any knowledge of the context in which the apparent 'accident' had occurred, Lewis would not have suspected that it all amounted to murder. But it *had* been murder, he felt sure of that; and four hours earlier he had taken personal responsibility for initiating the whole apparatus of yet another murder enquiry. Same SOCOs as in the Sutton Courtenay murder, same pathologist, same everything; but with almost every sign of immediate activity over when, just before 3 p.m., Morse finally put in an appearance, very soon to be seating himself in Mrs Bayley's north-facing sitting room on the ground floor.

'Northamptonshire faring any better?' he asked the senior SOCO.

'Next year, perhaps,' said Eddie Andrews pessimistically.

'You'd be out of a job without me,' continued Morse. 'Just like Dr Hobson here.'

But the unsmiling pathologist could find little place in her heart for any banter and ignored the comment. As did Edwards.

The gloomy room was suddenly empty, apart from Sergeant Lewis. 'You said there wasn't any danger of *him* being murdered, sir.'

Morse could find no satisfactory answer, and stared silently out of the window until Mrs Bayley came in with (for Morse) wholly unwelcome cups of coffee and the same two digestive biscuits that Barron would have eaten with his over-sugared tea.

'You mentioned to Sergeant Lewis what you saw from the window? The one above this, wasn't it?'

She nodded. 'It made such a vivid imprint on the, er . . .'

'Retina?' suggested Lewis.

'Thank you, Sergeant. I *did* myself once work in the Oxford Eye Hospital.' She turned to Morse. 'You'll think me a silly old woman, but it reminded me of something I saw quite a few years ago now in one of the Sundays. There were these outline drawings sent in by readers and you had to guess what they were; and one of them always stuck in my, er . . .' (This time Lewis desisted.) She took a pencil and without permission made a quick little drawing in Lewis's notebook:

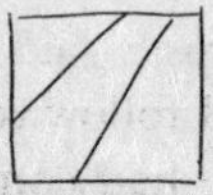

'Can't you guess, Inspector?' Her eyes twinkled.

Morse frowned, about to suggest something wildly inappropriate when the undeterred Lewis intervened:

'Giraffe walking past a window?'

'You clever man.'

'No!' Lewis smiled deprecatingly. 'I'd seen it before.'

He took a pencil and made an equally quick little drawing underneath:

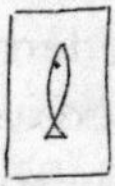

'Aristocratic sardine in a tin!' she cried triumphantly.

'You clever woman!'

She shook her head. 'I'd seen it before.'

Morse sounded wearily impatient. 'I'm very sorry to interrupt the fun, Mrs Bayley, but . . .'

'Of course. Forgive me!'

'Which way was your, er, giraffe walking? Left to right? Right to left?'

'Left to right – exactly like I've drawn it, Inspector.'

'So if the ladder fell across the window from left to right, the bottom of the ladder must have slipped from right to left – that is, from your point of view here in the house, Mrs Bayley?'

'I'm not quite sure I follow you.'

'I mean, if someone had come along and given the ladder a hefty kick at the bottom, he'd probably have been coming from' (Morse pointed to the right) 'the centre of Burford, say, to' (Morse pointed vaguely to the left) 'wherever this road leads to?'

'Bourton on the Water.'

'Thank you, Lewis!'

'But we know that, sir – about the ladder, I mean. They found him six or seven yards to the right of the front door. That's from Mrs Bayley's point of view of course,' he added mischievously.

'Yes!' whispered the lady of the household, as so vividly she recalled that terrible sight, with the red Stanley knife lying there beside the shattered skull.

Morse was looking far from pleased. Even less so when a further cup of coffee was suggested. The room had become chillier, and he shivered slightly as he got to his feet. It was time for the clichés:

'If you *do* remember anything else – anything odd – anything unusual – anything at all . . .'

And suddenly she *had* remembered something. It was Morse's involuntarily shivering shoulders that had jogged – yes, *jogged* – her memory.

The jogger.

'There *was* something a bit unusual. We don't get many people jogging here – we're all a bit too old. But there was one this morning, about a quarter-to-eight. He'd pulled the hood of his tracksuit over his head as if he was feeling the cold a bit.'

'Or wasn't anxious to be recognized,' added Morse quietly.

'Perhaps *you* could recognize him though, Inspector. You see, he was wearing a very distinctive pair of training shoes. *Red*, they were.'

*

The two policemen left with appropriate expressions of gratitude; and with the two digestive biscuits still untouched on the circular tray, beside two cups, one of them full, of stone-cold coffee.

Chapter Forty-Three

For coping with even one quarter of that running course known as 'Marathon' – for coping without frequent halts for refreshment or periodic bouts of vomiting – a man has to dedicate one half of his youthful years to quite intolerable training and endurance. Such dedication is not for me

(Diogenes Small, 1797–1805,
The Joys of Occasional Idleness)

After Lewis had turned right at the junction of Sheep Street and High Street and slipped the marked police car into the queue up to the A40 roundabout, Morse pointed peremptorily to the right, to the Cotswold Gateway Hotel.

Seated at a wall-settle in the bar, Morse tasted his pint of cask-conditioned ale and proclaimed it 'not so bad'. And Lewis, seated opposite, sipped his iced orange juice and said nothing.

Morse looked sourly out of sorts.

'Just nip and get me a packet of cigarettes, Lewis. Dunhill, if they've got them. I don't seem to . . .' In time-honoured fashion, he patted his trouser-pockets with little prospect, as it seemed, of finding any funds therein.

'I thought you'd stopped,' ventured Lewis, as minutes later Morse peeled off the cellophane.

'First today!' said Morse as with obvious gratification he inhaled deeply.

In turn, Lewis took a deep breath himself:

'You mustn't get cross with me if—'

'Certainly not.' Morse pushed his empty glass across the table.

Waiting at the bar, Lewis was rehearsing his carefully formulated sentence; was ready with it once he took his seat again.

'You mustn't be cross with me, sir, but—'

'Someone's been round to Mrs Barron? You've seen to that?'

'Dixon, yes. With WPC Towle – she's an experienced officer.'

'PC Towle, you mean. They're all PCs now, whatever the sex. Stands for Politically Correct.'

For the umpteenth time in his working life with Morse, Lewis knew that any potentially favourable wind had suddenly stopped blowing for him; and that it would be Morse who would now be sailing serenely on, whatever the state of the weather. As he did now:

'Something worrying you, Lewis?'

'Yes. Something *is*. We started off with two murders and you said you knew who the murderer was. And now this murderer of yours gets murdered himself and . . .'

'And there's not all that much point in sitting around in a pub all day just thinking about things. Is that what you're saying?'

'Yes! Why don't we sit back and look at what we've *got* – look at the *evidence*?'

'You're talking to me in italics, Lewis.'

'All right! But don't you think it *is* time – to start again – at the *beginning*?'

'No,' said Morse (no italics). 'Let's start with those red trainers.'

'All right. Good news that. There can't be more than a dozen people in Oxfordshire who've got a pair like that. Give us a few days. We'll find him. Guaranteed!'

'Let's hope you're right. Bit odd, though. Quarter-to-eight? And still running when Barron fell at ten-past-ten?'

'We're not all as unfit as you.'

'What? I could have run a marathon in that time. Once.'

Lewis smiled quietly to himself as Morse continued: 'You know, what worried me about the murders of Flynn and Repp was how anyone could have got away from that car without people noticing all the blood on his clothes. Then it struck me. Barron could have got away with it easily. His overalls were already covered in red – covered in the maroon paint from Debbie Richardson's out-house – *before* the murders. Nobody's going to worry about what he looks like, not in Lower Swinstead anyway. It's not exactly like spilling a bottle of Claret over your white tuxedo on the *QE2*. Is it now?'

'I wouldn't know, sir.'

'Being too clever, am I?'

'Perhaps.'

'You see, I thought *he* was clever, Barron. And in

spite of what some of these criminologists say, some criminals *are* clever.'

Lewis agreed. 'Pretty clever of our murderer to knock him off his ladder: no weapon, no fingerprints . . .'

'Mm.' Morse drained his beer and stood up. 'You will be glad to know that the brain is now considerably clearer, although I am still, if it's of interest to you, exceedingly puzzled as to why our murderer should decide to draw almost inevitable attention to himself by wearing such a conspicuous pair of plimsolls and running around Burford for two and a half hours.'

'Truth is, sir, some of 'em *aren't* all that clever. We both know that.'

By the time they were back at Kidlington HQ, the strangely disturbing news was already beginning to filter through.

Not that Morse himself was to be in his office that late Monday afternoon, for he had instructed Lewis to drop him off at his flat in North Oxford. He longed for some music: some Mozart (though not *Eine Kleine Nachtmusik*), some Wagner (though not the *Ride of the Valkyries*), some Vivaldi even (though not *The Four Seasons*), or some Vaughan Williams (though not *The Lark Ascending*).

Most especially not *The Lark Ascending*, since Morse (as we have seen) had already spent enough of his time with the dawn that day.

Chapter Forty-Four

CLINTON WINS ON BUDGET, BUT MORE LIES AHEAD

(From *USA's Best Newspaper Headlines*, 1997)

Sergeant Dixon swallowed the last of the jam-filled, sugar-coated doughnut: 'I'm beginning to think he's losing his marbles. First he says we go and bring Barron in – and the next thing is we're telling his missus he's croaked it.'

Sergeant Lewis looked up. 'How did she take it?'

'Not very well. Kate was very good with her but . . .'

'Her GP knows?'

'Yep. And she's got her mum and sister there, so . . . The kids though, innit? Poor little buggers: six and four.'

'Easier for them, I suppose.'

'Perhaps so. I just had the feeling though, you know, the marriage wasn't all that . . .' Dixon held out a shaky right hand, like that of a man with delirium tremens.

'What gave you that impression?'

Dixon tapped his right temple with a firmer finger. 'Experience, mate.'

He got up, walked over to the canteen counter, and looked hopefully along the glass shelves.

*

Lewis was summoned to Caesar's tent just after 5.30 p.m.

'Sorry state of affairs, Lewis, when a man can't even get a round of golf in on a Monday afternoon!'

'I just thought you ought to—'

'Winning I was. Two up at the turn. The swing really in the groove. And then . . .'

'I'm sorry, sir. But as I say I thought—'

'Where's Morse?'

'He, er, just went back home for a while.'

'Best place for him. Nothing but disaster since he took over things.'

'It was *you* wanted him,' said Lewis gently.

'Too clever – that's Morse's trouble! Time he jacked it in – like me. Make way for these bright young buggers checking in through the fast-track. It's all degrees these days, Lewis, and DNA, and . . .'

'Clipboards?'

Strange smiled sympathetically. 'Old Morse doesn't like clipboards much, does he?'

'No.'

'You'll miss him when he goes, won't you?'

'Is he going?'

'You'll be a richer man, for certain.'

Lewis made no reply.

'Did he have a couple of beers out at Burford?'

'Just the one.'

'Remarkable! And who paid for that, pray?'

'Oddly enough, *he* did.'

Strange looked across the desk shrewdly. 'Know

something, Lewis? You're nearly as big a liar as that American President.'

For the next ten minutes, and with no further lies, Lewis told the Chief Superintendent as much as he or anyone else (including Morse?) could know about the deliberate murder of J. Barron, Builder (and increasingly, as it appeared, Decorator) of Lower Swinstead.

'Mm!'

Strange contemplated the phone awhile; then rang Morse. But the ex-directory number was engaged. A minute later, he rang again; and, a minute later, again. Still engaged.

'Taken his phone off the bloody hook. Typical! He's supposed to be solving an assortment of murders.'

'He's a bit tired, sir. I don't think he's been sleeping very well.'

'Hardly surprising, is it? Having to get up for a pee every half hour?'

'I don't think it's *just* that.'

'What d'you mean?' Strange's voice was sharper.

'Well, nothing really.'

'*Out* with it, Lewis.'

'Just that sometimes perhaps it almost seems as if he doesn't really care all that much . . .'

'Interesting!'

For a while Strange pondered matters. Then decided: 'Go and knock him up!'

'Couldn't we give him a rest, just for today?' suggested a diffident Lewis. 'Not much *he* can do for the minute, is there? Not much *you* can do, either.'

'Mm. You could be right.'

'Why not get back to the golf course?'

'Because, Lewis – *because* I've let him off the hook. Three up at the turn . . .'

'I thought you said it was *two* up, sir.'

'Did I?'

Strange reached for the phone and rang Morse's number yet again.

Still engaged.

He stood up and repeated Lewis's words: 'Not much *you* can do, either. Why don't you just bugger off home. Eggs and chips, what?'

For a good deal of these exchanges between Strange and Lewis, Deborah Richardson had been standing, head tilted, in the narrow passageway at the back of the property, wondering whether she'd been sensible in choosing that particular shade of maroon for the newly established out-house. Two of the re-plastered walls had received their first coat – several weekends ago now – and they reminded her, according to the light, either of blackcurrant jam or of blood.

She thought she'd probably change things.

The phone rang.

She reached it at the sixth ring.

The arrangements, unusually involved, took a little while to get sorted out.

Once they were, she felt almost unprecedentedly excited.

Chapter Forty-Five

Nunquam ubi sub ubi!

After he had locked the door behind them she immediately, albeit a little nervously, commented upon the civilized appearance of the bachelor flat, listening with half an ear to a love-duet from one of the operas, although she had no idea which one; standing appreciatively for a while in front of a reproduction of *The Milkmaid*, although she had only just heard of Vermeer; looking wide-eyed along the shelves and shelves and shelves of books that lined three of the walls there; noticing too, although not herself a particularly houseproud woman, the thin layer of dust on the CD player and the thicker layer along the top of the skirting boards.

On the glass-topped coffee table there stood a chilled bottle of champagne, with two sparklingly bright glasses on their coasters beside it.

As quietly bidden, she sat down, the hem of the mini-dress riding more than halfway up her black-stockinged thighs as languidly she crossed her lengthy legs. Then, as he untwisted the wire at the top of the bottle, she turned away, holding the palms of her hands over her ears.

'No need for that,' he said. 'I'm an expert.'

Tilting the bottle to 45 degrees, he turned the cork

sharply, pulling only slightly – and that was it. Out! He filled the two glasses, sat opposite her, raised his glass, and said, 'Cheerio!'

It seemed to her a strange thing to say. 'Hello!' would surely have been more appropriate? It was obviously something he'd stored away in his verbal baggage from a period at least twenty-five years (she decided) earlier than her own.

Not that *that* mattered.

She sipped the champagne; sipped it again; and concluded, although she knew nothing whatever of Bruts and Crus, that it might well be fairly expensive stuff.

'Specially bought for the occasion?'

'No. I won it in a raffle.'

She took a further sip, then drank off the rest in a single draught. 'Lovely!'

He leaned forward and refilled her glass.

'Are you trying to get me drunk?'

'It might even things up a bit.'

'Mind if I smoke?'

'No. I'll join you.'

'You took a lot of trouble about gettin' me here – '

'Don't you like taxis?'

' – and I've never been told exactly what to wear before.'

He surveyed her vertically striped brown-and-white dress, and counted the button-holes: seven of them, the top three straining across her breasts.

'I like buttons. I've read that "unbuttoning" was Philip Larkin's favourite present participle.'

She let it go, fairly certain that she understood, and slowly unfastened the top button of her dress. 'I shall expect a fee, you know that.'

'Fee? You mean as well as the taxi and the champagne?'

She nodded, and pointed to the bottle. 'Will one be enough, do you think?'

'I won *two* in the raffle. The other one's cooling in the fridge.'

She drained her second glass, and sat back in the deeply comfortable settee, unfastening the second button as he again refilled her glass.

She patted the cushion beside her. 'Come and sit next to me.'

'In a little while. It's just that I'd like to get my fill of sitting here and lusting after you.'

She smiled. 'I wonder how we would have been together?'

'Know something? You've just quoted T. S. Eliot, virtually verbatim.'

She let it go, fairly certain that Eliot was a poet. But there wasn't much poetry out there – not in the world in which she moved. It all made her feel pleasingly important and decidedly sexy. Something more, too. As she tilted the third glass of champagne into her lipstick-moistened mouth; as she worked the third button of her dress loose; as she looked down at her bra-less breasts now almost fully exposed, she felt an animal sense of her own power – and she felt *good.*

He was right, though. She was enjoying teasing him, and he was enjoying being teased. No need for that rush to sexual congress the great majority of men (she knew full well) preferred.

'You know,' she said, 'I thought first of all when you rang that you wanted to ask me about the murders.'

'Afterwards, don't you think?'

She uncrossed her legs and leaned forward to light another cigarette. 'No. Let's get the inquisition over. Where's the bedroom, by the way?'

He pointed to a door on his left. 'Top sheet turned back in a very neat hypotenuse.'

She let it go, for her own mathematics had stopped well short of Pythagoras.

'I didn't ask you here for any grilling – you know that. But there *is* one thing I'd like you to tell me.'

'Fire away.'

'I think you've got a good idea who murdered Harry. And if you *have*, I'd like you to tell me.'

'But I don't – not for certain, I don't.' She recrossed the legs that a little earlier had been provocatively open.

'Go on!'

'It's just . . . well, I reckon perhaps it was Johnnie – *might* have been, anyway.'

'Why do you think that?'

'Somethin' he said and . . . well, you get the vibes sometimes.'

He seemed to know nothing of 'vibes' – interested only in strictly verbal significations.

'What exactly *did* he say?'

'Nothin' really. Nothin' I'm going to tell you, anyway.'

'When was this?'

'Sat'day night.'

'He was with you then?'

'Yes.'

'Did he often call round?'

'Quite often.'

'He'd been taking his time with your building alterations?' He drank the rest of the only glass of champagne he'd allowed himself – drank it swiftly, like a man in a pub who knows that if he stays any longer the next round will surely be his, and who therefore decides to depart.

'And you went to bed – quite often – with Barron?'

What the hell! If this fellow just so happened to be more gentle, more interesting, more articulate than some of her occasional partners – so bloody what!

'Yes!' She said it defiantly. 'Pretty good in bed he was, too!'

'I'm sorry,' he said slowly, 'but Mr Barron's dead.'

'You thought I didn't know?'

'How *did* you know?'

'Come off it! I wasn't born yesterday.'

He got to his feet and stepped over to sit beside her. For a while he held her right hand lightly in his; then, with his own right hand he refastened the top three buttons of the dress he'd specifically requested her to wear above no underwear.

Then he left the room and she heard his voice on the telephone: 'Radio Taxis? . . . One of your drivers, as soon as you can . . . to Burford . . . on my account, please . . . Morse.'

The two recently re-filled glasses of champagne – the one for her, and the one for him – remained untasted on the top of the coffee-table that had been polished so carefully before the arrival of Miss Debbie Richardson.

Chapter Forty-Six

> For the clash between the Classical and the Gothic revivals, visitors might go to the top end of Beaumont Street and compare the Greek glory of the Ashmolean on the left with the Gothic push of the Randolph Hotel on the right
>
> (Jan Morris, *Oxford*)

THE SPIRES RESTAURANT in the Randolph Hotel is an impressively elegant affair. A full complement of Oxford College crests is mounted in a frieze around the room, the regal ambience of the place relieved by the soft lighting of flambeaux on the brown-papered walls, and by two central chandeliers, holding similar flambeaux, that hang from the high-beamed ceiling. Twenty or so tables are spaciously arranged there, cross-draped with maroon tablecloths, and laid with gleaming silver-ware, sparkling wine glasses, and linen serviettes of a pale-ochre colour. The chairs, of uniform style, are upholstered in a material of bottle-green; and the colour combination of the room *in toto* has appealed to many (if not to all) as an unusually happy one. Two large windows on the room's northern side overlook Beaumont Street, with the Ashmolean Museum and the Taylorian Institute just across the way; whilst those seated beside three equally large windows on the eastern side look out on to the Martyrs'

Memorial, with St John's and Balliol Colleges beyond it, sharing with their fellow diners a vista of St Giles', the widest street in Oxford and visually one of the most attractive avenues in England.

At 7.15 that same evening, a man in the company of a much younger woman appeared to have eschewed either of these splendid views, for they had chosen a table (set for three) on the restaurant's west and windowless side, and now sat with their backs partly turned on the sprinkling of other early diners – like people who had no real objections to being seen, perhaps, but equally had no wish to draw attention to themselves.

At 7.25 p.m., the man was again consulting his wristwatch when a black-tied waiter asked if they would like a further drink while they waited.

Though expensive, the cocktail they had each been drinking was, in the young woman's judgement, 'absolutely yummy' – Cognac, Kümmel, Fraise Liqueur, topped with chilled champagne – and she nodded. Might just as well be happy about something.

'Same again,' said Frank Harrison. 'Ailish cocktails.' And when the waiter was gone: 'Where the hell's he got to? I've not got all bloody evening.'

'You've got to get back tonight, Dad?'

'That's got nothing to do with it. Seven-fifteen is seven-fifteen!'

'His hearing's not getting any better, you know. He probably thought you said seven-fifty.'

'Who's ever ordered a dinner for seven-fifty, for Christ's sake?'

For the moment Sarah said nothing further, looking

around her and enjoying the regal dignity of the restaurant. And in truth her father's tetchy impatience with Simon was not wholly displeasing to her. There had ever been a closer bond between herself and her father than with her mother; and, in turn, a very much closer bond between Simon and his mother than with his father. But such things were not spoken of freely in families; and it was better that way. Quite why she had always felt possessive about her father, she could not explain well even to herself. But she remembered clearly when she'd first been conscious of it: when she had crept silently downstairs late one night with a party in full swing below; and when, unseen herself, she'd watched her father kissing a young woman in the kitchen. She had cried herself to sleep that night. Only six, she'd been, but she could have murdered the woman. Disbelief? Shock? Outrage? All three mixed together, like a cocktail . . . like a cocktail topped up with a little chilled jealousy.

Simon appeared at 7.48. Like his father, not looking particularly in love with life.

'You're both early?' he ventured, as he took his seat. 'Seven-fifty, wasn't it?'

'Forget it!' His father passed over a menu.

'I could do with a drink first, Dad.'

'Just read the question-paper!'

Simon looked down at the succulent-sounding selections: *To Start . . . To Continue . . . Dessert . . . Beverages* – and felt a little happier, until Harrison père, brusquely ruling out starters, called over the waiter and put in their order for the main courses: Guinea Fowl; Calves'

Liver; Steak (medium). 'And a bottle of some decent Claret.'

'Just one?' queried Simon. 'Three of us?'

'Sarah's driving.'

'Aren't *you* driving, Dad?' asked Sarah.

'I don't really need my daughter to tell me what I can drink, thank you very much.'

Sarah put down her menu and stood up slowly. 'Excuse me a minute! I'm just off to . . .'

But before making her way to the Ladies' Powder Room, Sarah Harrison stopped at Reception.

'Can I ring one of your guests from here?'

'Of course.' The young girl smiled. 'Just ring the room number.' She pointed to the phone at the side of the desk.

'The name's Harrison – F. Harrison.'

'The receptionist tapped a few keys and looked at her video-screen.

'Yes. That's right.'

'Can you just give me the room number?'

'I'm sorry. I can't do that. It's strict company policy—'

'I'm his daughter, for God's sake!'

'Just a minute!' The girl moved away and the phone on the desk sprang to life when she returned: 'All yours.'

Sarah picked up the phone and listened, wondering what on earth she was going to say. But she needn't have bothered.

'Hellóho.' It was a female, husky, transatlantic voice.

Sarah put down the phone, a sudden glint of fury in her eyes.

She returned to the table to find father and brother,

heads close together, in what seemed a significant conversation. But there the exchanges stopped – whether because of her own return or the contemporaneous arrival of the main courses, Sarah was uncertain.

Thereafter the food was appreciatively consumed, the few transmensal exchanges wholly mundane and perfunctory, the bottle of Claret rapidly going and going and soon wholly gone.

'Another bottle, Dad?' suggested Simon.

'No!'

'I came on the *bus* – I'm going *back* on the bus.'

'But Dad's got to drive back to London, remember? Anyway I thought we were all supposed to keep sober tonight. Isn't that why we're here?'

'It *was*, yes. Just keep your voice down, will you? And read this. Simon's already seen it. Pretty quick off the mark, some of these local reporters.'

Sarah looked down at the copy of the *Oxford Mail* passed across to her, the lower half of the back page folded over to show the LATEST NEWS column:

> Thousands of families evacuated as Hurricane Georges lashes Florida Keys with torrential downpours and winds of over 120 m.p.h.
>
> Huge tailback on A40 as lorry carrying thousands of gallons of cows' blood overturns near Eynsham
>
> Local builder John Barron of Lower Swinstead pronounced dead on arrival at JR2 after falling from ladder in Sheep Street, Burford

Chapter Forty-Seven

Different things can add up in different ways whilst reaching an identical solution, just as 'eleven plus two' forms an anagram of 'twelve plus one'

(Margot Gleave, *A Classical Education*)

A WEALTH OF police personnel and well-targeted enquiries had borne swift if, here and there, unexpected evidence – evidence which Sergeant Lewis (alone in his office late that Monday evening) was able to shift and to categorize at his own pace. Thus far, the facts, and the glosses on the facts, formulated themselves as follows in Lewis's mind:

First. The shiny orange-red Stanley knife had been purchased, together with other items, from a hardware shop in Burford on the Saturday of the previous week (receipt unearthed in Barron's Expenses File). Barron could still have been a murderer – of course he could! – but quite certainly *not* with the knife he'd used that same morning as he stood almost atop the topmost section of the ladder and twisted the blade into the rotting, unresisting sill of the dormer window in Sheep Street.

Second. The stains on the overalls Barron had been wearing that morning had quite certainly *not* been human blood; but almost certainly smears of paint patented under the brand-name Cremosin, two-pint tins of which were found in Barron's garage, a space now used exclusively for building and decorating materials.

Third. On the morning of the Friday when Flynn and Repp had been murdered, Barron had left home around his usual time to spend some of the morning in Thame, where two properties were inviting tenders for renovation, for which Barron had been keen to submit his own estimates. Necessarily, of course, this evidence had been taken from Barron's wife, Linda; and yet (already) a dated parking ticket for four hours that morning (South Oxon DC, Cattle Market) had been found in Barron's van – evidence, if anything, to substantiate the claim that the builder had paid for a fairly extensive stay in the centre of Thame on July the 24th.

Fourth. There appeared, as yet, no evidence whatever that Barron had received any monies from anywhere to match the payments so regularly stashed into the balances of both Flynn and Repp. In short, *if* Barron had been the third man – *if* he had duly received his own share of the spoils for the conspiracy of silence – there was no sign of it, so far.

They were not in any way decisive, these findings and non-findings. The trouble was they all seemed to be pointing in the same direction.

Or were they?

For example (thought Lewis), it was surely to be expected that Barron would have got rid of the murder weapon and bought himself a new knife if in fact he *had* used the former for the murders.

For example (thought Lewis), it was most unlikely that Barron had only one pair of overalls. And if someone with an extravagantly fanciful mind (Morse!) could entertain the idea that a pair of white overalls covered with red paint was a good disguise for a soaking of blood . . . well, it *could* be, perhaps.

For example (thought Lewis), why buy a four-hour parking ticket in Thame on the day of the murders unless to create an alibi? Builders would usually have little difficulty in parking outside the properties in question. All right, parking was getting a nightmare everywhere, even for police cars, but . . .

For example (thought Lewis), why shouldn't Barron, like Flynn perhaps, have received his pay-offs in bank-notes, and kept them? No need to pay them into a bank or a building society. Why not put them in the loft? In the wardrobe? In a milk jug in the fridge? Like a few other self-employed builders, Barron might well be playing a canny little game with casual receipts, with ready-cash payments, with VAT evasions. And, if so, he would certainly not be over-anxious to account for any largish sums of money regularly entrusted to some official depository.

Lewis himself had felt pretty certain that Barron was their man; Morse was absolutely convinced. And yet the evidence thus far gathered seemed to be stacking up a little bit the wrong way. Lewis knew it. He had ever been a champion of the cumulative-evidence approach to crime: a piece-by-piece aggregation against a suspect that gradually mounted into an impressively documented pile that could be forwarded to the DPP. All right! Morse's method was occasionally very different. Yet many of the murders that the pair of them had solved together had been relatively uncomplicated: no real mystery, no real cunning, no real deviousness, no carefully woven web of deceit. Domestic stuff, next-door-neighbour stuff, most of it, with the husband returning home unexpectedly from work and finding his spouse abed with postman, milkman, gasman . . . builder?

But whichever way one looked at things, any direct evidence *against* the builder was proving surprisingly difficult to come by.

At 8.45 p.m., tired and hungry, Lewis decided that whatever further developments there were to be – and they were coming in all the time – he would have to take a break; and he drove home to Headington. But only after trying Morse's number once more. Ringing tone. No answer.

Morse came into HQ three-quarters of an hour later, and rang Lewis's home number immediately. Ringing tone. Answer.

Resignedly, about to start his eggs and chips, Lewis brought Morse up to date with the information received, suggesting that it was, at this point, all a bit ambivalent and equivocal, although in truth Lewis made use of neither of these epithets himself.

Morse sounded mildly interested, giving his own

verdict in somewhat pompous terms. He asserted that the character of the human condition was indeed 'ambiguity', the virtually inseparable mixture of the true and the false. But in the present case such apparent contradictions could be explained so very easily – in fact in exactly the way Lewis himself had just explained them. 'And,' continued Morse, 'you can be quite sure of one thing – no, two things: Barron murdered the pair of 'em; then somebody murdered Barron. Get that clear in your head, and we might make a bit of progress. OK? I'll see you in the morning.'

'Sir! Before you ring off. We tried to get you several times earlier but there was the engaged tone all the time.'

'That's funny. I only remember making the one call.'

'I thought perhaps – you know, you seemed a bit whacked . . .'

'You'd be wrong, Lewis. I *nearly* spent some time in bed. Not quite, though. Goodnight.'

The dramatic news came in at twenty minutes to midnight, as Morse sat at home making out a rough draft of his will. He'd no immediate relatives remaining, none at all; and therefore instructions for the post-mortem dissemination of all his worldly goods should not present too much of a complication. Nor did they. And he was writing out a fairish copy of a simple second draft – when the phone rang.

'What?'

. . .

'*What?*'

. . .

It was two minutes later before he spoke again: 'I'll be over straightaway.'

Chapter Forty-Eight

We trust we are not guilty of sacrilege in suggesting that the teaching of Religious Knowledge in some schools would pose an almighty challenge even for the Almighty Himself

(From the Introduction to *Religious Education in Secondary Schools: 1967–87*, HMSO)

Roy Holmes, aged fifteen, was a crudely disruptive pupil at school, a truculently unco-operative son in the Witney Street house he shared with his invalid mother, and a menace wherever he walked in the wider community. He took drugs; he was an inveterate and skilful shoplifter; he regularly snapped the stems of newly planted trees striving to establish themselves; he spat disgusting gobbets of phlegm on most of the pavements in Burford. In short, Roy Holmes was an appalling specimen of humankind. He deserved to have no real friends at all in life; and he had none.

Except one.

Ms Christine Coverley, aged twenty-seven, in her second year at Burford Secondary School, was not an impressive personage. A small, skinny, flat-chested, spotty-chinned, mousy-haired woman, she could scarcely have expected admirers anywhere – either among her fellow male members of staff, or among the motley collection of pupils, especially the boys, she was timetabled to teach. And, indeed, she had no such admirers.

Except one.

To complicate her incompetence as a teacher, she had been appointed *faute de mieux* to teach Religious Knowledge, a task wholly beyond her ability. Her classes taunted her mercilessly; and on more than one occasion such was the uproar in her classroom that teachers in adjacent rooms had barged in – only to find, with deep embarrassment, that a nominal teacher was already present there; and with even deeper embarrassment for Ms Coverley herself, resulting in fevered nightmares and anguish of soul that was often unbearable. One class, 4 Remove (Holmes's class), was even worse than the others – a group of pagan halfwits, of both sexes, whose interest in the pronouncements of major and minor prophets alike was nil. Over the year her hebdomadal clash with these monsters had been a terrifying ordeal; and the situation was quite hopeless. But no – not quite hopeless. Each night of term she would kneel in her bedsit and beseech the Almighty to grant her some deliverance from such despair. And one day her prayer had been answered.

In the middle of the summer term, at the end of one of her spectacularly disastrous lessons with 4 Remove, her eyes smarting with tears of humiliation, she had stopped the cocky, surly Holmes as he was about to leave the room:

'Roy! I know I'm useless. I *wouldn't* be though – if I got a bit of help, but I don't get any help from anyone.

I just want some help. And there's someone who *could* help me so easily if he wanted to. *You*, Roy!'

She turned away, wiped her moist cheeks, picked up her books, and left the empty classroom.

But Roy Holmes stood where he was, immobile. For the first time in his life someone had asked him for help – *him* – the despair of mother, vicar, social workers, headmaster, police; and suddenly he'd felt oddly, unprecedentedly moved, conscious somewhere deep inside himself of a compassion he'd never known and could scarcely recognize.

If, as Ms Coverley believed, her God sometimes moved in a mysterious way, it was not quite so dramatic as the way in which Roy Holmes was soon to move. In the next RK lesson one of the boys in the back row had been particularly foul-mouthed and disruptive, whilst Holmes had remained completely silent. After school that day, the youth in question returned home with a bleeding mouth, two broken teeth, and one bruised and hugely swollen eye. No one knew who was responsible. But then no one needed to know; since everyone knew who was responsible.

The nightmares were over, and Ms Coverley's last few weeks of the summer term were almost happy ones. Yet she knew that she was not the stuff that teachers are made of, and her resignation was received with relief by the headmaster. For the time being she decided to stay on in Burford, renewing the let on her ground-floor bedsit for a further two months.

The bell rang at 11.15 p.m. and Roy Holmes, somewhat the worse for drink or drugs or both, stood at the door when she opened it. His words were the words she had used to him, almost exactly so:

'I just want some help. And there's someone who can help me, if she wants to. You!'

It wasn't a lot he had to say; not a lot *she* had to say to the duty-sergeant, half an hour later, when she rang Burford Police Station; and not a lot when *he*, in turn, rang Thames Valley HQ, almost immediately put through to the home number of the man in charge of the enquiry into the death of J. Barron, Builder.

Roy Holmes, a pupil of Burford Secondary School, aged fifteen, living at 29A Witney Street, had been riding his mountain bike along the footway on the southern side of Sheep Street at approximately 10 a.m. that Monday, 3 August. By the youth's own admission he was showing off, expectorating regularly, terrorizing any pedestrians, riding no-handed – when he'd decided to defy all superstition and ride beneath the ladder he saw in front of him – when he'd badly misjudged whatever he'd misjudged – when he'd collided sharply with the bottom of the ladder – when the whole thing had jerked sideways – and when a man had toppled from the top of the ladder and landed on the compacted pathway outside 'Collingwood' . . .

Chapter Forty-Nine

'God save thee, ancient Mariner!
From the fiends, that plague thee thus! –
Why look'st thou so?' – 'With my cross-bow
I shot the Albatross.'

(Coleridge, *The Rime of the Ancient Mariner*)

THE FOLLOWING MORNING, Morse had been early summoned to the presence, summoned to Caesar's tent.

'Won't do, will it, Morse. Just won't do! You tell us to go and bring Barron in. And why? Because you say he's knifed Flynn and Repp. Fine! There's three of 'em, you say, originally involved in the cover-up over the Harrison murder, three of 'em prepared to stick to their stories – for a fee of course. Then suddenly we find two of 'em murdered, and somebody – *somebody*, Morse – thinks this'll be as good an opportunity as any to finish off number three. So whoever this somebody is, he decided he's been forking out way over the odds anyway, and he goes ahead with his plan. He's been living with three albatrosses round his neck, and suddenly he finds somebody else has cut the strings off *two* of 'em. Too good an opportunity to be missed. All adds up, doesn't it? Except, matey, for one thing: Barron's death turns out to be a bloody *accident*. Just some teenage lout . . .'

Strange took a breather, gulped down the last of his coffee, and stuck another chocolate biscuit in his mouth: 'Fancy a coffee?'

'No.'

'They'll be open in an hour, you mean?'

'Fifty minutes, actually.'

Strange suddenly sounded extremely pleased with himself: 'Did you actually say "actually", Morse?'

Oh dear.

It was Strange who broke the ensuing silence. 'Where are we, in all this?' he asked softly.

'I dunno. I felt convinced that the same fellow – Barron – had murdered both of them, both Flynn and Repp. I thought the motive was a pretty familiar one – money. You know, there's nothing much worse in life than people doing the same job and getting paid at different rates. It happens in every office, in every profession in the land. Anger . . . jealousy . . . bitterness . . . usually controllable but potentially dynamite. And I thought Barron had found out he wasn't doing half so well as his partners in crime.'

'And who exactly is this golden goose?'

'You know that as well as I do.'

'I do?'

'Oh, yes,' replied Morse quietly.

A knock at the door heralded PC Kershaw, the fast-track recruit with a First in History from Keble who'd driven Morse out to Sutton Courtenay, and whose duties for the present consisted mostly of supplying the Chief Superintendent with regular coffee and chocolate biscuits.

'Anything I can do for you, sir?'

'Yes,' growled Strange. 'Bugger off!' Then, turning back to Morse: 'Are you making *any* progress?'

'Early days. We've not even had the final path reports yet. Life's full of surprises.'

'And disappointments.'

'That too, yes.'

'Well if it *wasn't* Barron . . .'

'Dunno. But I'm sure the key figure in both cases is one and the same person – the man who was in bed with Yvonne Harrison the night she was murdered.'

'You don't think it was Repp?'

'No. As I see it, Repp had been recce-ing the property, maybe for several nights. It was going to be a gift for any professional burglar like him. And he knew pretty well all that went on that night—'

'Knew the fellow who was in bed with Yvonne?'

'Yes. But I don't think it was Repp or any other burglar who disturbed the bondage session that evening. I think that was somebody else. And I think it's most likely that our lover-boy knew that someone else.'

'And in your book Barron was the lover-boy?'

'Well, he was doing a job for her – hanging about the place quite a bit – strong, good-looking sort of fellow – the husband away a good deal of the time . . .'

'But I'll say it again – what if it *wasn't* Barron?'

'Plenty of other candidates, surely?'

'Oh yes?'

Morse measured his words carefully. 'I think that anyone meeting Yvonne Harrison, if she turned things on a bit – anyone, including me – would have given a month's beer money – '

'A week's in your case.'

' – for an hour or two between the sheets, or between the bedposts, or between anywhere else. By, er, by all accounts she was a . . . well, let's say she had the same effect on men as they tell me Viagra has on the impotent, or the victims of chronic erectile dysfunction, as they're known these days.'

'Really! So for all we know, this chap could have been a client from North Wales or somewhere.'

'More probably South Wales, sir.'

'And much more probably, somebody local.'

'Agreed.'

'Any ideas?'

'Well, the only fellow I've met in that little community who's topped up with surplus testosterone is the landlord of the Maiden's Arms.'

'You've interviewed him?'

'No.'

'Why not?'

'Because I'm still trying to come to terms with the fact that it *wasn't* Barron. You see I still think he's the key to all this ridiculously complex business. But complex only because those involved deliberately *made* it complex.'

'Barron's phone calls, you mean? No luck there?'

'No. Change of BT office, change of procedure, change of monitoring, files re-classified . . . no hope! Wouldn't help anyway. All Barron said was that he'd rung her and the number was engaged; and then rung her again and the call wasn't answered. Neat, wasn't it? No record of anything.'

'He was lying, you think?'

'Yes.'

'What about the burglar alarm?'

'Thunderstorm, possibly – that sets 'em off.'

'There wasn't a thunderstorm that night.'

'No? Probably a cat then – they set 'em off too.'

'They hadn't got a cat.'

'Oh.'

Strange lumbered to his feet. 'Look! You surely don't still think Barron's your man, do you?'

Morse smiled. '*Don't I?*'

Chapter Fifty

I can't tell a lie – not even when I hear one
(John Bangs, 1862–1922)

In the world of detective fiction, alibis are frequently concocted in order to mystify the reader. In what is called the 'real' world they usually provide an invaluable method of eliminating a few runners in an already limited field, thereby affording the police a better prospect of backing the likely winner. For (except in Morse's mind) an alibi is an alibi: if someone is seen in one place at one particular time, it seems highly improbable that this same someone may be seen in some other place at the *same* time. Yet it is sometimes difficult adequately to corroborate an alibi – viz, that plea of the criminal to have been in another place at the material time; and alibis may well be doubted, closely checked, and indeed, on occasion, be spectacularly broken.

This in various ways.

It is highly unlikely, for example, that a well-focused video camera will be in operation in that first particular place; and even if it is, some smart electronic alec may well be able to doctor the evidence. Almost always, therefore, corroboration will depend on the testimony of eyewitnesses who, even if honest, can be the victims of tricks of memory over times and sightings; *or*, on the testimony of witnesses who are dishonest, and are willing to fabricate falsehoods – for friends, perhaps, or for a fee. The alibi problem is further complicated by the confident assertion of some mystic sects that one *can*, in fact, be in two places simultaneously, although the police are grateful that such bizarre beliefs are currently not widely embraced.

Morse himself championed the view that all alibis should probably be ignored in the first instance, on the not illogical grounds that if just *one* of them were suspect, it was sensible to assume that all of them were . . .

Such views (with variants) Sergeant Lewis had heard several times before, and it was therefore with some diffidence that he broached the subject the following morning.

'Don't you reckon it would be a good idea to get all these alibis sorted out a bit clearer?'

'A bit more clearly, Lewis.'

'The night Mrs Harrison was murdered, the morning Flynn and Repp were murdered—'

'And don't forget Monday morning.'

'Barron, you mean? You surely don't still think—?'

Morse held up his right hand in surrender. 'You're right, perhaps. Let's make a list. Well, you make a list. Ready?'

He steepled his slim fingers in front of him and stared into the middle distance, though with little observable enthusiasm in his eyes:

'Frank Harrison
Simon Harrison
Sarah Harrison
Harry Repp
John Barron . . .'

'That's the short-list?'

Morse nodded.

'OK. First I'll recheck where they all were, or where they were all supposed to be, first when Mrs Harrison—'

'Already been done. You've read the files.'

'Weren't checked very thoroughly though, some of 'em.'

'Long time ago, Lewis. People forget or want to forget or pretend to forget.'

'A day like that though, when she was murdered? Biggest day in village history. Everybody remembers where they were, like when Kennedy was assassinated.'

'Nonsense, Lewis! People remember where they were and what they were doing at the time they *heard* of things like that. Agreed. But what else? Do you remember what you were doing for the rest of the day when Kennedy was shot? Do you?'

'No. I take your point, sir.'

'Who are you thinking of particularly?'

'Well the family got away with some pretty flimsy alibis, didn't they? Especially Simon and Sarah. No one seems to have checked them much at all.'

'Ye-es.'

'Simon said he got home from work about a quarter-past five, had a meal, then went down to the ABC cinema in George Street to see *The Full Monty*. Still had his ticket if I remember rightly.'

Morse nodded and Lewis continued:

'Sarah? She was at a Diabetes Conference in the Radcliffe Infirmary that day – no doubt about that. And after it had finished she went over the road to the Royal Oak for a drink with a few friends – no doubt about that either – and then left for her flat in Jericho at about a quarter-to-seven, where she listened to *The Archers*, had a long hot bath, watched the *Nine O'Clock News*, and then had an early night.'

'Making no mention in the course of her evidence that she had a phone call in the middle of the evening, as a result of which she tore down to the ABC Cinema, bought a ticket for *The Full Monty* – '

'Probably no seats left that night, sir.'

' – bought a ticket and promptly tore it across the middle and then tore out of the place – '

'Sir! Not so much of this tearing about all over the shop! She'd sprained her ankle just before then and she'd probably be hobbling—'

' – she hobbled out of the cinema with a very valuable little alibi in her pretty little hand.'

'Alibi for Simon, you mean?'

'Or for herself.'

'You're losing me again, sir.'

'I'm losing myself. Don't worry.'

'What about Frank Harrison?'

'You tell *me*!'

'Well, anyone who finds the body first is usually

going to be number one in your book, I know that. But there's no doubt about Paddy Flynn being on taxi-shift from 8 p.m. that night. He was seen on and off by his fellow-drivers as well as being contacted at regular intervals from base. No doubt either about him picking up Frank Harrison about eleven from Oxford railway station. But that's not to say – *is* it, sir? – that Harrison had just got off a train at the railway station. It would be the most natural thing in the world for anyone to *think* he had, but . . .'

Morse smiled. 'Could hardly have put it better myself. But somebody paid Flynn for something. So it was probably for something that happened after eleven o'clock. And there was only one person with Flynn then: Frank Harrison. And he's the only one of the whole bunch with the sort of money to buy Flynn off.'

'*And* buy Repp off, if we're right about him being there that night. Harrison must be earning, well . . .'

'A little more than you are, Lewis, yes. In fact he got a bonus – a *bonus* – of £85,000 last year. Seems he was sorting out his bank's involvement in the Nazi confiscation of Jewish assets, and his bosses were more than pleased with him.'

'How on earth do you know that?'

'Aren't we supposed to be detectives?'

Lewis pursued the matter no further. 'So, what do you think?'

'Waste of time as far as the children are concerned. But it might help to look at their father again.'

'You think it was Harrison who murdered his wife?'

'I dunno.'

'You think he murdered Flynn and Repp?'

'He had enough reason to. He couldn't go on forking out indefinitely.'

'So we'd better have a careful check on wherever *he* was that Friday morning.'

'Well, wherever else he was he wasn't in his London office.'

'How on earth—?'

'What else can I tell you?' asked Morse wearily.

'I've just asked you. Do you think he murdered Flynn and Repp?'

'He could have done. But somehow I don't believe he did.'

'So who . . .?'

'I keep telling you, Lewis. My modest bet is still on Barron.'

'Shouldn't we be looking a bit more into their backgrounds? Repp's? Flynn's? Barron's?'

'I don't think we're going to get anything more out of Debbie Richardson.'

'Why do you say that?'

'Just a feeling, Lewis. Just a feeling.'

'What about Flynn?'

Morse nodded. 'You're right. He was being paid for something. Exactly what, though . . . Yes. Leave that to me.'

'What about Barron? Shall I leave that to you, as well?'

'No, no! The less I have to do with the women in this case the better. You go along. And if you can find out more about where he was or where he was supposed to be on both those days . . . Yes, you do that!'

'All right. But don't you think we ought to widen the net, sir? Haven't we got any other suspects?'

'Tom Biffen, perhaps?'

Lewis's eyebrows shot up. 'You mean—?'

'The landlord of the Maiden's Arms, no less. We'll go out and interview him together once we get a chance. You'll be able to buy me a pint.'

'But wasn't it a Tuesday when Mrs Harrison was murdered?'

'You're right, yes.'

'Well, he always goes out fishing on Tuesdays, Biffen – dawn to dusk.'

'Really? How on earth do you know that?'

'Aren't we supposed to be detectives, sir?'

Chapter Fifty-One

Once cheated, wife or husband feels the same; and where there's marriage without love, there will be love without marriage

(Benjamin Franklin, *Poor Richard's Almanack*)

At 9.30 a.m. the following day, Mrs Linda Barron stepped back from the threshold, nodding rather wearily as Lewis produced his ID. In the kitchen, he accepted her offer of instant coffee.

She was a brunette of medium height, slightly overweight, with a small, cupid-lipped mouth, wearing a blue-striped kitchen apron over skirt and blouse.

Lewis decided she was coping with life, just about.

The smallish kitchen was cluttered with shelves and cupboards, the floor-space additionally limited by the usual appliances: cooker, dishwasher, fridge, microwave, washing machine. Lewis immediately noticed the damp patch of crumbling ceiling over the cooker. Same old story! Husband a plumber, and a tap-washer never gets fixed; husband a builder, and there's a two-year wait before a bit of re-plastering gets done . . . Difficult to say, offhand, whether the Barrons were better or worse off than they appeared.

From experience, Lewis had learned never to try his hand at commiseration or counselling; but when he questioned her, he did so in the kindly fashion that was his wont. He asked her tactfully about the times and places relevant to her husband's alibis; more tactfully about the family finances; most tactfully about the state of her marriage.

Alibis? On the two key dates she could be of little help. Mondays to Fridays he usually got home about 6 p.m., when she'd have a cooked meal ready for him. Between 8 and 9 p.m. he'd quite often go out for a pint or two, either down at the local or sometimes at a pub in Burford. But he wasn't a big drinker. She knew he'd rung up Mrs Harrison on the night of her murder – something about roofing tiles – but he'd not been able to get through. Tried twice – he'd told her so; the police knew all about that, though: it had been important evidence. On the second key date, the Friday, he'd gone off to Thame in the morning, she remembered that. He'd been asked for an estimate on some work there, and he'd gone over to size up the job. She didn't know – didn't ask – what he'd done after that; but he was back home at the usual sort of time. He always was on Fridays, because it was eggs-and-chips day – his favourite meal.

Mr J. Barron, Builder, was going up in Lewis's esteem.

Money? They were OK. For the past three years or so houses were selling fairly freely again; and mobility in the housing market always meant new owners wanting some renovation or structural changes: conservatories, extensions, garages, loft-conversions, patios. Yes, the past few years had been fairly good for them: she knew that better than he did. Her part in the business, for which she took a small official salary, was to look after the books: tax returns, invoices, VAT, expenses, bad debts – everything. If he was ever in the habit of accepting cash instead of the usual cheque-payments, she wasn't aware of it; and quite certainly neither of them was sufficiently bright in business-finance to be able to exploit any tax loopholes. She knew nothing about any regular payments in cash. ('What payments?') She'd have known if any envelopes had arrived through the post, because the mail was invariably delivered *after* he'd set off for work every morning. They had a joint account; and he had a separate private account, with an overdraft facility of £2,000.

Mr J. Barron, Builder, Lewis decided, was hardly in the Gates or the Soros brackets.

Marriage? It was only here that Linda Barron was less than fluent in her answers.

'Would you say the pair of you had a "tight" marriage?'

'. . . Perhaps not, no.'

'Was he ever unfaithful?'

'Aren't *most* men?'

'Not all of them,' said Lewis quietly.

She shrugged her shoulders.

'*Was* he?'

'. . . He may have been.'

'Do you think he ever had an affair with Mrs Harrison?'

'. . . No.'

'Would you have known?'

She smiled bleakly. 'Probably.'

'What about you, Mrs Barron? Were *you* ever unfaithful?'

'. . . Once or twice.'

'With Harry Repp?'

'God, no! I hardly knew him.'

'Tom Biffen?'

'. . . Once. He called one afternoon about eighteen months ago to bring a leg of lamb Johnnie won in the raffle. And . . .'

'What happened?'

'Do I *have* to tell you, Sergeant?'

'No. No, you don't, Mrs Barron.'

Wedlock for the Barrons (Lewis agreed with Dixon) did not appear to have been a wholly idyllic affair.

As he left, Lewis noticed on the wall in the hallway a framed photograph of a strong, fine-looking man in military uniform.

'Your husband?'

She nodded; and the rust-flecked hazel eyes were filmed with tears.

Chapter Fifty-Two

With a gen'rous ol' pal who will pick up the tab
It's always real cool in a nice taxi-cab
(J. Willington Spoole, *Mostly on the Dole*)

IF LEWIS'S (MORSE-INITIATED) interview had been a task of some fair difficulty, Morse's own (self-appointed) mission was wholly straightforward – the single problem being that of finding a parking-space in a car-cluttered Warwick Street, just off the Iffley Road.

In the outer office of Radio Taxis were seated two young ladies, their telephones, keyboards, and VDUs in front of them, with maps of Oxford, Oxfordshire, and the UK, pinned on the walls around. Morse was ushered through into the inner sanctum, where a six-foot, strongly built man of fifty or so, his short, dark hair greying at the temples, introduced himself:

'Jeff Measor, Company Secretary. How can I help?'

'Flynn, Paddy Flynn, he used to work for you – until you sacked him.'

Yes. Measor remembered him well enough. Flynn had worked for the company for just over a year. It was generally agreed that he'd been a competent driver, but he'd never fitted very happily into the team. There'd been several complaints from clients, including the reported 'Just help me get these bitches out of here!' request to the doorman at The Randolph, where three giggly and slightly unstable young ladies were attempting to alight. And, yes, a few other complaints about his less-than-sympathetic rejoinders to clients when sometimes (quite inevitably so) traffic-jams had caused his cab to be late. But Flynn had been a punctual man himself, invariably clocking in on time – one of those dedicated night-drivers who far preferred the 6 p.m.–2.30 a.m. shift. He'd known Oxford City and the surrounding area well – a big factor in taxi work; and there'd been no suspicion of his driving innocent clients on some roundabout route just to jump up the fare.

'Could he have fiddled a few quid here and there?'

'Not so easy these days. Everything's computerized in the cab. But I suppose . . .'

'How?'

'Well, let's say if he's cruising around the City Centre and gets a fare and doesn't clock it in. Just takes the cash and then goes back to cruising round as if he's been doing nothing else all the time . . .'

'Did he do that sort of thing?'

'Not that I know of.'

Morse was looking increasingly puzzled. 'He seems to have been a reasonably satisfactory sort of cabbie, then.'

'Well . . .'

'So why did you sack him?'

'Two things, really. As I said, he wasn't a good advertisement for the company. We always tell our drivers about the importance of friendliness and courtesy; but he wasn't quite . . . he always seemed a bit surly, and I doubt he ever swapped a few cheerful words with any of his passengers. Man of few words, Paddy Flynn. Not always though, by all accounts.'

'No?'

'No. Seems he used to do the rounds of the pubs and clubs – Oxford, Reading and so on – with a little group. Played the clarinet himself, and introduced things with a bit of Irish blarney. Quite popular for a while, I think, 'specially in those pubs guaranteeing music being played as loud as possible.'

Morse looked pained as Measor continued: 'Anyway, he just didn't fit in here. No one really liked him much. Simple as that!'

'*Two* things though, you said?' prompted Morse gently.

For the first time the articulately forthright Company Secretary was somewhat hesitant:

'It's a bit difficult to explain but . . . well, he never quite seemed up to coping with the radio side of the job. Still very important, the radio side is, in spite of all this latest technology. You know the sort of thing: we'll be phoning from the office here and asking one of the drivers if he's anywhere near Headington or Abingdon Road or wherever . . . Mind you, Inspector, the radio's not all *that* easy: distortion, interference, crackle, feedback, traffic-noise . . . You've certainly got to have your wits about you – and, well, he just couldn't quite cope with it well enough.'

'It doesn't seem all that much of a reason for sacking him, though.'

'It's not exactly like that, Inspector. You see, I don't myself employ drivers directly. They're contracted out to me. And so if I say to any owner of a taxi, or a group of taxis, "Look, there's no more work for you here" – well, that's it. It's like sub-contracting work on a building site. If I want to sack one of my staff here though, in the office, I'll have to give one verbal – recorded – and two written warnings.'

'No problems with Flynn, then?'

'Oh, no. And glad to see the back of him. Everybody was. One day he was here . . .'

'. . . and the next day he was gone,' added Morse slowly, as he thanked the Company Secretary – and felt that long familiar shiver of excitement along his shoulders.

Chapter Fifty-Three

At which period there were gentlemen and there were seamen in the navy. But the seamen were not gentlemen; and the gentlemen were not seamen

(Macaulay, *History of England*)

For Morse, that early evening followed much the same old pattern: same sort of bundle of ideas abounding in his brain; same impatience to reach that final, wonderfully satisfying, penny-dropping moment of insight; same old pessimism about the future of mankind; same old craving for a dram of Scotch that could make the world, at least for a while, a kindlier and a happier place; same old chauffeur – Lewis.

It was just after 6.30 p.m. when they were shown up a spiral flight of rickety stairs to the small office immediately above the bar of the Maiden's Arms. Around the walls, several framed diplomas paid tribute to the landlord's expertise and the cleanliness of his kitchen, although the untidy piles of letters and forms that littered the desk suggested a less than methodical approach to the hostelry's paperwork.

'Quick snifter, Inspector?'

'Later, perhaps.'

'Mind if I, er . . .?' Biffen reached behind him and poured out a liberal tot of Captain Morgan. 'You make me feel nervous!' Knocking back the neat rum in a single swallow, he smacked his lips crudely: 'Ahh!'

'Royal or Merchant?' asked Morse.

'Bit o' both.' But Biffen seemed disinclined to discuss his earlier years at sea, and came to the point immediately: 'How can I help you, gentlemen?'

So Morse told him: for the moment the village seemed to be at the centre of almost everything; and the pub was at the centre of village life and gossip; and the landlord was always going to be at the centre of the pub; so if . . .

For Lewis, Morse's subsequent interrogation seemed (indeed, was) aimless and desultory.

But Biffen had little to tell.

Of *course* the villagers had talked – still talked – talked all the time except when that media lot or the police came round. No secret, though, that the locals knew enough about Mrs H's occasional and more than occasional liaisons; no secret that they listened with prurient interest to the rumours, the wilder and wackier the better, concerning Mrs H's sexual predilections.

It was left to Lewis to cover the crucial questions concerning alibis.

The day of Mrs H's murder? Tuesday, that was. And Tuesday was always a special day – a sacrosanct sort of day. (He'd mentioned it earlier.) His one day off in the week when he refused to have anything at all to do with cellarage, bar-tending, pub-meals – fuck 'em all! Secretary of the Oxon Pike Anglers' Association, he was. Had been for the past five years. Labour of love! And every Tuesday during the fishing season he was out all day, dawn to dusk. Back late, almost always, though he couldn't say exactly when that day. No one had questioned him at the time. Why should they? He'd pretty certainly have met a few of his fellow-anglers but . . . what the hell was all this about anyway? Was he suddenly on the suspect-list? After all this time?

Thomas Biffen's eyes had hardened; and looking across at the brawny tattooed arms, the ex-boxer Sergeant Lewis found himself none too anxious ever to confront the landlord in a cul-de-sac.

Biffen was a family man? Well, yes and no, really. He'd been married – still was, in the legal sense. But his missus had gone off four years since, taking their two children with her: Joanna, aged three at the time, and Daniel, aged two. He still regularly gave her some financial support; always sent his kids something for their birthdays and Christmas. But that side of things had never been much of a problem. She was living with this fellow in Weston-super-Mare – fellow she'd known a long time – the same fellow in fact she'd buggered off with when they'd broken up.

'Whose fault was that?' asked Morse quietly.

Biffen shrugged. 'Bit o' both, usually, innit?'

'She'd been seeing someone else?'

Biffen nodded.

'Had *you* been seeing someone else?'

Biffen nodded.

'Someone local.'

'What's that got to do with it?'

It was Morse's turn to shrug.

'Well . . . Chap's got to get his oats occasionally, Inspector.'

'Mrs Harrison?'

Biffen shook his head. 'Wouldna minded, though!'

'Mrs Barron?'

'Linda? Huh! Not much chance there – with *him* around? SAS man, he was. Probably slice your prick off if he copped you mucking around with his missus.'

Lewis found himself recalling the photograph of the confident-looking young militiaman.

'Debbie Richardson?' suggested Morse.

'Most people've had a bit on the side with her.'

'You called yourself occasionally? While Harry was inside?'

'Once or twice.'

'Including the day after he was murdered.'

'Only to take a bottle – I told you that.'

'You fancied her?'

'Who wouldn't? Once she's got the hots on . . .'

Morse appeared to have lost his way, and it was Lewis who completed the questioning: 'Where were you earlier on the Friday when Flynn and Repp were murdered?'

'In the morning? Went into Oxford shopping. Not much luck, though. Tried to get a couple of birthday presents. You'd hardly credit it, but both o' my kids were born the same day – 3rd o' September.'

'Real coincidence.'

'Depends which way you look at it, Sergeant. Others'd call it precision screwing, wouldn't they?'

It was a crude remark, and Morse's face was a study

in distaste as Biffen continued: 'Couldn't find anything in the shops though, could I? So I sent their mum a cheque instead.'

Downstairs, it was far too early for any brisk activity; but three of the regulars were already foregathered there, to each of whom Biffen proffered a customary greeting.

'Evening, Mr Bagshaw! Evening, Mr Blewitt!'

One of the warring partners allowed himself a perfunctory nod, but the other was happily intoning a favourite passage from the cribbage litany: 'Fifteen-two; fifteen-four; two's six; three's nine; and three's twelve!'

With an 'Evening, Mr Thomas!' the landlord had completed his salutations.

In response, the youth pressed the start-button yet again, his eyes keenly registering the latest alignment of the symbols on the fruit machine.

'Now! What's it to be, gentlemen? On the house, of course.'

'Pint of bitter,' said Morse, 'and an orange juice. Want some ice in it, Lewis?'

A bored-looking barmaid folded up the *Mirror*, and pulled the hand-pump on the Burton Ale.

Chapter Fifty-Four

The time you won your town the race
We chaired you through the market-place;
Man and boy stood cheering by,
And home we brought you shoulder-high.

To-day, the road all runners come,
Shoulder-high we bring you home,
And set you at your threshold down,
Townsman of a stiller town

(A. E. Housman,
A Shropshire Lad, XIX)

It was just after 7.30 p.m. that same evening in the car park of the Maiden's Arms that Morse, after admitting to a very strange lapse of memory in missing *The Archers*, suddenly decided on a new line of enquiry that seemed to Lewis (if possible) even stranger: 'Drive me round to Holmes's place in Burford.'

'Why—?' began a weary Lewis.

'Get *on* with it!'

The ensuing conversation was brief. 'What did you make of Biffen, sir?'

'He decided to enlist in the ranks of the liars, like the rest of 'em.'

'Well, yes . . . if Mrs Barron was telling me the truth.'

'Probably not important anyway.'

Lewis waited a while. 'What *is* important, sir?'

'Barron! That's what's important. I'm still not absolutely sure I was on the wrong track but . . .'

'. . . but it looks as if you were.'

Morse nodded.

'What did you make of—?'

'Concentrate on the driving, Lewis! They're not used to Formula-One fanatics round here.'

A blurred shape slowly formed through the frosted glass of the front door, its green paint peeling or already peeled, which was finally opened by a pale-faced, wispily haired woman of some fifty-plus summers.

Lewis paraded his ID. 'Mrs Holmes?'

With hardly a glance at the documentation, the woman neatly reversed her wheelchair and led her visitors through the narrow, bare-floored, virtually bare-walled passageway – for indeed there was just the one framed memento of something on the wall to the left.

'I suppose it's about Roy?' She spoke with the dispirited nasal whine of a Birmingham City supporter whose team has just been defeated.

In the living room, in a much-frayed armchair, sat a youth smoking a cigarette, drinking directly from a can of Bass, a pair of black-stringed amplifiers stuck in his ears.

He vaguely reminded Morse of someone; but that was insufficient to stop him taking an intense and instant dislike to the boy, who had made no attempt to straighten his lounging sprawl, or to miss a single lyric from the latest rap record – until he saw Morse's lips speaking directly to him.

'Wha'?' Reluctantly Roy Holmes removed one of the ear-pieces.

'Why didn't you answer the door yourself, lad, and give your mum a break?'

The youth's eyes stared back with cold hostility. 'Couldn't 'ear it, could I? Not wi' this on.'

No Brummy accent there; instead, the Oxfordshire burr with its curly vowels.

His mother began to explain. 'It's the police, Roy—'

'Again? Bin there, 'aven't I. Made me statement. What more do they want? Accident, wonnit? I didn't try to 'ide nuthin. What the fuck?'

Morse responded quietly to the outburst. 'We appreciate your co-operation. But do you know what you've made of yourself in life so far? Shall I tell you, lad? You're about the most uncouth and loutish fourteen-year-old I've ever—'

'*Fifteen*-year-old,' interposed Mrs Holmes, more anxious, it seemed, to correct her son's natal credentials than to deny his innate crudity. 'Fifteen on March the 26th. Got it wrong in the papers, didn't they?'

'Well, well! Same birthday as Housman.'

Silence.

'*And*' (Morse now spoke directly to the mother) 'he'll be able to smoke in a year's time, and go to the pub for a pint a couple of years after that – if you give him some pocket-money, Mrs Holmes. Because I can't see him earning anything much himself, not in his present frame of mind.'

If Lewis had earlier noticed the tell-tale sign of drug dependency in the boy's eyes, he now saw a wider blaze of hatred there; and was sure that Morse was similarly and equally aware of both, as Mrs Holmes switched her wheelchair abruptly around and faced Morse aggressively:

'It was an accident – could happen to anybody – he didn't mean no trouble – like he *said* – like he *told* you . . . That's right, isn't it, Roy?'

'Leave me be!'

'Perhaps it wasn't you we came to Burford to see.'

For a few seconds there was a look of bewilderment, of anxiety almost, on Roy Holmes's face. Then, draining his can of beer, he got to his feet, and left the room.

Seconds later the front door slammed behind him with potentially glass-shattering force.

'What time will he be back?' asked Lewis.

She shrugged her narrow shoulders.

'You worry about him?'

'Everybody worries about him.'

'How long's he been on drugs?'

'Year – over a year.'

'How does he pay for them?'

'You tell *me*.'

'Not much of a son, is he?' said Morse.

She shook what once must have been a very pretty head with a gesture of desperation.

'Does he get the money from you?'

'I've got nothing to give him. He's not stupid. He knows that.'

'But . . .?' Morse pointed to the empty beer can; the empty packet of cigarettes.

'I dunno.'

Morse got to his feet. Lewis too.

'How long . . .?' Morse nodded to the wheelchair.

'Six years.'

Morse stopped in front of the one framed picture in the dingy hallway. Not a picture, though. A diploma.

Oxfordshire, Buckinghamshire, Berkshire
Athletics Association

This is to certify that in the annual three-counties cross-country championships held in Cutteslowe Park, Oxford, on the 19th March, 1974, the winner of the ladies event from a field of seventy-two runners was:

ELIZABETH JANE THOMAS

Congratulations!
Signed: *Monty Hillier* (Assn. Pres.)

For the second time that day Lewis noticed a film of tears in a woman's eyes; and for the second time that day Morse felt a shudder of excitement run along his shoulders.

Before they left, Morse turned to the erstwhile

athlete. 'The gods haven't smiled on you much, have they?'

'Not that I've noticed.'

'It's important for your son to do exactly what they've told him – with his Police Protection Order. You know that?'

'I suppose so.'

'And if you want cheering up a bit, Mrs Holmes, I'll tell you a big secret: I was about his age when I started drinking myself. A year younger, in fact.'

But the confession appeared to bring little comfort to the woman manoeuvring her wheelchair to the front door.

Morse gave her his card. 'One last thing. If there's anything you've forgotten to tell me? Anything you've not been willing to tell me . . . ?'

As the two detectives walked along the litter-strewn path up to a wooden front gate stripped of all but two of its vertical slats, Lewis's mind puzzled itself over those last few words. But Morse seemed deep in thought; and any questions for the moment, he knew, would be wholly inopportune.

Chapter Fifty-Five

Wherefore seeing we also are compassed about with so great a cloud of witnesses, let us lay aside every prejudice and error that doth so easily beset us

(*Letter to Hebrews*)

In his own way, Lewis was not unhappy that Morse had failed to put in his usual, comparatively early appearance the following morning. His own preferred programme of alibi-confirmation had earlier (as we have seen) been endorsed by Morse, albeit with muted enthusiasm; and Lewis was content to pursue such a programme solo.

It now appeared that Morse's simplistic hypothesis – that of casting Barron as a double murderer – was wholly discounted. It would have been convenient, certainly, if it *had* been Barron; and if Barron in turn had been murdered by whoever was behind . . . well, behind everything, really. Frank Harrison, say. And why *not* Frank Harrison? In Lewis's betting-book he was the one runner in the field with the requisite bank balance to fork out the regular dollops of hush-money. But with the potential collapse of global equity markets, such a bank balance might soon not be looking so healthy. And one of the laws of economics, as Lewis knew, was that people with pots of money could easily *lose* pots of money, including the person who hitherto had seen it as a matter of self-interest to divert some proportion of such monies to others: to Flynn, to Repp, perhaps to Barron. Then, almost miraculously, two of them had been crossed off the pay-roll; and if the third one . . .

Lewis could understand Morse's thinking perfectly well. But it had been wrong, as the great man had (virtually) admitted the previous evening. There had been that dramatic development in the case: Barron's death had been an accident. And the coincidence of Barron being knocked off a ladder *by accident* at virtually the same time someone else had planned to murder him *by criminal design* had clearly struck even Morse (a confirmed believer in coincidence) as quite extraordinarily improbable.

So what was needed now was a bit of old-fashioned procedure: some immediate phone calls; some speedy arrangements of interviews; some urgent checking of alibis. And so fortunate was Lewis that by 9.45 he had written down a firm timetable:

10.15 a.m. – interview with Simon Harrison (Jordan Hill)
11.15 a.m. – interview with Frank Harrison (Randolph)
12.15 p.m. – interview with Sarah Harrison (Ratcliffe Infirmary)

Back in HQ just after 2 p.m. (still no news from Morse) Lewis looked down, not without some satisfaction, at the notes he had made:

SIMON H

Friday 24 July: at his desk all a.m. – lunch in canteen – back at his desk till 4 p.m. when he took bus down to Summertown dentist (¾ hr). Home c. 6 p.m. Plenty of witnesses on and off all day, it seems.
Monday 3 Aug: (day off work) a.m. drove via M40 → Stokenchurch hoping for siting of red kite there – tried earlier in the year at Llandudno – both trips unsuccessful (keen bird-watcher). Back for lunch in White Hart (Wytham) – witnesses would include landlord etc.

Impossible for him to have been in on the Flynn/Repp murders. *Could* have pushed Barron off the ladder, if we wanted him for that, which we don't. Deafer than I thought and lip-reads a lot. Names a big problem: Flynn OK, but Repp and Barron hard for him – its something to do with the labial consonents (so he says). Intelligent, bit too *intense*, loner (?).

FRANK H

Friday 24 July: meeting in London office 10–11.45 a.m. with four colleagues. (Check!)
Monday 3 Aug: at Randolph (booked in the day before). Breakfast 7.50–8.40 a.m. (approx) with 'partner' (real honey acc. to Ailish at the bar.) Car apparently not moved from Resident's garage that day.

As suspect? Same as SH (see above). Smart business exec. type, pleasant enough, bit abrupt, not short of the pennies – asked me to join him in glass of champange (£7 a go!) Thinning on top, thickening in middle. Seems used to getting what he wants in life.

SARAH H

Friday 24 July: at BDA Conference in Manchester with boss – arr 12.30 p.m. ret 9.50 p.m. – rail both ways. Forget her!
Monday 3 Aug: consultant duties at Diabetes Centre in Ratcliffe Inf. Saw ten patients. Lunch in League of Fiends cafeteria. Forget her!

Attractive, clever, but perhaps hard streek somewhere?

Yes! Lewis felt pleased with his morning's work; and even more pleased with his afternoon's work, after he'd typed up the notes, correcting four of the six misspellings and tidying up one or two of the punctuational blemishes. There remained quite a bit of checking to be done, but none of it would be particularly onerous, and most of it probably unnecessary. The general upshot was unambiguous. None of the Harrison clan had murdered Flynn or Repp. Two of the three *could* have been on the scene when Barron was killed but neither of them had murdered him, because *no one* had murdered him. That was the only thing in the whole tragic business that now seemed wholly incontrovertible.

Chapter Fifty-Six

Have I Got News For You!
(TV programme title)

In nowise was Lewis surprised to meet Dixon in the police canteen.

'Busy day?'

'Well, yes and no really. Morse rang me up early—'

'He *what*?' spluttered Lewis.

'Well, early for me. Wanted me to check out on a few things, didn't he?'

'Such as?'

'Well, names of those going to lip-reading classes these last few years.'

'Simon Harrison, you mean?'

'Didn't say, did he? No problem, though. Just got the lists photocopied, didn't I?'

'What else?'

'Well, funny really. He wanted me to find out who Flynn's dentist was—'

'He *what*?'

'Well, easy that. Then to find out something about that Mrs Holmes – you know, before she was married . . . before she had her accident.'

Yes, Lewis could understand that.

'Then to ring that SOCO chap Andrews, the one who was out at Sutton Courtenay. Ask him to get a bit of a move on – you know, give him a kick up the arse, like, about the fingerprints. Morse got him to take Barron's, you knew that, didn't you?'

'Of course I knew that!' lied Lewis, euphoria fading fast.

'Well, there we are then. I suppose old Morse was just hoping, you know . . .'

Yes, Lewis knew exactly what Morse had been hoping.

'Has Andrews found anything?'

'Well, still working on it, isn't he? Messy old job, he said. Soon as he had any news though . . . Anyway I called round and stuck the stuff through the door. He was there, I reckon. The telly was on—'

'What?'

'Yeah, pretty certain of it. But he didn't come to the door. Odd sort of chap, isn't he?'

But the introductory 'Well's and the inquisitorial clausulae, (hallmarks of every Dixon sentence) had become too tiresome; and Lewis was glad when the canteen intercom cut across the conversation:

'Message for Chief Inspector Morse or Sergeant Lewis: Please ring Northampton SOCOs immediately. I repeat. Message for . . .'

Where are you, Dixon, in the hierarchy here? I'll tell you, mate. Nowhere – no bloody where – that's where!

Yet Lewis left such ungracious thoughts unspoken, jumping to his feet and leaving Dixon where he was, cheeks now jammed once more with a doughnu

Two minutes later Lewis was through to an exultant Andrews, who wasted no time in breaking the dramatic news: there was a 'hit' – yippee! – a match of fingerprints! In the car. Two sets – definite, distinct. The prints of J. Barron, Builder of Lower Swinstead!

As he walked back to the canteen (Morse's phone still engaged) Lewis reflected on his brief exchange of views with Andrews. Morse had asked for any news to be communicated to him direct, and if necessary at his home number, though as both men knew there'd been little chance of that. Yet the situation was now perfectly clear; and Lewis freely conceded that Morse's early conviction that Barron had been involved in the murders seemed wholly vindicated. No room for more than three people in the cluttered stolen car, surely? And since neither Flynn nor Repp had stepped out of that car alive, the discovery of that third set of prints, Barron's, was of momentous significance: *Barron himself had been in the car.* The logic sounded pretty childish when it was put like that but . . .

Andrews's guess had been that Morse had suddenly fallen into some deep slumber after – well, after whatever; and Dixon's guess that he'd been watching TV with the volume too high. But the latter explanation seemed unlikely. Morse could (Lewis succumbed to his second unworthy thought that day) *could* have purchased some pornographic video; but would he have been able to master the operating instructions? Doubtful – especially having no children (better still, grandchildren) to explain things to him. Morse seldom watched TV anyway, or so he claimed. Just the news. Just occasionally.

Lewis finished his coffee, slowly coming to terms with the extraordinary news he'd just received: that Barron was a murderer – the second thing in the whole tragic business that now seemed wholly incontrovertible.

He rang Morse once again. If the call wasn't answered, he would drive down and see the situation for himself because he was getting a little worried.

The phone was ringing.

The call was answered.

Chapter Fifty-Seven

Ah, could thy grave, at Carthage, be!
Care not for that, and lay me where I fall!
Everywhere heard will be the judgement-call:
But at God's altar, oh! remember me
(Matthew Arnold)

MORSE OPENED THE front door. 'And there's me hoping for a rest day, like they tell me they have in the middle of test matches.'

But, in truth, he had not tried overhard to have much of a rest day . . .

Early that morning (as we have seen) he had rung Sergeant Dixon and given him a list of duties.

At 10 a.m. he had received a middle-aged, palely intelligent gentleman from Lloyds Bank, a guru on (inter alia) Wills, Dispositions, Codicils, and Covenants.

'From what you tell me, Mr Morse, you're not exactly going to bequeath a large fortune, are you? And with no relatives, no immediate dependants, no unmanageable debts – well, you might just as well write down a few things on half a page of A4. Save yourself money that way. Do it now, if you like. Just write a few simple sentences – "I leave the house to blank, the bank balance to blank, the books and records to blank, the residual estate to blank." That'll cover things for now – and you say you *do* want things covered? Just sign it, I'll witness it, and I'll see it's carried through, in case, you know . . . Then we can flesh it out a bit later.'

'No problems really then?'

'No. We shall, as a bank, charge a small commission of course. But you expected that.'

'Oh yes, Mr Daniel. I'd expected that,' said Morse.

At 11.15 a.m. he had taken the 2A bus down the Banbury Road as far as Keble Road, where he alighted and walked across the Woodstock Road to the Radcliffe Infirmary, where he was directed up to an office on the first floor.

'Yes? How can I help you?' The woman behind the desk seemed to be a fairly important personage with carefully coiffured grey hair and carefully clipped diction.

'I'm thinking of leaving my body to the hospital.'

'You've come to the right place.'

'What's the drill?'

She took a form from a drawer. 'Just fill this in.'

'Is that all?'

'Make sure you tell your wife and your children and your GP. You'll avoid quite a few problems that way.'

'Thank you.'

'Of course, I ought to tell you we may not *want* your body. The situation does, er, fluctuate. But you'd expected that.'

'Oh yes, I'd expected that,' said Morse.

'And you must make sure you die somewhere fairly locally. We can't come and collect you from Canada, you know.'

Perhaps it was a bleak joke.

'No, of course not.'

It had been a joyless experience for Morse, who now walked slowly down St Giles' towards The Randolph. He'd thought at the very least they'd have shown a little gratitude. Instead, he felt as though they were doing *him* a favour by agreeing (provisionally!) to accept a corpse that would surely be presenting apprentice anatomists and pathologists with some appreciably interesting items: liver, kidneys, lungs, pancreas, heart . . .

In the Chapters' Bar, Ailish Hurley, his favourite barmaid, greeted him in her delightful Irish brogue; and two pints of bitter later, as he walked round into Magdalen Street and almost immediately caught a bus back up to the top of the Banbury Road, he felt that the world was a happier place than it had been half an hour earlier.

Once home, he treated himself to a small(ish) Glenfiddich, deciding that his liquid intake of calories that lunchtime would nicely balance his dosage of insulin. Yes, things were looking up, and particularly so since the phone hadn't rung all day. What a wonderful thing it would be to go back to the days pre telephone (mobile and immobile alike), pre FAX, pre e-mail!

And, to cap it all, he'd bought himself a video – in front of which, in mid afternoon, he'd fallen fairly soundly asleep, though at some point half-hearing, as he thought, a slippery flop through the letter-box.

*

It was an hour later when he opened the envelope and read Dixon's notes on Simon Harrison; on Paddy Flynn; on Mrs Holmes.

Interesting!

Interesting!

Interesting!

And very much as he'd thought . . .

Only one thing was worrying him slightly. Why hadn't Lewis been in touch? He didn't want Lewis to get in touch but . . . perhaps he did want Lewis to get in touch. So he rang Lewis himself only to discover that the phone was out of order. Or was it? He banged the palm of his right hand against his forehead. He'd rung Dixon early that morning from the bedroom; then he'd had to go downstairs to check an address in the phone book, finishing the call there, and forgetting to replace the receiver in the bedroom. He'd done it before. And he'd do it again. It was not a matter of any great moment. He'd ring Lewis himself – not that he had anything much to say to him; not for the minute anyway.

He was about to pick up the phone when the doorbell rang.

CHAPTER FIFTY-EIGHT

It remains quite a problem to play the clarinet with false teeth, because there is great difficulty with the grip (this may even result in the plate being pulled out!). In addition there are problems with the breathing, because it is difficult to project a successful airstream

(Paul Harris, *Clarinet Basics*)

'BEEN TRYING TO get you all day, sir.'

'I've had other things to do, you know.'

'You just said you'd wanted a rest day.'

'Come in! Fancy a quick noggin?'

Lewis hesitated. 'Why not?'

'Ye gods! You must have had a bad day – or was it a good day?'

'I've had a *good* day, and so have you.'

Morse now listened quietly to the extraordinary news from Andrews, though without any sign of triumphalism.

Equally quietly he slowly read through Lewis's typed reports. Then read them a second time.

'Your orthography has come on enormously since they put that spell-check system into the word-processor.'

'Don't *you* have any problems with spellings – sometimes?'

'Only with "proceed".'

'Where does this all leave us, sir?'

'Things are moving fast.'

'We're getting near the end, you mean?'

'We were always near the end.'

'So what do you think happened?'

'Shan't ever know for certain, shall we? With all three of them dead, all three of them murdered—'

'Only *two*, surely?'

'If you say so, Lewis. If you say so.'

'You're not suggesting—?'

But Morse was not to be deflected:

'There were three people who had a vested interest in Yvonne Harrison's murder: Repp, Barron, and Flynn. Repp – because he'd been casing the property for a burglary; because he happened to be there on the night of the murder; and because he *knew who the murderer was.* Barron – a man with an SAS background, who'd found a woman who could gratify his sexual fantasies, and who also *knew who the murderer was* – because he was the fellow in bed with Yvonne that night. Flynn – the fellow who lied about the events that night and who, like the other two, *knew who the murderer was.* The three of them had got their clutches into the only person who could pay their price, the person who *did* pay their price: Frank Harrison. *He* was becoming a fatter and fatter cat in his banking business, so they thought – and, rightly it seems. So they were ready to up the stakes. And on the day Repp was released, they'd agreed to meet and co-ordinate some plan of action. But things went wrong. Pretty certainly they somehow discovered that they'd each been treated differently – *dangerously* differently; and bitterness, jealousy, rivalry, all surfaced, and there was one almighty row. I've said all this before! They'd stopped, perhaps in a lay-by along the A34 – take your pick! – and Barron got his Stanley knife out and threatened Flynn, the man who'd just happened to be at the taxi-rank that night, and who was now overplaying his hand. And soon it must have occurred to the other two that half a cake is considerably better than a third of one; and Flynn was murdered and dumped at Redbridge in those black bags, the ones the owner of the car was originally going to cart off to the rubbish dump.'

'Waste Disposal Centre.'

'After that? Who knows? But suddenly the situation was becoming more dangerous still. If half a cake is better than a third, what about a whole cake? So the two of them must have wrangled about the best way to capitalize on Flynn's beneficial departure . . . But how and why and when and where things went on from there, I've no more idea than you have – and that's not saying much, is it?'

'No,' said Lewis flatly.

Morse looked at his sergeant, and smiled wearily:

'You're annoyed, aren't you?'

'Annoyed? What about?'

'Dixon.'

'Why didn't you *tell* me?'

'You'd've accused me of wasting police resources. Do you know what I got him to do today?'

'Vaguely.'

'Well, let me tell you, specifically. First, I asked him to do a bit of fourth-grade clerical stuff at Oxpens, and get copies of those attending lip-reading classes these last five years. And he did it. Very efficiently. He found Simon Harrison's name there, for three years; and Paddy Flynn's there, for two years – overlapping. *Very* interesting that, because they must have known each other!

'Second, I asked Dixon to find out more about Flynn. Flynn was known as an amateur entertainer round the local pubs and clubs in Oxfordshire, playing the clarinet and compèring his little pop group. Till about three years ago, when things started to go wrong: he began to experience trouble with his hearing – something that later compromised his job with Radio Taxis; *and* at about the same time, according to the post-mortem details, he had a lot of dental trouble which meant he had to have all his top-front teeth extracted. And that's not a good thing for a clarinet-player.'

'It's not?'

'Well-known fact. Louis Armstrong had the same sort of trouble.'

'He was a *trumpet*-player!'

'Same *sort* of thing! Then I asked Dixon to look into Mrs Holmes's background. I had the impression when we spoke to her that she might have been a most attractive woman when she was younger; and I just wondered . . . I got Dixon to check up on her, that's all. Seems she used to live in Lower Swinstead before she moved to Burford and, well, look at things for yourself.'

Lewis read Dixon's notes:

Elizabeth Jane Thomas (b. 7.11.53)	
1976 (Feb.)	Son b. (Alan) illeg.
1983 (March)	Son b. (Roy) illeg.
1983 (Dec.)	m. Kenneth Holmes (Registry Office)
1991 (Sept.)	Husband killed in pile-up on A40 – same accident that caused all her trouble

'They don't call them "illegitimate" these days, and it should be "Register" Office.'

Morse nodded. 'You're missing the main point, though.'

'I am?'

'Remember when we were in the village pub? Remember Biffen greeting his customers?'

Yes. Lewis remembered that 'Evening, Mr Thomas': the young fellow forever playing the fruit machine, the young fellow who had spoken to him in the car park.

'You mean they're half-brothers? Roy Holmes and Alan Thomas?'

'Why not *full* brothers – with the same father? I knew there was something familiar about young Holmes . . . Anyway, there it is. Elizabeth Thomas was an unmarried mum in the village; Alan was already seven when his younger brother was born; and everybody knew him as Alan *Thomas.* So he kept the name when his mother married a few months later, and kept it when he went along with the family to live in Burford.'

'Interesting enough – but is it important?'

'I don't know,' said Morse slowly. 'I just don't know. But it throws up one or two new ideas.'

'If you say so, sir. Aren't you going to offer me another Scotch, by the way?'

What a strange day it had been! Even stranger, perhaps, in that Morse now left his own glass unreplenished.

'Shall I tell you something else, Lewis? You'd never believe it, but I've been watching the telly this afternoon. I picked up one of those RSPB videos.'

'You mean you know how to work the machine?'

'It's Strange's fault. Genuine bird-watcher, Strange! He told me the sparrow population in North Oxford's down by fifty per cent these last few years; and he told me the sparrow-hawks along Squitchey Lane are getting fatter. So I bought this video on birds of prey – you know, eagles, falcons, hobbies, merlins, red kites . . . did you hear me, Lewis? *Red kites.*'

Lewis looked puzzled. 'I'm not with you.'

'Your interview with Simon Harrison. He's a phoney bird-watcher, that fellow. Said he'd been off to Llandudno to try to spot a red kite. Llandudno! He meant *Llandovery,* Lewis – that was the only home of the red kite in the UK until they introduced a few near Stokenchurch.'

'I didn't know you were an expert—'

'I'm not. And nor is Simon Harrison. His alibi for

Monday morning's worthless. He wouldn't know a red kite from a red cabbage.'

Unaccustomedly relaxed, Lewis sipped his Glenfiddich and involuntarily repeated an earlier comment: 'Interesting enough – but is it *important*?'

'I just don't know,' said Morse slowly, himself now involuntarily repeating an earlier comment: 'But it throws up one or two new ideas . . .'

'Perhaps they've *all* been telling us a few lies, sir . . . except Mrs Barron, perhaps.'

Morse smiled. 'Don't you mean *especially* Mrs Barron?'

Chapter Fifty-Nine

Wherever God erects a house of prayer,
The Devil always builds a chapel there;
And 'twill be found, upon examination,
The latter has the largest congregation
(Daniel Defoe,
The True-born Englishman)

Mrs Linda Barron walked steadily up the aisle between the small assembly of mourners, her arm linked through that of her mother, both women dutifully dressed in bible-black suits . . .

On the whole, it hadn't been quite the ordeal she'd expected: in practical terms, the shock of it all continued to cocoon a good half of her conscious thoughts; whilst emotionally she had long since accepted that her love for her husband was as dead as the man who had been lying there in the coffin – until mercifully the curtains had closed, and the show was over. He would have enjoyed the hymn though, 'He Who Would Valiant Be', for he had been valiant enough (she'd learned that from his army friends) – as well as vain and domineering and unfaithful. Yes, she'd found herself moved by the hymn; and the tears ought to have come.

But they hadn't.

Outside, in the clear sunshine, she whispered

quickly into her mother's ear. 'Remember what I said. The kids are fine, if anybody asks. OK?'

But the grandmother made no reply. She was the very last person in the world to let the little ones down, especially the one of them. As for Linda, she girded up her loins in readiness for the chorus of commiseration she would have to cope with.

And indeed several of the family and friends of her late husband, J. Barron, Builder, had already emerged through the chapel doors, including Thomas Biffen, Landlord, whose creased white shirt was so tight around the neck that he had been forced to unfasten the top button beneath the black tie; including the perennial opponents, Alf and Bert, who had exchanged no words in the chapel, but whose thoughts were perhaps in tune during the service as each of them must have mused on their imminent mortality, and the prospects of encountering that great cribbage-player in the sky.

Including Frank Harrison.

Chief Superintendent Strange, who had been seated in the back row next to Morse, was the last but one to leave. His thoughts had roamed irreverently throughout the short service, and the superannuated minister's apparent confidence in the resurrection of the dead had filled him more with horror than with hope. He thought of his wife and of her death, and experienced that familiar sense of the guilt that still remained to be expiated. The hymn was all right, although he'd gone himself for 'Praise, My Soul, the King of Heaven' in the Instructions For My Funeral stapled to his last will and testament. But on the whole he dreaded church services almost as much as did the man seated beside him; and he could think of nothing more detestable than a funeral.

Morse himself had been sickened by the latest version (Series Something) of the Funeral Service. Gone were those resonant cadences of the AV and the Prayer Book: those passages about corruption putting on incorruptibility and the rest of it, which as a youth he'd found so poignant and powerful. They'd even had a cheerful hymn, for heaven's sake! Where was that wonderfully sad and sentimental hymn he'd chosen for his own farewell: 'O Love That Wilt Not Let Me Go'? Chosen, that is, before he'd recently decided to leave his body for medical science, although that decision itself was now in considerable doubt. In particular that little clause in sub-section 6 of Form D1 still stuck in his craw: 'Should your bequest be accepted . . .'

He pointedly avoided the priest who'd presided – a man (in Morse's view) excessively accoutred in ecclesiastical vestments, and wholly lacking in any sensitivity to the English language. But he did have a quick word of sympathy with the widow, shaking her black-gloved hand firmly before turning to her mother.

'Mrs Stokes?' he asked quietly.

'Yes?'

Morse introduced himself. 'My sergeant called to see your daughter – '

'Oh yes.'

' – when you were there looking after the children, I believe. Very kind of you. Must be a bit wearisome . . . I wouldn't know, though.'

'It's a pleasure really.'

'Who's looking after them today?'

'Oh they're, er . . . you know, a friend, a neighbour. Won't be for long anyway.'

'No.'

Morse turned away, following in Strange's steps towards the car park.

She was lying, of course – Morse knew that. There was only one of the Barron children at home that day; as there had been when Lewis had called. The elder of the two, Alice, was away somewhere. That much, though very little else, Lewis himself had been able to learn from the Barrons' GP the previous day. Morse thought he knew why, and another piece of the jigsaw had slipped into place.

'Hello! Chief Inspector Morse, isn't it? My daughter tells me she saw you recently. But perhaps you don't know me.'

'Let's say we've never been officially introduced, Mr Harrison.'

'Ah! You *do* know me. I know you, of course, and Sergeant Lewis has been to see me. You probably sent him.'

'As a matter of fact I did.'

'I realize you weren't yourself involved in my wife's murder case but, er . . .'

Harrison was by some three inches or so the taller of the two, and Morse felt slightly uncomfortable as a pair of pale-grey eyes, hard and unsmiling, looked slightly down on him.

'. . . but I'd heard about you. Yvonne spoke about you several times. She'd looked after you once when you were in hospital. Remember?'

Morse nodded.

'Quite taken by you, she was. "A sensitive soul" – I think that's what she called you; said you were interesting to talk to and had a nice voice. Told me she was going to invite you out to one of her, er, soirées. When I was away, of course.'

'I should hope so. Wouldn't have wanted any competition, would I?'

'*Did* you have any competition?'

'The only time I ever met Yvonne again was in the Maiden's Arms,' said Morse gently, unblinking blue eyes now looking slightly upward into the strong, clean-shaven face of Harrison senior.

As Strange struggled to squeeze his bulk between seat and steering wheel, Morse looked back and saw that the funeral guests were almost all departed. But Linda Barron stood there still, in close conversation with Frank Harrison – both of them now stepping aside a little as another black Daimler moved smoothly into place outside the chapel, with another light-brown, lily-bedecked coffin lying lengthways inside, the polished handles glinting in the sun.

Morse found himself pondering on the funeral. 'I wonder why *he* put in an appearance.'

'Who? Frank Harrison? Why shouldn't he? Lived in the same village – had him in to do those house repairs—'

'Knew his wife had been in bed with him.'

'Fasten your seat-belt, Morse!'

'Er, before we drive off, there's something—'

'Fasten your seat-belt! Know what that's an anagram of, by the way? "Truss neatly to be safe." Clever, eh? Somebody told me that once. You probably.'

For a few seconds Morse looked slightly puzzled.

'Couldn't have been me. It's got to be "belts". Otherwise there's one "s" short.'

'Just put the bloody thing on!'

But Morse left the bloody thing off as he looked directly ahead of him and completed his earlier sentence: 'Just before we drive off, sir, there's something I ought to mention. It's about Lewis. I'm fairly sure he's beginning to get some odd ideas about my being involved in some way with Yvonne Harrison.'

It was Strange's turn to look directly ahead of him.

'And you think I wasn't aware of that?' he asked quietly.

Chapter Sixty

Have respect unto the covenant: for the dark places of the earth are full of the habitations of cruelty
(*Psalm* 74, v. 20)

ONCE IN CHARLTON KINGS, a suburb on the eastern side of Cheltenham, Sergeant Lewis had followed the map directions carefully (he loved that sort of thing), turning right from the A40 through a maze of residential streets, and finally driving the unmarked police car past the sign on the white-washed wall beside the gateway – 'Sisters of the Covenant: Preparatory Boarding School for Girls' – and along the short gravelled drive that led to a large, detached Georgian house.

Destination reached; and purpose, shortly afterwards, fulfilled.

With a few extra suggestions from Morse, Lewis had found it comparatively easy to fill in most of the picture. The Barrons' GP had professional and wholly proper reasons for his guarded reticence. But other sources had been considerably less cautious with their help and information: the Burford Social Services, the NSPCC, the headmistress of the village primary school, the local Catholic priest, and, last of all, the middle-aged nun, dressed in a chocolate-brown habit and white wimple, who was expecting him and who found little difficulty in answering his brief, pointed questions.

Five nuns, all of them resident, looked after the school, which was specifically dedicated to the physical and spiritual well-being of girls between the ages of four and eleven (currently eighteen of them) who for varied reasons – poverty, indifference, criminality, cruelty – had been ill-used in their family homes. In spite of a modest benefaction, the school was a place of limited resources, at least in human terms; and was appropriately designated 'Private', with the majority of parents paying fees of between £1,000 and £1,500 per term.

Alice Barron, yes – now aged six – was one of the pupils there, referred to the school by her mother. She had been abused: not sexually, it seemed; but certainly physically; certainly psychologically.

No, Alice was not one of our Lord's brightest intellects; in fact she was in some ways a slow-witted child. This may have been the result of her home environment, but probably only partially so. Her younger sister (the teaching staff had learned) was as bright as the proverbial button; and such a circumstance could well have accounted to some degree for an impatient, expectant, aggressive parent to have . . .

'The father, you mean?'

'You're putting words into my mouth, Sergeant.'

'But if you were a betting woman – which I know you're not, of course . . .'

'What on earth makes you think that?' Her eyes momentarily glinted with humour. 'But if I *were*, I would not be putting much money on the mother, no.'

'How are the accounts for each term settled?'

'I looked that up, as you asked me. I can't be quite sure, but I suspect it's been in cash.'

'Isn't that unusual?'

'Yes, it is.'

'Does Alice know about her father's death?'

'Not yet, no.'

'Do you think this whole business is going to . . .?'

'Difficult to tell, isn't it? She's improving, right enough. She's stopped wetting her bed, and she doesn't scream so loudly in the night.'

'But if you were going to have another bet?'

'If I were a bookmaker, I'd lay you even money on it.'

As he drove back up to the A40, Lewis felt fairly sure he knew only a quarter as much about horse-racing (and probably about life) as Sister Benedicta.

CHAPTER SIXTY-ONE

character (n.) handwriting, style of writing: Shakes. *Meas. for M.* Here is the hand and seal of the Duke. You know the character, I doubt not

(Small's *Enlarged English Dict.* 18th ed.)

BACK AT HQ Lewis found a handwritten note for his personal attention:

> Well worthwhile going to the crem. One or two interesting conversations and one or two new ideas (or is it one?). Super and I off to have a jug (or is it two?). Tell anybody who wants me that I'm out to lunch and shan't be available till tomorrow morning – no Monday morning. M.

It was in Morse's hand, that small, neatly formed upright script that was recognizable anywhere; as indeed, for that matter, was Strange's hand – large, spidery, with a perpetual list to starboard, and often only semi-legible.

But Lewis was unconcerned. He would type up a report on his wholly satisfactory morning's work. And then he would sit back and let things slowly sink in, for it had now become clear that the Repp–Flynn–Barron mystery was solved. Completely solved now, with the knowledge that it was Linda Barron who had taken the hush-money; Linda Barron who must have insisted that if her husband ever thought of syphoning some of it off for himself she would expose him for the child-abuser that he was, and expose him to Social Services, to the police, to the folk in the village, to the Press. And she would have meant it, for she was past caring. My God, yes! And Barron had agreed.

Yes . . .

The big moments in the case were over; and he rang Mrs Lewis and asked her to have the chip-pan ready half an hour earlier than usual.

Yes . . .

In a strange kind of way, his confidence in himself had grown steadily throughout the present case, in spite of a few irritations like Dixon! *And* there was that one thing that had been interesting him and troubling him, in equal measure, for some considerable time now. Very soon he'd have to face up to telling Morse of his suspicions. But not just yet. He'd need to know a bit more about the Harrison murder first; especially about the contents of that fourth green box-file which had mysteriously added itself to the documents in the case, and which now sat alongside the other three on a shelf in Morse's office. Perhaps a bit later that afternoon, since Morse was unlikely to return.

What if he did, anyway?

Yes . . .

Lewis sat back after typing his report, his thoughts dwelling on the case that to all intents and purposes had now closed. He *was* right, wasn't he? But there were just one or two tiny items he hadn't as yet checked; and he knew that his conscience would be niggling him about them. No time like the present.

But not much luck. Still, those alibis for the Monday morning didn't much matter any longer. Or rather *non*-alibis, since neither Harrison Senior nor Harrison Junior had any alibi at all. And whilst Sarah Harrison did have an alibi, it still remained unchecked.

He rang the Diabetes Centre in the Radcliffe Infirmary, with almost immediate if unexpected success, since Professor Turner (clearly not a Monday–Friday medic) now confirmed everything that Miss Harrison herself had affirmed: 'In fact, Sergeant, she had to take over some of my patients mid-morning when I was summoned by my superiors—'

'Do you have any superiors, sir?'

On reflection, Lewis was more than a little pleased with that last question: just the sort of thing Morse would have asked. Was he, Lewis, just a little – after all this time – moving gradually nearer to Morsean wavelength?

At a quarter-past four he walked along the corridor to Morse's office, to cast a fresh eye (so he promised himself) on that bizarre, that puzzling, that haunting evening of Yvonne Harrison's murder – the source of so much trouble and tragedy.

Very soon he was virtually certain that he had seen none of the contents of that fourth box-file before; and had convinced himself that this was not merely a matter of some redistribution of the case-documents. The file contained the sort of personal items that many women, and doubtless many men, keep in one of the locked drawers of their desks or bureaux, often with some sense of guilt.

There were all the usual things that from experience Lewis had known so well: letters, many of them in their original envelopes, some from women, most of them from men; photographs, many of them of Yvonne herself (one topless) with a variety of men-friends; postcards from many a quarter of the globe, but mostly from Greece and Switzerland; three slim (unopened) bottles of perfume; various receipts for the purchase of ultra-expensive clothes and shoes. But for all the variety of material there, the box was scarcely half-full, and Lewis took his time. He looked at the photographs reasonably quickly (not quite so quickly at one of them, perhaps), before reading slowly (though not as slowly as Morse would have done) through the letters.

Then he saw it:

> that they would prefer to be ill in hospital and nursed by you than to be in full health and never see you again. I join them. You have monopolized my thoughts these last few days, ever since you promised – remember? – to get in touch once I was discharged. But no invitation, no phone call, no letter, nothing.

> If you have decided that it was all just a temporary infatuation, and if, on your part, it was nothing more than that – so be it. Just for a while longer though, let me look through my mail each morning in the hope

That was all. Just one small page of a longer letter. No date, no address, no salutation, no valediction, no name – nothing. And yet everything. Because the letter was written in that small, neatly formed upright script that was recognizable everywhere in the Thames Valley Police HQ.

As he re-read the page, Lewis was suddenly aware of another presence in the office; and looked up to find Chief Inspector Morse standing silently in the doorway.

Chapter Sixty-Two

Don't tell me, sweet, that I'm unkind
Each time I black your eye,
Or raise a weal on your behind –
I'm just a loving guy.

We both despise the gentle touch,
So cut out the pretence;
You wouldn't love it half as much
Without the violence
(Roy Dean, *Lovelace Bleeding*)

ANYONE WISHING TO take up Morse's earlier promise of being available the following Monday morning would have been disappointed, since he had put in no appearance by lunchtime. Yet he was not idle during those morning hours; and any visitor to the bachelor flat would have found him seated at his desk for much of the time; and for a fair proportion of that time found him writing quite busily and (as we have seen) very neatly. His old typewriter (with its defective 'e' and 't's) sat at his elbow; but he had never mastered the keyboard-skills with any real confidence, and he wrote now in long-hand with a medium-blue Biro.

For Priority Consideration

Several things have happened these last few days which have prompted me to put down in writing my own thoughts on the present state of play.

First, I've been waking up every day recently, after some nightmarish nights, with a premonition that some disaster is imminent. Whether death comes into such a category, I'm not sure. I can't agree with Socrates, though, that death is a blessing devoutly to be wished, even if it is (as I hope it is, as I believe it is) one long completely dreamless sleep. For the very fact of being alive is surely the best thing that's happened to (almost) all of us.

Second, the last murder case entrusted to the pair of us has been (one or two loose ends though) satisfactorily resolved. Repp and Flynn were murdered by Barron, and the murderer himself is now dead. So any further insight into the original Harrison murder from *their* angles is wholly precluded.

Third, I'm certain that Frank Harrison has been the paymaster. It's high time we brought him into HQ for intensive questioning, either directly about the murder of his wife, or at the very least about some culpable complicity of her murder.

Fourth, I'm also convinced that Yvonne H was murdered by one of her own family. Nothing else makes any sense at all, not to me anyway. That murder was not premeditated: few of them are. It was committed spontaneously, viciously, involuntarily perhaps, by whichever of the three it was who found Yvonne Harrison in a situation that was utterly unexpected – kinkiness, perversion, degradation, all rolled up into one.

On the face of it, the husband is the outsider of the three, so you will appreciate, Lewis, that in my book he's the favourite. It's the 'why' that worries me, though. He wasn't and isn't anybody's fool, and he must have known more than enough about his wife's tastes in bondage and possibly masochism. So I just can't see blazing jealousy as his motive, especially since, as I strongly suspect, he regularly experienced the (reported) joys of extra-marital sex himself.

A confession here.

Quite a few times I've found myself looking at the faces of people concerned with this case and thinking I'd seen them somewhere before. I thought it might be the result of interbreeding in a small community – no wonder some of the villagers are pretty tight-lipped! And I was right. That fruit-machine addict, for example: *Allen* Thomas. That's how you spell his name by the way, Lewis. I found it in the village-school records: Allen Alfred Thomas. Unusual these days, that spelling of 'Allen'. And 'Alfred' belongs more to the first half of the century, doesn't it? I also found out (well, Dixon found out) that the Christian names of Elizabeth Jane Thomas's father were 'Harold Alfred'; and that someone else in the village had a father with the Christian names 'Joseph Allen'. That someone else was Frank Harrison. And (believe me!) *he* was the father of the lad, and Elizabeth decided to give him a couple of

Christian names that, at least for herself, could confer some little pretence of legitimacy on her illegitimate son. (I wonder if his father gives him a fruit-machine allowance?)

Let's turn to the Harrison children.

Either of them *could* have murdered their mother. What would be the motive, though? I just can't see Sarah suddenly turning to murder because she finds her mother abed with one of her many lovers. What does it really matter to her that her mother enjoys a bit of biting and bondage occasionally? Shocked and disgusted? Yes, she'd certainly have been both. But driven to murder? No. There's something about her, though – something that tells me that she's up to her very smooth neck in things.

What about Simon Harrison? As we know he's always been a bit of a mummy's darling: a boy disadvantaged because of early deafness; a boy always needing extra understanding and extra love, and who found it (hardly surprisingly) from his mother. I'd guess myself that for Simon this relationship had always been very precious. Sacrosanct almost. I'd also guess that he had no notion whatsoever of his mother's idiosyncratic tastes in sexual gratification. Then one night, the night of the murder, he'd driven out to see her. And why not? Just to say hello, perhaps? Like his sister, he had a key to the front door, and he entered the house and disturbed the copulating couple – copulating in the most extraordinary circumstances; and he would have been shocked and disgusted (like his sister) but heartbroken, too, and disillusioned and betrayed. His mother performing those things with some plebeian local builder!

Where does all this lead us? First and foremost to an early, long-overdue, full-scale interview with Frank Harrison. Not too early though. Our colleagues got nowhere with him and we, Lewis, are a pair of bloodhounds very late on the scene, with the scent gone very cold.

Fifth, there's this business of the letter you found in the Harrison file. As I told you, I take full responsibility for the fact that some items originally discovered at the Harrison murder scene were subsequently, as they say, found to be missing. It was embarrassing for me to talk to you about this and I know that you in turn found it equally embarrassing to—

Morse laid down his pen and answered the phone: 'Lewis! What do you want?'

'You OK, sir?'

'Why shouldn't I be?'

'It's just that – well, you know that animal charity shop on the corner of South Parade and Middle Way . . .'

'I am *not* an animal-lover, Lewis.'

'Well, people leave things there, by the door, things for the shop to sell for charity—'

'Get *on* with it!'

'Guess what one of the shop assistants found when she got to work this morning?'

'Pair of handcuffs?'

'Pair of *something*, sir. Pair of red trainers! Almost brand new. This woman had read in the *Oxford Mail* about the Burford jogger and she thought . . .'

'You know something, Lewis? That's very interesting. Very interesting indeed. I'll be with you straightaway.'

Chapter Sixty-Three

With much talk will they tempt thee, and smiling upon thee will get out thy secrets
(*Ecclesiasticus*, ch. XIII, v. 11)

'You know, come to think of it, Lewis, we could do all of this now, couldn't we? Just the two of us.'

'No Dixon?'

'No Dixon.'

Lewis smiled outwardly and inwardly as he looked down at the action plan. It seemed to him a sensible and fair division of a good deal of labour. For example, he himself had spoken only very briefly with Sarah Harrison; Morse had not as yet spoken at all with Simon Harrison. Both matters now to be dealt with. And all leading up to the two of them, Morse and Lewis, meeting Frank Harrison a.s.a.p. after these and a few other checks and visits had been made. Harrison! – 'the corner-stone, the kingpin, the pivot', as Morse had asserted, before running out of synonyms. 'We've got plenty of time for all this – well, no, perhaps we haven't. So we can be pretty direct, but not sharp. Smile occasionally. No aggressiveness, no hostility, no belligerence,' Morse had asserted, before running out of synonyms again.

It all suited Lewis nicely. If Morse's philosophy in life was to aim high even if the target was altogether missed, he personally preferred to aim low in the hope at least of hitting something.

The voluntary (mornings only) help at the Oxford Animal Sanctuary Shop (Gifts Welcome) lived only a few hundred yards away in Osberton Road: a widow, a cat-lover, an intelligent witness – Mrs Gerrard. It was just that, as every weekday morning, she'd walked down to South Parade to buy the *Daily Telegraph*, about 8 o'clock before opening the shop, and she'd seen this –

'Yes?' Lewis smiled.

' – well, this youngish fellow – smartly dressed, suit and tie – and he put this Sainsbury's plastic bag in the doorway there. She couldn't describe him any better than that really; but she remembered his car, parked for a few seconds on the double-yellows alongside the shop. She wouldn't have noticed that either – except that it was the same make as hers, a Toyota Carina, P-Reg, a different colour though: hers was a turquoisy colour, his was silvery-grey. The trainers she had put carefully aside, under the counter in the shop.

No one in North Oxford with a Toyota was likely to drive unnecessarily far afield for any servicing and repairs, since there was a specialist garage in Summertown itself; and it took Lewis only a few minutes to learn that the owner of a silvery-grey P-Reg Carina was a regular and esteemed customer of the company, a man named Simon Harrison.

*

Simultaneously Morse was driving himself in the Jaguar through the low range of open hills that border Oxfordshire and Gloucestershire. His old pathologist friend, Max, had once told him that two pleasures grew ever deeper with advancing age, the pleasures of the belly and the pleasures of natural beauty. And Morse found himself concurring with the latter proposition as he turned right at the roundabout and drove down into Burford.

Christine Coverley was clearly surprised to see him, and clearly not happy.

'It's all a bit untidy—'

Morse smiled. 'Can I come in?'

'I haven't got long, I'm afraid.'

'It won't take long, I promise.'

'How can I . . .?'

'What were you doing last Monday morning? Between, say, nine and eleven?'

'Not the faintest, have I? Nobody could remember exactly—'

'Did you go out – for a newspaper, shopping, seeing someone?'

'I don't know. Like I say—'

'Can you have a look in your diary for me?'

'That wouldn't help.'

'What *would* help?'

'I don't know what you're getting at. Look, Inspector.' She glanced down at her wristwatch with what appeared incipient panic. 'Could we talk some other time, *please*? You see I've got—'

But it was too late.

There was the scratch of a key in the Yale lock and the front door was quickly opened and as quickly closed, and a youth entered from the narrow hallway to stand in the doorway of the single bed-sit room.

With staring eyes he looked first at Morse and then at Christine Coverley: 'What the fuck?'

'You haven't increased your word-power much since we last—' began Morse. But Roy Holmes had disappeared even more rapidly than he'd appeared.

In the stillness that followed the crash of the front door closing, Morse sat down in one of the armchairs, and gestured the speechless schoolmistress to seat herself in the other.

'Please tell me all about it,' he said, with no hint of aggressiveness or any of its synonyms. 'If you don't, I'm sorry but I shall have to take you down to Police HQ.'

After his twinkling Irish eyes had scrutinized Lewis's ID, Mr Tony Marrinan, the manager of The Randolph, was wholly co-operative; and very soon the outline of Frank Harrison's recent stay was revealed. Double-room booked with, as staff recalled her, a sultrily attractive if less than attractively mannered partner – late twenties, perhaps; meals taken together quite regularly in the Spires Restaurant – details available, if Sergeant Lewis wanted to see them.

As Sergeant Lewis did.

The pair had breakfasted together on each morning except the Monday, and Lewis was fairly soon looking at that day's Good Morning Breakfast chit, its details having been transferred immediately to the hotel's computer before being placed on a spike and then at the end of the day transferred to the accounts department upstairs for a limited period, as a check if any guest should query an entry on the final bill.

Interesting! Especially the bottom half of the chit:

Continental	☑	Full	☐
Date	3/8/98	Time	8.20
Table No.	7	Covers	1
Room No.	210	Waiter	C.M.
Room Charge	☑	Other	☐
Guest Name:	HARRISON		
Signature:			

'Covers', as Lewis learned, signified how many had been at the table: on the other chits it had the figure '2' beside it. But on the Monday morning just the one of them, and the restaurant manager remembered which one of them: 'It was the lady. I think Mr Harrison may have been feeling a little tired.'

Before he left the hotel, Lewis had a word with the chambermaid who had looked after Room 210, discovering that for much of the time over the period in question the DO NOT DISTURB notice had hung over the outside door-knob.

'And the bed looked as if it had been slept in each night?' (Lewis tried to smile knowingly.)

'Oh yes, sir. Oh yes.'

Perhaps the restaurant manager was right. Perhaps

Mr Harrison's stay in Oxford had been a busy and tiring one.

For one reason or another.

Before driving back to HQ, Morse called in at the Maiden's Arms, in the hope of finding Alf and Bert, Lower Swinstead's answer to 'Bill and Ben'. The time was now just after 2.30 p.m.; and Morse expected that they would be gone by then. But he was lucky; or at least half-lucky.

Bert, it seemed, had 'got the screws', and Alf was sitting alone by the window, slowly sipping the last of his beer, and readily accepting Morse's offer of 'one for the road'.

'Lost his nerve!' confided Alf. 'Lost the last five times we've a' been playing. Lost his nerve!'

'Like me to give you a quick game? Just the one?'

Morse had determined to lose the challenge in as swift and incompetent a manner as possible. But unfortunately the gods were smiling broadly on his hands; and very soon, *malgré lui*, he had won the single encounter by the proverbial street.

Unfortunately?

Oh no. For Alf appeared to recognize in his opponent a player of supreme skills; and instead of his wonted sullen silence on such occasions, he was soon speaking with unprecedented candour about life there in the village in general, and in particular about the Harrisons – with the result that after twenty minutes

Morse had learned more than any other police officer before him from any of the locals in Lower Swinstead.

'Did Frank ever come in the pub here with other women?'

'Never. In Lon'on most of his time, weren't he?'

'What about Simon?'

'He come in sometimes, but he never had no reg'lar girlfriend. Bit of a loner, Simon.'

'What about Sarah?'

'Lovely, she were – not seen her though this last coupla years. In fact, last time I seen her was here in the pub – sort of guest appearance singing with a pop group. Nice voice, she had, young Sarah.'

'Did she come in with any boyfriends?'

'Did she? I'll tell you summat – she did. Could've had anybody she wanted, I reckon.'

'Who did she want?'

Alf chuckled. 'Didn't want me – Bert neither! One or two was luckier though, mister.'

The light in Alf's old eyes suddenly sparked, like the coals on a fire that were almost ready to sink back to an ashen-grey; and he nodded his head – just as Bert, in his turn, would have nodded across the cribbage-board.

Enviously.

With the consulting rooms all taken up with a series of interviews for diabetes students, Lewis sat with Sarah Harrison behind a curtain in the Blood-Testing Room.

'Did you see your father while he was staying at the Randolph last week?'

'I always see my father when he comes to Oxford. In fact, I had a meal with him one evening.'

'So you get on well with him?'

Lewis's smile was not reciprocated, and she almost spat her reply at him: 'What the hell's *that* supposed to mean?'

'I'm not sure really. It's just that I've got a list of questions here from Chief Inspector Morse – by the way, I think you know him . . . ?'

'I've met him *once*.'

'Well he's asked me to ask you – not very well phrased, that – '

'What's he want to know?'

'What the relationships were like in your family.'

'I can't speak for Simon – you must ask *him*. If you mean did I have any preference? No. I loved Mum, and I loved, *love*, Dad. Some children love both their parents, you know.'

'You never felt that your mother loved Simon a bit more than she loved you – you know, because he was a bit handicapped, perhaps because he needed more affection than you did?'

There was a silence before Sarah answered the question; and as Lewis looked at her he realized how attractive she must have appeared to all the men and boys in the village; how attractive she was now, and would be for many years to come, in whatever place she found herself.

'You know I've never thought of it quite like that

before, but yes . . . I suppose you could be right, Sergeant Lewis.'

After leaving the Maiden's Arms, where the fruit machine had stood unwontedly and unprofitably silent, Morse called on Allen (*sic*) Thomas at his home in Lower Swinstead. Alf had told him where to go: the lad was sure to be there. He'd not be at work, because he'd never done a hand's turn in his life.

And Alf was right.

The dingy room was untidy and undusted, with three empty cans on the top of the TV and a hugely piled ash-tray on the arm of the single armchair. But Thomas (the facial resemblance between him and Roy Holmes so very obvious to him now) was a paragon of civility compared with the crudity of that sibling of his, and Morse found himself feeling more pro than anti the unshaven youth in front of him.

'How often do you keep in touch with your dad?' began Morse.

The cigarette that had been dangling from Thomas's loose mouth fell to the carpet; and although it was swiftly retrieved the damage had been done. Thomas knew it. And Morse knew it. And fairly soon the truth, or what Morse took to be half of the truth, had started to surface.

Yes, Elizabeth Holmes was his natural mother.

Yes, Roy Holmes was his stepbrother – or his real brother – he'd never really known.

Yes, he kept in touch with his natural father, and his natural father kept in touch with him: Frank Harrison, yes – he'd always known that.

No. His father had never sent him what could loosely be called a fruit-machine allowance.

No. His father had never asked him to keep him regularly informed about any developments in the enquiries into Yvonne Harrison's murder.

No. He'd had no contact whatever recently either with his father or his mother or his brother.

Morse was half-smiling to himself as finally he drove back to Oxford, knowing beyond any peradventure that the No No No was in reality a Yes Yes Yes.

In the semi-co-ordinated strategy earlier agreed between the pair of them, Lewis's last allotted task had been some further enquiries into the balances and business activities of Mr Frank Harrison. Somewhat trickier than anticipated though. Yet far more exciting, as Lewis discovered after depositing (as agreed) the Sainsbury's bag, with contents, in Morse's office late that same afternoon, and ringing the London offices of the Swiss Helvetia Bank.

Reaching the senior manager surprisingly speedily.

Being informed that he, Lewis, ought really to get to London immediately and urgently.

Deciding to go.

Using the siren (one of Lewis's greatest joys) if he

found himself stuck, as he knew he would be, amidst the capital's inevitable gridlocks.

Morse took the red trainers from the bag and placed them on Simon Harrison's desk.

'These yours?'

'Pardon? What shorts?'

The interview wasn't going to be easy, Morse conceded that. Yet already the suspicion had crossed his mind that any deaf man, and especially a canny deaf man, might occasionally pretend to mis-hear in order to give himself a little more time to consider an awkward question.

'Your car, Mr Harrison? Toyota, P-Reg?'

'It ought to be what, Inspector?'

'Llandudno? Mean anything to you?'

'Did you know, you say? Didn't know?'

'The time for playing games is over, lad,' said Morse quietly. 'Let's start at the beginning again, shall we?' He pointed to the trainers. 'These yours?'

The truth, or what Morse took to be half of the truth, was fairly soon out.

The teenaged Simon had known Barron well enough because the builder had done a few things around the house, including a big structural job on the back patio. Frequently he'd found Barron in the kitchen having a mug of coffee with his mother, and he'd sensed that Barron fancied her. Jealous? Yes, he'd been jealous. Angry, too, because his mother had once confided in him that she found Barron a bit of a creep.

Then, so very recently, there'd been this upsurge of interest in his mother's murder, bringing with it a corresponding upsurge in his hatred of Barron.

Yes, he'd bought the trainers – £70! No, he'd not driven out to Stokenchurch that Monday morning. He'd driven out to Burford instead, where he knew that Barron was working.

Here Morse had interrupted. 'How did you know that?'

'Pardon?'

Was it a genuine plea? Morse was most doubtful, but he repeated the question with what he trusted was legible enunciation, conscious as he had been throughout of Simon's eyes upon his lips.

'He told me himself. You see, I wanted the outside of my flat, er . . . you know, the windows, doors . . . they were all getting a bit . . . Anyway, I asked him if he could do it and he said he'd come round and give me an estimate after he'd finished his next job. And I don't know why but he just happened to mention where it was, that's all.'

Morse nodded dubiously. Even if it wasn't the truth, it wasn't a bad answer. And Simon Harrison continued his unofficial statement:

He'd just felt – well, murderous. Simple as that. He'd always suspected that Barron was involved somehow in his mother's murder, and he was conscious of an ever-increasing hatred for the man. So he'd decided to go and see if Barron *was* there, in Sheep Street, balanced precariously (as he hoped) on the top of an extended ladder, painting the guttering or something. And he was.

Morse made a second interruption: 'So why didn't you . . .?'

Simon understood the inchoate query immediately, and for Morse his answer had the ring of truth about it:

'I wanted to make sure he *could* be pushed off. I'd noticed when he was doing Mum's roof that he used to anchor the top of his ladder to the troughing or chimney stack or something. And he'd done the same there, in Sheep Street – I could see it easily. So even if I'd had the guts to do it, the ladder wouldn't have fallen. *He* might have done, agreed, but . . . Anyway, I was a nervous wreck when I got back home; and when I read in the *Oxford Mail* that Mrs Somebody-or-other had mentioned seeing a jogger there wearing red trainers . . . I should have put them in the dustbin. Stupid, I was! But they'd cost me – well, I told you. And I've always loved animals, so . . . well, that's it really.'

Although less than convinced by what sounded a suspiciously shaky story, Morse was adequately impressed by the manner of the pleasantly spoken young man. Had he been as vain as Morse and many other mortals, he would probably have grown his hair fairly long over his temples in order to conceal his hearing-aids. But Harrison's dark hair was closely cropped, framing a clean-shaven face that seemed honest. Or reasonably so.

Asking Harrison to remind him of his home address and telephone number, Morse got to his feet and prepared to leave.

'You'll have to make an official statement, of course.'

'I realize that, yes.'

Morse pushed the trainers an inch or two further across the desk.

'You might as well keep them now. I only wish I were as fit as you.'

Was there a glint of humour in Simon's eyes as, in turn, he got to his feet?

'Fit a shoe, did you say, Inspector?'

Morse let it go. The man's hearing was very poor, little doubt of that. Which made it surprising perhaps that a mobile phone lay on the desk beside him.

On his second impulse that day, Morse drove down to North Oxford and stopped momentarily outside Simon Harrison's small property at 5 Grosvenor Street. The replacement windows with their aluminium frames had clearly been installed there fairly recently – frames whose glory (as advertised) was never to need any painting at all.

Courteously if somewhat cautiously received, Lewis listened carefully as one of the Bank's important personages spelled out the situation with (as was stressed) utter confidentiality, with appropriate delicacy, and with (for Lewis) a leavening of incomprehensible technicalities. In simple terms it amounted to this: Mr

Frank Harrison, currently on furlough, was currently also, if unofficially, on suspension from his duties with the Bank on suspicion, as yet unsubstantiated, of misappropriation of monies: viz. an unexplained black hole of some £520,000 in his department's Investment Portfolios.

Chapter Sixty-Four

Refrain to-night
And that shall lend a kind of easiness
To the next abstinence: the next more easy;
For use almost can change the stamp of nature
(Shakespeare, *Hamlet*)

SLOANE SQUARE . . . GRIDLOCK . . . Siren . . . Gridlock . . . Siren . . .

It is not a matter for any surprise that car drivers occasionally contract one of the minor strains of the road-rage virus – even that patient man in the siren-assisted police car who finally pulled over on to the hard shoulder of the M40 and rang his chief.

'Been stuck in traffic, sir. Be with you in about an hour.'

'Lewis! Can't you hear the wireless? It's five-past seven – bang in the middle of *The Archers*. It can wait, surely!'

Lewis supposed it could; and would have said so. But the phone was dead.

Wireless! Huh! Everybody called it a 'radio' these days – well, everybody except Morse and one or two of the old 'uns, like Strange. Yes, come to think of it, Morse and Strange were the oldest of the HQ lot, with Strange six months the older, and due for retirement that next month.

The road was free and Lewis drove fast. It could wait – of course it could – the news about Harrison Senior. Perhaps it didn't matter all that much; and as Morse frequently reminded him nothing really mattered very much at all in the end. But he was looking forward to a swapping of notes. There had been some interesting developments, certainly on his own side; and he doubted not that Morse's researches that day had generated a few new ideas. Not that they needed any more high-flown ideas really, he decided, as a sudden torrential downpour called for more terrestrial concentration. He reduced his speed to 80 m.p.h.

At 7.20 p.m. Morse was sitting back in the black-leather armchair, knowing that only a few of the pieces in the jigsaw remained to be fitted. Earlier in the case the top half of the puzzle had presented itself as a monochrome blue, like the sky earlier that evening, although of late the weather had become sultry, as though a thunderstorm were brewing. But the jigsaw's undifferentiated blue had been duly broken by a solitary seagull or two, by a piece of soft-white cloud, and later perhaps (when Lewis arrived?) by what Housman so memorably had called 'the orange band of eve'. He felt almost happy. There was something else, too: he would quite certainly wait until that arrival before having his first drink of the day. It was quite easy really (as he told himself) to refrain from alcohol for a limited period.

The storm reached North Oxford fifty minutes later,

travelling from the south-west at a pace commensurate with Lewis's speed along the M40.

It may have had something to do with Wagner, but Morse enjoyed the intensity and the electricity of a thunderstorm, and he watched with deep pleasure the plashing rain and the dazzling flashes in the lightning-riven sky. From his viewpoint by the window of his flat, a slightly sagging telephone-wire cut the leaden heavens in two; and he watched as a succession of single drops of rain ran along the wire before finally falling off, reminding him of soldiers crossing a river on rope-harness, and finally dropping off on the other side. As he had once done himself.

Crossing the river . . .

His mother would never speak of 'dying': always of 'crossing the river'. It was a pleasing conceit; a pleasing metaphor. If he'd been a poet, he might have written a sonnet about that telephone-wire just outside. But Morse wasn't a poet. And the storm now ceased as suddenly as it had started.

And the front-door bell was ringing.

It was after 10 p.m. when, with Lewis now gone, Morse took stock of the situation – with renewed interest, though (truth to tell) with little great surprise. Lewis had declined the offer of alcohol, and Morse had decided to prolong his own virtually unprecedented abstinence. He felt tired, and at 10.30 p.m. decided that he would be early abed. So many times had he been counselled that beer made a lumpy mattress, that spirits made a hard pillow, and that in general alcohol was the stuff that nightmares were made of. So, if that were true, he could perhaps expect to be sleeping the sleep of the just that night. It would be a new experience.

He put on the RSPB video, and once again watched the wonderful albatross gliding effortlessly across the Antarctic wastes. So relaxing . . .

At 11.15 he switched off the bedroom light and turned as ever on to his right-hand side, conscious of a clear head, a freshness of mind, and a gently slumbrous lassitude.

Wonderful.

In spite of his occasional disillusionment about being cast up on to the shores of light in the first place, it would be wholly untrue to say that Morse was over-eager to embark upon that final journey to that further land. Indeed, like the majority of mortals, he was something of a hypochondriac; and that night he found himself becoming increasingly fearful about his own physical well-being. Or ill-being.

The illuminated green figures on the alarm clock showed 2.42 a.m. when he finally abandoned the unequal struggle. His mind was an uncontrollable whirligig at St Giles' Fair, and the indigestion-pains in his chest and in his arms were hard and unrelenting. He got up, poured himself a glass of Alka-Seltzer, poured himself a glass of the single malt, took up his medium-blue Parker pen, and resumed the exegesis he'd been writing when Lewis had interrupted him, deciding however to cross out the last (and uncompleted) sentence:

> 'It was embarrassing for me to talk to you about this and I know that you in turn found it equally embarrassing to—

There would be ample time to put that part of the record straight in the days ahead.

Tomorrow and tomorrow and tomorrow . . .

CHAPTER SIXTY-FIVE

Jealousy is that pain which a man feels from the apprehension that he is not equally beloved by the person whom he entirely loves

(Addison, *The Spectator*)

Simon H is not a good liar, and I dragged some of the truth out of him. He is genuinely very deaf, and the telephone must always be a nightmare for him. So what's he got a mobile for? Even people with good hearing often have trouble with one. But, remember, even someone who's stone-deaf can communicate to some degree with someone on the other end, because he's always able to *speak* if not to hear.

Many people must have wanted Barron dead. And no one more so than Frank Harrison, who'd learned that Barron would soon be working up at some giddy height in a quietish street in Burford. The job had been mentioned, among other places no doubt, in the Maiden's Arms. And one person in that pub was in regular communication with Frank H: Allen Thomas, that soon-to-be-married youth who regularly wastes his substance on the fruit machine. How come? Like so many others in this case, he's dependent on Frank H – his father, remember! – who (rumour!) has just bought him a small flat in Bicester, and who has pretty certainly been making him a regular allowance for many years.

The plan had been a reasonably simple one – with one snag. Both the Harrisons, Senior and Junior, had some knowledge of Barron's ladder-technique from the several times he had worked at the family home: specifically his habit of tying the top of his ladders to something firm up there in the heights. It would seem likely that he'd do the same again, and there'd be little point in giving the ladder one great hefty push if it wouldn't topple to the ground. Some recce was therefore required; and Simon picked up his father that Monday morning in Oxford and drove him the twenty miles to Burford, leaving the car at the western end of Sheep Street, and then jogging up and down the opposite side of the street in tracksuit and trainers, noting that Barron was moving the ladder along every twelve minutes or so, and predictably re-roping the top each time. The only possibility then was to catch Barron after he'd *re*-climbed the ladder and was refixing the rope. A minute or so? Not much more. But enough. Simon's job was to phone his father, mobile to mobile, and just say 'Now!'. Nothing else. He hadn't the spunk he says (I believe him) to perform the deed himself; and it was his father, also in jogging kit, who would run along the pathway there and topple Barron to a death that in Simon's view was fully deserved and long overdue.

That was the plan. Something like it. So I believe.

But the countdown had been aborted because (Simon himself a witness) a bicycle, the front wheel jerked up repeatedly from the ground, was lurching its way along the path, and under the ladder, *and into* the ladder. Surplus to requirements therefore was the plan the Harrisons had plotted. Or so we are led to believe. Why such a proviso? Because I shall be surprised if any plan devised by the opportunistic Frank Harrison has ever come to a sorry nothing. Is it possible therefore that the accident of Barron's death was not quite so 'accidental' after all? Already Frank Harrison had accomplished something far more complex – his manipulation of the evidence surrounding his wife's murder, when it was imperative for him to establish one crucial fact: that no other living soul was present when he went into his house that night. But three other people knew this fact was untrue; and all three of them – whichever way intercommunication was effected – were subsequently rewarded for their roles in the conspiracy of complicity and silence.

Back to my proviso.

Can it be that Frank Harrison trawled his net even wider and dragged in the cyclist who sent Barron down to his death, the boy Holmes – the brother of Harrison's son Allen?

We turn now to the Harrison clan itself.

Our researchers have given us several pointers to the relationships within that family. The marriage itself had long been loveless: he with a string of mistresses in his Pavilion Road flat in London; she with a succession of straight or kinky but always besotted bedmates, with whom she fairly regularly dallied with mutual delight. And, doubtless, profit. Of the two children, Simon was clearly the mother's favourite – a boy who had battled bravely with his disability; a boy for whom his mother had found an affection considerably deeper than that for her daughter Sarah – a young lady who was very attractive physically, very bright academically, very talented musically, who from her early years had almost everything going for her, and who (unlike her brother) needed far less of her mother's tender loving care. Both children, as well as their parents, were probably fully aware of the imbalance here; and tacitly and tactfully accepted it.

At the time of their mother's murder, both the children had left home several years earlier. Sarah had already qualified as a doctor specializing with considerable distinction in the treatment of diabetes. And Simon had landed a surprisingly good job in publishing, and was now financially independent – if not emotionally independent, because he still yearned for that unique love his mother had always shown him; a love that had meant everything to him in those long years of an ever-struggling school-life in which he knew with joyous assurance that it was he – Simon! – who'd acquired the monopoly of a mother's love, more of it even than his father had ever had. He called to see her regularly, of course he did. But she probably always insisted that he rang her beforehand. No reason to ask why, surely? Simon was completely unaware of his mother's vespertinal divertissements.

But Frank certainly knew all about them, and they served as some sort of excuse and justification for his own adulterous liaisons. He didn't much care anyway. Perhaps he could shrug things off fairly easily. But Simon couldn't. Simon turned up unexpectedly one evening and found his mother lying on that very same bed where as a young boy (perhaps as an older boy?) he'd snuggled in beside her when his dad was away; and where he'd seen a man straddled across her on his elbows and his knees.

I doubt it had been exactly like that, though. More likely he'd seen a man bouncing down the stairs towards him, jerking up his trousers and fastening up his flies. A man he knew: Barron! Then he'd found his mother lying in the bedroom there: naked, gagged, handcuffed, with a pornographic video probably still running on the TV. Shell-shocked with disbelief and disillusionment, in the white heat of a furious jealousy – yes! – *he murdered his mother.*

Chapter Sixty-Six

We might now be stepping through a dark door with no bottom on the other side, and fall flat on our faces

(A member of the Honolulu City Council, quoted by the Press Corps)

Conscious that he was writing with increasing fluency, Morse poured himself another tumbler of single malt, and resumed his narrative:

With regard to events immediately thereafter, we can only guess. But at some point Simon rang his father in predictable panic. He had very few people he could call on. But he *could* call on his father – and there was a special loop-system on the telephone there. And Frank H got to the house as quickly as any man could have done that night. His BMW *was* in for servicing, that was checked; and I now believe (a bit late in the day) that the sequence of events was precisely as he claimed: taxi → Paddington; train → Oxford; Oxford (enter Flynn!) → Lower Swinstead.

Then? Probably we'll never really know. But five people, three of them now dead, *they* knew: Barron, who'd been disturbed *in medio coitu*; Flynn, the petty crook who just happened to be on hand; Repp, the burglar who'd been watching the property all evening; Frank H; and Simon H himself. Simon doesn't seem to me the calibre of fellow who could stay long at such a ghastly scene on his own; and I think it's more than likely that his father rang Sarah and told her to get along there post-haste, on the way buying a cinema ticket as an alibi for Simon. Certainly when I met Sarah I felt strongly that she probably knew who had murdered her mother. The trouble was that the three outsiders also knew: Repp and Barron, who were both local men – and Flynn, who'd met Simon in the lip-reading classes at Oxpens, and who must have seen him there that night.

What then was the family plan of campaign?

The two (or three) of them were determined to create the maximum amount of confusion – their only hope. The murder couldn't be concealed; but the waters around it could be made so muddied that any investigation was likely to shoot off into several blind alleys. We may postulate that a gag was tied around Yvonne's mouth (as I recall the report: 'no longer tight as if she had worked it looser in her desperation'); that a pair of handcuffs was snapped around her wrists; that one of the panes of the french window was smashed in from the outside. Why Yvonne's carefully folded clothes were not scattered all over the floor, I just don't know, because 'attempted rape' would have seemed a wholly probable explanation of the murder.

When and how the circling vultures closed in for

their shares of the kill – your guess, Lewis, is (almost) as good as mine. Some early liaison there must have been with Barron in order to establish the telephone alibi. Flynn probably just stayed around that night – a petty crook going through a bad patch, and naming his price immediately. I suspect that Repp, a real pro, held his hand for a couple of days or so before threatening to spill at least half the can of beans . . . unless he could be persuaded otherwise.

Whatever the case, financial arrangements were made, and as far as we know faithfully met. After the murder of his wife, much money was diverted from the assets of Frank H into other channels, although I'm still surprised to learn that there may well have been some serious misappropriation of funds at the Swiss Helvetia Bank.

All of which leaves one or two (or three!) points unresolved.

First, the burglar alarm. Now on his train-trip from London Frank H must have had thoughts galore. Several times he would have phoned home from the train, and *Sarah* must surely have been there to take the calls. And it was probably from the back of the taxi that Frank had the clever idea of ringing Sarah and telling her he would be ringing again, when the taxi was only half a minute or so from home, and asking her (Flynn wouldn't have heard, would he?) to turn on the burglar alarm. It *was* a clever idea, let's agree on that. It certainly and understandably caused huge confusion in the original police enquiry. The only person not wholly confused was Strange. It was he, from the word go, who suggested that the alarm might well have been set off deliberately by the murderer himself. (Never under-rate that man, Lewis!)

The time, as Morse saw, was 3.40 a.m., almost exactly one hour after he'd started writing. He was feeling pleasantly tired, and he knew he would slip into sleep so easily now. Yet he wanted to go (as Flecker had said) 'always that little further'; and perhaps more immediately to the point he wanted to pour himself a further Scotch – which he did before resuming.

There is one more thing to consider, and it is of vital importance, as well as being (almost!) the only thing about which I was less than honest with you. That is, the extraordinary relationship between a drink-doped, drug-doped juvenile lout and an insignificant-looking little schoolma'am: between Roy Holmes and Christine Coverley. Something must have happened, probably at school, which had forged a wholly improbable but strangely strong bond between them – including a sexual relationship (she confessed as much). That's the reason she stayed on in Burford after the end of the summer term. Why is this important? Because we have been making one fundamental assumption in our enquiries which thus far has been completely unverified by any single independent witness. But truth will out! And first, and forthwith, we shall call in on Ms

Coverley for further questioning. How wise it was to hold our horses before facing Frank Harrison with a whole

(Here the narrative breaks off.)

Morse, who had been deeply asleep at his study desk, his head pillowed on folded arms, jerked awake just before 7.30 a.m., feeling wonderfully refreshed.

Life was a funny old business.

Chapter Sixty-Seven

To run away from trouble is a form of cowardice; and, whilst it is true that the suicide braves death, he does it not for some noble object but to escape some ill

(Aristotle, *Nicomachean Ethics*)

THE FOLLOWING MORNING Lewis was pleased with himself. Before Morse arrived, he'd turned to the *Police Gazette*'s 'Puzzle Corner', and easily solved the challenge there:

> What initially would an intelligent cyclist's thought be on studying the following list of operas by Verdi?
>
> *Tosca*
> *Aida*
> *Nabucco*
> *Don Carlos*
> *Ernani*
> *Macbeth*

'Initially' – that was the clue; and once you twigged it, the answer stared you in the face vertically.

Morse made an appearance at 9.10 a.m., looking (in Lewis's view) a little fitter than of late.

'Want to test your brain, sir?'

'Certainly not!'

Lewis pushed the puzzle across the desk, and Morse considered it, though for no more than a few seconds:

'Do *you* know the answer?'

'Easy! "Initially", sir – that's what you've got to think about. Just look at the first letters. Cyclist? Get it?'

'I thought the question was what would an *intelligent* cyclist's thought be.'

'I don't quite follow.'

'Not difficult surely, Lewis? You've just got the answer wrong, that's all. Any intelligent cyclist, any bright bus-driver – anyone! – would think exactly the same thing immediately.'

'They would?'

'The *question*'s phoney. Based on a false premise, isn't it? Based on the assumption that the facts you've been given are true.'

'You mean they're not?'

'*Tosca*? Written by *Verdi*?'

Oh dear! 'You were quick to spot that.'

Morse grinned. 'Not really. They often ask me to submit a little brain-teaser to the *Gazette*.'

'You mean—?'

Morse nodded. 'And talking of false premises, that's been a big part of our trouble. We've both been trying to check up on such a lot of things, haven't we? But there's *one* thing we've been prepared to accept without one ha'p'orth of evidence. So we'll get on to that without delay. Couple of cars we'll need. I'll just give Dixon a ring—'

Lewis got to his feet. 'I can deal with all that, sir.'

'Si' down, Lewis! I want to talk to you.'

Through the glass-panelled door Dixon finally saw the silhouette moving towards him: a woman in a wheelchair who brusquely informed him that she knew nothing of the whereabouts of her son. He had not been home the previous evening. He had a key. He was sometimes out all night, yes. No, she didn't know where. And if it was of any interest to the police, she didn't care – didn't bloody well *care*.

There was no reply to PC Kershaw's importunate ringing and knocking. But at last he was able to locate the mildly disgruntled middle-aged woman who looked after the two 'lets'; and who accompanied him back to the ground-floor flat. She appeared to have little affection for either of the two lessees, although when she opened the door she must have felt a horrified shock of sympathy with one of them.

Christine Coverley lay supine on a sheepskin rug in front of an unlit electric-fire. She was wearing a summery, sleeveless, salmon-pink dress, her arms very white, hands palm-upwards, with each of her wrists slashed deeply and neatly across. A black-handled kitchen-knife lay beside her left shoulder.

Young Kershaw was unused to such horrors; and over the next few days the visual image was to refigure repeatedly in his nightmares. Two patches on the rug were deeply steeped in blood; and Kershaw was reminded of the Welsh hill-farm where he'd once stayed and where the backs of each of the owner's sheep had been daubed with a dye of the deepest crimson.

No note was found by Kershaw; indeed no note was found by anyone afterwards. It was as if Christine had left this world with a despair she'd found incommunicable to anyone: even to her parents; even to the uncouth lout who penetrated her so pleasurably now, though at first against her will; even to the rather nice police inspector who'd seemed to her to understand so much about her. Far too much . . . including (she'd known it!) the fact that she had lied. Roy could never have been cycling along Sheep Street when Barron fell to his death because at that very moment he had been in bed with her . . .

Chapter Sixty-Eight

It is not the criminal things which are hardest to confess, but the ridiculous and the shameful

(Rousseau, *Confessions*)

LEWIS HAD NOT been surprised – no, certainly not that. But disappointed? Yes. Oh yes! And Morse had been aware of his reaction, clearly anticipating it, yet saying nothing to lessen the impact of the revelation. The relationship between them would never be quite the same again, Lewis realized that. It wasn't at all the fact that Morse had driven out one evening (two evenings? ten evenings?) to meet a seductively attractive woman. Lewis had seen the sharply focused photographs of her body stretched out on the bed that night; and it could be no great wonder that many a man, young and old alike, had lusted after a woman such as that. No, it was something else. It was the out-of-character, under-hand way that Morse had allowed the dishonest subterfuge to linger on and on from the beginning of the case.

Indeed Morse had been less than wholly forthcoming in his confession even now, Lewis was fairly sure of it. Yes, Morse agreed, he *had* gained access to the file containing the intimate correspondence addressed to Y H. Yes, he *had* 'appropriated' the handcuffs, police handcuffs, with a number stamped on them that could easily be traced back to the officer issued with them, in this case to Morse himself. And yes (he readily admitted it) he *had* 'withdrawn' the relevant sheet of the issue-numbers kept at HQ. As far as the partial letter was concerned (Morse accepted immediately that it was in his own hand) Lewis had hoped, in an old-fashioned sort of way, that Morse had in fact *never* been invited to Lower Swinstead, in spite of his own plea for some communication from her; in spite of that almost schoolboyish business about looking through his mail every morning in the hope of finding something from her. And that was about it. Morse had wanted to cover up something of which he was rather ashamed and very embarrassed; just wanted his own name, previously his own good name, never to be associated with the life – and the death – of Yvonne Harrison. He'd been careless about leaving that single page of a longer letter but (as he asked Lewis to agree) it was hardly an incriminating piece of evidence. What Morse stoutly refused to accept was that what he had done, however cowardly and dishonest and foolish, had in any way jeopardized the course of the original enquiry, which he now had the nerve to assert had been conducted with almost unprecedented incompetence. Such arrogance was of course not all that unusual; yet in the present circumstances it seemed to Lewis quite gratuitously cheap.

Leaving all such considerations aside though, what stuck in Lewis's throat was that initial, duplicitous refusal on Morse's part to have anything to do with the original case. Agreed, once he had been drafted on to what seemed to both Lewis and Strange the second half of the *same* case, Morse had risen to his accustomed heights of logical analysis and depths of human understanding. Agreed, he had (as usual) been several furlongs ahead of the field – and, for once, on the right racecourse from the 'off'.

Who else but Morse could have put forward the quite extraordinary hypotheses made earlier that morning about the murder of J. Barron, Builder? The hypothesis (seemingly confirmed) that Roy Holmes – who'd do almost anything to *get* drugs and who'd do absolutely anything when he was *on* drugs – was having a sexual relationship with Christine Coverley; the hypothesis (seemingly confirmed) that the weirdly incongruous partnership had resulted from some incident or series of incidents at school; that the youth had agreed, for money, to make a statement to the police about a supposedly accidental collision with a high ladder – a statement that was wholly untrue, because Roy Holmes had been nowhere near Sheep Street that morning; the hypothesis (to *be* confirmed!) that it was Frank Harrison who had murdered Barron, and who had engineered an ingenious scheme whereby all suspicion would be diverted both from himself and from Simon – the scheme itself probably prompted by another son, by Allen Thomas, who regularly gathered a good deal of information from his vantage-point in the Maiden's Arms and who regularly passed it on to his father, the man at the centre of everything.

Lewis nodded to himself. No wonder Frank Harrison had gone to earth somewhere. Not for long though, surely. He had nowhere to go; nowhere to hide. Airports and seaports had been apprised of his passport number, and photographs would be on their way. Unless it was too late.

It was Morse's suggestion that the two of them together should interview Roy Holmes and Christine Coverley, with Lewis invited to do most of the talking with the youth. 'I detest him, Lewis! And you're better at that sort of things than I am.' It was flattering, but it didn't work. Morse was sadly wrong if he thought he could so easily re-establish some degree of integrity in the eyes of his sergeant.

In mid-morning, Lewis left the office without asking Morse if he would like a coffee. He knew that the omission would be noted; he knew that Morse would feel the hurt.

Not so.

When Lewis returned ten minutes later, he found Morse leaning back and beaming happily.

'Fetch me a coffee, will you, Lewis! No sugar – we diabetics, you know . . . Something to celebrate.' *The Times* was folded back in quarters in front of him, the crossword-grid completely filled in. 'Six and a half minutes! I've never done it quicker.'

'Shouldn't that be "more quickly"?'

'Good man! You're learning at last. You see it's a question, as I've told you, of the comparative adjective and the comparative adverb. If you say—'

The phone rang.

Dixon.

For the moment Roy Holmes was not to be found: he wasn't at home; he wasn't anywhere. Did Morse want him to keep looking?

'What the hell do you think?' Morse had snapped at him. 'You remember the old proverb? If at first you don't succeed, don't take up hang-gliding.'

The brief telephone conversation pleased Lewis, and for a few seconds he wondered if he was being a little unfair in his judgement on Morse. But only for a few seconds.

'Not the only one we can't find, sir.'

'Frank Harrison, you mean? Ye-es. I'm a bit puzzled about him. He might be a crook – he *is* a crook – but he's not a fool. He's an experienced, hard-nosed, single-minded, rich banker, and if you're all those things you don't suddenly put your fingers in the—'

The phone rang.

Kershaw.

Morse listened, saying nothing; but the eyes that lifted to look across the desk into Lewis's face, if not wholly surprised, seemed very disappointed and very sad. Much as two hours earlier Lewis's own eyes had looked.

In mid-afternoon (Morse was no longer at HQ) the phone rang.

Swiss Helvetia Bank.

'Could we speak to Superintendent Lewis, please?'

'Sergeant Lewis speaking.'

Chapter Sixty-Nine

Sec. Off.:	Antonio, I arrest thee at the suit of Count Orsino.
Ant.:	You do mistake me, sir.
First Off.:	No, sir, no jot.

(Shakespeare, *Twelfth Night*)

At 5.20 p.m. he was still standing beside his minimal hand-luggage a few yards from the Euro-Class counter at Heathrow's Terminal 4, looking around him with as yet dismissable anxiety, but with gradually increasing impatience. 5.10 p.m. – that was when they'd agreed to meet, giving them ample time, once through the fast-track channel, to have some gentle relaxation together in the British Airways Lounge before boarding the 18.30 Flight 338.

Paris . . .

A long time ago he and Yvonne had gone to Paris on their honeymoon: lots of love, lots of sex, lots of sightseeing, lots of food and wine. A whole fortnight of it, although he'd known even then that just a week of it would have been rather better. It was not difficult (he already knew it well) to get bored even in the presence of a mistress; and he'd begun to realize on that occasion that it was perfectly possible to grow just a little wearied even in the company of a newly wed wife. There had been one or two incidents, too, when he'd thought Yvonne was experiencing similar thoughts . . . especially that time one evening when she'd quite obviously been exchanging long looks with a moustachioed Frenchman who looked exactly like Proust. He'd called her 'a flirtatious bitch' when they got to their hotel room; and when she'd glared back at him and told him they'd make a 'bloody good pair' one way or another . . .

There would be no trouble like that with Maxine: only two and a half days – just right, that! And she was a real honey, a law professor from Yale, aged forty-two, divorced, a little over-sexed, a little overweight, and hugely desirable.

She finally appeared, pulling an inordinately large suitcase on wheels.

'You're late!' His tone was a combination of anger and relief; and he immediately moved forward ahead of her to the back of the short queue at the First-Class counter.

'You didn't get my message, did you? I tried and tried—'

'Like I told you? On the mobile?'

'It wasn't working. I think you'd forgotten—'

'Christ!' Harrison took his mobile from an inside pocket, tapped a few digits, then another few; then repeated the blasphemy: 'Christ! I'd had enough of the bloody mobile recently and—'

'And you forgot that we'd agreed—'

'Sorry! Say you'll forgive me!'

He looked down at her squarish, slightly prognathic face, her dark-brown silky hair cut short in a fringe across her broad forehead and above the quietly gentle eyes that were becoming tearful now, perhaps from her hectic rush, perhaps from the undeserved brusqueness of his greeting, but perhaps above all from the knowledge that his love for her homodyned only with the waves of that physical lust which so often excited him. Yet the brief holiday had been *her* choice, and she knew that she wouldn't regret having made it. She enjoyed being with him: he was good fun and intelligent and well read and still handsome and still excellent in bed and – yes! – he was rich.

They moved nearer the counter, neither of them too anxious to speak – a phenomenon not uncommon with persons queuing, as if their concentration were required for the transactions ahead. But she volunteered some incidental information:

'Accident there was, near Stokenchurch, and I tried to—'

Gently he ran a hand through her silken hair. 'Sweetheart? Forget it!'

'It's just that we must have been stuck there half an hour and we saw – one of the other passengers pointed it out – a beautiful bird of prey there. A red kite.'

'Tell me later!'

There was now just the one business-suited man in front of them.

'Where have you booked us?'

'The best.'

'And the best air-tickets—?'

'Sh! Nothing but the best for you. Why not? Just think of me! No wife. No blackmailing kids. No problems at work. Nothing to spend money on for a day or two – except on you. I'm a rich man, sweetheart. I thought I'd told you.'

'Tickets, please?'

The smiling young lady scrutinized the perfectly valid tickets.

'Passports, please?'

The young lady scrutinized the perfectly valid passports.

'Smoking?'

'Non-smoking.'

'Window-centre? Centre-aisle?'

'Centre-aisle.'

'Luggage?'

Frank Harrison lugged the great case on to the trackway beside the desk.

'Only the one?'

'Yes.'

'You know where the club-lounge is?'

'Yes.'

'Enjoy your flight, sir, and enjoy your stay in Paris!'

He handed her a glass of champagne, and two glasses clinked. 'Here's to a wonderful little break together. Ritz – here we come!'

He leaned across and kissed her on the soft, unlip-sticked mouth – a long, yearning kiss. His eyes closed. Her eyes closed.

'Mr Harrison?' A tap on the shoulder. 'Mr Frank Harrison?'

'What—?'

A uniformed police officer stood beside the small table: 'I'm sorry, sir, but we need to speak to you. Routine check.'

'Thames Valley Police, is this?'

'That's right, sir.'

'What exactly—?'

'It's not *just* that. Your employers want to speak to you as well.'

Harrison's eyes squinted in bewilderment.

'What the hell do *they* want? I'm on official furlough, for God's sake. They'll have to wait till I get back.'

'Will you come this way, sir? Please!'

A second uniformed policeman – young, dark-haired – stood just inside the entrance to the executive lounge; was still standing there a quarter of an hour later when Maxine, after drinking the one and then the other glass of champagne, went over to speak to him.

'Do you mind telling me, Officer, by whose authority—?'

'Not mine, miss,' said PC Kershaw. 'Please believe me. I also am a man *under* authority.'

'You haven't answered my question.'

'I'm from Thames Valley – we both are.'

'Who sent you here?'

'The CID.'

'Who?'

'Chief Inspector Morse.'

'Who's he when he's in his office?'

'He's an important man.'

'Very important?'

'Oh yes!' Kershaw nodded with a reverential smile.

'You talk as if he's God Almighty.'

'Some people think he is.'

'Do you?'

'Not always.'

'How long will you be keeping Mr Harrison?'

'I just don't know, Mrs Ridgway.'

Maxine poured herself a further glass of champagne, and pondered as she sat alone at the small table. They knew *her* name too . . .

He wasn't a particularly lucky man to associate with, Frank Harrison. The last time she'd been with him, over a year ago, he'd had that phone call from – well, he'd never said who from – to tell him that his wife had been murdered . . .

She was tempted to get up and – well, just leave. Just get out of there. Her case was on the plane by now though – suits, dresses, lingerie, shoes – but it *could* be returned perhaps? She still had her handbag with its far more important items: cards, keys, diary, money . . .

But she felt sure the PC at the door would never let her out. That's why he was there. Why else?

An announcement over the lounge Tannoy informed her that first-class passengers for British Airways Flight 338 to Paris should now proceed to Gate 3; and a dozen or so people were draining their drinks and gathering up their hand luggage. But for Maxine Ridgway it was now a feeling of deep sadness that had overtaken those earlier minutes of indecision and despair. She was no fool. She knew by heart the rôle she'd been asked to play in the Ritz; and she'd accepted the bargain, because it *would* have been a bargain.

She was not even bothering to wonder what she should do next when she heard the voice behind her: 'Come on, sweetheart! You heard the announcement. Gate 3.'

With her mind in a mingled state of amazement and relief, she picked up her hand luggage and followed him to the exit-doors, where there was now no sign of PC Kershaw, the man who had seemed to have a greater familiarity with Holy Writ than she had herself.

'Routine check, that's all,' asserted Frank Harrison. 'Just like the man said.'

Chapter Seventy

I cried for madder music and for stronger wine,
But when the feast is finished and the lamps expire,
Then falls thy shadow, Cynara! the night is thine;
And I am desolate and sick of an old passion,
Yea hungry for the lips of my desire:
I have been faithful to thee, Cynara! in my fashion
(Dowson, *Non Sum Qualis Eram*
Bonae Sub Regno Cynarae)

'LET HIM GO, Kershaw. Let him catch his flight.'

'You think that's wise, sir?'

'*What?*'

'I just wondered—'

'Look, lad! If I ever have to look to you as a fount of wisdom, it'll be the day you're dry behind the ears. Is that clear?'

'Sir!'

Morse put down the phone. It was 6.10 p.m.

'Do you think that was fair, sir?' asked Lewis.

'Probably not,' conceded Morse.

It had been Lewis, an hour earlier, who had received the call from the Bank: profound apology; embarrassing recantation; chagrin unspeakable! Over £500,000 indeed was still unaccountably missing; but not, *not* from Harrison's department. Enquiries subsequent to Lewis's visit had now established that any embezzlement or misappropriation of funds was most definitely not to be laid at the door of one of the Bank's most experienced, most trusted, most valued blah blah blah.

It was a call in which Morse was most interested, now repeating (with some self-congratulation) what he had earlier maintained: that Frank Harrison might well be, most likely *was*, capable of murder; but that it was quite out of character, definitely *infra dignitatem*, for him to stoop to cooking the books and fiddling the balance-and-loss ledgers.

'Do you think you may be wrong, sir?'

'Certainly not. He'll be back from Paris, believe me! There's no hiding-place for him. Not from me, there isn't.'

'You think he murdered his wife?'

'No. But he knows who did. *You* know who did. But we've got to get some evidence. We've been checking alibis – recent ones. But we've got to check those earlier alibis again.'

'Who are you thinking of?'

'Of whom am I thinking?' (Morse recalled the suspicion he'd voiced in his earlier notes.) 'I'm thinking of the only other person apart from Frank Harrison who had a sufficient motive to kill Yvonne.'

'You mean—?'

'Do you ever go to the pictures?'

'They don't call it the "pictures" any more.'

'I went to the pictures a year and a bit ago to see *The Full Monty*.'

'Surely not your sort of—?'

'*Exactly* my sort of thing. I laughed and I cried.'

'Oh yes.' (The penny had dropped.) 'Simon Harrison said he'd gone—'

' "Said", yes.'

'Said he'd gone with someone else, didn't he? A girlfriend.'

'Wasn't checked though, as far as I can see.'

'Understandable, isn't it? Nobody ever really thought of someone inside the family—'

'Oh yes they did. Frank Harrison was one of their first suspects.'

'But with those signs of burglary, the broken window, the burglar alarm . . .'

Morse nodded. 'At first almost everything pointed to an outside job. But then it slowly began to look like something else: a lover, a tryst, a sex-session, a quarrel, a murder . . .'

'And now we're coming back to the family, you say.'

'No one seems to have bothered to get a statement from the young lady Simon Harrison took to the pictures that evening.'

'Perhaps we could still trace her, sir?'

'Yes.'

'It's a long time ago though. She'd never remember—'

'Of course she would! It was all over the papers: "Woman Murdered" – and she'd been with that same woman's son the evening when it happened. She could never forget it!'

'It's still a long time—'

'Lewis! I don't eat all that much as you know. But when I'm cooking for myself – '

(Lewis's eyebrows rose.)

' – I always make sure the plate's hot. I can't abide eating off a cold plate.'

'You mean we could heat the plate up again?'

'The plate's already hot again. She's still around. She's a proud, married mum now living in Witney.'

'How do you know all that?'

'You can't do *everything* yourself, Lewis.'

'Dixon, you mean?'

'Good man, Dixon! So we're going to see her tonight. Just you and I.'

'You think Simon murdered his mum.'

'No doubt about that. Not any longer, Lewis,' said Morse quietly.

'Just because he found her in bed with someone . . .'

'With Barron. I *know* that, Lewis.'

Never before had Lewis been so hesitant in asking Morse a question:

'Did . . . did Mrs Harrison ever tell *you* that she was . . . seeing Barron?'

Morse hesitated – hesitated for far too long.

'No. No, she never told me that.'

Lewis waited a while, choosing his words carefully and speaking them slowly: 'If she *had* told you, would *you* have been as jealous as Simon Harrison?'

Again Morse hesitated. 'Jealousy is a dreadfully corrosive thing. The most powerful motive of all, in my view, for murder – more powerful than—'

The phone rang once more and Morse answered.

Kershaw.

'They'll soon be winging their way across the channel, sir. Anything more you want me to do?'

'Yes. Have a pint of beer, just the one, then bugger off home.'

Morse put down the phone.

'Good man, Kershaw! Bit of an old woman though. Reminds me of my Aunt Gladys in Alnwick, my last remaining relative. Well, she was. Dead now.'

'I think he'll do well, yes.'

'Kershaw? Should do. He got a First in History from Keble.'

'Bit more than me, sir.'

'Bit more than me, Lewis.'

The phone was ringing again.

Strange.

'Morse? You've let him out of the country, I hear?'

'Yes. We need a bit more time and a bit more evidence before we bring him in.'

'I agree,' said Strange, unexpectedly. 'No good just . . .'

'He'll be back for the day of reckoning.'

'You think so?'

'I know so.'

'And in the interim?'

'He'll be having a beano – kisses, wine, roses. "But when the feast is finished and the lamps expire . . ." You know the Dowson poem, sir?'

'Course I bloody do!'

'Well, I don't think he'll ever be really happy with any of these other women of his.'

'This one sounds like a bit of all right though.'

'I'd still like to bet he wakes up in the small hours sometimes and thinks back on the woman he loved more than any of them, feeling a bit desolate – '

' – and sick of an old passion.'

'Exactly.'

'Yvonne, you mean?'

'No, not Yvonne, sir. Elizabeth – Elizabeth Jane Thomas.'

Chapter Seventy-One

What more pleasant setting than the cinema for sweetly deodorized bodies to meet, unzip, and commune?

(Malcolm Muggeridge,
The Most of Malcolm Muggeridge)

Sylvia Marsden (née Prentice) was temporarily living with her mother in a pleasantly appointed semi on a housing estate at Witney. And it was her mother (Lewis had phoned earlier) who had answered the door and shown the two detectives into the lounge where the buxom Sylvia, blouse open, was breast-feeding a very new baby – not in the slightest degree disconcerted to be thus interrupted in her maternal ministrations, one hand splayed across an engorged nipple, the fingers of the other playing lovingly around the lips of the suckling infant.

An awkwardly embarrassed Morse moved slowly round the room, simulating deep interest in the tasteless bric-a-brac that cluttered every surface and shelf in the brightly decorated room; whilst Lewis stood above the mother and child, smiling quasi-paternally and drawing the back of his right index-finger lightly across the cherubic cheek:

'Little treasure, isn't he? What's his name?'

'She's a she, actually – aren't you, Susie?'

'Ah yes, of course!'

Morse temporarily declined to take a seat but accepted, strangely enough, the offer of coffee, and began his questioning whilst looking through the window on to the neatly kept back garden.

'We're just having to make one or two further enquiries, Mrs Marsden—'

'Call me Sylvia!'

'It's about one of your former boyfriends—'

'Simon, yes, I know. That Sergeant Dixon told me. Nice man, isn't he? He got on ever so well with Mum.'

Morse nodded, aware of the probable reason. 'It's a long time ago now, I realize . . .'

'Not really. Not for me it isn't. The night Simon's mum was murdered? Can't forget something like that, can you?'

'That's good news, Sylvia. Now that night, that evening, the 9th—'

'Oh no! You've got it wrong. It was the 8th – the night Mrs Harrison was murdered. I'm quite sure of that. My birthday, wasn't it? Simon took me to the ABC in Oxford. Super film! All about these male strippers—'

'Did the police ever ask you about it?'

'No. Why should they?'

Sylvia rebuttoned her blouse, and as Morse turned at last to face her, Lewis could see the disappointment on his face.

Mrs Prentice (née Jones) who had clearly been listening keenly from the adjacent kitchen, now brought in two cups of coffee. 'I can remember that,' she volunteered. 'Like she says, that was your birthday, wasn't it, Sylv?'

'How did you find Simon, Mrs Prentice?' asked Lewis.

'I liked him. He used to come in sometimes but I think he felt a bit . . . you know, with his hearing.'

'He didn't come in that night?'

'No. I remember it well. Like Sylv says – well, not something you forget, is it? I saw him though, after he'd brought her back. And I heard the pair of 'em whispering on the doorstep. Nice boy, really. Could have done worse, couldn't you, Sylv?'

'I did *better*, Mum, OK?'

Clearly there was less than complete family agreement on the merits of baby Susie's official father and Morse swallowed his coffee quickly and, as ever, Lewis followed his chief's lead dutifully.

In the car outside they sat for some time in silence.

'You knew it was the 8th, sir. Why—?'

'Just to test her memory.'

There was another long silence.

'Looks as if we've been wrong, sir.'

'Looks as if *I've* been wrong.'

'Alibis don't come much better than that.'

'No.'

'You know when Mrs Whatshername said she heard the pair of 'em whispering outside, she probably heard more of the conversation than Simon ever did!'

Morse nodded with a wry grin. 'You don't think there's any chance that somebody bribed our Sylvia and Sylvia's mum . . . ?'

'Not the remotest. Do you?'

'No.'

'Where do we go from here, sir?'

'You can drop me off at the Woodstock Arms or . . .'

'No. I meant with the *case*, sir.'

'. . . or perhaps the Maiden's Arms.'

It seemed that Morse was hardly listening.

'I know you're disappointed, sir, but—'

'Disappointed? Nonsense!'

Some light-footed mouse had just scuttled across his scapulae; and when Lewis turned to look at him, it seemed as if someone had switched the electric current on behind his eyes.

'Yes, Lewis. Just drive me out to Lower Swinstead.'

Chapter Seventy-Two

Below me, there is the village, and looks how quiet and small!
And yet bubbles o'er like a city, with gossip, scandal, and spite

(Tennyson, *Maud*)

UNWONTEDLY IN A car, Morse was almost continuously talkative as they drove along: 'Do you know that lovely line of Thomson's about villages "embosomed soft in trees"?'

'Don't even know Thomson,' mumbled Lewis.

'Remarkable things! Strange, intimate little places where there's more going on than anybody ever dreams of. You get illicit liaisons, hopeless love affairs, illegitimate offspring, wife-swopping, interbreeding, neighbourly spite, class warfare – all that's for the insiders, though. If you're on the outside, they refuse to have anything to do with you. They clamp up. They present a united defensive front because they've got one thing in common, Lewis: the village itself. They're all members of the same football club. They may loathe each other's guts for most of the week, but come Saturday afternoon when they put on the same football shirts . . . Well, the next village better look out!'

'Except Lower Swinstead doesn't have a football team.'

'What are you talking about? They're *all* in the football team.'

Lewis drove down the Windrush Valley into Lower Swinstead.

'They don't all clamp up, anyway. Not to you, they don't. Compared with some of our lads you've squeezed a carton of juice out of 'em already.'

'But there's more squeezing to do, Lewis – just a little.'

Unwontedly in a pub, Morse had already taken out his wallet at the bar, and Lewis raised no objection.

'Pint of bitter – whatever's in the best nick.'

'It's all in the best nick,' began Biffen.

'And . . . orange or grapefruit, Lewis?'

The fruit machine stood idle and the cribbage-board was slotted away behind the bar. But the place was quite busy. Most of the customers were locals; most of them people who'd earlier been questioned about the Harrison murder; most of them members of the village team.

On the pub's noticeboard at the side of the bar, underneath 'Live Music Every Saturday', was an amateurishly printed yellow poster advertising the current week's entertainment:

8.30–11.30 p.m.
DON'T MISS IT
The widely acclaimed folk-singer
CYNDI COOK
with the ever popular
3 R's
Randy, Ray, Rick

'Popular?' asked Morse of the landlord.

'Packed out we are, every Sat'day.'

'Ever had Paddy Flynn and his group playing here?'

'Paddy who?'

'Flynn – the chap who was murdered.'

'Ah yes. Read about it, o'course. But I don't think he were ever here, Inspector. You know, fifty-odd groups a year and – how many years is it I've—'

'Forget it!' snapped Morse.

'The beer OK?'

'Fine. How's Bert, by the way? Any better?'

'Worse. Quack called to see him yesterday – just after we'd opened – told Bert's boy the old man oughta go in for a few days, like – but Bert told 'em he wasn't going to die in no hospital.'

For someone who knew almost nothing about some things, Thomas Biffen seemed to know an awful lot about others.

'Where does he live?' asked Morse.

*

It was Bert's son, a man already in his late fifties, who showed Morse up the narrow steepish steps to the bedroom where Bert himself lay, propped up against pillows, the backs of his hands, purple-veined and deeply foxed, resting on the top of the sheet.

'Missing the cribbage, I bet!' volunteered Morse.

The old face, yellowish and gaunt, lit up a little. 'Alf'll be glad of a rest. Hah!' He chuckled deeply in his throat. 'Lost these last five times, he has.'

'You're a bit under the weather, they tell me.'

'Still got me wits about me though. More'n Alf has sometimes.'

'Still got a good memory, you mean?'

'Allus had a good memory since I were at school.'

'Mind if I ask you a few things? About the village? You know . . . gossip, scandal . . . that sort of thing? I had a few words with Alf, but I reckon his memory's not as sharp as yours.'

'Never was, was it? Just you fire away, Inspector. Pleasure!'

Lewis, who had been left in the car, leaned across and opened the passenger door.

'Another member of the local football team?'

Morse smiled sadly and shook his head. 'I think he's in for a transfer.'

'What exactly did he—?'

'Get me home, Lewis.'

*

On the speedy journey back to Oxford, the pair spoke only once, and then in a fairly brief exchange:

'Listen, Lewis! We know exactly where Frank Harrison is; who's with him; how long he's booked in at his hotel; when his return flight is. So. I want you to make sure he's met at Heathrow.'

'If he comes back.'

'He'll be back. I want *you* to meet him. Charge him with anything you like, complicity in the murder of his missus; complicity in the murder of Barron – please yourself. Anything! But bring him back to me, all right? I've seldom looked forward—'

Morse suddenly rubbed his chest vigorously.

'You OK, sir?'

Morse made no reply immediately. But after a few miles had perked up considerably.

'Just drop me at the Woodstock Arms!'

'Do you think—?'

'And present my apologies to Mrs Lewis. As per usual.'

Lewis nodded as he turned right at the Woodstock Road roundabout.

As per usual.

In Paris, in the Ritz, later that same evening – a good deal later – Maxine Ridgway was finding it difficult to finish the lobster dish and almost impossible to drink another mouthful of the expensive white wine that looked to her exactly the colour and gravity of urine. She was tired; she was more than a little tipsy; she was slightly less than breathlessly eager for another bout of sexual frolicking on their king-size bed. And Frank, too, (she'd sensed it all evening) had been strangely reticent and surprisingly sober.

She braved the exchange: 'You're not quite your usual self tonight, Frank.'

'Why do you say that?'

'It's that business at Heathrow, isn't it?'

Frank leaned across the table and placed his right hand on her arm. 'I'll be OK soon, sweetheart. Don't worry! And I ought to tell you something: you're looking absolutely gorgeous!'

'You think so?'

'Why do you reckon all the waiters keep making detours round our table?'

'Tell me!'

'To have a look down the front of your dress.'

'Don't be silly!'

'You hadn't noticed?'

'Frank! It's been a long day – and I'm just so tired . . . so tired.'

'Not *too* tired, I hope? *Nicht zu müde*?'

'No, darling.'

'You don't want a sweet? A coffee?'

'No.'

'Well, you go up. I'll be with you soon. I've just got a couple of private phone calls to make. And I want to think for a little while – on my own, if you don't mind? And make sure you put that see-through thing on, all right? The one that'll send the garçon ga-ga when he brings our breakfast in the morning.'

'You've arranged that?'

Frank Harrison nodded; and watched the backs of her legs as she left the table.

Yes, he'd arranged for breakfast in their room.

He'd arranged everything.

Almost.

CHAPTER SEVENTY-THREE

When I have fears that I may cease to be
Before my pen has glean'd my teeming brain . . .
(Keats, *Sonnet*)

SLOWLY MORSE WALKED homeward from the Woodstock Arms, disappointed (as we have seen) if not wholly surprised, that the favourite in the Harrison Stakes had fallen (like Devon Loch) within sight of the winning-post. But now, at last (or so he told himself) Morse guessed the whole truth. And feeling pleasingly over-beered, he had earlier taken the unusual step of ordering a bar snack, and had enjoyed his liberally horse-radished beef sandwiches. He thought he would probably sleep well enough that night. After a while. Not just for a minute though. Truth was that he felt eager to continue (to finish off?) the notes he'd already been making on the Harrison murder, just in case something happened; just in case no one would be aware of the sweetly logical solution that had formulated itself in his mind that day.

Much earlier (Morse knew it) he should have paid far more attention to the thing that had puzzled him most about the Harrison murder: *motive.* Until now, Simon had fitted that bill pretty well, since Morse was sure that the mother–son relationship had been very close; much *too* close. Good thinking, that! Then, that very afternoon, a busty lusty lass sitting with Simon in the three-and-sixpennies had innocently scuppered his carefully considered scheme of things.

Once home, Morse poured himself a modestly liberal measure of Glenfiddich, and changed into a gaudily striped pair of pyjamas that blossomed in white and purple and red . . . before continuing, indeed completing, his written record.

This evening in Lower Swinstead I spoke at quite some length with Mr Bert Bagshaw. Why did I not follow my first instincts? Had I done so, I would have realized that any clues to that (most elusive) motivation for the murder of Yvonne Harrison would ever be likely to lie in the immediate locality itself, rather than in some external rape or alien burglary. Hardy's yokels usually knew all about the goings on in the Wessex villages; and their rôle is paralleled today by the likes of the Alfs and the Berts in the Cotswold public houses. Although I now know who murdered Yvonne Harrison, it will not be easy to prove the guilt of the accused party. I am reminded of the Greek philosopher Protagoras, who found it difficult to be dogmatic about the existence of the gods, partly because of the obscurity of the subject matter, and partly because of the brevity of human life.

But herewith I give my final thoughts on the murder of Yvonne Harrison, that crisply uniformed nurse who looked after me in hospital once (but once!) with such tempting, loving care . . .

He finished writing an hour later at 12.45 a.m.

Or perhaps, to be accurate, he wrote no more thereafter.

At which hour Lewis was somewhat uneasily asleep, not at all sure in his mind whether things were going well or going ill. Morse had insisted that it should be he, Lewis, who would be on hand when Frank Harrison and his lady passed through Arrivals at Heathrow. No problem there though. Still thirty-six hours to go before the scheduled British Airways flight was due to land, and Morse had been adamant that Harrison *would* be on that flight, and not flitting off to Kathmandu or the Cayman Islands. Yet one thing was ever troublously disturbing Lewis's thoughts: the real nature of the puzzling and secret relationship that had clearly existed between Morse and Yvonne Harrison.

Chapter Seventy-Four

We are adhering to life now with our last muscle – the heart

(Djuna Barnes, *Nightwood*)

Morse awoke at 2.15 a.m., his forehead wet with sweat, an excruciating ache along the whole of his left arm running up as far as his neck and jaw, a tightly constricting corselet of pain around his chest. He managed to reach the bathroom sink where he vomited copiously. Thence, in pathetically slow degrees, he negotiated the stairs, one by one – finally reaching the ground-floor telephone, where he dialled 999, and in a remarkably steady voice selected the first of the Ambulance Fire Police options. He was seated on the lime-green carpet beside the front door, its Yale lock and bolts now opened, when the ambulance arrived six minutes later.

It all happened so quickly.

After being attached to a portable heart-monitor, after a pain-killing injection, after chewing an aspirin, after having his blood pressure taken, Morse found himself lying, contentedly almost, eyes open, on a stretcher in the back of the ambulance.

Beside him a paramedic was looking down with well-disguised anxiety at the ghastly pallor of the face and the lips of a purple-blue: 'We'll just get the docs to have a look at you. We'll soon be there. Don't worry.'

Morse closed his eyes, conscious that life had always been a bit of a worry and seemed to have every likelihood of so continuing now . . .

He should perhaps have rung Lewis from upstairs – Lewis had a flat-key – instead of ringing 999.

But then, he realized, Lewis wouldn't have had all that medical equipment, now would he?

He'd been a little disappointed that he'd heard no ambulance siren.

But then, he realized, there wouldn't be all that much traffic, even in Oxford, at such an early hour, now would there?

Soon, he knew it, they'd be asking for his 'Religion'.

But then, he realized, it wouldn't take too long for him (or them) to write down 'None' in some appropriate box, now would it?

'Next of Kin', too. Trickier that though, because the penultimate member of the Morse clan had recently died, aged ninety-two.

But then it wouldn't take too long to write down 'None' again.

And there were more cheerful things to contemplate. Perhaps Nurse Harrison would be there in the ward again to sit by his bed in the small hours . . .

But then, he realized, Yvonne Harrison was now dead.

Perhaps Sister McQueen would be on duty to pull him through again?

But then, he realized, she was away for a month in far Carlisle, tending a frail, demanding mother.

The kindly paramedic held him down gently as he tried to sit up on the stretcher.

'Lewis! I must see Sergeant Lewis.'

'Of course. We'll make sure you see him as soon as they've had a quick look at you. We're nearly there.'

The night nurse in the 'goldfish-bowl', at the right of the Emergencies Entrance, watched as the automatic double-doors opened and the paramedics wheeled the latest casualty through, deciding immediately that Resuscitation Room B was the place for the newcomer. Quickly she bleeped the Senior House Officer.

The next ten minutes saw swift and methodical action: blood samples were promptly despatched somewhither; chest X-rays were taken; an electrocardiograph test had firmly established that the patient had suffered a hefty anterior myocardial infarct. But it was time for another move; and the activities of a young and kindly nurse with a clipboard, dutifully requesting details of medical history, next of kin, religion, and the like, were mercifully cut short by a specialist nurse who with all speed supervised an urgent transfer.

Morse had always delighted in sesquipedalian terminology, since his education in the Classics had given him much insight into the etymology of words more than a foot-and-a-half long. And now, as he lay in the Coronary Care Unit, he listened with interest to the words being spoken around him: thrombolysis;

tachycardia, strepto-something-something. One thing was certain: much was happening and was happening quickly again. As if there were little time to spare . . .

Were angels male or female? They'd started off life as male, surely? So there must have been a sort of trans-sexual interim when . . . Morse's mind was wondering . . . What gender was the Angel of Death then, whom he now saw standing at the right-hand side of his bed, with a nurse holding one gently restraining hand on a softly feathered wing, and the other hand on his own shoulder.

Morse awoke to full consciousness again, opened his eyes, and found Lewis's hand on his shoulder.

'Sorry to disturb you, sir.'

'You? What the 'ell are you doing here?'

'One o' the paras – knew who you were – and heard you say, you know . . .'

Morse nodded, and smiled.

'How you doing, sir?'

'Fine! It's just a case of mis-identity.'

'I mustn't be long. They've told me just a coupla minutes, you know.'

'Why's that?' asked Morse wearily.

'They say you need, you know, a lot of rest.'

'*Lew*-is! Why do you keep saying "you know" all the time?'

'Not said "actually" yet though, have I?'

'When you go up to bring Harrison in today—'

'Tomorrow, sir.'

'You sure?'

'Quite sure.'

'Don't forget! *I'm* doing the interviewing.'

Lewis turned to find Nurse Shelick standing behind him. 'Please!' her lips mouthed, as she looked down on Morse's intermittently closing eyes.

'Shan't be a second, nurse.'

He bent down and whispered: 'Anything I can do, sir?'

Morse's eyes were still closed, but he seemed to regain some of his earlier coherence.

'Yes. Second drawer down on the right. There's a Carlisle number for Sister McQueen. Give her a ring. Not today though . . . like you say, tomorrow. Just say I'm . . .'

Lewis prepared to go. 'Leave it to me, sir, and . . . keep a stout heart! Promise me that!'

Morse opened his eyes briefly. 'That's what my old father used to say.'

'So you *will*, won't you, sir?'

Morse nodded slowly. 'I'll try. I'll try ever so hard, my old friend.'

Lewis was checking back the tears as he walked away from the Coronary Care Unit, and failed to hear Nurse Shelick's quiet 'Goodbye'.

Chapter Seventy-Five

> The cart is shaken all to pieces, and the rugged road is very near its end
>
> (Dickens, *Bleak House*)

THAT SAME DAY was to be the longest and almost the unhappiest in Lewis's life. At 6.30 a.m. he drove out to Police HQ and sat quietly in Morse's office, the Harrison case the last thing that concerned him. At 7 a.m. he rang the JR2 and learned that Morse's condition was 'Critical but stable', although he had little real idea what that might signify on the Coronary Richter Scale.

Strange, early apprised of Morse's hospitalization, came in at 8 a.m., himself immediately ringing the JR2, and impatiently asking several questions – and being given the same answer as Lewis: 'Critical but stable'. As much was being done as humanly possible, Strange learned, and any visit was, at present, quite out of the question. For the minute it was all tests and further treatment. The ward had the police number of Sergeant Lewis, and would ring if . . . if there was any news.

Morse was fully conscious of what was going on around him. He felt fairly sure that he was dying, and pretended to himself that he would face death with at least some degree of dignity, if not with equanimity. He had been seated beside his old father when he'd died, and heard him reciting the Lord's Prayer, as if it were some sort of insurance policy. And Morse wondered whether his own self-interest might possibly be served by following suit. But if by any freak of chance there *was* an Almighty, well, He'd understand anyway; and since, in Morse's view, there wasn't, he'd be wasting his really (at this time) rather precious breath. No. The long day's task was almost done, and he knew that he must sleep . . .

At 1.30 p.m. the consultant looked down on the sleeping man. There had been no positive reaction from the comprehensive tests and treatments; no success from the diuretic dosages that should have cleared the fluid that was flooding the lungs; no cause for the slighest optimism from the echo-cardiogram.

He sat at the desk there and wrote:

> 'Clinical evidence that the heart is irreparably damaged; kidney failure already apparent. Without specific request from n.o.k. in my judgement inappropriate to resuscitate'

The nurse beside him read through what he had written.

'Nothing else we can do, is there?'

The consultant shook his head. 'Pray for a miracle,

that's about the only hope. So if he asks for anything, let him have it.'

'Even whisky?'

'Why do you say that?'

'He's already asked for a drop.'

'Something we don't stock in the pharmacy, I'm afraid.'

The nurse smiled gently to herself after the consultant had left, for someone had already slipped a couple of miniature Glenfiddichs into the top of Morse's bedside table; and there'd only been the one visitor.

Seated outside a café on the Champs Elysées, Maxine Ridgway clinked her glass across the table. It had been a splendid lunch and she felt almost happy.

'Thank you! You're a terrible, two-timing fellow – you know that. But you're giving me a wonderful time. You know that, too.'

'Yes, I do know. Trouble is the time's gone by so quickly.'

'No chance of staying another few days? Day or two? Day?'

'No. We're back in the morning as scheduled. I've got a meeting I've agreed to attend.'

'A board meeting?'

'No, no. Much more interesting. A meeting with a chief inspector of police. I've met him once before, only the once, at a funeral; and then only very briefly. But he's – well, he's a bit like me, in a way, I suppose.

He'd never run away from anyone, I reckon; and I'd never forgive myself if I ran away from him.'

Maxine looked over at Frank Harrison, and realized for the first time in their relationship that she was probably in love with the man. In those early heady days it had been all Daimlers and diamonds; but she would always have chosen the wine and the roses of these last forty-eight hours . . .

Suddenly she sensed that she was never going to see him again, and she yearned at that moment to be alone with him, and to give herself to him.

'Let's go back to the hotel, Frank.'

'What? On a beautiful sunny afternoon like this?'

'Yes!'

Frank Harrison leaned across and placed his right hand on her bare shoulder. 'Shall I tell you a secret, my darling? I was about to suggest exactly the same thing myself.'

It was a happy moment.

But a moment only.

Harrison got to his feet.

'I've just got to make a phone call first.'

'You can ring from the room.'

'No, it's a private call.'

'And you don't want me to—?'

'No, I don't.'

'If he asks for anything,' that's what the consultant said. And when Morse made his second request (the first already granted) the nurse rang Police HQ immediately. Lewis and Strange – Morse wanted to see them.

Perhaps she had given the two names in alphabetical order, but Lewis hoped it had been in order of preference – a hope though that had probably been unjustified, he thought, as he stood waiting at the back of the unit, since it had clearly been Strange who had been first on Morse's visiting list.

'Right old mess you've got yourself into, Morse!'

'Looks like it, I'm afraid.'

'You're in the best of hands, you know that.'

'I'm going to need a bit more than that.'

'Look, Morse. Don't you think it would be a good thing . . . don't you think I ought—?'

But Morse was shaking his head in some agitation.

'No! Please! If you really want to help . . .'

'Course! Course, I do!'

'Can you ask Lewis . . . ?'

'Course! Just you keep hold of the hooks, old mate! And that's an order. Don't forget I'm still your superior officer.'

'Lewis!' Morse spoke the name very quietly but quite clearly. His eyes were open, and his lips moved as if he were about to say something.

But if such were the case, he never said it; and Lewis decided to do what so many people have done beside a hospital bed; decided to speak a few comforting thoughts aloud:

'You've got the top load of quacks in Oxfordshire

looking after you, sir. All you've got to do – promise me! – is to do what they say and . . . And what I really want to say is thank-you for . . .'

But Lewis could get no further.

And in any case Morse had closed his eyes and turned his head away to face the pure-white wall.

Just a little word from Morse would have been enough.

But it wasn't to be.

A nurse was standing beside him, testing his lip-reading skills once more: 'I'm afraid we must ask you to go . . .'

At 4.20 p.m. Morse seemed to rally a little, and held his hand up for the nurse.

'I'm allowed a drop more Scotch?' he whispered.

She poured out the miserably small contents of the second miniature and held a jug of water over the glass.

'Yes?'

'No,' said Morse.

She put her arm around his shoulders, pulled him towards her, and held the glass to his lips. But he sipped so little that she wondered whether he'd drunk a single drop; and as he coughed and spluttered she took the glass away and for a few moments held him closely to her, and felt profoundly sad as finally she eased the white head back against the pillows.

For just a little while, Morse opened his eyes and looked up at her.

'Please thank Lewis for me . . .'

But so softly spoken were the words that she wasn't quite able to catch them.

The call came through to Sergeant Lewis just after 5 p.m.

Chapter Seventy-Six

Say, for what were hop-yards meant,
Or why was Burton built on Trent?
Oh many a peer of England brews
Livelier liquor than the Muse,
And malt does more than Milton can
To justify God's ways to man

(A. E. Housman,
A Shropshire Lad)

BEFORE LEAVING FOR Heathrow, Lewis had informed Chief Superintendent Strange that it would not be at all sensible, in fact it would be wholly inappropriate, for him to continue as a protagonist, virtually *the* protagonist, in the Harrison case: he was exhausted mentally, physically, emotionally; and, well . . . he just begged for a rest. And Strange had granted his request.

'I'm going to put someone in charge who's considerably more competent than you and Morse ever were.'

'Yourself, sir?'

'That's it,' smiled Strange sadly. 'You have two or three days off – from tomorrow. You could take the missus to South Wales.'

'I said I needed a rest, sir! And there are one or two things that Morse . . .'

'Make a few calls you mean – yes. And go through his diary and see what dates . . .'

'I don't think there'll be many of those.'

'You don't?' asked Strange quietly.

'And I haven't got much of a clue how he was going to tackle Frank Harrison.'

Strange lumbered round the table and placed a vast hand on Lewis's shoulder. 'You've got a key?'

Lewis nodded.

'Just bring Harrison Senior straight to me. Then . . .'

Lewis nodded. He was full up to the eyes; and left without a further word.

On journeys concerned with potential criminals or criminal activity, CID personnel were never advised, and were seldom permitted, to travel alone. And the following morning Lewis was not wholly unhappy to be travelling alongside a familiar colleague, albeit alongside Sergeant Dixon. After the first few obligatory words, the pair of them had lapsed into silence.

There was never likely to be any risk of missing the returning couple at the Arrivals exit. Nor was there. And it was Lewis who read from his prepared notes, as unostentatiously as he could: 'Mr Frank Harrison, it is my duty as a police officer to inform you that I am authorized to remand you into temporary custody on two counts: first, on suspicion of the murder of Mr John Barron of Lower Swinstead on the 3rd of August, 1998; second, on suspicion of the murder of your wife,

Yvonne Harrison, on the 8th July 1997. It is also my duty to tell you—'

'Forget it, Sergeant. You told me what to expect. Just a couple of favours though, if that's all right? Won't take long.'

'What have you got in mind?' In truth, Lewis had neither the energy nor the enthusiasm to initiate any determined pursuit had Frank Harrison and partner decided to make a dash for it and vault the exit-barriers. But that was never going to happen. Nor did it.

'Well, it's the car, first of all. I left it—'

'All taken care of, sir. Or it will be.'

'Thank you. Second thing, then. You know the one thing I really missed in Paris? A pint of real ale, preferably brewed in Burton-on-Trent. The bars are open here and . . .'

'OK.'

Dixon stood beside him as Harrison ordered a pint of Bass and a large gin and tonic (and, of course, nothing else) whilst Lewis sat at a nearby table, momentarily alone with Maxine Ridgway.

'You know,' she said very firmly, 'you're quite wrong about one thing. I don't know too much about Frank's life, but it does just so happen I was with him the night that his wife was murdered. We were together in his London flat! I was there when the phone rang and when he ordered a taxi to Paddington—'

Frank Harrison was standing by the table now: 'Why don't you learn to keep your mouth shut, woman!' But his voice was resigned rather than angered, and if he had contemplated throwing the gin and tonic in her face, it was only for a second or two.

He sat down and drank his beer.

The damage had been done.

In the back of the police car as it returned to Oxford, Lewis realized, with an added sadness, that Morse had been wholly wrong, as it now transpired, in his final analysis of the Harrison murder. Frank Harrison, if his lady-friend were to be believed, just could *not* have murdered his wife that night; and the police must have been right, in the original enquiry, to cross him off their suspect list. It had all happened before, of course – many a time! – when Morse, after the revelation of some fatal flaw in his earlier reasoning, would find his mind leaping forward, suddenly, with inexplicable insight, towards the ultimate solution.

But those days had now gone.

It was not until the car was passing through the cutting in the Chilterns by Stokenchurch that Harrison spoke:

'Red kite country this is – now. Did you know that, Sergeant?'

'As a matter of fact I did, yes. I'm not into birds myself though. The wife puts some nuts out occasionally but . . .'

It may hardly be seen as a significant passage of conversation.

Harrison spoke again just after Dixon had turned off the M40 on to the A40 for Oxford.

'You know, I'm looking forward to seeing Morse again. I met him at Barron's funeral, but I don't think we got on very well . . . My daughter, Sarah, knows him though. He's one of her patients at the Radcliffe. She tells me he's a strange sort of fellow in some ways – interesting though, and *very* bright, but perhaps not taking all that good care of himself.'

Lewis remained silent.

'Why didn't he come up to Heathrow himself? Wasn't that the original idea?'

'Yes, I think it was.'

'Are we meeting at St Aldate's or Kidlington?'

'He won't be meeting you anywhere, sir. Chief Inspector Morse is dead.'

CHAPTER SEVENTY-SEVEN

Dear Sir/Madam

Please note that an entry on the Register of Electors in your name has been deleted for the following reason:

DEATH

If you have any objections, please notify me, in writing, before the 25th November, 1998, and state the grounds for your objection.

Yours faithfully

(Communication from Carlow County Council
to an erstwhile elector)

AFTER RETURNING TO HQ Lewis gave Strange an account of the quite extraordinary evidence so innocently (as it seemed) supplied by Maxine Ridgway.

But he could do no more.

For he had nothing more to give.

Unlike Morse, who had always professed enormous faith in pills – pills of all colours, shapes, and sizes – Lewis could hardly remember the last time he'd taken anything apart from the Vitamin C tablet he was bullied to swallow each breakfast-time. It had therefore been something of a surprise to learn that Mrs L kept such a copious supply of assorted medicaments; and retiring to bed unprecedentedly early that evening he had swallowed two Nurofen Plus tablets, and slept like the legendary log.

At 10 a.m. the following day he drove up to the mortuary at the JR2.

The eyes were closed, but the expression on the waxen face was hardly one of great serenity, for some hint of pain still lingered there. Like so many others contemplating a dead person, Lewis found himself pondering so many things as he thought of Morse's mind within the skull. Thought of that wonderful memory, of that sensitivity to music and literature, above all of that capacity for thinking laterally, vertically, diagonally – whateverwhichway that extraordinary brain should decide to go. But all gone now, for death had scattered that union of component atoms into the air, and Morse would never move or think or speak again.

Feeling slightly guilty, Lewis looked around him. But at least for the moment his only company was the dead. And bending down he put his lips to Morse's forehead and whispered just two final words: 'Good-bye, sir.'

CHAPTER SEVENTY-EIGHT

. . . & that I be not bury'd in consecrated ground
& that no sexton be asked to toll the bell
& that no murners walk behind me at my funeral
& that no flours be planted on my grave . . .

(Thomas Hardy,
The Mayor of Casterbridge)

MORSE HAD ALWAYS been more closely attuned to life's adagios than its allegros; and his home reflected such a melancholic temperament. The pastel-coloured walls, haunted by the music of Wagner, Bruckner, and Mahler, were decorated with sombre-toned reproductions of Rembrandt, Vermeer, and Atkinson Grimshaw; and lined, in most rooms both upstairs and down, with long shelves of the poets and the novelists.

The whole place now seemed so very still as Lewis picked up two pints of semi-skimmed Co-op milk from the porch, picked up four letters from the doormat, and entered.

In the study upstairs there were several signs (as Lewis already knew) of a sunnier temperament: the room was decorated in a sun-bed tan, terracotta, and white, with a bright Matisse hanging on the only wall free of the ubiquitous books, CDs, and cassettes. A red angle-lamp stood on the desk with, beside it, a bottle of Glenfiddich, virtually empty, and a cut-glass tumbler, completely empty. Morse had timed his exit fairly satisfactorily.

Lewis sat down and quickly looked through the letters: BT; British Diabetic Association; Lloyds Bank; Oxford Brookes University. Nothing too personal perhaps in any of them, but he left them there unopened. He fully realized there would be quite a few details to be sorted out soon by someone. Not by him though. He had but the single mission there.

In the second drawer down on the right, he found six photographs and took them out. An old black-and-white snap of a middle-aged man and woman, the man showing facial lineaments similar to Morse's. A studio portrait of a fair-haired young woman, with a written message on the back: 'Like you I wish so much that things could have been different – love always – W'. Another smaller photograph, with a brief sentence in Morse's own hand: 'Sue Widdowson before she was arrested'. A holiday shot of a young couple on a beach somewhere, the dark-headed bronzed young woman in a white bikini smiling broadly, the young man's right arm around her shoulders, and (again) some writing on the back 'I only *look* happy. I miss you like crazy!!! Ellie'. Clipped to a photograph of a smartly attractive woman, in the uniform of a hospital sister, was a brief letter under a Carlisle address and telephone number: 'I understand. I just can't help wondering how we would have been together, that's all. *I'd* have had to sacrifice a bit of independence too you know! Always remember my love for you. J.' Only the one other photograph: that of Morse and Lewis standing next to each other beside the Jaguar, with no writing on the back at all.

Lewis tried the Carlisle number; with no success.

On the floor to the right of the desk lay a buff-coloured folder, its contents splayed out somewhat, as if perhaps it may have been knocked down accidentally; and he picked it up. On the front was written: 'For the attn. of Lewis'.

The top sheet was the printed FORM D1/D2, issued by the Department of Human Anatomy in South Parks Road, the second section duly signed by the donor; and countersigned by the same man who had witnessed the validity of the second single sheet of A4 to which Lewis now turned his attention:

MY WILL

I expressly forbid the holding of any religious service to mark my death. Nor do I wish any memorial service to be arranged thereafter. If any persons wish to remember me in any way, let it be in their thoughts.

If these handwritten paragraphs have any legal validity, as I am assured they do, my estate may be settled with little difficulty. I no longer have any direct next-of-kin, and even if I have, it makes no difference.

My worldly goods and chattels comprise: my flat (now clear of mortgage); its contents (including a good many rare first editions); two insurance policies; and the monies in my two accounts with Lloyds Bank. The total assets involved I take to be somewhere in the region of £150,000 at current rates and values.

It is my wish that the said estate, after appropriate charges, be divided (like Gaul) into three parts, in equal amounts (unlike Gaul) with the beneficiaries as follows:

(a) The British Diabetic Association

(b) Sister Janet McQueen (see address book)
(c) Sergeant Lewis, my colleague in the Thames Valley CID.

For several minutes, Lewis sat where he was, unmoving, but deeply moved. Why in heaven Morse should have shown such bitterness toward the Church, he couldn't know; and wouldn't know. And why on earth Morse had remembered *him* with such . . .

His thoughts still in confusion, Lewis tried the Carlisle number again; again without success.

He washed out the empty tumbler in the bathroom, and returned to the study, where he poured himself the last half-inch of Glenfiddich, sat down again, silently raised his glass, and drained it.

He looked down at the several sheets of paper remaining in the folder, marked on the first page 'Notes on the Harrison Case', and all written in Morse's hand, that same small upright script that Lewis had found in the Harrison files. He'd go through it all later though. For the moment he placed the other two single sheets on the top, and was preparing to leave, when he opened the second drawer down again, took out the photograph of the Jaguar, and slipped it into the folder – on top of everything else.

And noticed something else there, pushed to the back of the drawer.

A pair of handcuffs.

CHAPTER SEVENTY-NINE

Heaven has no rage like love to hatred turned,
Nor hell a fury like a woman scorned
(Congreve, *The Mourning Bride*)

If you're guilty, you'll have to prove it
(Groucho Marx)

LEWIS FINISHED READING through the folder early that same evening. Most of it he'd known about already. It was only when he'd come to the last three sheets that he was aware of the wholly new tenor of Morse's thinking.

> But herewith I give my final thoughts on the murder of Yvonne Harrison, that crisply uniformed nurse who looked after me in hospital once (but once!) with such tempting, loving care.
>
> From the start of this case, one person stood out high above the others in firmness of purpose, daring, and clarity of mind: Frank Harrison. He was still sexually attracted to Yvonne, but she was no longer attracted to him; indeed one night in hospital she told me that she used to hook her foot over her own side of the mattress to establish a sort of no-man's land between them. But she remained a woman obsessively interested in sex, both as prac-

tising participant and addicted voyeur. (She had mentioned to me some Amsterdam videos. But although I looked quite carefully through the scores of videos there, I could find nothing. I suspect they were innocently disguised under such labels as *The Jungle Book* or *Cooking with Herbs*.)

Now clearly Frank Harrison was – is – someone with a very strong sexual drive, and doubtless he claimed his marital rights on his spasmodic periods at home. But inevitably, when they were away from each other, Yvonne knew what he was up to, just as he knew what she was up to. And for that reason, I can find no compelling motive for Frank Harrison to have murdered his wife. There *might* have been the opportunity, for all we know. But his alibi was uncontested, since there seemed no reason to suspect the firm and explicit evidence of the man Flynn, who claimed to have picked him up from Oxford Station and driven him out to his home to Lower Swinstead.

It is now my view (I look forward to interviewing Frank H on the matter) that Flynn was not in fact paid for fixing his taxi-times for the purpose of Harrison's alibi. He was paid for something different.

Until so very recently I thought that Simon must have murdered his mother. He had ample motive if he found his beloved mum in bed with the local builder – God help us! And the other facts fitted that hypothesis neatly: he was known to Repp, the local shady character familiar to everyone around, as well as being a regular at the Maiden's Arms; known to Barron, of course; and also known to Flynn, because the pair of them had attended lip-reading classes together.

As you know, I was wrong.

But there was someone else who had an even more compelling motive, with the other facts fitting equally convincingly: Sarah Harrison. What motive could *she* have had? Simply this: that she and Barron had been secret lovers for a year or so before Yvonne's murder. I learned something about this from two most unlikely witnesses – from Alf and Bert, denizens of the Maiden's Arms. Particularly from Bert, who had seen the two of them together, both at the Three Pigeons in Witney and at the White Hart in Wolvercote, when he was playing away in the cribbage-league. I've little doubt that others in Lower Swinstead knew about it too, but they all kept their mouths shut. On that fateful evening, Sarah called home unexpectedly, and found her secret lover in bed with her mother – God help us! She was already known to Repp, as well as to Barron, of course. But where does that opportunistic fellow Flynn fit into the picture this time? There is now ample proof that he knew Sarah fairly well, because in the years before the murder the pair of them had performed in a pop group together in several pubs and clubs in West Oxfordshire (some details are known) although never as it happens at the Maiden's Arms.

And that's almost it, Lewis.

There remains just the one final matter to settle. The murder weapon was never found. But the path-report, as you'll recall, gave some indication of the type of weapon used. There were perhaps two blows only to Yvonne's head. The first rendered the right cheek-bone shattered and the bridge of the nose broken. The second, the more vicious and it seems the fatal blow, crashed across the base of the skull, doubtless as Yvonne tried to turn her head away in desperate self-defence. The suggestion made was that some sort of 'tubular metal rod' was in all probability the cause of such injuries.

An arm-crutch!

How do I know this? I don't. But I shall be inordinately surprised if I am not very close indeed to the truth. And – how many times has this happened? – it was you, Lewis, who did the trick for me again! Remember? You were reining back some fanciful notions of mine about Sarah tearing down to the cinema to buy a ticket, and you said that she wasn't going to be tearing about anywhere that night, because she'd sprained her ankle rather badly; and that if she were doing anything it would be *hobbling* about. Yes. Hobbling about on one of those metal arm-crutches they'd probably issued her with from the Physiotherapy Department. (Will you find out, Lewis, if and when the arm-crutch was returned?)

I realize that it won't be easy to establish Sarah's guilt, but we've got the long-awaited interview with her father to look forward to. He'll be a worthy opponent, I know that, but I'm beginning to suspect that even *he* has almost had enough by now. If I'm over-optimistic about such an outcome, there'll still be Sarah herself. It will be a surprise if the pair of them haven't been in close touch in recent days and weeks, and I've got a feeling that like her father she's almost ready herself to emerge from the hell she must have been going through for so long. Quite apart from judicial convictions and punishments, guilt brings its own moral retribution. We all know that.

One thing is certain. This will be – has been – my last case. I am now determined to retire and to take life a little more gently and sensibly. We've tackled so many cases together, old friend, and I'm very happy and very proud to have worked with you for so long.

That's it. The time is now 12.45 a.m., and suddenly I feel so very weary.

All the manuscript notes were with Strange within the half-hour.

And Lewis had nothing further to do with the investigation.

Chapter Eighty

I am retired. I am to be met with in trim gardens. I am already come to be known by my vacant face and careless gesture, perambulating at no fixed pace nor with any settled purpose. I walk about; not to and from

(Charles Lamb, *Last Essays of Elia*)

It seemed there was little to cloud the bright evening at the end of August, that same year, when Strange held his retirement party. The Chief Constable (no less!) had toasted his farewell from the Force, paying a fulsome tribute to his colleague's many years of distingished service in the Thames Valley CID, crowned, as it had been, with yet another significant triumph in the Yvonne Harrison murder case.

For his part, Strange had spoken reasonably wittily and blessedly briefly, and had included a personal tribute to Chief Inspector Morse:

'I don't think we're going to see his like again in a hurry, and people of lesser intellect like me should be grateful for that. And it's good to have with us here his faithful friend and, er, drinking-companion' (muted amusement) 'Sergeant Lewis' (Hear-Hear! all round). 'Morse had no funeral service and no memorial service, just as he wished; but I make no apology for remembering him here this evening because, quite simply, he had the most brilliant mind I ever encountered in the whole of my police career . . . Well now. All that remains for me is to thank you for coming along to see me off; to say thank you for the lawnmower and the book' (he held aloft a copy of Sir David Attenborough's *The Life of Birds*) 'and to remind you there's a splendid buffet next door, including a special plate of doughnuts for one of our number.' (Much laughter, and much subsequent applause.)

Lewis had clapped as much as the rest of them, but he had no wish to stay too long amid the back-slapping and the reminiscences; and soon made his way upstairs to the deserted canteen where he sat in a corner drinking an orange juice, wishing to be alone with his thoughts for a while . . .

The conclusion to the Harrison case had proved pretty much, though far from exactly, as Morse had predicted. Two hours after her father had been taken to HQ for questioning, Sarah Harrison (refusing to see her father) had presented herself voluntarily and made a full confession to the murder of her mother, making absolutely no apology for anything – except for causing her father (she knew it!) all that pain and agony of spirit. What would happen to her now, she said, would not really amount to imprisonment at all; but, in a curious sort of way, to a kind of liberation.

And perhaps it had been much the same, albeit rather later, for Frank Harrison himself, who (less eloquently than his daughter) had by degrees unburdened himself of his manifold sins and wickednesses, including the subsequent murder of his wife's lover, John Barron . . .

His actions, after receiving his daughter's frantic, frenetic phone call on the night of Yvonne's murder, had been straightforward. Train to Oxford; then taxi to Lower Swinstead, whence Barron had long since fled; and where Repp, though still around, remained unseen. Harrison had paid off Flynn, expecting him to drive away forthwith; thereafter very quickly dispatching his distraught daughter home. Coolly and ruthlessly he'd taken over. Confusion! – that was the only hope; and the only plan. Yvonne was already handcuffed, presumably for some bizarre bondage session, and what a blessing that had been! He'd tied a gag lightly around her mouth; gone on to the patio and smashed in the glass of the french window from the outside before unlocking it; he'd turned the lights on, every one of them, and yanked out the TV and the telephone leads, both upstairs and down; and finally, with illogical desperation, he'd decided to activate the burglar alarm, since even if no one heard it, it would be recorded (so he believed).

He'd done enough. Almost enough. Just the police now. He *had* to ring the police, immediately; and suddenly he realized he *couldn't* ring them – he'd just made sure of that himself. But there was his mobile, the mobile on which he'd already rung Sarah several times from the train and once from Flynn's taxi. He could always *lose* it though: and the longer he waited to ring for help, the better the chances for that confusion he'd tried so hard to effect. In detective stories he'd often read of the difficulties pathologists encountered in establishing the time parameters for any murder. Yes! He'd just go up to the main road and walk (run!) the half-mile or so to the next house. Which indeed he was doing when he heard the voice at the gate that led to the drive. He remembered Flynn's words exactly:

'I t'ink you moight be needin' a little help, sorr?' . . .

Epilogue

Certainly the gods are ironical: they always punish one for one's virtues rather than for one's sins

(Ernest Dowson, *Letters*)

'DIDN'T YOU WANT any food?'

'No thank you, sir. I've got a meal waiting at home.'

'Ah yes. Of course.'

'And I didn't particularly want to watch Dixon eating doughnuts.'

'No, I understand.' Strange lowered himself rather gingerly on to the inappropriately small chair opposite. 'Talking of eating, Lewis, what the hell's eating *you*, pray?'

As he'd requested (and as we have seen) Lewis had nothing further to do with the Harrison case. He had tried, and with some considerable success, to distance himself from the whole affair, even from thinking about it. There was just that one persistent, niggling worry that tugged away at his mind like some over-indulged infant tugging away at its mother's skirts in a supermarket: the knowledge that Morse, on his own admission, and for the first time in their collaboration, had acted dishonestly and dishonourably.

He looked up at Strange.

'What makes you think something's eating me?'

'Come *on*, Lewis! I wasn't born yesterday.'

So Lewis told him.

Told him of the unease he'd felt from the beginning of the case: that Morse had known far too little about it, and then again far too much; that Morse had originally voiced such vehement opposition to taking on the case, and yet had spent the last days of his life doing little else than trying to fathom its complexity.

'And that's all that's been bothering you?'

'*All*?'

'Look! Tell me! What's the very *worst* thing you think he could have done? There's this attractive nurse pulling him through a serious illness in hospital – a place where patients can get a bit low, and a bit vulnerable. Nurses, too, for that matter. And she fell for him a bit—'

'How do you know that?'

'She told me so. She told me one night in hospital when she was looking after *me*! Morse fell for *her* a bit, too – anybody would! – and after he's discharged he writes and asks her why she's not been in touch with him. But she doesn't write back, although she keeps his letter. Know why, Lewis? Because she doesn't really know how to cope with being in love herself.'

'How do you know *that*?'

'Does it matter? When she was murdered – well, you know the rest. Morse was on another case at the time – you were on it *with* him, for God's sake! And he said it was too much for the pair of you to take on another.'

'Only after he'd found his own letter.'

'Lewis!'

'Only after he'd recognized the handcuffs.'

'*Lewis!* Listen! Nothing Morse did then – *nothing* – affected that enquiry in the slightest way. Yvonne had kept some letters from her men-friends, the kinkies and the straights alike. She certainly didn't keep any from Barron. Maybe because he never wrote any, I dunno. Maybe because she just didn't want to.'

'Just the ones from her favourite clients.'

'You know that. You've seen them.'

'Some of them,' said Lewis slowly.

'Well I saw *all* the bloody letters!'

'Including the one from Morse.'

'Not a crime you know, writing a letter. It was immaterial anyway, as I keep trying to tell you.' Strange looked exasperated. 'It's just that it would have been awkward, wouldn't it? Bloody awkward! I wanted to protect the silly sod. You never thought he was a *saint*, did you?'

Lewis was silent for a while. No. He'd never thought of Morse as a possible candidate for sanctification.

But there was something wrong about what he'd just heard.

'So *you* saw the letter before *Morse* saw it, is that what you're saying?'

'Morse *never* saw the letter, not till you showed him that page of it. You see, Lewis, *I* took it – not Morse.'

'And you didn't check—'

'Couldn't have done, could I? It was a longish letter. But I didn't read it, so I wouldn't have spotted if there was any gap.'

'So it was you who kept some of the evidence separate?'

'Afraid so, yes. I was scared stiff one of *my* letters might be there, if you want the truth. And as things turned out it just became impossible for me to put that stuff back in the folder while the original enquiry was still going on.'

'So you got a new box-file when the case was re-opened . . .'

Strange nodded. 'Always felt guilty about it but—'

'Why didn't Morse spot the page you'd missed?'

'Perhaps he didn't look all that carefully. Not his way usually, was it? Perhaps he wasn't too interested in the literary shortcomings of her other admirers. Not very fond of spelling mistakes, now was he . . . ? or perhaps he just felt the letters were too private, like he'd hoped his own letter would be. How do *I* know? What I do know is that he wasn't looking for a list of lovers who might have been in bed with Yvonne that night. Somehow he was convinced he *knew* who the man was. He told me who it was; and he told you who it was. And he was right.'

Lewis nodded.

But the supermarket-brat was giving a final tug.

'Plenty of letters and none of them any help, I agree, sir. But just the one pair of handcuffs! And Morse realized there'd be no problem in tracing them, so he destroyed the issue-list. And we both know why, don't we, sir? *Because they were his.*'

'Come off it, Lewis! There's a hundred and one worse things in life than him giving some bloody cuffs he'd never used once in his life to some woman who'd asked him for them – whatever the reason.'

Slowly shaking his head, Lewis stared down at the canteen carpet disconsolately.

'It's just that he seems not quite the man . . .'

'And you can't forgive him for that.'

'Course I can forgive him! Just a bit of a jolt, that's all. Can't you understand that? After all those years we were together?'

'That's what's *really* eating you, isn't it? Be honest! It's just that you don't think as much of old Morse as you used to.'

'Not quite as much, no.'

Strange struggled to his feet. 'Must be off. Good to talk. I'd better get back downstairs.'

Lewis got to his feet. 'Mrs Lewis sends her very best wishes, sir.'

The two policemen shook hands, and the interesting exchange was apparently over.

But not so.

Halfway to the canteen exit, Strange suddenly turned round and came back to the table.

'Do you remember those issue-lists for handcuffs, Lewis?'

'It's a long time ago . . .'

'Well, they're just handwritten lists, kept up to date in a series of columns: date, name, rank, serial number. Just like this.' Strange took a folded sheet of A4 from an inside pocket. 'But you remember the serial-number on the pair you found in Morse's drawer?'

'Nine-two-two.'

He handed the sheet to Lewis. 'You've got a good memory!'

'Where did you get this?'

'Someone took it from HQ, Lewis. Morse did!'

Lewis looked down at the list, but could find no mention of Morse's name. Could see another name though – at the seventh entry down, along with the other details in the neatly ruled lines:

3 June '68	Strange	PC	734	922

'You mean. . .?'

'I *mean*, Lewis, that Morse knew I was having an affair with Yvonne Harrison. I don't know how he knew, but he always tended to know things, didn't he? He pinched that form, and he kept it till after the wife's funeral. Then he gave it to me. Said it would be useless without the cuffs, which he said *he* was going to keep anyway, just in case I ever did anything bloody stupid. And he said exactly what I said to you a few minutes ago: nothing – *nothing* – that happened then had affected the enquiry in the slightest way. Is that clear, Lewis?'

Yes it *was* clear. 'You're saying that all Morse did was to save you . . . and save Mrs Strange . . .'

'It would have broken her to pieces,' said Strange very quietly. 'And me. Would have broken both of us to pieces.'

'She never knew?'

'Never had the faintest idea. Thanks to Morse.'

Lewis was silent.

'Just like you, eh? About lots of things. You never had the faintest idea, for example, that I re-opened the Harrison case on the basis of a couple of bogus telephone calls, now did you?'

'You mean—?'

'I mean there *were* no telephone calls. I made 'em up myself. Both of 'em.'

'I just didn't realize . . .'

'Nobody did, except Morse of course. He guessed straightaway. But I'd like to bet he never told you! He just didn't want to let me down, that's all.'

'Why didn't he tell me all this though? It would have made such a lot of difference . . . at the end . . .'

'I dunno. Always an independent sod, wasn't he? And always had that great big streak of loyalty and integrity somewhere deep inside him. But you don't need me to tell you that. So he was never worried too much about what people thought of him. He certainly didn't give two monkeys what *I* thought of him, at least most of the time. In fact the only person he did want to think well of him was *you*, Lewis. So let me tell you something else. It's one helluva job having to live with guilt, as I've done. Almost everybody discovers the same, you know that. Frank Harrison did, didn't he? Sarah Harrison, too. It's something I hope you'll never have to go through yourself. Not that you ever will. Nor did Morse though. He once told me that the guiltiest he ever felt in his life was when a couple of the lads saw him flicking through a girlie magazine in the Summertown newsagent's. So . . . So just keep thinking well of him, Lewis – that's all I ask.'

The former Chief Superintendent lumbered across the still-deserted canteen to join the jollifications below.

But Lewis sat where he was.

Apart from the middle-aged woman at the counter reading the *Sun*, there seemed no one else there. And after looking around him as guiltily as Morse must have done in the Summertown newsagent's, for a little while, in his desolation, he wept silently.

THE WENCH IS DEAD

For
Harry Judge,
lover of canals, who introduced me to
The Murder of Christine Collins,
a fascinating account of an
early Victorian murder,
by
John Godwin.
To both I am deeply indebted.
(Copies of John Godwin's publication are obtainable
through the Divisional Librarian, Stafford
Borough Library.)

Thou hast committed –
Fornication; but that was in another country,
And besides, the wench is dead
(Christopher Marlowe, *The Jew of Malta*)

Acknowledgements

The author and publishers wish to thank the following who have kindly given permission for use of copyright materials:

Map of Oxford Canal reproduced by permission of Oxfordshire Museum Services;

Century Hutchinson Limited for extracts from *Adventures in Wonderland* by David Grayson;

Faber and Faber Ltd for extracts from 'Little Gidding' from *Four Quartets* by T. S. Eliot;

David Higham Associates Limited on behalf of Dorothy L. Sayers for extracts from *The Murder of Julia Wallace*, published by Gollancz;

Methuen London Limited for extracts from *A Man's a Man* by Bertolt Brecht;

Oxfordshire Health Authority for extracts from *Handbook for Patients and Visitors*;

Oxford Illustrated Press for extracts from *The Erosion of Oxford* by James Stevens Curl;

E. O. Parrott for extracts;

Routledge, Chapman and Hall for extracts from *Understanding Media* by Marshall McLuhan;

The Society of Authors on behalf of the Bernard Shaw Estate for extracts from *Back to Methuselah,* published by Longman.

Every effort has been made to trace all the copyright holders but if any have been inadvertently overlooked, the author and publishers will be pleased to make the necessary arrangement at the first opportunity.

THE OXFORD CANAL

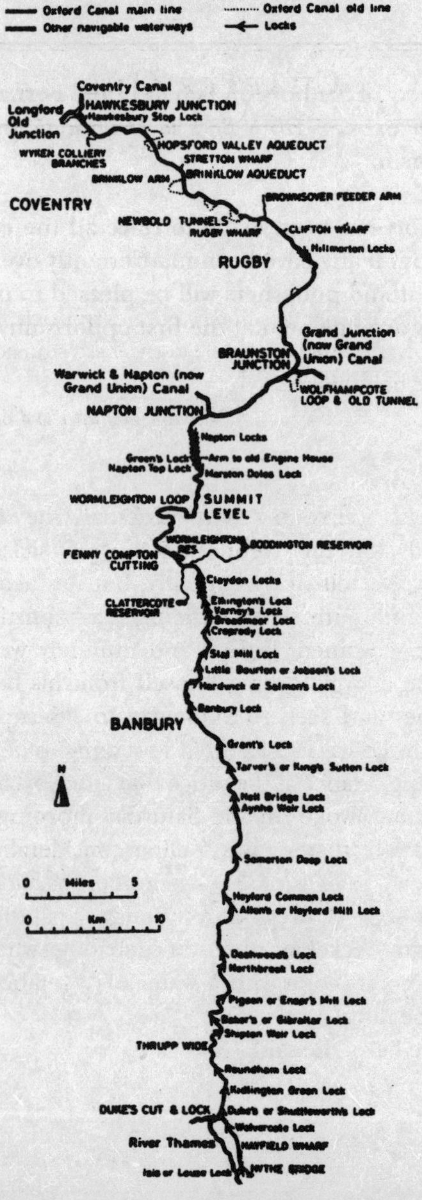

Oxford Canal main line
Other navigable waterways
Oxford Canal old line
Locks
Coventry Canal
HAWKESBURY JUNCTION
Hawkesbury Stop Lock
Longford Old Junction
WYKEN COLLIERY BRANCHES
HOPSFORD VALLEY AQUEDUCT
STRETTON WHARF
BRINKLOW AQUEDUCT
BRINKLOW ARM
COVENTRY
BROWNSOVER FEEDER ARM
NEWBOLD TUNNELS
RUGBY WHARF
CLIFTON WHARF
Hillmorton Locks
RUGBY
Grand Junction (now Grand Union) Canal
BRAUNSTON JUNCTION
Warwick & Napton (now Grand Union) Canal
WOLFHAMPCOTE LOOP & OLD TUNNEL
NAPTON JUNCTION
Napton Locks
Green's Lock
Arm to old Engine House
Napton Top Lock
Marston Doles Lock
WORMLEIGHTON LOOP
SUMMIT LEVEL
WORMLEIGHTON RES.
BODDINGTON RESERVOIR
FENNY COMPTON CUTTING
Claydon Locks
CLATTERCOTE RESERVOIR
Elkington's Lock
Varney's Lock
Broadmoor Lock
Cropredy Lock
Slat Mill Lock
Little Bourton or Jobson's Lock
Hardwick or Salmon's Lock
Banbury Lock
BANBURY
Grant's Lock
Tarver's or King's Sutton Lock
N
Nell Bridge Lock
Aynho Weir Lock
Somerton Deep Lock
0 Miles 5
0 Km 10
Heyford Common Lock
Allen's or Heyford Mill Lock
Dashwood's Lock
Northbrook Lock
Pigeon or Enser's Mill Lock
Baker's or Gibraltar Lock
Shipton Weir Lock
THRUPP WIDE
Roundham Lock
Kidlington Green Lock
DUKE'S CUT & LOCK
Duke's or Shuttleworth's Lock
Wolvercote Lock
River Thames
HAYFIELD WHARF
Isis or Louse Lock
HYTHE BRIDGE

CHAPTER ONE

Thought depends absolutely on the stomach; but, in spite of that, those who have the best stomachs are not the best thinkers

(*Voltaire, in a letter to d'Alembert*)

INTERMITTENTLY, ON THE Tuesday, he felt sick. Frequently, on the Wednesday, he *was* sick. On the Thursday, he felt sick frequently, but was actually sick only intermittently. With difficulty, early on the Friday morning – drained, listless, and infinitely weary – he found the energy to drag himself from his bed to the telephone, and seek to apologize to his superiors at Kidlington Police HQ for what was going to be an odds-on non-appearance at the office that late November day.

When he awoke on the Saturday morning, he was happily aware that he was feeling considerably better; and, indeed, as he sat in the kitchen of his bachelor flat in North Oxford, dressed in pyjamas as gaudily striped as a Lido deckchair, he was debating whether his stomach could cope with a wafer of Weetabix – when the phone rang.

'Morse here,' he said.

'Good morning, sir.' (A pleasing voice!) 'If you can hold the line a minute, the Superintendent would like a word with you.'

Morse held the line. Little option, was there? No option, really; and he scanned the headlines of *The Times* which had just been pushed through the letter-box in the small entrance hall – late, as usual on Saturdays.

'I'm putting you through to the Superintendent,' said the same pleasing voice – 'just a moment, please!'

Morse said nothing; but he almost prayed (quite something for a low-church atheist) that Strange would get a move on and come to the phone and say whatever it was he'd got to say . . . The prickles of sweat were forming on his forehead, and his left hand plucked at his pyjama-top pocket for his handkerchief.

'Ah! Morse? Yes? Ah! Sorry to hear you're a bit off-colour, old boy. Lots of it about, you know. The wife's brother had it – when was it now? – fortnight or so back? No! I tell a lie – must have been three weeks, at least. Still, that's neither here nor there, is it?'

In enlarged globules, the prickles of sweat had re-formed on Morse's forehead, and he wiped his brow once more as he mumbled a few dutifully appreciative noises into the telephone.

'Didn't get you out of bed, I hope?'

'No – no, sir.'

'Good. Good! Thought I'd just have a quick word, that's all. Er . . . Look here, Morse!' (Clearly Strange's thoughts had moved to a conclusion.) 'No need for you to come in today – no need at all! Unless you feel suddenly very much better, that is. We can just about cope here, I should think. The cemeteries are full of indispensable men – eh? Huh!'

'Thank you, sir. Very kind of you to ring – I much appreciate it – but I am officially off duty this weekend in any case—'

'Really? Ah! That's good! That's er . . . *very* good, isn't it? Give you a chance to stay in bed.'

'Perhaps so, sir,' said Morse wearily.

'You say you're *up*, though?'

'Yes, sir!'

'Well you go back to bed, Morse! This'll give you a chance for a jolly good rest – this weekend, I mean – won't it? Just the thing – bit o' rest – when you're feeling a bit off-colour – eh? It's exactly what the quack told the wife's brother – when was it now . . .?'

Afterwards, Morse thought he remembered concluding this telephone conversation in a seemly manner – with appropriate concern expressed for Strange's convalescent brother-in-law; thought he remembered passing a hand once more over a forehead that now felt very wet and very, very cold – and then taking two or three hugely deep breaths – and then starting to rush for the bathroom . . .

It was Mrs Green, the charlady who came in on Tuesday and Saturday mornings, who rang treble-nine immediately and demanded an ambulance. She had found her employer sitting with his back to the wall in the entrance-hall: conscious, seemingly sober, and passably presentable, except for the deep-maroon stains down the front of his deckchair pyjamas – stains that in both colour and texture served vividly to remind her of the dregs in the bottom of a coffee percolator. And she knew exactly what *they* meant, because that thoughtlessly cruel doctor had made it quite plain – five years ago now, it had been – that if only she'd called him immediately, Mr Green might still . . .

'Yes, that's right,' she heard herself say – surprisingly, imperiously, in command: 'just on the southern side of the Banbury Road roundabout. Yes. I'll be looking out for you.'

At 10.15 a.m. that same morning, an only semi-reluctant Morse condescended to be helped into the back of the ambulance, where, bedroom-slippered and with an itchy, grey blanket draped around a clean pair of pyjamas, he sat defensively opposite a middle-aged, uniformed woman who appeared to have taken his refusal to lie down on the stretcher-bed as a personal affront, and who now sullenly and silently pushed a white enamel kidney-bowl into his lap as he vomited copiously and noisily once more, while the ambulance climbed Headley Way, turned left into the grounds of the John Radcliffe Hospital complex, and finally stopped outside the Accident, Casualty, and Emergency Department.

As he lay supine (on a hospital trolley now) it

occurred to Morse that he might already have died some half a dozen times without anyone recording his departure. But he was always an impatient soul (most particularly in hotels, when awaiting his breakfast); and it might not have been quite so long as he imagined before a white-coated ancillary worker led him in leisurely fashion through a questionnaire that ranged from the names of his next of kin (in Morse's case, now non-existent) to his denominational preferences (equally, alas, now non-existent). Yet once through these initiation rites – once (as it were) he had joined the club and signed the entry forms – Morse found himself the object of considerably increased attention. Dutifully, from somewhere, a young nurse appeared, flipped a watch from her stiffly laundered lapel with her left hand and took his pulse with her right; proceeded to take his blood-pressure, after tightening the black swaddling-bands around his upper-arm with (for Morse) quite needless ferocity; and then committing her findings to a chart (headed MORSE, E.) with such nonchalance as to suggest that only the most dramatic of irregularities could ever give occasion for anxiety. The same nurse finally turned her attention to matters of temperature; and Morse found himself feeling somewhat idiotic as he lay with the thermometer sticking up from his mouth, before its being extracted, its calibrations consulted, its readings apparently unsatisfactory, it being forcefully shaken thrice, as though for a few backhand flicks in a ping-pong match, and then being replaced, with all its earlier awkwardness, just underneath his tongue.

'I'm going to survive?' ventured Morse, as the nurse added her further findings to the data on his chart.

'You've got a temperature,' replied the uncommunicative teenager.

'I thought *everybody* had got a temperature,' muttered Morse.

For the moment, however, the nurse had turned her back on him to consider the latest casualty.

A youth, his legs caked with mud, and most of the rest of him encased in a red-and-black-striped Rugby jersey, had just been wheeled in – a ghastly-looking Cyclopean slit across his forehead. Yet, to Morse, he appeared wholly at his ease as the (same) ancillary worker quizzed him comprehensively about his life-history, his religion, his relatives. And when, equally at his ease, the (same) nurse put him through his paces with stethoscope, watch, and thermometer, Morse could do little but envy the familiarity that was effected forthwith between the young lad and the equally young lass. Suddenly – and almost cruelly – Morse realized that she, that same young lass, had seen him – Morse! – exactly for what he was: a man who'd struggled through life to his early fifties, and who was about to face the slightly *infra-dignitatem* embarrassments of hernias and haemorrhoids, of urinary infections and – yes! – of duodenal ulcers.

The kidney-bowl had been left within easy reach, and Morse was retching violently, if unproductively, when a young houseman (of Morse's age, no more than half) came to stand beside him and to scan the reports of ambulance, administrative staff, and medical personnel.

'You've got a bit of nasty tummy trouble – you realize that?'

Morse shrugged vaguely: 'Nobody's really told me anything yet.'

'But you wouldn't have to be Sherlock Holmes to suspect you've got something pretty radically wrong with your innards, would you?'

Morse was about to reply when the houseman continued. 'And you've only just come in, I think? If you could give us – Mr, er, *Morse*, is it? – if you give us a chance, we'll try to tell you more about things as soon as we can, OK?'

'I'm all right, really,' said the duly chastened Chief Inspector of Police, as he lay back and tried to unloose the knot that had tied itself tight inside his shoulder muscles.

'You're *not* all right, I'm afraid! At best you've got a stomach ulcer that's suddenly decided to burst out bleeding' – Morse experienced a sharp little jerk of alarm somewhere in his diaphragm – 'and at worst you've got what we call a "perforated ulcer"; and if that *is* the case . . .'

'If that *is* the case . . .?' repeated Morse weakly. But the young doctor made no immediate answer, and for the next few minutes prodded, squeezed, and kneaded the paunchy flesh around Morse's abdomen.

'Found anything?' queried Morse, with a thin and forced apology for a grin.

'You could well lose a couple of stone. Your liver's enlarged.'

'But I thought you just said it was the stomach!'

'Oh yes, it is! You've had a stomach haemorrhage.'

'What's – what's that got to do with my liver?'

'Do you drink a lot, Mr Morse?'

'Well, most people have a drink or two most days, don't they?'

'Do you drink a *lot*?' (The same words – a semitone of exasperation lower.)

As non-commitally as his incipient panic would permit, Morse shrugged his shoulders once more: 'I like a glass of beer, yes.'

'How many pints do you drink a week?'

'A week?' squeaked Morse, his face clouding over like that of a child who has just been given a complex problem in mental multiplication.

'A day, then?' suggested the houseman helpfully.

Morse divided by three: 'Two or three, I suppose.'

'Do you drink spirits?'

'Occasionally.'

'What spirits do you drink?'

Morse shrugged his tautened shoulders once again: 'Scotch – sometimes I treat myself to a drop of Scotch.'

'How long would a bottle of Scotch last you?'

'Depends how big it was.'

But Morse immediately saw that his attempt at humour was ill appreciated; and he swiftly multiplied by three: 'Week – ten days – about that.'

'How many cigarettes do you smoke a day?'

'Eight . . . ten?' replied Morse, getting the hang of things now and smoothly dividing by three.

'Do you ever take any exercise – walking, jogging, cycling, squash . . .?'

But before Morse could switch back to his tables, he reached for the kidney-bowl that had been left within reach. And as he vomited, this time productively, the houseman observed with some alarm the coffee-grounds admixed with the tell-tale brightly crimsoned specks of blood – blood that was de-oxygenated daily with plentiful nicotine and liberally lubricated with alcohol.

For some while after these events, Morse's mind was somewhat hazy. Later, however, he could recall a nurse bending over him – the same young nurse as earlier; and he could remember the beautifully manicured fingers on her left hand as she flipped the watch out again into her palm; could almost follow her thoughts as with contracted brow she squinted at the disturbing equation between his half-minute pulse-rate and the thirty-second span upon her watch . . .

At this point Morse knew that the Angel of Death had fluttered its wings above his head; and he felt a sudden *frisson* of fear, as for the first time in his life he began to think of dying. For in his mind's eye, though just for a second or two, he thought he almost caught sight of the laudatory obituary, the creditable paragraph.

CHAPTER TWO

Do you know why we are more fair and just towards the dead? We are not obliged to them, we can take our time, we can fit in the paying of respects between a cocktail party and an affectionate mistress – in our spare time

(*Albert Camus,* The Fall)

WHEN MORSE AWOKE the following morning, he was aware of a grey dawn through the window of the small ward, to his left; and of a clock showing 4.50 a.m. on the wall above the archway to his right, through which he could see a slimly attractive nurse, sitting in a pool of light behind a desk, and writing in a large book. Was she writing, Morse wondered, about *him*? If so, there would be remarkably little to say; for apart from one very brief bout of vomiting in the small hours, he had felt, quite genuinely, so very much better; and had required no further attention. The tubing strapped to his right wrist, and stretching up to the saline-drip bottle hooked above his bed, was still dragging uncomfortably against his skin most of the time, as if the needle had been stuck in slightly off-centre; but he'd determined to make no mention of such a minor irritant. The awkward apparatus rendered him immobile, of course – at least until he had mastered the skills of the young man from the adjacent bed who had spent most of the previous evening wandering freely (as it seemed) all over the hospital, holding his own drip high above his head like some Ethiopian athlete brandishing the Olympic torch. Morse had felt most self-conscious when circumstances utterly beyond his control had finally induced him to beg for a 'bottle'. Yet – thus far – he had been spared the undignified palaver of the dreaded 'pan'; and he trusted that his lack of solid nutriment during the preceding days would be duly acknowledged with some reciprocal inactivity by his bowels. And so far so good!

The nurse was talking earnestly to a slightly built, fresh-faced young houseman, his white coat reaching almost to his ankles, a stethoscope hooked into his right-hand pocket. And soon the two of them were walking, quietly, unfussily, into the ward where Morse lay; then disappearing behind the curtains (drawn across the previous evening) of the bed diagonally opposite.

When he'd first been wheeled into the ward, Morse had noticed the man who occupied that bed – a proud-looking man, in his late seventies, perhaps, with an Indian Army moustache, and a thin thatch of pure-white hair. At that moment of entry, for a second or two, the old warrior's watery-pale eyes had settled on Morse's face, seeming almost to convey some faint message of hope and comradeship. And indeed the dying old man would certainly have wished the new patient well, had he been able to articulate his intent; but the rampaging septicaemia which had sent a bright-pink suffusion to his waxen cheeks had taken from him all the power of speech.

It was 5.20 a.m. when the houseman emerged from behind the curtains; 5.30 a.m. when the swiftly summoned porters had wheeled the dead man away. And when, exactly half an hour later, the full lights flickered on in the ward, the curtains round the bed of the late Colonel Wilfrid Deniston, OBE, MC, were standing open, in their normal way, to reveal the newly laundered sheets, with the changed blankets professionally mitred at the foot. Had Morse known how the late Colonel could not abide a chord of Wagner he would have been somewhat aggrieved; yet had he known how the Colonel had committed to memory virtually the whole poetic corpus of A. E. Housman, he would have been most gratified.

At 6.45 a.m. Morse was aware of considerable activity in the immediate environs of the ward, although initially he could see no physical evidence of it: voices, clinking of crockery, squeaking of ill-oiled wheels – and finally Violet, a happily countenanced and considerably overweight West Indian woman hove into view pushing a tea-trolley. This was the occasion, clearly, for a pre-dawn beverage, and how Morse welcomed it! For the first time in the past few days he was conscious of a positive appetite for food and drink; and already, and with envy, he had surveyed the jugs of water and bottles of squash that stood on the bedside tables of his fellow-patients, though for some reason not on the table of the man immediately opposite, one Walter Greenaway, above whose bed there hung a rectangular plaque bearing the sad little legend NIL BY MOUTH.

'Tea or coffee, Mr Greenaway?'

'I'll just settle for a large gin-and-tonic, if that's all right by you.'

'Ice and lemon?'

'No ice, thank you: it spoils the gin.'

Violet moved away massively to the next bed, leaving Mr Greenaway sans ice, sans everything. Yet the perky sixty-odd-year-old appeared far from mortified by his exclusion from the proceedings, and winked happily across at Morse.

'All right, chief?'

'On the mend,' said Morse cautiously.

'Huh! That's exactly what the old Colonel used to say: "On the mend". Poor old boy!'

'I see,' said Morse, with some unease.

After Greenaway's eyes had unclouded from their appropriate respect for the departed Colonel, Morse continued the dialogue.

'No tea for you, then?'

Greenaway shook his head. 'They know best, though, don't they?'

'They do?'

'Wonderful – the doctors here! And the nurses!'

Morse nodded, hoping indeed that it might be so.

'Same trouble as me?' enquired Greenaway confidentially.

'Pardon?'

'Stomach, is it?'

'Ulcer – so they say.'

'Mine's perforated!' Greenaway proclaimed this fact with a certain grim pride and satisfaction, as though a combination of the worst of disorders with the best of physicians was a cause for considerable congratulation. 'They're operating on me at ten o'clock – that's why I'm not allowed a drink, see?'

'Oh!' For a few seconds Morse found himself almost wishing he could put in some counter-claim for a whole gutful of mighty ulcers that were not only perforated but pierced and punctured into the bargain. A more important matter, however, was now demanding his attention, for Violet had effected a U-turn and was (at last!) beside his bed.

She greeted her new charge with a cheerful grin. 'Morning, Mr, er' (consulting the Biro'd letters on the name-tab) 'Mr Morse!'

'Good morning!' replied Morse. 'I'll have some coffee, please – two spoonfuls of sugar.'

'My, my! *Two – sugars!*' Violet's eyes almost soared out of their whitened sockets towards the ceiling; then she turned to share the private joke with the grinning Greenaway. 'Now, look you here!' (reverting to Morse): 'You can't have no coffee nor no tea nor no sugar neither. Oh right?' She wagged a brown forefinger at a point somewhere above the bed; and twisting his neck Morse could see, behind his saline apparatus, a rectangular plaque bearing the sad little legend NIL BY MOUTH.

Chapter Three

Flowers, writing materials, and books are always welcome gifts for patients; but if you wish to bring food or drink, do ask the Sister, and she will tell you what is advisable

(*Oxford Health Authority,* Handbook for Patients and Visitors)

Detective Sergeant Lewis came into the ward just after seven o'clock that Sunday evening, clutching a Sainsbury carrier-bag with the air of a slightly guilty man walking through the Customs' shed; and at the sight of his old partner, Morse felt very glad, and just a little lachrymose.

'How come you knew I was here?'

'I'm a detective, sir – remember?'

'They phoned you, I suppose.'

'The Super. He said you sounded awful poorly when he rang yesterday morning. So he sent Dixon round, but you'd just been carried off in the ambulance. So he rang me and said I might like to see if the NHS is still up to scratch – see if you wanted anything.'

'Something like a bottle of Scotch, you mean?'

Lewis ignored the pleasantry: 'I'd've come in last night, but they said you weren't to have any visitors – only close relatives.'

'I'll have you know I'm not quite your "Orphan Annie", Lewis. I've got a great-aunt up in Alnwick somewhere.'

'Bit of a long way for her to come, sir.'

'Especially at ninety-seven . . .'

'Not a bad fellow, Strange, is he?' suggested Lewis, after a slightly awkward little pause.

'Not when you get to know him, I suppose,' admitted Morse.

'Would you say *you've* got to know him?'

Morse shook his head.

'Well?' said Lewis briskly. 'How *are* things? What do they say's the trouble?'

'Trouble? No trouble! It's just a case of mistaken identity.'

Lewis grinned. 'Seriously, though?'

'Seriously? Well they've put me on some great big round white pills that cost a couple of quid a time, so the nurses say. Do you realize you can get a very decent little bottle of claret for that price?'

'What about the food – is that all right?'

'Food? *What* food? Except for the pills they haven't given me a thing.'

'No drink, either?'

'Are you trying to set back my medical progress, Lewis?'

'Is that what – what *that* means?' Lewis jerked his eyes upwards to the fateful warning above the bed.

'That's just precautionary,' said Morse, with unconvincing nonchalance.

Lewis's eyes jerked, downwards this time, towards the carrier-bag.

'Come on, Lewis! What have you got in there?'

Lewis reached inside the bag and brought out a bottle of lemon-and-barley water, and was most pleasantly surprised to witness the undisguised delight on Morse's face.

'It was just that the missus thought – well, you know, you wouldn't be allowed to drink – to drink anything else much.'

'*Very* kind of her! You just tell her that the way things are I'd rather have a bottle of that stuff than a whole crate of whisky.'

'You don't mean that, do you, sir?'

'Doesn't stop you telling her, though, does it?'

'And here's a book,' added Lewis, withdrawing one further item from the bag – a book entitled *Scales of Injustice: A Comparative Study of Crime and its Punishment as Recorded in the County of Shropshire, 1842–1852.*

Morse took the thick volume and surveyed its inordinately lengthy title, though without any obvious enthusiasm. 'Mm! Looks a fairly interesting work.'

'You don't mean that, do you?'

'No,' said Morse.

'It's a sort of family heirloom and the missus just thought—'

'You tell that wonderful missus of yours that I'm very pleased with it.'

'Perhaps you'll do me a favour and leave it in the hospital library when you come out.'

Morse laughed quietly; and Lewis was strangely gratified by his chief's reactions, and smiled to himself.

He was still smiling when an extraordinarily pretty young nurse, with a freckled face and mahogany-highlighted hair, came to Morse's bedside, waved an admonitory finger at him, and showed her white and beautifully regular teeth in a dumbshow of disapproval as she pointed to the lemon-and-barley bottle which Morse had placed on his locker-top. Morse, in turn, nodded his full appreciation of the situation and showed his own reasonably regular, if rather off-white, teeth as he mouthed a silent 'OK'.

'Who's that?' whispered Lewis, when she had passed upon her way.

'That, Lewis, is the Fair Fiona. Lovely, don't you think? I sometimes wonder how the doctors manage to keep their dirty hands off her.'

'Perhaps they don't.'

'I thought you'd come in here to cheer me up!'

But for the moment good cheer seemed in short supply. The ward sister (whom Lewis had not noticed as he'd entered – merely walking straight through, like everyone else, as he'd thought) had clearly been keeping her dragon's eye on events in general, and in particular on events around the bed where the dehydrated Chief Inspector lay. To which bed, with purposeful stride, she now took the few steps needed from the vantage point behind the main desk. Her left hand immediately grasped the offending bottle on the locker-top, while her eyes fixed unblinkingly upon the luckless Lewis.

'We have our regulations in this hospital – a copy of them is posted just outside the ward. So I shall be glad if you follow those regulations and report to me or whoever's in charge if you intend to visit again. It's absolutely vital that we follow a routine here – try to understand that! Your friend here is quite poorly, and we're all trying our vairy best to see that he gets well again quickly. Now we canna do that if you are going to bring in anything *you* think might do him good, because you'd bring in all the *wrong* things, OK? I'm sure you appreciate what I'm saying.'

She had spoken in a soft Scots accent, this grimly visaged, tight-lipped sister, a silver buckle clasped around her dark-blue uniform; and Lewis, the colour tidally risen under his pale cheeks, looked wretchedly uncomfortable as she turned away – and was gone. Even Morse, for a few moments, appeared strangely cowed and silent.

'Who's that?' asked Lewis (for the second time that evening).

'You have just had an encounter with the embittered soul of our ward sister – devoted to an ideal of humourless efficiency: a sort of Calvinistic Thatcherite.'

'And what she says . . .?'

Morse nodded. 'She is, Lewis, in charge, as I think you probably gathered.'

'Doesn't have to be so *sharp*, does she?'

'*Forget* it, Lewis! She's probably disappointed in her love-life or something. Not surprising with a face—'

'What's her name?'

'They call her "Nessie".'

'Was she born near the Loch?'

'*In* it, Lewis.'

The two men laughed just a little; yet the incident had been unpleasant and Lewis in particular found it difficult to put it behind him. For a further five minutes he quizzed Morse quietly about the other patients; and Morse told him of the dawn departure of the ex-Indian-Army man. For still another five minutes, the two men exchanged words about Police HQ at Kidlington; about the Lewis family; about the less-than-sanguine prospects of Oxford United in the current soccer campaign. But nothing could quite efface the fact that 'that bloody sister' (as Morse referred to her) had cast a darkling shadow over the evening visit; had certainly cast a shadow over Lewis. And Morse himself was suddenly feeling hot and sweaty, and (yes, if he were honest) just a fraction wearied of the conversation.

'I'd better be off then, sir.'

'What else have you got in that bag?'

'Nothing—'

'Lewis! My stomach may be out of order for the minute but there's nothing wrong with my bloody ears!'

Slowly the dark clouds began to lift for Lewis, and when, after prolonged circumspection, he decided that the Customs Officer was momentarily off her guard, he withdrew a small, flattish bottle, wrapped in soft, dark-blue tissue-paper – much the colour of Nessie's uniform.

'But not until it's *official* like!' hissed Lewis, palming

the gift surreptitiously into Morse's hand beneath the bedclothes.

'Bell's?' asked Morse.

Lewis nodded.

It was a happy moment.

For the present, however, the attention of all was diverted by another bell that sounded from somewhere, and visitors began to stand and prepare for their departure: a few, perhaps, with symptoms of reluctance; but the majority with signs of only partially concealed relief. As Lewis himself rose to take his leave, he dipped his hand once more into the carrier-bag and produced his final offering: a paperback entitled *The Blue Ticket*, with a provocative picture of an economically clad nymphet on the cover.

'I thought – I thought you might enjoy something a little bit lighter, sir. The missus doesn't know—'

'I hope she's never found you reading this sort of rubbish, Lewis!'

'Haven't read it *yet*, sir.'

'Well, the, er, title's a bit shorter than the other thing . . .'

Lewis nodded, and the two friends shared a happy grin.

'Time to go, I'm afraid!' The Fair Fiona was smiling down at them, especially (it seemed) smiling down at Lewis, for whom every cloud was suddenly lifted from the weather-chart. As for Morse, he was glad to be alone again; and when the ward finally cleared of its last visitor, the hospital system smoothly, inexorably, reorientated itself once more to the care and treatment of the sick.

It was only after further testings of pulse and blood pressure, after the administration of further medicaments, that Morse had the opportunity (unobserved) of reading the blurb of the second work of literature (well, literature of a sort) which was now in his possession:

> Diving into the water, young Steve Mingella had managed to pull the little girl's body on to the hired yacht and to apply to her his clumsy version of the kiss-of-life. Miraculously, the six-year-old had survived, and for a few days Steve was the toast of the boat clubs along the Florida Keys. After his return to New York he received a letter – and inside the letter a ticket from the young girl's father, the playboy proprietor of the city's most exclusive, expensive, and exotic night-spot, a club specializing in the wildest sexual fantasies. The book opens as Steve treads diffidently across the thick carpeted entrance of that erotic wonderland, and shows to the topless blonde seated at Reception the ticket he has received – *a ticket coloured deepest blue*...

Chapter Four

> My evening visitors, if they cannot see the clock, should find the time in my face
>
> (*Emerson,* Journals)

Half an hour after Lewis's departure, Fiona came again to Morse's bedside and asked him to unfasten his pyjama bottoms, to turn over on his left side, and to expose his right buttock. Which orders having been obeyed (as Morse used to say when he studied the Classics), the unsmiling Nessie was summoned to insert a syringe of colourless liquid into his flank. This insertion (he could see nothing over his right shoulder) seemed to Morse to have been effected with less than professional finesse; and he heard himself grunt 'Christ!' when the plunger was pressed, his body twitching involuntarily as what felt like a bar of iron was implanted into his backside.

'You'll feel a wee bit sleepy,' was the laconic comment of the Loch Ness Monster; and Fiona was left to pour some disinfectant on to a piece of gauze, which she proceeded to rub vigorously across and around the punctured area.

'She'd have landed a top job in Buchenwald, that woman!' said Morse. But from the uncomprehending look on her face, he suddenly realized that Nazi concentration camps were as far back in the young nurse's past as the relief of Mafeking was in his own; and he felt his age. It was forty-four years now since the end of the Second World War . . . and this young . . . nurse . . . could only be . . . Morse was conscious of feeling very weary, very tired. 'What I mean is . . .' (Morse pulled his pyjama bottoms up with some difficulty) '. . . she's so . . . sharp!' Yes, Lewis had used that word.

'Did you realize that was my very first injection? Sorry if it hurt a bit – I'll get better.'

'I thought it was . . .'

'Yes, I know.' She smiled down at him and Morse's eyelids drooped heavily over his tired eyes. Nessie had said he'd feel a wee bit . . . weary . . .

His head jerked down against his chest, and Fiona settled him against the pillows, gently looking at him as he lay there, and wondering for the dozenth time in her life why all the men who attracted her had either been happily married long, long since, or else were far, far, far too old.

Morse felt a soft-fingered hand on his right wrist, and opened his eyes to find himself staring up into the face of an extraordinary-looking personage. She was a very small woman, of some seventy-five to eighty summers, wispily white-haired, her face deeply wrinkled and unbeautiful, with an old-fashioned NHS hearing-aid plugged into her left ear, its cord stretching down to a battered appliance in the pocket of a dirty, loose, grey-woollen cardigan. She appeared naïvely unaware that any apology might perhaps be called for in wakening a weary patient. Who was she? Who had let her in? It was 9.45 p.m. by the ward clock and two night nurses were on duty. Go away! Go away, you stupid old crow!

'Mr Horse? Mr Horse, is it?' Her rheumy eyes squinted myopically at the Elastoplast name-tag, and her mouth distended in a dentured smile.

'Morse!' said Morse. 'M-O . . .'

'Do you know, I think they've spelt your name wrong, Mr Horse. I'll try to remember to tell—'

'Morse! M-O-R-S-E!'

'Yes – but it *was* expected, you know. They'd already told me that Wilfrid had only a few days left to live. And we all do get older, don't we? Older every single day.'

Yes, yes, clear off! I'm bloody tired, can't you *see*?

'Fifty-two years, we'd been together.'

Morse, belatedly, realized who she was, and he nodded more sympathetically now: 'Long time!'

'He *liked* being here, you know. He was so grateful to you all—'

'I'm afraid I only came in a couple of days ago—'

'That's exactly why he wanted me to thank *all* of you – all his old friends here.' She spoke in a precise, prim manner, with the diction of a retired Latin mistress.

'He was a fine man . . .' began Morse, a little desperately. 'I wish I'd got to know him. As I say, though, I only got in a day or two ago – stomach trouble – nothing serious . . .'

The hearing-aid began to whistle shrilly, picking up some internal feedback, and the old lady fiddled about ineffectually with the ear-piece and the control switches. 'And that's *why*' (she began now to talk in intermittent italics) 'I've got this little *book* for you. He was *so* proud of it. Not that he *said* so, of course – but he *was*. It took him a very long time and it was a *very* happy day for him when it was printed.'

Morse nodded with gratitude as she handed him a little booklet in bottle-green paper covers. 'It's very kind of you because, as I say, I only came in—'

'Wilfrid would have been *so* pleased.'

Oh dear.

'And you will *promise* to read it, won't you?'

'Oh yes – certainly!'

The old lady fingered her whistling aid once more, smiled with the helplessness of a stranded angel, said 'Goodbye, Mr Horse!' and moved on to convey her undying gratitude to the occupant of the adjacent bed.

Morse looked down vaguely at the slim volume thus presented: it could contain no more than – what? – some twenty-odd pages. He would certainly look at it later, as he'd promised. Tomorrow, perhaps. For the moment, he could think of nothing but closing his weary eyes once more, and he placed *Murder on the Oxford Canal*, by Wilfrid M. Deniston, inside his locker, on top of *Scales of Injustice* and *The Blue Ticket* – the triad of new works he'd so recently acquired. Tomorrow, yes . . .

Almost immediately he fell into a deep slumber, where he dreamed of a long cross-country race over the fields of his boyhood, where there, at the distant finishing-line, sat a topless blonde, a silver buckle clasped around her waist, holding in her left hand a pint of beer with a head of winking froth.

Chapter Five

> This type of writing sometimes enjoys the Lethean faculty of making those who read it forget to ask what it means, or indeed if it means anything very substantive
>
> (*Alfred Austin,* The Bridling of Pegasus)

THE ENDOSCOPY, PERFORMED under a mild anaesthetic at 10 o'clock the following morning (Monday), persuaded the surgeons at the JR2 that in Morse's case the knife was probably not needed; their prognosis, too, was modestly encouraging, provided the patient could settle into a more cautiously sober and restrictive regimen for the months (and years) ahead. Furthermore, as a token of their muted optimism, the patient was that very evening to be allowed one half-bowl of oxtail soup and a portion of vanilla ice-cream – and for Morse any gourmand *à la carte* menu could hardly have been more gloriously welcome.

Lewis reported to Sister Maclean at 7.30 p.m., and was unsmilingly nodded through Customs without having to declare one get-well card (from Morse's secretary), a tube of mint-flavoured toothpaste (from

Mrs Lewis), and a clean hand-towel (same provenance). Contentedly, for ten minutes or so, the two men talked of this and that, with Lewis receiving the firm impression that his chief was recovering rapidly.

Fiona the Fair put in a brief appearance towards the end of this visit, shaking out Morse's pillows and placing a jug of cold water on his locker.

'Lovely girl,' ventured Lewis.

'You're married – remember?'

'Done any reading yet?' Lewis nodded towards the locker.

'Why do you ask?'

Lewis grinned: 'It's the missus – she was just wondering . . .'

'I'm half-way through it, tell her. Riveting stuff!'

'You're not serious—'

'Do you know how to spell "riveting"?'

'What – one "t" or two, you mean?'

'And do you know what "stools" are?'

'Things you sit on?'

Morse laughed – a genuine, carefree, pain-free laugh. It was good to have Lewis around; and the vaguely puzzled Lewis was glad to find the invalid in such good spirits.

Suddenly, there beside the bed, re-mitreing the bottom right-hand corner of the blankets, was Sister Maclean herself.

'Who brought the jug of water?' she enquired in her soft but awesome voice.

'It's all right, Sister,' began Morse, 'the doctor said—'

'Nurse Welch!' The ominously quiet words carried easily across the ward, and Lewis stared at the floor in pained embarrassment as Student Nurse Welch walked warily over to Morse's bed, where she was firmly admonished by her superior. Free access to liquids was to be available only w.e.f. the following dawn – *and not before*. Had the student nurse not read the notes before going the rounds with her water-jugs? And if she had, did she not realize that no hospital could function satisfactorily with such sloppiness? If it mightn't seem important on *this* occasion, did the student nurse not realize that it could be absolutely vital on the *next*?

Another sickening little episode; and for Lewis one still leaving a nasty taste when a few minutes later he bade his chief farewell. Morse himself had said nothing at the time, and said nothing now. Never, he told himself, would he have reprimanded any member of his own staff in such cavalier fashion in front of other people: and then, sadly, he recalled that quite frequently he had done precisely that . . . All the same, he would have welcomed the opportunity of a few quiet words with the duly chastened Fiona before she went home.

There was virtually no one around in the ward now: the Ethiopian athlete was doing the hospital rounds once more; and two of the other patients had shuffled their way to the gents. Only a woman of about thirty, a slimly attractive, blonde-headed woman (Walter Greenaway's daughter, Morse guessed – and guessed correctly) still sat beside her father. She had given Morse a quick glance as she'd come in, but now hardly appeared to notice him as she made her way out of the ward, and pressed the 'Down' button in front of the top-floor lifts. It was her father who was monopolizing her thoughts, and she gave no more than a cursory thought to the man whose name appeared to be 'Morse' and whose eyes, as she had noticed, had followed her figure with a lively interest on her exit.

The time was 8.40 p.m.

Feeling minimally guilty that he had not as yet so much as opened the cover of the precious work that Mrs Lewis had vouchsafed to his keeping, Morse reached for the book from his locker, and skimmed through its first paragraph:

> 'Diversity rather than uniformity has almost invariably been seen to characterize the criminal behaviour-patterns of any technologically developing society. The attempt to resolve any conflicts and/or inconsistencies which may arise in the analysis and interpretation of such patterns (see Appendix 3, pp. 492 ff.) is absolutely vital; and the inevitable reinterpretation of this perpetually variable data is the raw material for several recent studies into the causation of criminal behaviour. Yet conflicting strategic choices within heterogeneous areas, starkly differentiated creeds, greater knowledge of variable economic performances, as well as physical, physiological, or physiognomical peculiarities – all these

> facts (as we shall maintain) can suggest possible avenues never exhaustively explored by any previous student of criminal behaviour in nineteenth-century Britain.'

'Christ!' muttered Morse (for the second time that evening). A few years ago he might possibly have considered persevering with such incomprehensible twaddle. But no longer. Stopping momentarily only to marvel at the idiocy of the publisher who had allowed such pompous polysyllaby ever to reach the compositor in the first place, he closed the stout work smartly – and resolved to open it never again.

As it happened, he was to break this instant resolution very shortly; but for the moment there was a rather more attractive proposition awaiting him in his locker: the pornographic paperback which Lewis (praise the Lord!) had smuggled in.

A yellow flash across the glossy cover made its promise to the reader of Scorching Lust and Primitive Sensuality – this claim supported by the picture of a superbly buxom beauty sunning herself on some golden-sanded South Sea island, completely naked except for a string of native beads around her neck. Morse opened the book and skimmed (though a little more slowly than before) a second paragraph that evening. And he was immediately aware of a no-nonsense, clear-cut English style that was going to take the palm every time from the sprawling, spawning, sociological nonsense he had just encountered:

'She surfaced from the pool and began to unbutton her clinging, sodden blouse. And as she did so, the young men all fell silent, urging her – praying her! – in some unheard but deafening chorus, to strip herself quickly and completely – their eyes now rivetted to the carmined tips of her slimly sinuous fingers as they slipped inside her blouse, and so slowly, so tantalizingly, flicked open a further button . . .'

'Christ!!' It was the third time that Morse had used the same word that evening, and the one that took the prize for blasphemous vehemence. He leaned back against his pillows with a satisfied smile about his lips, clasping to himself the prospect of a couple of hours of delicious titillation on the morrow. He could bend those covers back easily enough; and it would be no great difficulty temporarily to assume the facial expression of a theological student reading some verses from the Minor Prophets. But whatever happened, the chances that Chief Inspector Morse would ever be fully informed about crime and its punishment in nineteenth-century Shropshire had sunk to zero.

For the moment, at any rate.

He replaced *The Blue Ticket* in his locker, on top of *Scales of Injustice* – both books now lying on top of the hitherto neglected *Murder on the Oxford Canal*, that slim volume printed privately under the auspices of The Oxford and County Local History Society.

*

As Morse nodded off once more, his brain was debating whether there was just the one word misspelled in the brief paragraph he had just read. He would look it up in Chambers when he got home. Lewis hadn't seemed to know, either . . .

Chapter Six

I enjoy convalescence. It is the part that makes the illness worth while

(*G. B. Shaw,* Back to Methuselah)

At 2 a.m. the inevitable occurred; but fortunately Morse managed to attract the quick attention of the nurse as she'd flitted like some Nightingale around the darkened wards. The noise of the curtains being drawn around his bed sounded to Morse loud enough to rouse the semi-dead. Yet none of his fellow-patients seemed to stir and she – the blessed girl! – had been quite marvellous.

'I don't even know which way up the thing should go,' confided Morse.

'Which way *round*, you mean!' Eileen (such was her name) had whispered, as she proceeded without the slightest embarrassment to explain exactly how the well-trained patient would negotiate this particular crisis. Then, leaving him with half a roll of white toilet-paper, and the firm assurance of a second coming within the next ten minutes, she was gone.

It was all over – consummated with a bowl of warm

water and a brief squirt of some odoriferous air-freshener. Whew! Not half as bad as Morse had feared – thanks to that ethereal girl; and as he smiled up gratefully at her, he thought there might have been a look in her eyes that transgressed the borders of perfunctory nursing. But Morse would always have thought there was, even if there wasn't; for he was the sort of man for whom some area of fantasy was wholly necessary, and his imagination followed the slender Eileen, as elegantly she walked away: about 5′ 8″ in height – quite tall really; in her mid-twenties; eyes greenish-hazel, in a delicately featured, high-cheekboned face; no ring of any sort on either hand. She looked so good, so wholesome, in her white uniform with its dark-blue trimmings.

Go to sleep, Morse!

At 7.30 a.m., after breakfasting on a single wafer of Weetabix with an inadequate pour-over of semi-skimmed milk (and no sugar), Morse noted with great satisfaction that the NIL BY MOUTH embargo was now in abeyance, and he poured himself a glass of water with the joy of a liberated hostage. There followed for him, that morning, the standard readings of pulse-rate and blood-pressure, a bedside wash in a portable basin, the remaking of his bed, the provision of a fresh jug of water (!), a flirting confab with Fiona, the purchase of *The Times*, a cup of Bovril from the vivacious Violet, and (blessedly) not a single spoke stuck in the hospital machinery from the *éminence grise* installed at the seat of power.

At 10.50 a.m. a white-coated cohort of consultant-cum-underlings came to stand around his bed, and to consider the progress of its incumbent. The senior man, after briefly looking through Morse's file, eyed the patient with a somewhat jaundiced eye.

'How are you feeling this morning?'

'I think I'll live on for a few more weeks – thanks to you,' said Morse, with somewhat sickening sycophancy.

'You mention here something about your drinking habits,' continued the consultant, unimpressed as it appeared with such spurious gratitude.

'Yes?'

'You drink a lot.' It was a statement.

'That's a lot, you think?'

The consultant closed the file with a sigh and handed it back to Nessie. 'During my long years in the medical profession, Mr Morse, I have learned that there are two categories of statistics which can invariably be discounted: the sexual prowess of those suffering from diabetes mellitus; and the boozing habits of our country's middle management.'

'I'm not a diabetic.'

'You will be if you keep drinking a bottle of Scotch a week.'

'Well – perhaps not *every* week.'

'You sometimes drink *two* a week, you mean?'

There was a twinkle in the consultant's eye as he waved his posse of acolytes across to the bed of the weakly Greenaway, and sat himself down on Morse's bed.

'Have you had a drop yet?'

'Drop of what?'

'It's a dreadful give-away, you know' (the consultant nodded to the locker) ' – that tissue paper.'

'Oh!'

'Not *tonight* – all right?'

Morse nodded.

'And one further word of advice. Wait till Sister's off duty!'

'She'd skin me alive!' mumbled Morse.

The consultant looked at Morse strangely. 'Well, since you mention it, yes. But that wasn't what I was thinking of, no.'

'Something worse?'

'She's about the most forbidding old biddy in the profession; but just remember she comes from north of the border.'

'I'm not quite sure . . .'

'She'd probably' (the consultant bent down and whispered in Morse's ear) ' – she'd probably draw the curtains and insist on fifty-fifty!'

Morse began to feel more happily settled; and after twenty minutes with *The Times* (Letters read, Crossword completed), one-handedly he folded back the covers of *The Blue Ticket*, and moving comfortably down against his pillows started Chapter One.

'Good book?'

'So-so!' Morse had not been aware of Fiona's presence, and he shrugged non-committally, holding the pages rigidly in his left hand.

'What's it called?'

'Er – *The Blue – The Blue City.*'

'Detective story, isn't it? I think my mum's read that.'

Morse nodded uneasily. 'Do *you* read a lot?'

'I used to, when I was young and beautiful.'

'This morning?'

'Sit up!'

Morse leaned forward as she softened up his pillows with a few left hooks and right crosses, and went on her way.

'Lovely girl, isn't she?' It wasn't Lewis this time who made the obvious observation, but the stricken Greenaway, now much recovered, and himself reading a book whose title was plain for all to see: *The Age of Steam.*

Morse pushed his own novel as unobtrusively as possible into his locker: it was a little disappointing, anyway.

'*The Blue Ticket* – that's what it is,' said Greenaway.

'Pardon?'

'You got the title wrong – it's *The Blue Ticket.*'

'Did I? Ah yes! I, er, I don't know why I'm bothering to read it, really.'

'Same reason I did, I suppose. Hoping for a bit of sex every few pages.'

Morse grinned defeatedly.

'It's a bit of a let-down,' went on Greenaway in his embarrassingly stentorian voice. 'My daughter sometimes brings me one or two books like that.'

'She was the woman – last night?'

The other nodded. 'In library work ever since she was eighteen – twelve years. In the Bodley these last six.'

Morse listened patiently to a few well-rehearsed statistics about the mileage of book-shelving in the warrens beneath the Bodleian; and was already learning something of the daughter's *curriculum vitae* when the monologue was terminated by cleaners pushing the beds around in a somewhat cavalier fashion, and slopping their mops into dingily watered buckets.

At 1.30 p.m., after what seemed to him a wretchedly insubstantial lunch, Morse was informed that he was scheduled that afternoon to visit various investigative departments; and that for this purpose the saline-drip would be temporarily removed. And when a hospital porter finally got him comfortably into a wheelchair, Morse felt that he had certainly climbed a rung or two up the convalescence ladder.

It was not until 3.30 p.m. that he returned to the ward, weary, impatient, and thirsty – in reverse order of severity. Roughly, though oddly painlessly, a silent Nessie, just before going off duty, had reaffixed into his right wrist the tube running down from a newly hung drip; and with the eyes of a now fully alert Greenaway upon him, Morse decided that Steve Mingella's sexual fantasies might have to be postponed a while. And when a small, mean-faced Englishwoman (doubtless Violet's understudy) had dispensed just about enough viscous liquid from her tureen to cover the bottom of his soup bowl, Morse's earlier euphoria had almost evaporated. He wouldn't even be seeing Lewis – the latter (as he'd told Morse) taking out the missus for some celebration (reason unspecified). At 7.05 p.m. he managed to sort out his headphones for *The Archers*; and at 7.20 p.m., he decided to dip into the late Colonel's *magnum opus.* By 7.30 p.m. he was so engrossed that it was only after finishing Part One that he noticed the presence of Christine Greenaway, the beautiful blonde from the Bodley.

Chapter Seven

Murder on the Oxford Canal

The author wishes to acknowledge the help he has so freely received from several sources; but particularly from the Bodleian Library, Oxford; from the *Proceedings of the North Oxford Local History Society*; and from the *Court Registers* of the City of Oxford Assizes, 1859 and 1860.

Further details of the trials mentioned in the following pages may be found in the editions of *Jackson's Oxford Journal* for 20th and 27th August, 1859; and of the same journal for 15th and 22nd April, 1860.

PART ONE

A Profligate Crew

THOSE WHO EXPLORE the back-streets and the by-ways of our great cities, or indeed our small cities, will sometimes stumble (almost literally, perhaps) upon sad memorials, hidden in neglected churchyards – churchyards which seem wholly separated from any formal ecclesiastical edifice, and which are come across purely by accident at the far side of red-bricked walls, or pressed upon by tall houses – untended, silent, forgotten. Until recent years, such a churchyard was to be found at the lower end of the pretty little road in North Oxford, now designated Middle Way, which links the line of Summertown shops in South Parade with the expensively elegant houses along Squitchey Lane, to the north. But in the early nineteen-sixties most of those tomb-stones which had stood in irregular ranks in the Summertown Parish Churchyard (for such was its official name) were removed from their original, supra-corporal sites in order to afford a rather less melancholic aspect to those who were about to pay their deposits on the flats being built upon those highly desirable if slightly lugubrious acres. Each there in his narrow cell had once been laid, and each would there remain; yet after 1963 no one, for certain, could have marked that final resting place.

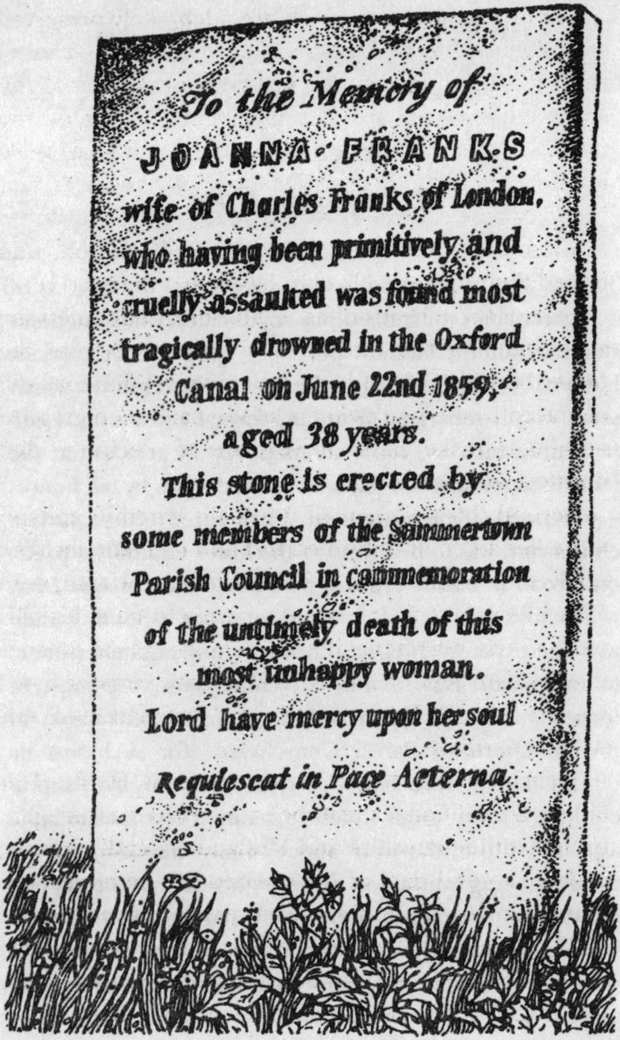
To the Memory of
JOANNA FRANKS
wife of Charles Franks of London,
who having been primitively and
cruelly assaulted was found most
tragically drowned in the Oxford
Canal on June 22nd 1859,
aged 38 years.
This stone is erected by
some members of the Summertown
Parish Council in commemoration
of the untimely death of this
most unhappy woman.
Lord have mercy upon her soul
Requiescat in Pace Aeterna

The few headstones which are adequately preserved and which are to be found – even to this day – leaning almost upright against the northern perimeter of the aforesaid enclave, are but one tenth or so of the memorials once erected there, in the second and third quarters of the nineteenth century, by relatives and friends whose earnest wish was to perpetuate the names of those souls, now perhaps known only to God, who passed their terrestrial lives in His faith and fear.

One of these headstones, a moss-greened, limestone slab (standing the furthest away but three from the present thoroughfare) bears an epitaph which may still be traced by the practised eye of the patient epigraphist – though make haste if you are to decipher that disintegrating lettering!

Beyond this poignant (if unusually lengthy) epitaph there lies a tale of unbridled lust and drunken lechery; a tale of a hapless and a helpless young woman who found herself at the mercy of coarse and most brutally uninhibited boatmen, during an horrendous journey made nearly one hundred and twenty years ago – a journey whose details are the subject-matter of our present narrative.

Joanna Franks hailed originally from Derby. Her father, Daniel Carrick, had been accredited as an agent to the Nottinghamshire and Midlands Friendly Society; and for a good deal of his married life he appears to have maintained a position as a reasonably prosperous and well-respected figure in his home community. Later, however – and certainly in the few years prior to the tragic death of his only daughter (there was a younger brother, Daniel) – he encountered a period of hard times.

Joanna's first husband was F. T. Donavan, whose family sprang from County Meath. He is described by one of his contemporaries as "an Irishman of many parts", and being a man of large physique we learn that he was familiarly (and predictably) known by the nickname of 'Hefty' Donavan. He was a conjurer by profession (or by one of them!) and appeared in many theatres and music-halls, both in London and in the provinces. In order to attract some badly needed publicity, he had at some unspecified date assumed the splendidly grandiloquent title of 'Emperor of all the Illusionists'; and the following theatre handbill was printed at his own expense to herald his appearance at the City of Nottingham Music Hall in early September 1856:

> 'Mr DONAVAN, citizen of the World and of Ireland, most humbly and respectfully informs all members of the upper and the lower nobilities, folk of the landed gentry, and the citizens of the historic district of Nottingham, that in view of his superior and unrivalled excellencies in MAGIC and DECEPTION, he has had conferred upon him, by the supreme conclave of the Assembly of Superior Magicians, this last year, the unchallenged title of EMPEROR of all the Illusionists, and

> this particularly by virtue of the amazing trick of cutting off a cockerel's head and then restoring the bird to its pristine animation. It was this same DONAVAN, the greatest man in the World, who last week diverted his great audience in Croydon by immersing his whole body, tightly secured and chained, in a tank of the most corrosive acid for eleven minutes and forty-five seconds, as accurately measured by scientific chronometer.'

Three years earlier Donavan had written (and found a publisher for) his only legacy to us, a work entitled *The Comprehensive Manual of the Conjuring Arts.* But the great man's career was beginning to prove progressively unsuccessful, and no stage appearances whatsoever are traceable to 1858. In that year, he died, a childless and embittered man, whilst on holiday with a friend in Ireland, where his grave now rests in a burial-plot overlooking Bertnaghboy Bay. Some time afterwards his widow, Joanna, met and fell deeply in love with one Charles Franks, an ostler from Liverpool.

Like her first, Joanna's second marriage appears to have been a happy one, in spite of the fact that times were still hard and money still scarce. The new Mrs Franks was to find employment, as a dressmaker and designers' model, with a Mrs Russell of 34 Runcorn Terrace, Liverpool. But Franks himself was less successful in his quest for regular employment, and finally decided to try his luck in London. Here his great expectations were soon realized for he was almost immediately engaged as an ostler at the busy George & Dragon Inn on the Edgware Road, where we find him duly lodged in the spring of 1869. In late May of that same year he sent his wife a guinea (all he could afford) and begged her to join him in London as soon as possible.

On the morning of Saturday, June 11th, 1859, Joanna Franks, carrying two small trunks, bade her farewell to Mrs Russell in Runcorn Terrace, and made her way by barge from Liverpool to Preston Brook, the northern terminus of the Trent and Mersey Canal, which had been opened some eighty years earlier. Here she joined one of Pickford & Co.'s express (or 'fly') boats[1] which was departing for Stoke-on-Trent and Fradley Junction, and thence, via the Coventry and Oxford Canals, through to London on the main Thames waterway. The fare of sixteen shillings and eleven pence was considerably cheaper than the fare on the Liverpool–London railway line which had been opened some twenty years earlier.

Joanna was an extremely petite and attractive figure, wearing an Oxford-blue dress, with a white kerchief around her neck, and a figured silk bonnet with a bright pink ribbon. The clothes may not have been new; but they were not inexpensive, and they gave to Joanna a very tidy appearance indeed. A very tempting appearance, too, as we shall soon discover.

[1] A 'fly' boat travels round the clock, with a double crew, working shifts, with horses exchanged at regular intervals along the canals.

The captain of the narrow-boat *Barbara Bray* was a certain Jack 'Rory' Oldfield from Coventry. According to later testimony of fellow boat-people and other acquaintances, he was basically a good-natured sort of fellow, of a blunt, blustery type of address. He was married, though childless, and was aged 42 years. The fellow-members of his crew were: the 30-year-old Alfred Musson, alias Alfred Brotherton, a tall, rather gaunt figure, married with two young children; Walter Towns, alias Walter Thorold, the 26-year-old illiterate son of a farm-labourer, who had left his home town of Banbury in Oxfordshire some ten years earlier; and a teenaged lad, Thomas Wootton, about whom no certain facts have come down to us beyond the probability that his parents came from Ilkeston in Derbyshire.

The *Barbara Bray* left Preston Brook at 7.30 p.m. on Saturday, 11th June. At Fradley Junction, at the southern end of the Mersey Canal, she successfully negotiated her passage through the locks; and at 10 p.m. on Sunday, 19th June, she slipped quietly into the northern reaches of the Coventry Canal, and settled to a course, almost due south, that would lead down to Oxford. Progress had been surprisingly good, and there had been little or no forewarning of the tragic events which lay ahead for the *Barbara Bray*, and for her solitary paying passenger – the small and slimly attractive person of Joanna Franks, for whom such a little span of life remained.

Chapter Eight

> Style is the hallmark of a temperament stamped upon the material at hand
>
> (*André Maurois,* The Art of Writing)

After reading these few pages, Morse found himself making some mental queries about a few minor items, and harbouring some vague unease about one or two major ones. Being reluctant to disfigure the printed text with a series of marginalia, he wrote a few notes on the back of a daily hospital menu which had been left (mistakenly) on his locker.

The Colonel's style was somewhat on the pretentious side – a bit too high-flown for Morse's taste; and yet the writing a good deal above the average of its kind – with a pleasing peroration, calculated to ensure in most readers some semi-compulsive page-turning to Part Two. One of the most noticeable characteristics of the writing was the influence of Gray's 'Elegy Written in a Country Churchyard' – a poem doubtless stuck down the author's throat as a lad in some minor public school, and one leaving him with a rather lugubrious view of the human lot. One or two *very* nice touches, though, and Morse was prepared to give a couple of ticks to that epithet 'supra-corporal'. He wished, though, he had beside him that most faithful of all his literary companions, *Chambers English Dictionary*, for although he had frequently met 'ostler' in crossword puzzles, he wasn't sure *exactly* what an ostler did; and 'figured' bonnet wasn't all that obvious, was it?

Thinking of writing – and writing books – old Donavan (Joanna's first) must have been pretty competent. After all, he'd 'found a publisher' for his great work. And until the last few years of his life, this literate Irish conjurer was seemingly pulling in the crowds at all points between Croydon and Burton-on-Trent . . . He must certainly have had *something* about him, this man of many parts. 'Greatest man in the World' might be going over the top a bit, yet a mild degree of megalomania was perhaps forgivable in the publicity material of such a multi-talented performer?

'Bertnaghboy Bay?' – Morse wrote on the menu. His knowledge of geography was minimal. At his junior school, his teachers had given him a few assorted facts about the exports of Argentina, Bolivia, Chile, and the rest; and at the age of eight he had known – and still knew (with the exception of South Dakota) – all the capital cities of the American States. But that was the end of his apprenticeship in that discipline. After winning a scholarship to the local grammar school, the choice of the three 'G's had been thrust upon him: Greek, German, or Geography. Little real choice, though, for he had been thrust willy-nilly into the Greek set, where the paradigms of nouns and verbs precluded any knowledge of the Irish counties. Where *was* – what was the name? – Bertnaghboy Bay?

It was paradoxical, perhaps, that Morse should have suddenly found himself so fascinated by the Oxford Canal. He was aware that many people were besotted with boat-life, and he deemed it wholly proper that parents should seek to hand on to their offspring some love of sailing, or rambling, or keeping pets, or bird-watching, or whatever. But in Morse's extremely limited experience, narrow-boating figured as a grossly over-rated activity. Once, on the invitation of a pleasant enough couple, he had agreed to be piloted from the terminus of the Oxford Canal at Hythe Bridge Street up to the Plough at Wolvercote – a journey of only a couple of miles, which would be accomplished (he was assured) within the hour; but which in fact had been so fraught with manifold misfortunes that the finishing line was finally reached with only five minutes' drinking-time remaining – and that on a hot and thirsty Sunday noon. That particular boat had required a couple of people – one to steer the thing and one to keep hopping out for locks and what the handbook called 'attractive little drawbridges'. Now, Joanna's boat had got four of them on it – five with her; so it must surely have been awfully crowded on that long and tedious journey, pulled slowly along by some unenthusiastic horse. Too long! Morse nodded to himself – he was beginning to get the picture . . . Far quicker by rail, of course! And the fare she'd paid, 16*s* 11*d*, seemed on the face of it somewhat on the steep side for a trip as a passenger on a working-boat. In 1859? Surely so! What would the rail-fare have been then? Morse had no idea. But there were ways of finding out; there were people who knew these things . . .

He could still see in his mind's eye the painting in the cabin in which he'd travelled, with its lake, its castle, its sailing boat, and range of mountains – all in the traditional colours of red, yellow, green. But what was it like to *live* in such boats? Boats that in the nineteenth century had been crewed by assortments of men from all over the place: from the Black Country; from the colliery villages around Coventry and Derby and Nottingham; from the terraced cottages in Upper Fisher Row by the terminus in Oxford – carrying their cargoes of coal, salt, china, agricultural produce . . . other things. *What* other things? And why on earth all those 'aliases'? Were the crewmen counted a load of crooks before they ever came to court? Did every one on the Canal have two names – a 'bye-name', as it were, as well as one written in the christening-book? Surely any jury was bound to feel a fraction of prejudice against such . . . such . . . even before . . . He was feeling tired, and already his head had jerked up twice after edging by degrees towards his chest.

Charge Nurse Eileen Stanton had come on duty at 9 p.m., and Morse was still sound asleep at 9.45 p.m. when she went quietly to his bedside and gently took the hospital menu from his hand and placed it on his locker. He was probably dreaming, she decided, of some *haute cuisine* from Les Quat' Saisons, but she would have to wake him up very shortly, for his evening pills.

Chapter Nine

> What a convenient and delightful world is this world of books – if you bring to it not the obligations of the student, or look upon it as an opiate for idleness, but enter it rather with the enthusiasm of the adventurer
>
> (*David Grayson,* Adventures in Contentment)

THE FOLLOWING MORNING (Wednesday) was busy and blessed. Violet's early offerings of Bran Flakes, semi-burnt cold toast, and semi-warm weak tea, were wonderfully welcome; and when at 10 a.m. Fiona had come to remove the saline-drip (permanently), Morse knew that the gods were smiling. When, further, he walked down the corridor now to the washroom, without encumbrance, and without attendant, he felt like Florestan newly released from confinement in Act 2 of *Fidelio.* And when with full movement of both arms he freely soaped his hands and face, and examined the rather sorry job he'd earlier made of shaving, he felt a wonderfully happy man. Once out of this place (he decided) he would make some suitable, not too startling, donation to the staff in general, and invite, in particular, his favourite nurse (odds pretty even for the moment between the Fair and the Ethereal) to that restaurant in North Oxford where he would show off his (limited) knowledge of modern Greek and order a Mezéthes Tavérnas menu, the one billed as 'an epicurean feast from first dip to final sweet'. Ten quid per person, or a little more; and with wine – and liqueurs, perhaps – and one or two little extras, £30 should cover it, he hoped . . . Not that the creamy-skinned Eileen would be on duty that night. Some domestic commitments, she'd said. 'Domestic?' It worried Morse, just a little. Still, so long as Nessie wasn't going to be prowling around . . . because Morse had decided that, in the interests of his convalescence, he might well twist the little bottle's golden cap that very night.

Back in the ward, the time passed, one could say, satisfactorily. A cup of Bovril at 10.30 a.m. was followed by a further recital from Mr Greenaway of his daughter's quite exceptional qualities – a woman without whom, it appeared, the Bodleian would have considerable difficulty in discharging any of its academic functions. After which, Morse was visited by one of the ten-a-penny dietitians in the place – a plain-looking, serious-souled young madam, who took him *seriatim* through a host of low-calorie vegetables on which he could 'fill up' *ad libitum*: asparagus; bamboo-shoots; beans (broad); beans (French); beans (runner); bean-sprouts; broccoli; Brussels sprouts; cabbage (various); cauliflower; celery; chicory; chives; courgettes; cucumber – and that was only the first three letters in the eternal alphabet of a healthy dietary. Morse was so impressed with the recital of the miraculous opportunities which awaited him that he even forebore to comment on the assertion that both tomato-juice and turnip-juice were wonderfully tasty and nutritious alternatives to alcoholic beverages. Dutifully, he sought to nod at suitable intervals, knowing deep down that he could, should, and bloody well *would*, shed a couple of stone fairly soon. Indeed, as an earnest of his new-found resolution, he insisted on only one scoop of potatoes, and no thickened gravy whatsoever, when Violet brought her lunch-time victuals round.

In the early afternoon, after listening to the repeat of *The Archers*, the most pleasing thought struck him: no work that day at Police HQ; no worries about an evening meal; no anxieties for the morrow, except perhaps those occasioned by his newly awakened consciousness of infirmity – and of death. But not that even *that* worried him too much, as he'd confessed to Lewis: no next of kin, no dependants, no need for looking beyond a purely selfish gratification. And Morse knew exactly what he wanted now, as he sat upright, clean, cool, relaxed, against the pillows. Because, strange as it may seem, for the present he wouldn't have given two Madagascan monkeys for a further couple of chapters of *The Blue Ticket*. At that moment, and most strongly, he felt the enthusiasm of the voyager – the voyager along the canal from Coventry to Oxford. Happily, therefore, he turned to *Murder on the Oxford Canal*, Part Two.

Chapter Ten

PART TWO
A Proven Crime

Although at the time there were a few conflicting statements about individual circumstances in the following, and fatal, sequence of events, the general pattern as presented here is – and, indeed, always has been – undisputed.

The 38-odd mile stretch of the Coventry Canal (of more interest today to the industrial archaeologist than to the lover of rural quietude) appears to have been negotiated without any untoward incident, with recorded stops at the Three Tuns Inn at Fazely, and again at the Atherstone Locks, further south. What can be asserted with well-nigh certitude is that the *Barbara Bray* reached Hawkesbury Junction, at the northern end of Oxford Canal, an hour or so before midnight on Monday, 20th June. Today, the distance from Hawkesbury Junction down to Oxford is some 77 miles; and in 1859 the journey was very little longer. We may therefore assume that even with one or two protracted stops along the route, the double crew of the 'fly' boat *Barbara Bray* should have managed the journey within about thirty-six hours. And this appears to have been the case. What now follows is a reconstruction of those crucial hours, based both upon the evidence given at the subsequent trials (for there were two of them) and upon later research, undertaken by the present author and others, into the records of the Oxford Canal Company Registers and the Pickford & Co. Archives. From all the available evidence, one saddening fact stands out, quite stark and incontrovertible: the body of Joanna Franks was found just after 5.30 a.m. on Wednesday, 22nd June, in the Oxford Canal – in the triangular-shaped basin of water known as 'Duke's Cut', a short passage through to the River Thames dug by the fourth Duke of Marlborough in 1796, about two and a half miles north of the (then) canal terminus at Hayfield Wharf in the city of Oxford.

For the moment, however, let us make a jump forward in time. After a Coroner's inquest at The Running Horses Inn (now demolished, but formerly standing on the corner of Upper Fisher Row by Hythe Bridge in Oxford) the four crew members of the *Barbara Bray* were straightly charged with the murder of Joanna Franks, and were duly committed to the nearby Oxford Gaol. In the preliminary trial, held at the Oxford Summer Assizes of August 1859, there were three indictments against these men: the wilful murder of Joanna Franks by throwing her into the canal; rape upon the said woman, with different counts charging different prisoners with being principals in the commission of the offence and the others as aiders and abettors; and the stealing of various articles, the property of her husband. To a man, the crew pleaded not guilty to all charges. (Wootton, the boy, who was originally charged with them, was not named in the final indictments.)

Mr Sergeant Williams, for the prosecution, said he should first proceed on the charge of rape. However, after the completion of his case, the Judge (Mr Justice Traherne) decided that there could be no certain proof of the prisoners having committed the crime, and the Jury was therefore directed to return a verdict of 'Not Guilty' on that charge. Mr Williams then applied to the Court for a postponement of the trial under the indictment for murder, until the next Assizes, on the grounds that a material witness, Joseph Jarnell, formerly a co-prisoner in Oxford Gaol, and previously committed for bigamy, could not be heard before the Court until he had obtained a free pardon from the Secretary of State. Oldfield, the boat's captain, was understood to have made some most important disclosure to Jarnell while the two men shared the same prison-cell. Although this request was strenuously opposed by Oldfield's Counsel, Mr Judge Traherne finally consented to the suggested postponement.

The Judge appointed for the second trial, held in April 1860, was Mr Augustus Benham. There was intense public feeling locally, and the streets leading to the Assize Court in Oxford were lined with hostile crowds. The case had also excited considerable interest among many members of the legal profession. The three prisoners appeared at the bar wearing the leather belts and sleeve waistcoats usually worn at that time by the canal boatmen, and were duly charged with "wilful murder, by casting, pushing, and throwing the said Joanna Franks into the Oxford Canal by which means she was choked, suffocated, and drowned". What exactly, we must ask, had taken place on those last few, fatal miles above the stretch of water known as Duke's Cut on the Oxford Canal? The tragic story soon began to unfold itself.

There are more than adequate grounds for believing that the journey from Preston Brook down to the top of the Oxford Canal at Hawkesbury was comparatively uneventful, although it soon became known that Oldfield had sat with Joanna in the cabin while the boat was negotiated through the Northwich and Harecastle Tunnels. However, from the time the *Barbara Bray* reached the lonely locks of Napton Junction – 30-odd miles down from Hawkesbury, and with Oxford still some 50 miles distant – the story appears to change, and to change (as we shall see) dramatically.

William Stevens, a canal clerk employed by Pickford & Co., confirmed[1] that the *Barbara Bray* reached the Napton Locks at about 11 a.m. on Tuesday 21st June, and that the boat remained there, in all, for about an hour and a half. "There was a woman passenger on board", and she complained immediately to Stevens about "the conduct of the men with whom she was driven to associate". It would, he agreed, have been proper for him to have logged the complaint (the

[1] Many of the facts in the account used here are taken from the *Court Registers* of the Oxford Assizes, 1860, and from the *verbatim* transcript of those parts of the trial reported in *Jackson's Oxford Journal*, April 1860 (passim).

Barbara Bray was, after all, a Pickford & Co. transport); but he had not done so, confining his advice to the suggestion that the woman should report forthwith to the Company offices in Oxford, where it should be possible for her to switch to another boat on the last leg of her journey. Stevens had witnessed some shouted altercations between Joanna and a member of the crew, and remembered hearing Joanna speak the words: "Leave me alone – I'll have nothing to do with you!" Two of the men (Oldfield and Musson, he thought) had used some utterly disgraceful language, although he agreed with Counsel for the defence that the language of almost all boatmen at these times was equally deplorable. What seemed quite obvious to Stevens was that the crew were beginning to get very much the worse for drink, and he gave it as his opinion that they were "making very free with the spirit which was the cargo". Before setting off, the woman had complained yet again about the behaviour of the men, and Stevens had repeated his advice to her to reconsider her position once the boat reached the terminus of the Oxford Canal – where a partial off-loading of the cargo was officially scheduled.

It appears, in fact, that Stevens's advice did not go unheeded. At Banbury, some twelve miles further down the canal, Joanna made a determined effort to seek alternative transport for the remainder of her journey. Matthew Laurenson, wharfinger at Tooley's Yard, remembered most clearly Joanna's "urgent enquiries" about the times of "immediate coaches to London – and coaches from Oxford to Banbury". But nothing was convenient, and again Joanna was advised to wait until she got to Oxford – now only some 20 miles away. Laurenson put the time of this meeting as approximately 6.30–7 p.m. (it is hardly surprising that times do not always coincide exactly in the court evidence – let us recall that we are almost ten months after the actual murder), and was able to give as his general impression of the unfortunate woman that she was "somewhat flushed and afeared".

As it happened, Joanna was now to have a fellow passenger, at least for a brief period, since Agnes Laurenson, the wharfinger's wife, herself travelled south on the *Barbara Bray* down to King's Sutton Lock (five miles distant); she, too, was called to give evidence at the trial. Recalling that there was "a fellow passenger aboard who looked very agitated", Mrs Laurenson stated that Joanna may have had a drink, but that she seemed completely sober, as far as could be judged – unlike Oldfield and Musson – and that she was clearly most concerned about her personal safety.

The tale now gathers apace towards its tragic conclusion; and it was the landlord of The Crown & Castle at Aynho (just below Banbury) who was able to provide some of the most telling and damning testimony of all. When Mrs Laurenson had left the boat three miles upstream at King's Sutton, it would appear that Joanna could trust herself with the drunken boatmen no longer, according to the landlord, who had encountered her at about 10 p.m. that night. She had arrived, on foot, a little earlier and confessed that she was so frightened of the lecherous drunkards on the *Barbara*

Bray that she had determined to walk along the tow-path, even at that late hour, and to take her chances with the considerably lesser evils of foot-pads and cut-purses. She hoped (she'd said) that it would be safely possible for her to rejoin the boat later when its crew might be a few degrees the more sober. Whilst she waited for the boat to come up, the landlord offered her a glass of stout, but Joanna declined. He had kept an eye on her, however, and noticed that as she sat by the edge of the canal she appeared to be secretly sharpening a knife on the side of the lock (Musson was later found to have a cut on his left cheek, and this could have been, and probably was, made with the same knife). As the boat had drawn alongside Aynho wharf, one of the crew (the landlord was unable to say which) had "cursed the eyes of the woman and wished her in hell flames, for he loathed and detested the very sight of her". As she finally re-boarded the boat, the landlord remembered seeing Joanna being offered a drink; and, in fact, he thought she might have taken a glass. But this evidence must be discounted wholly, since Mr Bartholomew Samuels, the Oxford surgeon who conducted an immediate *post-mortem*, found no evidence whatsoever of any alcohol in poor Joanna's body.

George Bloxham, the captain of a northward-bound Pickford boat, testified that he had drawn alongside Oldfield's boat just below Aynho, and that a few exchanges had been made, as normal, between the two crews. Oldfield had referred to his woman passenger in terms which were completely "disgusting", vowing, in the crudest language, what he would do with her that very night "or else he would burke her".[2] Bloxham added that Oldfield was very drunk; and Musson and Towns, too, were "rather well away, the pair of 'em".

James Robson, keeper of the Somerton Deep Lock, said that he and his wife, Anna, were awakened at about midnight by a scream of terror coming from the direction of the lock. At first they had assumed it was the cry of a young child; but when they looked down from the bedroom window of the lock-house, they saw only some men by the side of the boat, and a woman seated on top of the cabin with her legs hanging down over the side. Three things the Robsons were able to recall from that grim night, their evidence proving so crucial at the trial. Joanna had called out in a terrified voice "I'll not go down! Don't attempt me!" Then one of the crew had shouted "Mind her legs! Mind her legs!" And after that the passenger had resumed her frightened screams: "What have you done with my shoes – oh! please tell me!" Anna Robson enquired who the woman was, and was told by one of the crew: "A passenger – don't worry!", the crewman adding that she was having words with her husband, who was with her aboard.

Forbidding to Joanna as the tall lock-house must have appeared that midnight, standing sentinel-like above the black waters, it presented her with her one

[2] Burke was a criminal who had been executed some thirty years earlier for smothering his victims and then selling their bodies for medical dissection.

last chance of life – had she sought asylum within its walls.

But she made no such request.

At this point, or shortly after, it appears that the terrified woman took another walk along the tow-path to escape the drunken crew; but she was almost certainly back on board when the boat negotiated Gibraltar Lock. After which – and only some very short time after – she must have been out walking (yet again!) since Robert Bond, a crew-hand from the narrow-boat *Isis,* gave evidence that he passed her on the tow-path. Bond recorded his surprise that such an attractive woman should be out walking on her own so late, and he recalled asking her if all was well. But she had only nodded, hurriedly, and passed on into the night. As he approached Gibraltar Lock, Bond had met Oldfield's boat, and was asked by one of its crew if he had seen a woman walking the tow-path, the man adding, in the crudest terms, what he would do to her once he had her in his clutches once again.

No one, apart from the evil boatmen on the *Barbara Bray,* was ever to see Joanna Franks alive again.

Chapter Eleven

> 'Pon my word, Watson, you are coming along wonderfully. You have really done very well indeed. It is true that you have missed everything of importance, but you have hit upon the method
>
> (*Sir Arthur Conan Doyle,* A Case of Identity)

As with Part One, Morse found himself making a few notes (mentally, this time) as he read through the unhappy narrative. For some reason he felt vaguely dissatisfied with himself. Something was nagging at his brain about Part One; but for the present he was unable to put a finger on it. It would come back to him once he'd re-read a few pages. No hurry, was there? None. The theoretical problem which his mind had suddenly seized upon was no more than a bit of harmless, quite inconsequential amusement. And yet the doubts persisted in his brain: could anyone, *anyone,* read this story and not find himself questioning one or two of the points so confidently reported? Or two or three of them? Or three or four?

What was the normal pattern of entertainment for canal boatmen, like Oldfield, on those 'protracted stops' of theirs? Changing horses was obviously one of the key activities on such occasions, but one scarcely calculated to gladden every soul. Dropping in at the local knocking-shop, then? A likely port-of-call for a few of the more strongly sexed among them, most surely. And drink? Did they drink their wages away, these boatmen, in the low-beamed bars that were built along their way? How not? Why not? What else was there to do? And though drink (as the Porter once claimed) might take away the performance, who could gainsay that it frequently provoked the desire? The desire, in this case, to rape a beautiful woman-passenger.

So many questions.

But if sex was at the bottom of things, why were the rape charges dropped at the first trial? Agreed, there was no DNA biological fingerprinting in the 1850s; no genetic code that could be read into some desperate fellow's swift ejaculations. But even in that era, the charge of rape could often be made to stick without too much difficulty; and Confucius's old pleasantry about the comparative immobility of a man with his trousers round his ankles must have sounded just as hollow then as now. Certainly to the ears of Joanna Franks.

The footnote referring to the *Court Registers* had been a surprise, and it would be of interest, certainly to the sociologist, to read something of contemporary attitudes to rape in 1859. Pretty certainly it would be a few leagues less sympathetic than that reflected in Morse's morning copy of *The Times*: 'Legal Precedent in Civil Action – £35,000 damages for Rape Victim'.

Where were those Registers, though – if they still existed? They might (Morse supposed) have explained the Colonel's bracketed caveat about discrepancies. But *what* discrepancies? There must have been *something* in old Deniston's mind, something that bothered him just that tiny bit. The Greeks had a word for it – *parakrousis* – the striking of a slightly wrong note in an otherwise tuneful harmony.

Was that 'wrong note' struck by Mrs Laurenson, perhaps? Whatever the situation had been with Joanna, this Laurenson woman (with her husband's full assent, one must assume) had joined the *Barbara Bray* for the journey down to King's Sutton with – as the reader was led to believe – a boat-load of sexually rampant dipsomaniacs. Difficult to swallow? Unless of course the wharfinger, Laurenson, was perfectly happy to get rid of his missus for the night – or for any night. But such a line of reasoning seemed fanciful, and there was a further possibility – a very simple, and really rather a startling one: that the crew of the *Barbara Bray* had *not* been all that belligerently blotto at the time! But no. Every piece of evidence – surely! – pointed in the opposite direction; pointed to the fact that the boatmen's robes of honour (in Fitzgeraldian phrase) were resting, like the Confucian rapist's, only just above their boot-laces.

Boots . . . shoes . . .

What was all that about those shoes? Why were they figuring so repeatedly in the story? There would surely have been more intimate items of Joanna's wardrobe to pilfer if the crewmen had been seeking to effect some easier sexual congress. One of them *might*, perhaps, have been a clandestine foot-fetishist . . .

Morse, telling himself not to be so stupid, looked again at the last couple of pages of the text. A bit over-written, all that stuff about the sentinel-like old lock-house, looking out over the dark waters. Not bad, though: and at least it made Morse resolve to drive out and see it for himself, once he was well again. Unless the planners and the developers had already pulled it down.

Like they'd pulled down St Ebbe's . . .

Such were some of Morse's thoughts after reading his second instalment. It was quite natural that he should wish to eke out the pleasures afforded by the Colonel's text. Yet it must be admitted that, once again, Morse had almost totally failed to conceive the real problems raised by this narrative. Usually, Morse was a league and a league in front of any competitive intellects; and even now his thought processes were clear and unorthodox. But for the time being, he was far below his best. Too near the picture. He was standing where the coloured paints on the narrow-boat's sides had little chance of imposing any pattern on his eye. What he really needed was to stand that bit further back from the picture; to get a more synoptic view of things. 'Synoptic' had always been one of Morse's favourite words. Quickly Morse re-read Part Two. But he seemed to see little more in general terms than he had done earlier, although there were a few extra points of detail which had evaded him on the first reading, and he stored them away, haphazardly, in his brain.

There was that capital 'J', for example, that the Colonel favoured whenever he wished to emphasize the enormity of human iniquity and the infallibility of Jury and Judicature – like the capital 'G' the Christian Churches always used for God.

Then there were those journeys through the two tunnels, when Oldfield had sat with Joanna . . . or when, as Morse translated things, he put his arm around the frightened girl in the eerie darkness, and told her not to be afraid . . .

And those last complex, confusing paragraphs! She had been desperately anxious to get off the boat and away from her tipsy persecutors – so much seemed beyond any reasonable doubt. But, if so, why, according to that selfsame evidence, had she always been so anxious to get back *on* again?

Airy-fairy speculation, all this; but there were at least two things that could be factually checked. 'Nothing was convenient', it had said, and any researcher worth his salt could easily verify *that.* What *was* available, at the time Joanna reached Banbury? He could also soon discover how much any alternative route to London would have cost. What, for example, was the rail-fare to London in 1859? For that matter, what exactly had been the rail-fare between Liverpool and London, a fare which appeared to have been beyond the Franks's joint financial resources?

Interesting . . .

As, come to think of it, were those double quotation

marks in the text – presumably the actual words, directly transcribed, and reported *verbatim*, and therefore primary source material for the crewmen's trial. Morse looked through the interspersed quotations again, and one in particular caused his mind to linger: "coaches to London – and coaches from Oxford to Banbury". Now, if those were the *exact* words Joanna had used . . . *if* they were . . . Why had she asked for the times of coaches 'from Oxford to Banbury'? Surely, she should have been asking about coaches *from Banbury to Oxford.* Unless . . . unless . . .

Again, it all seemed most interesting – at least to Morse. What, finally, was he to make of that drink business? Had Joanna been drinking – or had she not? There was some curious ambivalence in the text; and perhaps this may have been in the Colonel's mind when he referred to 'a few conflicting statements'? But no – that was impossible. Mr Bartholomew Samuels had found no alcohol in Joanna's body, and that was that!

Or, rather, would have been, to most men.

The thought of drink had begun to concentrate Morse's mind powerfully, and with great circumspection and care, Morse poured a finger of Scotch into his bedside glass, with the same amount of plain water. Wonderful! Pity that no one would ever believe his protestations that Scotch was a necessary stimulant to his brain cells! For after a few minutes his mind was flooding with ideas – exciting ideas! – and furthermore he realized that he could begin to test one or two of his hypotheses that very evening.

That is, if Walter Greenaway's daughter came to visit.

Chapter Twelve

> Th' first thing to have in a libry is a shelf. Fr'm time to time this can be decorated with lithrachure. But th' shelf is th' main thing
>
> (*Finley Peter Dunne,* Mr Dooley Says)

As she walked down Broad Street at 7.40 a.m. the following morning (Thursday), Christine Greenaway was thinking (*still* thinking) about the man who had spoken to her the previous evening in Ward 7C on the top floor of the JR2. (It was only on rare occasions that she welcomed her father's pride in his ever-loving daughter!) It wasn't that she'd been obsessively preoccupied with the man ever since; but there had been a semi-waking, overnight awareness of him. All because he'd asked her, so nicely, to look up something for him in the Bodley. So earnest, so grateful, he'd seemed. And that was silly, really, because she'd willingly have helped him, anyway. That's why she'd become a librarian in the first place: to be able to locate some of the landmarks in the fields of History and Literature, and to provide where she could the correct map-references for so many curious enquiries. Even as a five-year-old, with her blonde plaits reaching half-way down her bony back, she'd envied the woman in the Summertown Library who similarly located tickets somewhere in the long drawers behind the high counter; envied, even more, the woman who stamped the dates in the front of the borrowed books, and inserted each little ticket into its appropriate, oblong folder. Not that she, Christine Greenaway, performed any longer such menial tasks herself. Almost forgotten now were those inevitable queries of who wrote *The Wind in the Willows*; for she, Christine, was now the senior of the three august librarians who sat at the northern end of the Bodleian's Lower Reading Room, where her daily duties demanded assistance to both senior and junior members of the University: checking slips, identifying shelf-marks, suggesting reference-sections, making and taking phone calls (one, yesterday, from the University of Uppsala). And over these last years she had felt a sense of importance and enjoyment in her job – of functioning happily in the workings of the University.

Of course, there had been some major disappointments in her life, as there had been, she knew, with most folk. Married at twenty-two, she had been a divorcee at twenty-three. No other woman on his part; no other man on hers – although there'd been (still were) so many opportunities. No! It was simply that her husband had been so immature and irresponsible – and, above all, so boring! Once the pair of them had got down to running a home, keeping a monthly budget, checking bank-statements – well, she'd known he could never really be the man for her. And as things now stood, she could no longer stomach the prospect of another mildly ignorant, semi-aggressively macho figure of a bed-mate. Free as she was of any financial worries, she could do exactly as she wished about issues that were important to *her*; and she had become a modestly active member of several organizations, including Greenpeace, CND, the Ramblers' Association, and the RSPB. Quite certainly, she would never join one of those match-making societies with the hope of finding a more interesting specimen than her former spouse. If ever she *did* look for another husband, he would have to be someone she could, in some way, come to *respect*: to respect for his conversation or his experience or his intellect or his knowledge or his – well, his anything at all, really, except a pride in his sexual prowess. So what (she asked herself) had all this got to do with *him*? Not much to look at, was he? Balding, and quite certainly carrying considerable excess weight around the midriff. Though, to be honest with herself, she was beginning to feel a grudging regard for those men who were just *slightly* overweight, perhaps because she herself seemed never able to put on a few pounds – however much she over-indulged in full-cream cakes and deep-fried fish and chips.

Forget him! Forget him, Christine!

Such self-admonition prevailed as she walked that morning down the Broad, past Balliol and Trinity on her left, before crossing over the road, just before Blackwell's, and proceeding, *sub imperatoribus*, up the semi-circular steps into the gravelled courtyard of the Sheldonian. Thence, keeping to her right, she walked past the SILENCE PLEASE notice under the archway, and came out at last into her real home territory – the Quadrangle of the Schools.

For many days, when six years earlier she had first started working at the Bodleian, she had been conscious of the beautiful setting there. Over the months and years, though, she had gradually grown over-familiar with what the postcards on sale in the Proscholium still called 'The Golden Heart of Oxford'; grown familiar, as she'd regularly trodden the gravelled quad, with the Tower of the Five Orders to her left, made her way past the bronze statue of the third Earl of Pembroke, and entered the Bodleian Library through the great single doorway in the West side, beneath the four tiers of blind arches in their gloriously mellowed stone.

Different today though – so very different! She felt once again the sharp irregularities of the gravel-stones beneath the soles of her expensive, high-heeled, leather shoes. And she was happily aware once more of the mediaeval Faculties painted over those familiar doors around the quad. In particular, she looked again at her favourite sign: SCHOLA NATURALIS PHILOSOPHIAE, the gilt capital-letters set off, with their maroon border, against a background of the deepest Oxford-blue. And as she climbed the wooden staircase to the Lower Reading Room, Christine Greenaway reminded herself, with a shy smile around her thinly delicious lips, why perhaps it had taken her so long to re-appreciate those neglected delights that were all around her.

She hung her coat in the Librarians' Cloakroom,

and started her daily duties. It was always tedious, that first hour (7.45–8.45 a.m.), clearing up the books left on the tables from the previous day, and ensuring that the new day's readers could be justifiably confident that the Bodley's books once more stood ready on their appointed shelves.

She thought back to the brief passages of conversation the previous evening, when he'd nodded over to her (only some six feet away):

'You work at the Bodleian, I hear?'

'Uh-huh!'

'It may be – it is! – a bit of a cheek, not knowing you . . .'

' – but you'd like me to look something up for you.'

Morse nodded, with a winsome smile.

She'd known he was some sort of policeman – things like that always got round the wards pretty quickly. His eyes had held hers for a few seconds, but she had been conscious neither of their blueness nor of their authority: only their melancholy and their vulnerability. Yet she had sensed that those complicated eyes of his had seemed to look, somehow, deep down inside herself, and *to like what they had seen.*

'Silly twerp, you are!' she told herself. She was behaving like some adolescent schoolgirl, smitten with a sudden passion for a teacher. But the truth remained – that for that moment she was prepared to run a marathon in clogs and calipers for the whitish-haired and gaudily pyjamaed occupant of the bed immediately opposite her father's.

Chapter Thirteen

Ah, fill the Cup: – what boots it to repeat
How Time is slipping underneath our Feet:
Unborn To-morrow, and dead Yesterday,
Why fret about them if To-day be sweet!
(*Edward Fitzgerald,* The Rubaiyat of Omar Khayyam)

HE'D BEEN RATHER vague, and it had been somewhat difficult precisely to assess what he wanted: some specific details about any assurance or insurance companies in the mid-nineteenth century – especially, if it were possible, about companies in the Midlands. Off and on, during the morning, it had taken her an hour or more to hunt down the appropriate catalogues; and another hour to locate the pertinent literature. But by lunch-time (praise be!) she had completed her research, experiencing, as she assumed, an elation similar to that of the scholars who daily dug into the treasury of her Great Library to extract their small nuggets of gold. She had found a work of reference which told her exactly what Morse (the man responsible for ruffling her wonted calm) had wanted her to find.

Just after twelve noon, with one of her female

colleagues, she walked over to the King's Arms, on the corner of Holywell Street – in which hostelry she was accustomed to enjoy her fifty-five minute lunch-break, with a single glass of white wine and a salmon-and-cucumber sandwich. It was when Christine got to her feet and offered to get in a second round of drinks, that her colleague eyed her curiously.

'You always said two glasses sent you to sleep.'

'So?'

'So I'll go to sleep as well, all right?'

They were good friends; and doubtless Christine would have given some castrated account of her visit to the JR2 the previous evening, had not another colleague joined them. Whereafter the three were soon engaged in happily animated conversation about interior decorating and the iniquity of current mortgage repayments.

Or two of them were, to be more accurate. And the one who had been the least lively of the trio found herself doing rather less work than usual that same afternoon. After carefully photocopying her finds, she wished the p.m. hours away, for she was impatient to parade the fruits of her research; and she just, simply – well, she just wanted to see the man again. That was all.

At 6.30 p.m. at her home in the village of Bletchington, some few miles out of Oxford, towards Otmoor, she slowly stroked red polish on to her smoothly manicured oval nails, and at 7 p.m. started out for the JR2.

Equally, from his own vantage point, Morse was looking forward to seeing Christine Greenaway once again. The previous evening he'd quickly appreciated her professionalism as she'd listened to his request, as she'd calculated how it might be implemented. In a more personal way he'd noted, too, the candour and intelligence of her eyes – eyes almost as blue as his own – and the quiet determination around her small mouth. So it was that at 7.25 p.m. he was sitting in his neatly re-made bed, newly washed, erect against his pillows, his thinning hair so recently re-combed – when his stomach suddenly felt as though it was being put through a mangle; and for two or three minutes the pain refused to relax its grinding, agonizing grip. Morse closed his eyes and squeezed his fists with such force that the sweat stood out on his forehead; and with eyes still shut he prayed to Someone, in spite of his recent conversion from agnosticism to outright atheism.

Two years earlier, at the Oxford Book Association, he had listened to a mournful Muggeridge propounding the disturbing philosophy of The Fearful Symmetry, in which the debits and the credits on the ledgers are balanced inexorably and eternally, and where the man who tries to steal a secret pleasure will pretty soon find himself queuing up to pay the bill – and more often than not with some hefty service-charges added in. What a preposterous belief it was (the sage had asserted) that the hedonist could be a happy man!

Oh dear!

Why had Morse ever considered the pleasure of a little glass? The wages of sin was death, and the night before was seldom worth the morning after (some people said). All mortals, Morse knew, were ever treading that narrow way by Tophet flare to Judgement Day, but he now prayed that the last few steps in his own case might be deferred at least a week or two.

Then, suddenly as it had come, the pain was gone, and Morse opened his eyes once more.

The clock behind Sister's desk (as earlier and darkly rumoured, Nessie was going to be on the night-shift) was showing 7.30 when the visitors began to filter through with their offerings stashed away in Sainsbury or St Michael carriers, and, some few of them, with bunches of blooms for the newly hospitalized.

Life is, alas, so full of disappointments; and it was to be an unexpected visitor who was to monopolize Morse's time that evening. Bearing a wilting collection of white chrysanthemums, a sombre-looking woman of late-middle age proceeded to commandeer the sole chair set at his bedside.

'Mrs Green! How very nice of you to come!'

Morse's heart sank deeply, and took an even deeper plunge when the dutiful charlady mounted a sustained challenge against Morse's present competence to deal, single-handedly, with such crucial matters as towels, toothpaste, talcum-powder, and clean pyjamas (especially the latter). It was wonderfully good of her (who could deny it?) to take such trouble to come to see him (*three* buses, as Morse knew full well); but he found himself consciously *willing* her to get up and *go.*

At five minutes past eight, after half a dozen 'I-really must-go's, Mrs G. rose to her poorly feet in preparation for her departure, with instructions for the care of the chrysanthemums. At last (at last!), after a mercifully brief account of her latest visit to her 'sheeropodist' in Banbury Road, Mrs G. dragged her long-suffering feet away from Ward 7C.

On several occasions, from her father's bedside, Christine Greenaway had half-turned in the course of her filial obligations; and two or three times her eyes had locked with Morse's: hers with the half-masked smile of understanding; his with all the impotence of some stranded whale.

Just as Mrs Green was on her way, a white-coated consultant, accompanied by the Charge Nurse, decided (inconsiderately) to give ten minutes of his time to Greenaway Senior, and then in some *sotto voce* asides, to confide his prognosis to Greenaway Junior. And for Morse, this hiatus in the evening's ordering was getting just about as infuriating as waiting for breakfast in some 'Fawlty Towers' hotel.

Then Lewis came.

Never had Morse been less glad to see his sergeant; yet he *had* instructed Lewis to pick up his post from the flat, and he now took possession of several envelopes and a couple of cards: Morse's shoes (his other pair) were now ready for collection from Grove Street; his car licence was due to be renewed within the next twenty days; a ridiculously expensive book on *The Transmission of Classical Manuscripts* now awaited him at OUP; a bill from the plumber for the repair of a malfunctioning stop-cock was still unpaid; the Wagner Society asked if he wanted to enter his name in a raffle for Bayreuth *Ring* tickets; and Peter Imbert invited him to talk in the new year at a weekend symposium, in Hendon, on inner-city crime. It was rather like a cross-section of life, his usual correspondence: half of it was fine, and half of it he wanted to forget.

At twenty-three minutes past eight, by the ward clock, Lewis asked if there was anything else he could do.

'Yes, Lewis. Please *go*, will you? I want to have five minutes with – ' Morse nodded vaguely over to Greenaway's bed.

'Well, if that's what you want, sir.' He rose slowly to his feet.

'It *is* what I bloody want, Lewis! I've just *told* you, haven't I?'

Lewis took a large bunch of white seedless grapes (£2.50 a pound) from his carrier-bag. 'I thought – we thought, the missus and me – we thought you'd enjoy them, sir.'

He was gone; and Morse knew, within a second of his going, that he would not be forgiving himself easily for such monumental ingratitude. But the damage was done: *nescit vox missa reverti.*

The bell rang two minutes later, and Christine came across to Morse's bed as she left, and handed him six large photocopied sheets.

'I hope this is what you wanted.'

'I'm ever so grateful. It's – it's a pity we didn't have a chance to . . .'

'I understand. I *do* understand,' she said. 'And you will let me know if I can do anything else?'

'Look . . . perhaps if we—'

'Come along now, please!' The Charge Nurse's voice

sounded to Morse almost as imperious as Nessie's as she walked quickly around the beds.

'I'm so grateful,' said Morse. 'I really am! As I say it's . . .'

'Yes,' said Christine softly.

'Will you be in tomorrow?' asked Morse quickly.

'No – not tomorrow. We've got some librarians coming from California—'

'Come along now, *please*!'

Mrs Green, Sergeant Lewis, Christine Greenaway – now all of them gone; and already the medicine-trolley had been wheeled into the ward, and the nurses were starting out on yet another circuit of measurements and medicaments.

And Morse felt sick at heart.

It was at 9.20 p.m. that he finally settled back against his piled pillows to glance quickly through the photocopied material Christine had found for him. And soon he was deeply and happily engrossed – his temporary despondency departing on the instant.

Chapter Fourteen

> Being in the land of the living was itself the survivor's privilege, for so many of one's peers – one's brothers and sisters – had already fallen by the wayside, having died at birth, at infancy or childhood
>
> (*Roy & Dorothy Porter,* In Sickness and in Health)

THE DOCUMENTS WHICH Morse now handled were just the thing (he had little doubt) for satisfying the original-source-material philosophy which was just then swamping the GCSE and A-level syllabuses. And for Morse, whose School Certificate in History (Credit) had demanded little more than semi-familiarity with the earliest models of seed-drills and similar agricultural adjuncts of the late eighteenth century, the reading of them was fascinating. Particularly poignant, as it appeared to Morse, was the Foreword to the *Insurance Guide and Hand-Book 1860* (bless the girl! – she'd even got the exact year) where the anonymous author stated his own determination to soldier along in 'this vale of tears' for as long as decently possible:

> 'Thus it is that all our efforts are forever required, not to surpass what we may call the biblical "par" for

> life – that famous "three-score years and ten" – but to come reasonably near to attaining it at all. For it is only by continuous vigilance and energy in the work for self preservation that the appointed average can be brought into view; and with good fortune and good sense (and God's grace) be achieved.'

It was interesting to find the Almighty in parenthesis, even in 1860, and Morse felt he would like to have known the author. Yet when that same author went on to assert that 'mortality had decreased by two-fifths between 1720 and 1820', Morse began to wonder what on earth such a bafflingly unscientific – indeed, quite nonsensical – statement might mean. What did seem immediately clear, as he read through the small print, was that people during those years were beginning to live rather longer, and that by the middle of the nineteenth century insurance companies were beginning to match this sociological phenomenon with increasingly attractive rates and premiums, in spite of the sombre statistics appended to each year, right up to the 1850s. Like 1853, e.g. – the figures for which Morse now considered. Of the half million or so departed souls reported in the pages of the Guide, 55,000 had died of consumption, 25,000 of pneumonia, 24,500 of convulsions, 23,000 of bronchitis, 20,000 of premature death and debility, 19,000 of typhus, 16,000 of scarlatina, 15,000 of diarrhoea, 14,000 of heart disease, 12,000 of whooping cough, 11,000 of dropsy, 9,000 of apoplexy, 8,500 of paralysis, 6,000 of asthma, 5,750 of cancer, 4,000 of teeth troubles, 3,750 of measles, 3,500 of croup, 3,250 of smallpox, 3,000 of (mothers) giving birth; and so on to the smaller numbers succumbing to diseases of brain, kidney, liver, and other perishable parts of the anatomy – and to old age! As he added up such numbers quickly in his head, Morse realized that about two-thirds of the 500,000 were unaccounted for; and he had to assume that even with a few more categories added ('murder' for one!) there must have been vast numbers of people in those days whose deaths were for some reason or other not specifically 'accounted for' at all, albeit being registered in the national statistics. Perhaps a lot of them were just not important enough to get their own particular malady spelled out on any death certificate; perhaps many of the physicians, midwives, nurses, poor-law-attendants, or whatever, just didn't know, or didn't want to know, or didn't care.

As he lay back on the pillows and thought of the circumstances besetting the luckless Joanna Franks, who had died neither of consumption nor pneumonia . . . nor . . . he suddenly fell into a sleep so deep that he missed his 10 p.m. Horlicks and his treasured digestive biscuit; and then he woke up again, somewhat less than refreshed, at 11.45 p.m., with a dry throat and a clear head. The lights in the ward were turned down to half power, and the other patients around him seemed contentedly asleep – apart from the man who'd been admitted late that afternoon and around whom the medical staff had been fussing with a rather ominous concern; the man who now lay staring at the ceiling, doubtless contemplating the imminent collapse of his earthly fortunes.

Nessie was nowhere to be seen: the desk was empty.

He'd just had a nasty little dream. He'd been playing cricket in his early days at Grammar School; and when it came to his turn to bat, he couldn't find his boots . . . and then when he did find them the laces kept snapping; and he was verging on a tearful despair – when he'd awoken. It might have been Mrs Green talking about her chiropody? Or was it Lewis, perhaps, who'd brought the card from the cobblers? Or neither of them? Was it not more likely to have been a young woman in 1859 who'd shouted, with her particular brand of terrified despair, 'What have you done with my shoes?'

He looked around again: the desk was still empty.

Surely he wasn't likely to imperil the well-being of the ward if he turned on his angle-lamp? Especially if focused directly into a small pool of light on his own pillows? No! Reading a book wasn't going to hurt anyone and the sick man had had *his* light on all the time.

Pushing in the button switch, he turned on his own light, with no reaction from anyone; and still no sign of Nessie.

Part Three of *Murder on the Oxford Canal* was close to hand; but Morse was reluctant to finish *that* too quickly. He remembered when he'd first read *Bleak House* (still to his mind the greatest novel in the English language) he'd deliberately decelerated his reading as the final pages grew ever thinner beneath his fingers. Never had he wanted to hang on to a story so much! Not that the Colonel's work was anything to wax all that lyrical about; and yet Morse *did* want to eke it out – or so he told himself. Which left the not displeasing possibility of a few further chapters of *The Blue Ticket* – with Mr Greenaway now fast asleep. The pattern of crime in nineteenth-century Shropshire had already joined the local legion of lost causes.

Morse was soon well into the exploits of a blonde who would have had arrows on her black stockings pointing northward and reading 'This way for the knickers' – that is, if she'd worn any stockings; or worn any knickers, for that matter. And it was amid much parading of bodies, pawing of bosoms, and patting of buttocks, that Morse now spent an enjoyable little interval of erotic pleasure; indeed, was so engrossed that he did not mark her approach.

'What do you think you're doing?'

'I was just—'

'Lights go out at ten o'clock. You're disturbing everyone on the ward.'

'They're all asleep.'

'Not for much longer, with you around!'

'I'm sorry—'

'What's this you're reading?'

Before he could do anything about it, Nessie had removed the book from his hands, and he had no option but to watch her helplessly. She made no comment, passed no moral judgement, and for a brief second Morse wondered if he had not seen a glint of some semi-amusement in those sharp eyes as they had skimmed a couple of paragraphs.

'Time you were asleep!' she said, in a not unkindly fashion, handing him back the book. Her voice was as crisp as her uniform, and Morse replaced the ill-starred volume in his locker. 'And be careful of your fruit juice!' She moved the half-filled glass one millimetre to the left, turned off the light, and was gone. And Morse gently eased himself down into the warmth and comfort of his bed, like Tennyson's lily sliding slowly into the bosom of the lake . . .

That night he dreamed a dream in Technicolor (he swore it!), although he knew such a claim would be contradicted by the oneirologists. He saw the ochre-skinned, scantily clad siren in her black, arrowed stockings, and he could even recall her lavender-hued underclothing. Almost it was the perfect dream! Almost. For there was a curiously insistent need in Morse's brain which paradoxically demanded a *factual* name and place and time before, in *fantasy*, that sexually unabashed freebooter could be his. And in Morse's muddled computer of a mind, that siren took the name of one Joanna Franks, provocatively walking along towards Duke's Cut, in the month of June in 1859.

When he awoke (was woken, rather) the following morning, he felt wonderfully refreshed, and he resolved that he would take no risks of any third humiliation over *The Blue Ticket*. With breakfast, temperature, wash, shave, blood-pressure, newspaper, tablets, Bovril, all these now behind him – and with not a visitor in sight – he settled down to discover exactly what had happened to that young woman who had taken control of his nocturnal fantasies.

Chapter Fifteen

PART THREE
A Protracted Trial

Joanna Franks's body was found at Duke's Cut at about 5.30 a.m. on Wednesday, 22nd June 1859. Philip Tomes, a boatman, said he was passing down-canal towards Oxford when he saw something in the water – something which was soon identified as, in part, a woman's gown; what else, though, he could not for the moment make out in the darkened waters. The object was on the side of the canal opposite the tow-path, and in due course he discovered it to be the body of a female, without either bonnet or shoes. She was floating alongside the bank, head north, feet south, and there was no observable movement about her. She was lying on her face, which seemed quite black. Tomes stopped his boat, and with a boat-hook gently pulled the body to the tow-path side, where he lifted it out of the water, in which latter task he was assisted by John Ward, a Kidlington fisherman, who happened to be passing alongside the canal at that early hour. In fact, it was Ward who had the presence of mind to arrange for the body, which was still warm, to be taken down to the Plough Inn at Wolvercote.

It appears from various strands of inter-weaving evidence, albeit some of it from the guilty parties themselves, that Oldfield and Musson (and, by one account, Towns also) left the *Barbara Bray* at roughly the point where Joanna met her death, and that they were seen standing together on the tow-path side of the canal just below Duke's Cut. A certain man passed by the area at the crucial time, 4 a.m. or just after, and both Oldfield and Musson, with great presence of mind, asked him if he had seen a woman walking beside the canal. The man had replied, as they clearly recalled, with a very definite "No!", and had made to get further on his way with all speed. Yet the two (or perhaps three) men had asked him the same question again and again, in rather an agitated manner.

(It is clear that this man's testimony could have been vital in substantiating the boatmen's claims. But he was never traced, in spite of wide-scale enquiries in the area. A man roughly answering his description, one Donald Favant, had signed the register at the Nag's Head in Oxford for either the 20th or the 21st June – there was some doubt – but this man never came forward. The strong implication must therefore remain, as it did at the time, that the whole story was the clever concoction of desperate men.)

Jonas Bamsey, wharfinger in the employ of the Oxford Canal Authority at Oxford's Hayfield Wharf, gave evidence at the trial that the *Barbara Bray* had duly effected its partial unloading, but that Oldfield had not reported the loss of any passenger – which quite certainly should have been the duty of the boat's captain under the Authority's Regulations. Instead, according to the scant and inconsistent evidence at this point, the boatmen do appear to have confided in some of their acquaintances in Upper Fisher Row, claiming that their passenger had been out of her mind; that she had committed suicide; and that on at least one occasion they had been called upon to save her from an attempted drowning on the journey down from Preston Brook.

Later that dreadful day, when the crew of the *Barbara Bray* came to negotiate the lock on the Thames at Iffley, two miles downstream from Folly Bridge, Oldfield spoke to the keeper, Albert Lee, and reported to him and his wife (coincidentally also named Joanna) that a passenger on his boat had been drowned; but that she was most sadly deranged, and had been a sore trial to him and his fellow crew-members ever since she had first embarked at Preston Brook. Oldfield was still obviously very drunk. Pressed to explain what he was seeking to say, Oldfield – asserted only that "It was a very bad job that had happened". The passenger was "off her head" and had been last seen by the crew off Gibraltar Lock. Yet Oldfield was vehemently unwilling to listen to Lee's suggestion of returning to Oxford to sort out the whole tragedy; and this made Lee more than somewhat suspicious. On the departure of the *Barbara Bray*, therefore, he himself immediately set off for Oxford, where he contacted the Pickford Office; and where the Pickford Office, in turn, contacted the Police Authority.

When the infamous boat finally arrived at Reading (for some reason, over two hours behind schedule) Constable Harrison was on hand, with appropriate support, to take the entire crew into custody, and to testify that all of them, including the youth, were still observably drunk and excessively abusive as he put them in darbies and escorted them to temporary cell-accommodation in the gaol at Reading. One of them, as Harrison vividly recalled, was vile enough to repeat some of his earlier invective against Joanna Franks, and was heard to mutter "Damn and blast that wicked woman!"

Hannah MacNeill, a serving woman at the Plough Inn, Wolvercote, testified that when the sodden body had been brought from the canal, she had been employed, under direction, to take off Joanna's clothes. The left sleeve was torn out of its gathers and the cuff on the same hand was also torn. Tomes and Ward, for their part, were quite firm in their evidence that they themselves had made no rips or tears in Joanna's clothing as they lifted her carefully from the water at Duke's Cut.

Katharine Maddison testified that she was a co-helper with Hannah MacNeill in taking off Joanna's drenched garments. Particularly had she noticed the state of Joanna's calico knickers which had been ripped right across the front. This garment was produced in Court; and many were later to agree that the production of such an intimate item served further to heighten the universal feeling of revulsion against those callous men who were now arraigned with her murder.

Mr Samuels, the Oxford surgeon who examined the body at the inquest, reported signs of bruising below the elbow of the left arm, and further indications of subcutaneous bruising below left and right cheekbones; the same man described the dead woman's face as presenting a state of "discoloration and disfigurement". Mr Samuels agreed that it was perhaps possible for the facial injuries, such as they were, to have been caused by unspecified and accidental incidents in the water, or in the process of taking-up from the water. Yet such a possibility was now seeming, both to Judge and Jury, more and more remote.

The youth Wootton then gave his version of the tragic events, and on one point he expressed himself forcefully: that Towns had got himself "good and half-seas-over" the night before Joanna was found, and that he was sound asleep at the time the murder must have occurred, for he (Wootton) had heard him "snoring loudly". We shall never be in a position to know whether Towns had forced Wootton to give this evidence to the Court – under some threat or other, perhaps. From subsequent developments, however, it seems clear that we may give a substantial degree of credence to Wootton's testimony.

Joseph Jarnell, the co-prisoner pending whose evidence the re-trial had been agreed, related to the Court the damning confessions Oldfield had betrayed whilst the two men shared a prison-cell. In essence such 'confessions' amounted to a rather crude attempt on Oldfield's part to settle the majority of blame for almost everything which had happened on Musson and Towns. But in spite of the man's earnest manner and the consistency of his account, Jarnell's story made little or no impression. Yet his testimony carried interest, if not conviction. Amongst the strongest of the fabrications which Oldfield had sought to put about was that Joanna Franks had in excess of fifty golden sovereigns in one of her two boxes; that Towns had discovered this fact, and that Joanna had found him rummaging through her trunks. She had threatened (so the allegation ran) to report him to the next Pickford Office if he did not mend his ways and make immediate apology and restoration. (Such nonsense was wholly discredited at the time, and may be safely discounted now.)

Together with many other items, the knife which Joanna had been observed sharpening was later found in one of her trunks, the cord of which had been cut, and which still remained untied. The assumption was that at some point the men had opened Joanna's belongings after the murder, and had replaced the knife in one of the trunks. It must certainly be considered a strong possibility that the men intended to steal some of her possessions, for as we have seen a charge of theft was included, in the most strongly worded terms, in the original indictment of the crew at the first trial in August 1859. It seems, however, that Prosecuting Counsel at the second trial were sufficiently confident to forgo such a charge and to concentrate their accusations on murder, since the lesser charge (difficult, in any case, as it would have been to substantiate) was subsequently excluded. We have seen a similar procedure operating, in the first trial, concerning the charges of rape; and perhaps it is of some strange and macabre interest to note that in the original trial the charges of both rape and theft (as well as murder) were made against each individual member of the crew – including the youth Wootton.

Out of all the evidence given at that memorable second trial at Oxford in April 1860, fairly certainly that of Charles Franks himself evoked the greatest feeling and the widest sympathy. The poor man was weeping aloud as he entered the witness-box, and it seemed as if it were almost beyond his physical powers to raise his eyes in order to bear the sight of the prisoners and to look upon their faces. He had obviously been deeply in love with Joanna, and turning his back on the vile men arraigned before the Court he explained how in consequence of some information he had come into Oxfordshire and seen his wife's dead body at the time of the inquest. For although it was dreadfully disfigured (here the poor fellow could not at all restrain his feelings) yet he knew it by a small mark behind his wife's left ear, a mark of which only a parent or an intimate lover could have known. Corroboration of identification (if, in fact, corroboration was needed) was afforded by the shoes, later found in the fore-cabin of the *Barbara Bray*, which matched in the minutest degrees the contours of the dead woman's feet.

At the conclusion of the hearing, and after a lengthy summing-up by Mr Augustus Benham, the Jury, under their duly appointed chairman, begged permission of his Lordship to retire to consider their verdict.

CHAPTER SIXTEEN

At a hotel facing the sea at Brighton, he ate a good breakfast of bacon and eggs, toast and marmalade; then took a stroll round the town before returning to the station and boarding a train for Worthing

(Court Record of evidence given in the trial of Neville George Clevely Heath, on the morning after the murder of Margery Gardner)

PERHAPS IT WAS the dream.

Whatever it was, Morse knew that something had at last prodded him into a slightly more intelligent appraisal of the Colonel's story, because he was now beginning to take account of two or three major considerations which had been staring at him all the while.

The first of these was the character of Joanna Franks herself. How had it come about – whatever the fortuitous, involuntary, or deliberate circumstances in which Joanna had met her death – that the crew of the *Barbara Bray* had insisted time and time again that the wretched woman had been nothing but one long, sorry trial to them all ever since she'd first jumped on board at

Preston Brook? How *was* it that they were still damning and blasting the poor woman's soul to eternity way, way *after* they had pushed her into the Canal and, for all Morse or anyone else knew, held her head under the black waters until she writhed in agony against their murderous hands no longer? Had a satisfactory explanation been forthcoming for such events? All right, there was still Part Four of the story to come. But so far, the answer was 'no'.

There was, though (as it now occurred to Morse), one possible dimension to the case that the good Colonel had never even hinted at – either through an excessive sense of propriety, or from a lack of imagination – namely that *Joanna Franks had been a seductive tease*: a woman who over those long hours of that long journey had begun to drive the crew towards varied degrees of insanity with her provocative overtures, and to foster the inevitable jealousies arising therefrom.

Come off it, Morse!

Yes, come off it! There was no evidence to support such a view. None! Yet the thought stayed with him, reluctant to leave. An attractive woman . . . boredom . . . drink . . . a tunnel . . . continued boredom . . . more drink . . . another tunnel . . . darkness . . . desire . . . opportunity . . . still more drink . . . and more Priapic promptings in the loins . . . Yes, all that, perhaps, the Colonel himself may have understood. But what if she, Joanna herself, had been the active catalyst in the matter? What if she had craved for the men just as much as they had craved for her? What (put it simply, Morse!) *what if she'd wanted sex just as badly as they did*?

What if she were the precursor of Sue Bridehead in *Jude the Obscure*, driving poor old Phillotson potty, as well as poor old Jude?

'Men's questions!' he heard a voice say. 'Just the sort of thoughts that would occur to an ageing MCP like you!'

There was a second general consideration which, from the point of view of criminal justice, struck Morse as considerably more cogent and a good deal less contentious. In the court-room itself, the odds did seem, surely, to have been stacked pretty heavily against the crew of the *Barbara Bray* – with 'presumption of innocence' playing decidedly second fiddle to 'assumption of guilt'. Even the fair-minded Colonel had let his prejudgements run away with him a little: already he'd decided that any ostensible concern on the part of the boatmen for the missing passenger (believed drowned?) was only shown 'with great presence of mind' in order to establish a semi-convincing alibi for themselves; already he'd decided that these same boatmen, 'still obviously very drunk' (and by implication still knocking it back at top-tipplers' rates) had manoeuvred their 'infamous' craft down the Thames to Reading without having the common decency to mention to anyone the little matter of the murder they'd committed on the way. Did (Morse asked himself) wicked men tend to get more *drunk* – or more *sober* – after committing such callous crimes? Interesting thought . . .

Yes, and there was a third general point – one that seemed to Morse most curious: the charges both of

Theft and of Rape had, for some reason, been dropped against the boatmen. Was this because the Prosecution had been wholly confident, and decided to go for the graver charge of Murder – with the expectation (fully justified) that they had sufficient evidence to convict 'Rory' Oldfield and Co. on the capital indictment? Or was it, perhaps, because they had too *little* confidence in their ability to secure conviction on the *lesser* charges? Obviously, as Morse seemed vaguely to remember from his schooldays, neither rape nor theft would have been considered too venial an offence in the middle of the last century, but . . . Or was it just possible that these charges were dropped because there was no convincing evidence to support them? And if so, was the indictment for murder entered upon by the Prosecution for one simple reason – that it presented the *only* hope of bringing those miserable men to justice? Certainly, as far as multiple rape was concerned, the evidence must have been decidedly dodgy – as the Judge in the first trial had pronounced. But what about theft? The pre-requisite of theft was that the aggrieved party possessed something worth the stealing. So what was it that poor Joanna had about her person, or had in either of her two travelling-boxes, that was worth the crime? The evidence, after all, pointed to the fact that she hadn't got a couple of pennies to rub together. Her fare for the canal-trip had been sent up from her husband in London; and even facing the terrible risks of travelling with a drunken, lecherous crew – certainly after Banbury had been reached – she had *not* taken, or not been *able* to take, any alternative means of transport to get to the husband who was awaiting her in the Edgware Road. So? So what had she got, if anything, that was worth stealing?

There were those shoes again, too! Did Joanna deliberately leave off her shoes? Did she enjoy the feel of the mud between her toes along the tow-path – like some bare-foot hippie on a watery walk round Stonehenge in the dawn?

What a strange case it had been! The more he thought about it, the greater the number of questions that kept occurring to Morse's mind. He had a good deal of experience in cases where the forensic and pathological evidence had been vital to the outcome of a court case. But he wasn't particularly impressed with the conclusions that (presumably) must have been drawn from Mr Samuels' comparatively scientific findings. For Morse (wholly, it must be admitted, without medical or scientific qualifications) the state of the dress, and the bruising described, would have been much more consistent with Joanna being held firmly from behind, with the assailant's (?) left hand gripping her left wrist; and his (her?) right hand being held forcibly across her mouth, where thumb and forefinger would almost invariably produce the sort of bruising mentioned in the recorded description.

What of this Jarnell fellow? The Prosecution must have been considerably impressed, at the first hearing, with his potential testimony. Why, otherwise, would anyone be willing to postpone a trial for six months – on the word of a gaolbird? Even the Colonel had given the fellow a good write-up! So why was it that when he duly turned up to tell his tale, at the second trial, no one wished to listen to him? Had there been something, some knowledge, somewhere, that had caused the court to discount, or at least discredit, the disclosures his cell-mate, Oldfield, had allegedly made to him? Because whatever accusations could be levelled against Oldfield, the charge of inconsistency was *not* amongst them. On three occasions, after Joanna's death, he had insisted that she was "out of her mind", "sadly deranged", "off her head" ... And there had, it appeared, been no conflict of evidence between the crewmen that on one occasion at least (did that mean two?) they had been called upon to save Joanna from drowning herself. The one vital point Jarnell disclosed was that Oldfield had not only protested his own innocence of the murder, but had also sought to shift all responsibility on to his fellow crewmen. Not, to be sure, a very praiseworthy piece of behaviour! Yet, *if Oldfield himself were innocent*, where else could he have laid the blame? At the time, in any case, no one had been willing to listen seriously either to what Jarnell or to what Oldfield might have to say. But if they were right? Or if *one* of them were right?

A curious little thought struck Morse at this point, and lodged itself in a corner of his brain – for future reference. And a rather bigger thought struck him simultaneously: that he needed to remember he was only playing a game with himself; only trying to get through a few days' illness with a happy little problem to amuse himself with – like a tricky cryptic crossword from *The Listener*. It was just a little worrying, that was all ... the way the dice had been loaded all the time against those drunkards who had murdered Joanna Franks.

And the niggling doubt persisted.

If they had . . .

Chapter Seventeen

The detective novelist, as a class, hankers after complication and ingenuity, and is disposed to reject the obvious and acquit the accused if possible. He is uneasy until he has gone further and found some new and satisfying explanation of the problem

(*Dorothy L. Sayers,* The Murder of Julia Wallace)

THE THOUGHT THAT the crewmen may not have been guilty of Joanna Franks's murder proved to be one of those heady notions that evaporate in the sunrise of reason. For if the crewmen had not been responsible, who on earth had? Nevertheless, it seemed to Morse pretty much odds-on that if the case had been heard a century later, there would have been no certain conviction. Doubtless, at the time, the jury's verdict had looked safe and satisfactory, especially to the hostile crowds lining the streets and baying for blood. But *should* the verdict have been reached? True, there was enough circumstantial suspicion to sentence a saint; yet no really *direct* evidence, was there? No witnesses to murder; no indication of *how* the murder had been committed; no adequately convincing motive for *why*.

Just a time, and a place, and Joanna lying face-downwards in Duke's Cut all that while ago.

Unless, of course, there were some passages of evidence not reported – either from the first or the second trial? The Colonel had clearly been rather more interested in the lax morals of the boatmen than in any substantiation of the evidence, and he could just have omitted the testimony of any corroborative witnesses who might have been called. Perhaps it would be of some interest – in this harmless game he was playing – to have a quick look through those Court Registers, if they still existed; or through the relevant copies of *Jackson's Oxford Journal*, which certainly *did* exist, as Morse knew, filed on microfiche in the Oxford Central Library. (Doubtless in the Bodley, too!) And, in any case, he hadn't finished the Colonel's book yet. Why, there might be much still to be revealed in that last exciting episode!

Which he now began to read.

Almost immediately he was conscious of Fiona standing beside him – the amply bosomed Fiona, smelling vaguely of the summer and strongly of disinfectant. Then she sat down on the bed, and he felt the pneumatic pressure of her against him as she leaned across and looked over his shoulder.

'Intereeeesting?'

Morse nodded. 'It's the book the old girl brought round – you know, the Colonel's wife.'

Fiona stayed where she was, and Morse found himself reading the same short sentence for the third, fourth, fifth time – without the slightest degree of comprehension – as her softness gently pressed against him. Was she conscious, herself, of taking the initiative in such memorable intimacy, however mild?

Then she ruined everything.

'I don't go in much for reading these days. Last book I read was *Jane Eyre* – for GCSE, that was.'

'Did you enjoy it?' (Poor, dear Charlotte had long had a special place in Morse's heart.)

'Pretty boring stuff. We just had to do it, you know, for the exam.'

Oh dear!

Crossing her black-stockinged legs, she took off one of her flat-heeled black shoes, and shook out some invisible irritant on to the ward floor.

'When do people take their shoes off?' asked Morse. 'Normally, I mean?'

'Funny question, isn't it?'

'When they've a stone in them – like you?'

Fiona nodded. 'And when they go to bed.'

'And?'

'Well – when they go paddling at Blackpool.'

'Yes?'

'When they sit watching the telly with their feet on the sofa – if they've got a mum as fussy as mine.'

'Anything else?'

'What do you want to know all this for?'

'If they've got corns or something,' persisted Morse, 'and go to the chiropodist.' ('Kyropodist', in Morse's book.)

'Yes. Or if their feet get sore or tired. Or if they have to take their tights off for some reason—'

'Such as?'

Morse saw the flash of sensuous amusement in her eyes, as she suddenly stood up, pulled his sheets straight, and shook out his pillows. 'Well, if you don't know at your age—'

Oh dear!

Age.

Morse felt as young as he'd ever done; but suddenly, and so clearly, he could see himself as he *was* seen by this young girl.

Old!

But his mood was soon to be brightened by the totally unexpected re-appearance of Sergeant Lewis, who explained that the purpose of his unofficial visit (it was 2.15 p.m.) was to interview a woman, still in intensive care, in connection with yet another horrendous crash on the A34.

'Feeling OK this morning, sir?'

'I shall feel a jolly sight better once I've had the chance of apologizing to you – for being so bloody ungrateful!'

'Oh yes? When was that, sir? I thought you were always ungrateful to me.'

'I'm just sorry, that's all,' said Morse simply and quietly.

Lewis, whose anger had been simmering and spitting like soup inadvertently left on the stove, had come into the ward with considerable reluctance. Yet when some ten minutes later he walked out, he felt the same degree of delight he invariably experienced when he knew that Morse needed *him* – even if it were only, as in this case, to do a bit of mundane research (Morse had briefly explained the case) and to try to discover if the Court Registers of the Oxford Assizes, 1859–60, were still available; and if so to see if any records of the trials were still extant.

After Lewis had gone, Morse felt very much more in tune with the universe. Lewis had forgiven him, readily; and he felt a contentment which he, just as much as Lewis, could ill define and only partly comprehend. And with Lewis looking into the Court Registers, there was another researcher in the field: a qualified librarian, who could very quickly sort out *Jackson's Oxford Journals.* Not that she was coming in that evening, alas!

Patience, Morse!

At 3 p.m. he turned once again to the beginning of the fourth and final episode in the late Colonel Deniston's book.

Chapter Eighteen

PART FOUR
A Pronounced Sentence

A BAILIFF WAS sworn in to attend the Jury, who immediately retired to the Clerk of Indictments' Room. After an absence of three-quarters of an hour, they returned to the Court; and, their names having been read over, every person appeared to wait with breathless anxiety for their verdict. In reply to the usual questions from Mr Benham, the foreman replied that the Jury was all agreed and that they were unanimous in finding each of the three prisoners at the bar GUILTY of the murder of Joanna Franks. It is said that no visible alteration marked the countenances of the crew on the verdict being given, except that Oldfield for the moment became somewhat paler.

The black coif, emblematical of death, was placed on the Judge's head; and after asking the prisoners if they had anything to say, he passed his sentence in the following awesome terms:

> 'Jack Oldfield, Alfred Musson, Walter Towns – after a long and patient hearing of the circumstances in this case, and after due deliberation on the part of the Jury, you have each and all of you been found guilty of the most foul crime of murder – the murder

of an unoffending and helpless woman who was under your protection and who, there is now no doubt as to believe, was the object of your lust; and thereafter, to prevent detection of your crime, was the object of your cruelty. Look not for pardon in this world! Apply to the God of Mercy for that pardon which He alone can extend to sinners who are penitent for their misdeeds, and henceforth prepare yourselves for the ignominious death which now awaits you. This case is one of the most painful, the most disgusting, and the most shocking, that has ever come to my knowledge, and it must remain only for me to pass upon you the terrible and just sentence of the Law, that you be taken whence you came, and from thence to the place of execution, and that you, and each of you, be hanged by the neck until you be dead, and that your bodies be afterward buried within the precincts of the prison and be not accorded the privilege of consecrated ground. And may God have mercy on your souls!'

After the trial was over, and sentence pronounced, the three men still persisted in maintaining their innocence. Indeed, Oldfield's wife, who visited the prison, was so agitated by her husband's protestations that "she herself was thrown into a sore fit".

It had seemed reasonably clear, from various statements including those of Oldfield and Musson that Towns had been somewhat less involved in the happenings on the canal journey than the other two. It was no surprise therefore, that some members of the legal profession now thought there was a case for the last-minute reconsideration of the sentence imposed upon Towns; so a letter setting forth their agreed view was taken to London by a barrister, and a special interview with the Secretary of State was obtained. As a result of such representations, Towns was reprieved at (almost literally) the eleventh hour. The good news was broken to him as the three men were receiving for the last time the Holy Sacrament from the Prison Chaplain. Towns immediately burst into a flood of tears, and taking each of his former associates by the hand kissed them affectionately, repeating "God bless you, dear friend!" "God bless you, dear friend!" He was later transported to Australia for life, where he was still alive in 1884 when he was seen and interviewed by one Samuel Carter (like Oldfield and Towns, a citizen of Coventry), who took a lively interest in local history and who wrote of his experiences on his return to England the following year.[1]

Oldfield and Musson were duly hanged in public at Oxford. According to the newspaper reports, as many as ten thousand people were estimated to have witnessed the macabre spectacle. It is reported that from an early hour men sat high on walls, climbed trees, and even perched on the roofs of overlooking houses in order to obtain a good view of those terrible events. A notice-board placed by the Governor in front of the gaol door stated that the execution would not proceed

[1] *Travels and Talks in the Antipodes,* Samuel Carter (Farthinghill Press, Nottingham, 1886).

until after eleven o'clock; but although this occasioned much disappointment among the spectators, it did not deter their continued attendance, and not a spare square-foot of space was to be found when, at the appointed hour, the execution finally occurred.

First to appear was the Prison Chaplain, solemnly reading the funeral service of the Church of England; next came the two culprits; and following them the Executioner, and the Governor, as well as some other senior officers from the prison. After the operation of pinioning had been completed, the two men walked with firm step to the platform, and ascended the stairs to the drop without requiring assistance. When the ropes had been adjusted round their necks, the Executioner shook hands with each man; and then, as the Chaplain intoned his melancholy service, the fatal bolt was drawn, and in a minute or two, after much convulsion, the wretched malefactors were no more. The dislocation of the cervical vertebrae and the rupture of the jugular vein had been, if not an instantaneous, at least an effective procedure. The gallows appeared to have sated the sadistic fascination of the mob once more, for there are no reports of any civic disorders as the great throng dispersed homewards on that sunlit day. It was later disclosed, though it had not been observable at the time, that Oldfield's last action in life had been to hand over to the Chaplain a postcard, to be delivered to his young wife, in which to the very end he proclaimed his innocence of the crime for which he had now paid the ultimate penalty.

Locally produced broadsheets, giving every sensational

detail of trial and execution, were very quickly on sale in the streets of Oxford – and were selling fast. They were even able to give a full account, with precise biblical reference, of the last sermon preached to the men at 6 p.m. on the Sunday before their hangings. The text, clearly chosen with ghoulish insensitivity, could hardly have brought the condemned prisoners much spiritual or physical solace: 'Yet they hearkened not unto me, nor inclined their ear, but hardened their neck: they did worse than their fathers' (*Jeremiah*, ch. 7, v. 26).

The horror felt by the local population at the murder of Joanna Franks did not end with the punishment of the guilty men. Many, both lay and clerical, thought that something more must be done to seek to improve the morals of the boatmen on the waterways. They were aware, of course, that the majority of boatmen were called upon to work on the Sabbath, and had therefore little or no opportunity of attending Divine worship. A letter from the Revd Robert Chantry, Vicar of Summertown Parish, was typical of many in urging a greater degree of concern amongst the boatmen's employers, and suggesting some period of time free from duties on the Sabbath to allow those having the inclination the opportunity of attending a Church service. Strangely enough, such attendance would have been readily possible for the crew-members of the *Barbara Bray* had Oxford been a regular port-of-call, since a special 'Boatmen's Chapel' had been provided by Henry Ward, a wealthy coal-merchant, in 1838 – a floating chapel, moored off Hythe Bridge, at which services were held on Sunday afternoons and Wednesday evenings. For Joanna Franks, as well as for her sorrowing husband and parents, it was a human tragedy that the sermon preached to the murderers on the Sunday prior to their execution was perhaps the first – as well as the last – they ever heard.

But it is all a long time ago now. The floating chapel has long since gone; and no one today can point with any certainty to the shabby plot in the environs of Oxford Gaol where notorious criminals and murderers and others of the conjecturally damned were once buried.

Chapter Nineteen

We read fine things but never feel them to the full until we have gone the same steps as the author
(*John Keats,* Letter to John Reynolds)

Morse was glad that the Colonel had ignored Doctor Johnson's advice to all authors that once they had written something particularly fine they should strike it out. For Part Four was the best-written section, surely, of what was proving to be one of the greatest assets in Morse's most satisfactory (so far) convalescence; and he turned back the pages to relish again a few of those fine phrases. Splendid, certainly, were such things as "sated the sadistic fascination"; and, better still, that "ghoulish insensitivity". But they were *more* than that. They seemed to suggest that the Colonel's sympathies had shifted slightly, did they not? Where earlier the bias against the boatmen had been so pronounced, it appeared that the longer he went on the greater his compassion was growing for that disconsolate crew.

Like Morse's.

*

It was such a good *story*! So it was no surprise that the Colonel should have disinterred the bare bones of this particular one from the hundreds of other nineteenth-century burial-grounds. All the ingredients were there for its appealing to a wide readership, if once it got its foot wedged in the doorway of publicity. Beauty and the Beasts – that's what it was, quintessentially.

At least as the Colonel had seen it.

For Morse, who had long ago rejected the bland placebos of conventional religion, the facility offered to errant souls to take the Holy Sacrament before being strangled barbarously in a string seemed oddly at variance with the ban on the burial of these same souls within some so-called 'holy ground'. And he was reminded of a passage which had once been part of his mental baggage, the words of which now slowly returned to him. From *Tess of the d'Urbervilles* – where Tess herself seeks to bury her illegitimate infant in the place where 'the nettles grow; and where all unbaptised infants, notorious drunkards, suicides, and others . . .' What was the end of it? Wasn't it – yes! – 'others of the conjecturally damned are laid'. Well, well! A bit of plagiarism on the Colonel's part. He really should have put quotation marks around that memorable phrase. Cheating just a little, really. Were there any other places where he'd cheated? Unwittingly, perhaps? Just a little?

Worth checking?

That floating chapel interested Morse, too, particularly since he had read something about it in a recent issue of the *Oxford Times*. He remembered, vaguely, that although the Oxford Canal Company gave regular monies towards its upkeep the boat on which it was housed had finally sunk (like the boatmen's hopes) and was terrestrialized, as it were, later in the century as a permanent chapel in Hythe Bridge Street; was now, at its latest conversion, metamorphosed to a double-glazing establishment.

Without looking back, Morse could not for the moment remember which of the other crew-members had been married. But it was good to learn that Oldfield's wife had stood beside her husband, for better or for worse. And a pretty bloody 'worse' it had turned out to be! How interesting it would have been to know something of *her* story, too. How Morse would like to have been able to interview her, then and there! The recipient (presumably she had been) of that terrible card addressed to her, and handed to the Chaplain at the very foot of the gallows, she must have found it well-nigh impossible to believe that her husband could commit so foul a deed. But hers had been only a small role in the drama: only a couple of walking-on appearances, the first ending with a dead faint, and the second with a poignant little message from the grave. Morse nodded rather sadly to himself. These days there would be a legion of reporters from the *News of the World*, the *Sunday Mirror*, and the rest, hounding the life of the poor woman and seeking to prise out of her such vital information as whether he'd snored, or been tattooed on either upper or nether limbs, or how frequently they'd indulged in sexual intercourse, or what had been the usual greeting of the loving husband after coming back from one of his earlier murderous missions.

We live in a most degenerate age, decided Morse. Yet he knew, deep down, what nonsense such thinking was. He was no better himself, really, than one of those scandal-sheet scouts. He'd just confessed – had he not? – how much he himself wanted to interview Mrs Oldfield and talk about all the things she must have known. And what (sobering thought!) what if *she* had invited each of them in, one after the other, separately – and asked for £20,000 a time?

No chance of any interview or talk now though – not with any of them . . . But, suddenly, it struck Morse that perhaps there was: Samuel Carter's *Travels and Talks in the Antipodes.* That might be a most interesting document, surely? And (it struck Morse with particular pleasure) it would certainly be somewhere on the shelves of the three or four great UK libraries, the foremost of which was always going to be the Bodleian.

Lewis had already been given his research project; and work was now beginning to pile up for his second researcher in the field: what with *Jackson's Oxford Journal,* and now Carter's book . . . Had the Colonel consulted that? Must have done, Morse supposed – which was a little disappointing.

That Friday evening, Morse was visited by both Sergeant Lewis and Christine Greenaway, the latter suddenly changing her mind and foregoing a cocktail reception in Wellington Square. No trouble at all. Just the opposite.

Morse was very happy.

Chapter Twenty

Those hateful persons called Original Researchers
(*J. M. Barrie,* My Lady Nicotine)

As usual when she went into Oxford on a Saturday, Christine Greenaway drove down to the Pear Tree roundabout and caught the Park-and-Ride bus. Alighting in Cornmarket, she walked up to Carfax, turned right into Queen's Street, and along through the busy pedestrian precinct to Bonn Square, where just past the Selfridges building she pushed through the doors of the Westgate Central Library. Among the wrong assumptions made by Chief Inspector Morse the previous evening was the fact that it would be sheer child's play for her to fish out the fiche (as it were) of any newspaper ever published, and that having effected such effortless entry into times past she had the technical skill and the requisite equipment to carry out some immediate research. She hadn't told him that the Bodleian had not, to the best of her knowledge, ever micro-filmed the whole of the nation's press from the nineteenth century, nor that she herself was one of those people against whom all pieces of electrical gadgetry waged a non-stop war. She'd just agreed with him: yes, it would be a fairly easy job; and she'd be glad to help – again. To be truthful, though, she was. Earlier that morning she'd telephoned one of her acquaintances in the Reference Section of the Westgate Central, and learned that she could have immediate access to *Jackson's Oxford Journal* for 1859 and 1860. How long did she want to book things for? One hour? Two? Christine thought one hour would be enough.

10.30–11.30 a.m., then?

Perhaps Morse had been right all along. It was going to be easy.

On the second floor of the Central Library, in the Local History and Study Area, she was soon seated on an olive-green vinyl chair in front of a Micro-Film-Reader, an apparatus somewhat resembling the upper half of a British Telecom telephone-kiosk, with a vertical surface, some two feet square, facing her, upon which the photographed sheets of the newspaper appeared, in columns about 2½ inches wide. No lugging around or leafing through heavy bound-volumes of unmanageable newspapers. 'Child's play.' The controls marked Focusing Image, Magnification, and Light Control had all been pre-set for her by a helpful young library assistant (male), and Christine had only to turn an uncomplicated winding-handle with her right hand to skip along through the pages, at whatever speed she wished, of *Jackson's Oxford Journal*.

She was relieved, nevertheless, to discover that the Journal was a weekly, not a daily publication; and very soon she found the appropriate columns relating to the first trial of August 1859, and was making a series of notes about what she found; and, like Morse, becoming more and more interested. Indeed, by the time she had finished her research into the second trial, of April 1860, she was fascinated. She would have liked to go back and check up a few things, but her eyes were getting tired; and as soon as the print began to jump along like a line of soldiers dressing by the right, she knew that what the splendid machine called the Viewer Operator had better have a rest. She'd found a couple of pieces of information that might please Morse. She hoped so.

She was looking quickly through her scribbled notes, making sure that she could transcribe them later into some more legible form, when she became aware of a conversation taking place only three or four yards behind her at the Enquiries desk.

'Yes, I've tried County Hall – no help, I'm afraid.'

'Your best bet I should think, then, is the City Archivists. They've got an office in—'

'They sent me here!'

'Oh!' The phone rang and the assistant excused himself to answer it.

Christine gathered up her notes, turned off the MFR (as it seemed to be known), and went up to the desk.

'We met yesterday evening—' began Christine.

Sergeant Lewis smiled at her and said, 'Hullo.'

'Seems I'm having more luck than you, Sergeant.'

'Augh! He always gives me the lousy jobs – I don't know why I bother – my day off, too.'

'And mine.'

'Sorry we can't help, sir,' said the assistant (another query dealt with). 'But if they've got no trace at the Archivists . . .'

Lewis nodded. 'Well, thanks, anyway.'

Lewis escorted Christine to the swing doors when the assistant had a final thought: 'You could try St Aldate's Police Station. I *have* heard that quite a lot of documents and stuff got housed by the police in the war' ('Which war?' mumbled Lewis, inaudibly) 'and, well, perhaps—'

'Thanks very much!'

'They can't really be *all* that helpful to the public, though – I'm sure you know—'

'Oh yes!'

But the phone had been ringing again, and now the attendant answered it, convinced that he'd sent his latest customer on what would prove a wholly unproductive mission.

When alone in crowded streets, Christine sometimes felt a little apprehensive; but she experienced a pleasing sense of being under protection as she walked back towards Carfax with the burly figure of Sergeant Lewis beside and above her. Great Tom was striking twelve noon.

'I don't suppose you fancy a drink—' began Lewis.

'No – not for me, thank you. I don't drink much, anyway, and it's a bit – bit early, isn't it?'

Lewis grinned: 'That's something I don't hear very often from the Chief.' But he felt relieved. He wasn't much good at making polite conversation; and although she seemed a very nice young lady he preferred to get about his business now.

'You like him, don't you? The "Chief", I mean?'

'He's the best in the business.'

'Is he?' asked Christine, quietly.

'Will you be going in tonight?'

'I suppose so. What about you?'

'If I find anything – which seems at the moment very doubtful.'

'You never know.'

Chapter Twenty-one

From the cradle to the coffin, underwear comes first
(*Bertolt Brecht,* The Threepenny Opera)

In the late 1980s the premises of the City Police HQ in St Aldate's were being extensively renovated and extended – and the work was still in progress when Sergeant Lewis walked in through the main door that Saturday morning. The Force had always retained its obstinately hierarchical structure, and friendships between the higher and the lower ranks would perhaps always be slightly distanced. Yet Lewis knew Chief Superintendent Bell fairly well from the old days up at Kidlington and was glad to find him in the station.

Yes, of course Bell would help if he could: in fact, the timing of Lewis's visit might be very opportune, because many corners and crannies had only just been cleared out, and the contents of scores of cupboards and dust-covered cases and crates had recently seen the light of day for the first time within living memory. Bell's orders on this had been clear: if any documents seemed even marginally worth the keeping, let them be kept; if not, let them be destroyed. But strangely, up to now, almost everything so newly rediscovered had appeared potentially valuable to *someone*; and the upshot was that a whole room had been set aside in which the preserved relics and mementos from the earliest days – certainly from the 1850s onwards – had been unsystematically stacked, awaiting appropriate evaluation by academic historians, sociologists, criminologists, local-history societies – and authors. In fact a WPC was in the room now, as Bell thought – doing a bit of elementary cataloguing; and if Lewis wanted to look around . . .

Explaining that this was her lunch-break, WPC Wright, a pleasant enough brunette in her mid-twenties, continued eating her sandwiches and writing her Christmas cards, waving Lewis to any quarter of the room he wished after he had briefly stated his mission.

'It's all yours, Sergeant. Or, at least, I wish it was!'

Lewis could see what she meant. Morse had given him a copy of the Colonel's work (several spares had been left on the ward); but for the moment Lewis could see little or no chance of linking anything that had occurred in 1860 with the chaotic heaps of boxes, files, bags, crates, and piles of discoloured, dog-eared documents that lay around. To be fair, it was clear that a start had been made on sorting things out, for fifty-odd buff-coloured labels, with dates written on them, were attached to the rather neater agglomeration of material that had been separated from the rest, and set out in some semblance of chronological order. But amongst these labels Lewis looked in vain for 1859 or 1860. Was it worth having a quick look through the rest?

It was at 1.45 p.m., after what had proved to be a long look, that Lewis whistled softly.

'You found something?'

'Do you know anything about this?' asked Lewis. He had lifted from one of the tea-chests a chipped and splintered box, about two feet long, by one foot wide, and about 9–10 inches deep; a small box, by any reckoning, and one which could be carried by a person with little difficulty, since a brass plate, some 4 inches by half an inch, set in the middle of the box's top, held a beautifully moulded semi-circular handle, also of brass. But what had struck Lewis instantly – and with wondrous excitement – were the initials engraved upon the narrow plate: 'J.D.'! Lewis had not read the slim volume with any great care (or any great interest, for that matter); but he remembered clearly the two 'trunks' which Joanna had taken on to the boat and which presumably had been found in the cabin after the crew's arrest. Up to that point, Lewis had just had a vague mental picture of the sort of 'trunks' seen outside Oxford colleges when the undergraduates were arriving. But surely it had said that Joanna was *carrying* them, hadn't it? And by the well-worn look of the handle it looked as if this box had been carried – and carried often. And the name of Joanna's first husband had begun with a 'D'!

The policewoman came over and knelt beside the

box. The two smallish hooks, one on each side of the lid, moved easily; and the lock on the front was open, for the lid lifted back to reveal, inside the green-plush lining, a small canvas bag, on which, picked out in faded yellow wool, were the same initials as on the box.

Lewis whistled once more. Louder.

'Can you – can we – ?' He could scarcely keep the excitement from his voice, and the policewoman looked at him curiously for a few seconds, before gently shaking out the bag's contents on to the floor: a small, rusted key, a pocket comb, a metal spoon, five dress-buttons, a crochet-hook, a packet of needles, two flat-heeled, flimsy-looking shoes, and a pair of calico knickers.

Lewis shook his head in dumbfounded disbelief. He picked up the shoes in somewhat gingerly fashion as if he suspected they might disintegrate; then, between thumb and forefinger, the calico knickers.

'Think I could borrow these shoes and the er . . .?' he asked.

WPC Wright eyed him once again with amused curiosity.

'It's all right,' added Lewis. 'They're not for me.'

'No?'

'Morse – I work for Morse.'

'I suppose you're going to tell me he's become a knicker-fetishist in his old age.'

'You know him?'

'Wish I did!'

'He's in hospital, I'm afraid—'

'Everybody says he drinks far too much.'

'A bit, perhaps.'

'Do you know him well, would you say?'

'Nobody knows him all *that* well.'

'You'll have to sign for them—'

'Fetch me the book!'

'—and bring them back.'

Lewis grinned. 'They'd be a bit small for me, anyway, wouldn't they? The shoes, I mean.'

Chapter Twenty-Two

Don't take action because of a name! A name is an uncertain thing, you can't count on it!

(*Bertolt Brecht*, A Man's a Man)

DURING THAT SAME Saturday which saw Sergeant Lewis and Christine Greenaway giving up their free time on his behalf, Morse himself was beginning to feel fine again. Exploring new territory, too, since after lunch-time he was told he was now free to wander along the corridors at will. Thus it was that at 2.30 p.m. he found his way to the Day Room, an area equipped with armchairs, a colour TV, table-skittles, a book-case, and a great pile of magazines (the top one, Morse noted, a copy of *Country Life* dating from nine years the previous August). The room was deserted; and after making doubly sure the coast was clear, Morse placed one of the three books he was carrying in the bottom of the large wastepaper receptacle there: *The Blue Ticket* had brought him little but embarrassment and humiliation, and now, straightway, he felt like Pilgrim after depositing his sackful of sin.

The surfaces of the TV set seemed universally

smooth, with not the faintest sign of any switch, indentation, or control with which to set the thing going; so Morse settled down in an armchair and quietly contemplated the Oxford Canal once more.

The question for the Jury, of course, had not been 'Who committed the crime?' but only 'Did the prisoners do it?'; whilst for a policeman like himself the question would always have to be the first one. So as he sat there he dared to say to himself, honestly, 'All right! If the boatmen didn't do it, *who did*?' Yet if that were now the Judge's key question, Morse couldn't see the case lasting a minute longer; for the simple answer was he hadn't the faintest idea. What he *could* set his mind to, though, was some considered reflection upon the boatmen's guilt. Or innocence . . .

A quartet of questions, then.

First. Was it true that a jury should have been satisfied, beyond any reasonable doubt, that the boatmen murdered Joanna Franks? Answer: no. Not one shred of positive evidence had been produced by the prosecution which could be attested in court by any corroborative witnesses to murder – and it had been on the count of murder that the boatmen had been convicted.

Second. Was it true that the prisoners at the bar had been afforded the time-honoured 'presumption of innocence' – the nominal glory of the British Legal System? Answer: it most definitely was not. Prejudgements – wholly pejorative prejudgements – had been rife from the start of the first trial, and the attitude of the law officers no less than the general public had been, throughout, one of unconcealed contempt for, and revulsion against, the crude, barely literate, irreligious crew of the *Barbara Bray*.

Third. Was it true that the boatmen, or some of them, were likely to have been guilty of something? Answer: almost certainly, yes; and (perversely) most probably guilty on the two charges that were dropped – those of rape and theft. At the very least, there was no shortage of evidence to suggest that the men had lusted mightily after their passenger, and it was doubtless a real possibility that all three – all four? – had sought to force their advances on the hapless (albeit sexually provocative?) Joanna.

Fourth. Was there a general sense – even if the evidence *was* unsatisfactory, even if the Jury *were* unduly prejudiced – in which the verdict was a reasonable one, a 'safe' one, as some of the jurisprudence manuals liked to call it? Answer: no, a thousand times no!

Almost, now, Morse felt he could put his finger on the major cause of his unease. It was all those conversations, heard and duly reported, between the principal characters in the story: conversations between the crew and Joanna; between the crew and other boatmen; between the crew and lock-keepers, wharfingers, and constables – all of it was *wrong* somehow. *Wrong, if they were guilty*. It was as if some inexperienced playwright had been given a murder-plot, and had then proceeded to write page after page of inappropriate, misleading, and occasionally contradictory dialogue. For there were moments when it looked as if it were Joanna Franks who was the avenging Fury, with the crewmen merely the victims of her fatal power.

Then, too, the behaviour of Oldfield and Musson *after* the murder seemed to Morse increasingly a matter of considerable surprise, and it was difficult to understand why Counsel for the Defence had not sought to ram into the minds of Judge and Jury alike the utter *implausibility* of what, allegedly, they did and said. It was not unknown, admittedly, for the odd psychopath to act in a totally irrational and irresponsible manner. But these men were *not* a quartet of psychopaths. And, above all, it seemed quite extraordinary to Morse that, even after (as was claimed) the crew had somehow and for some reason managed to murder Joanna Franks, they were – some twenty-four, thirty-six hours later – still knocking back the booze, still damning and blasting the woman's soul to eternity. Morse had known many murderers, but never one who had subsequently acted in such a fashion – let alone *four*. No! It just didn't add up; didn't add up at all. Not that it mattered, though – not really – after all these years.

Morse flicked open the index of the stout volume recording the misdeeds of Old Salopians, and his eye caught 'Shropshire Union Canal (The)'. He turned idly to the page reference, and there read through the paragraph, and with growing interest. (Well done, Mrs Lewis!) The author was still most horribly enmeshed in his barbed-wire style, still quite incapable of calling a spade anything else but a broad-bladed digging-tool; but the message was clear enough:

'With such an incidence of crime on the canals, it can scarcely be a source of surprise that we find countless instances of evasiveness, on the part of many of the boatmen, in matters such as the registering of names, both those of the boats they crewed and of their own persons. Specifically, with regard to the latter of these deceptions, we discover that many of those working both on the water and on the wharfs had a duality of names, and were frequently considerably better known by their 'bye-names' than by their christened nomenclature. For varied sociological reasons (some of which we have yet to analyse) it can more than tentatively be suggested that boatmen as a generality were likely to be potentially predisposed to the regular commission of crime, and certain it must be held that their profession (if such it may be called) afforded ample opportunities for the realization of such potentiality. Sometimes they sold parts of their cargoes, replacing, for example, quantities of coal with similar quantities of rocks or stone; frequently we come across recorded instances (see esp. SCL, *Canal and Navigable Waters Commission*, 1842, Vol. IX, pp. 61–4, 72–5, 83–6, *et passim*) of crewmen drinking from their cargoes of fine wines and whiskies, and refilling the emptied bottles with water. Toll officials, too, do not always appear blameless in these affairs, and could occasionally be bribed into closing their eyes . . .'

Morse's eyes were beginning to close, too, and he laid the book aside. The point had been made: boatmen were a load of crooks who often nicked bits of their cargoes. Hence Walter Towns, aka Walter Thorold, and the rest. All as simple as that – once you knew the answers. Perhaps it would *all* be like that one day, in that Great Computer Library in the Sky, when the problems that had beset countless generations of sages and philosophers would be answered immediately, just by tapping in the questions on some celestial key-board.

The youth with the portable saline-drip walked in, nodded to Morse, picked up a small TV control-panel from somewhere, and began flicking his way around the channels with, for Morse, irritating impermanence. It was time to get back to the ward.

As he was leaving his eyes roamed automatically over the book-case, and he stopped. There, on the lower row, and standing side by side, were the titles *Victorian Banbury* and *OXFORD* (Rail Centres Series). Having extracted both, he walked back. Perhaps, if you kept your eyes open, you didn't need any Valhallan VDUs at all.

Walter Algernon Greenaway had been trying, with little success, to get going with the *Oxford Times* crossword. He had little or no competence in the skill, but it had always fascinated him; and when the previous day he had watched Morse complete *The Times* crossword in about ten minutes, he felt most envious. Morse had just settled back in his bed when Greenaway (predictably known to his friends, it appeared, as 'Waggie') called across.

'You're pretty good at crosswords—'

'Not bad.'

'You know anything about cricket?'

'Not much. What's the clue?'

'"Bradman's famous duck".'

'How many letters?'

'Six. I saw Bradman at the Oval in 1948. He got a duck then.'

'I shouldn't worry too much about cricket,' said Morse. 'Just think about Walt Disney.'

Greenaway licked the point of his pencil, and thought, unproductively, about Walt Disney.

'Who's the setter this week?' asked Morse.

'Chap called "Quixote".'

Morse smiled. Coincidence, wasn't it! 'What was *his* Christian name?'

'Ah! I have you, sir!' said Waggie, happily entering the letters at 1 across.

Chapter Twenty-three

All that mankind has done, thought, gained, or been, it is all lying in magic preservation in the pages of books

(*Thomas Carlyle*)

Embarras de richesses – for Morse couldn't have chosen a more informative couple of books if he'd sauntered all day round the shelves in the local Summertown Library.

First, from *Victorian Banbury,* he gleaned the information that by about 1850 the long-distance stage-coach routes via Banbury to London had been abandoned, almost entirely as a result of the new railway service from Oxford to the capital. Yet, as a direct result of this service, coaches between Banbury and Oxford had actually *increased,* and regular and efficient transportation was readily available between Banbury and Oxford (only twenty miles to the south) during the 1850s and 1860s. Furthermore, the author gave full details of the actual stage-coaches that would have been available, on the day in question, and about which Joanna Franks must have made enquiry: quite certainly coach-horses would have been seen galloping southwards on three separate occasions in the earlier half of the following day, delivering passengers picked up at the Swan Inn, Banbury, to the Angel Inn in the High at Oxford. That for the sum of 2*s*/1*d*. Even more interesting for Morse was the situation pertaining at Oxford itself, where trains to Paddington, according to his second work of reference, were far more frequent, and far quicker, than he could have imagined. And presumably Joanna herself, at Banbury on that fateful day, had been presented with *exactly* the same information: no less than *ten* trains daily, leaving at 2.10 a.m., 7.50 a.m., 9 a.m., 10.45 a.m., 11.45 a.m., 12.55 p.m., 2.45 p.m., 4.00 p.m., 5.50 p.m., and 8.00 p.m. *Embarras du choix*. Admittedly, the fares seemed somewhat steep, with 1st-, 2nd-, and 3rd-class carriages priced respectively at 16*s*, 10*s*, and 6*s*, for the 60-odd-mile journey. But the historian of Oxford's railways was fair-minded enough to add the fact that there were also three coaches a day, at least up until the 1870s, making the comparatively slow journey to London via the Henley and Reading turnpikes: *The Blenheim* and *The Prince of Wales*, each departing at 10.30 a.m., with *The Rival* an hour later, the fare being a 'whole shilling' less than the 3rd-class railway fare. And where did they finish up in the metropolis? It was quite extraordinary. The Edgware Road!

So, for a few minutes Morse looked at things from Joanna's point of view – a Joanna who (as he had no option but to believe) was *in extremis*. Arriving at Banbury, as she had, in the latish evening, she would very soon have seen the picture. No chance of anything immediately, but the ready opportunity of a stay overnight in Banbury, in one of the taverns along the quayside, perhaps. Not four-star AA accommodation – but adequate, and certainly costing no more than 2*s* or so. Then one of the coaches to Oxford next morning – the book of words mentioned one at 9.30 a.m., reaching Oxford at about 1 p.m. That would mean no difficulty at all about catching the 2.45 p.m. to Paddington – or one of the three later trains, should any accident befall the horses. Easy! If she *had* eventually made a firm decision to escape her tormentors for good, then the situation was straightforward. 2*s* overnight, say, 2*s*/1*d* coach-fare, 6s 3rd-class rail-fare – that meant that for about 10s she was offered a final chance of saving her life. And without much bother, without much expense, she *could* have done so.

But she hadn't. Why not? Received wisdom maintained that she hadn't got a penny-piece to her name, let alone half a guinea. But had she nothing she could sell, or pawn? Had she no negotiable property with her? What *had* she got in those two boxes of hers? Nothing of any value whatsoever? Why, then, if that were so, could there ever have been the slightest suspicion of *theft*? Morse shook his head slowly. Ye gods! – how he wished he could have a quick look into one of those boxes!

It was tea-time, and Morse was not aware that his wish had already been granted.

Chapter Twenty-four

Magnus Alexander corpore parvus erat (Even Alexander the Great didn't measure up to the height-requirement of the Police Force)

(*Latin Proverb*)

Normal shifts for the staff at the JR2 were Early (07.45–15.45), Late (13.00–21.30) and Night (21.00–08.15). Always more of an owl than a lark, Eileen Stanton shared none of the common objections that were levelled against the Night shift: born with a temperament slightly tinged with melancholy, she was perhaps a natural creature of the dark. But this particular week had been unusual. And that day she was on Late.

Married at the age of nineteen and divorced at twenty, she was now, five years later, living out at Wantage with a man, fifteen years her senior, who had celebrated his fortieth birthday the previous evening (hence the re-arrangements). The party had gone splendidly until just after midnight when the celebrant himself had been involved in a pathetic little bout of fisticuffs, over *her*! Now, in films or on TV, after being knocked unconscious with a vicious blow from an iron bar, the hero has only to rub the sore spot for a couple of minutes before resuming his mission. But life itself, as Eileen knew, wasn't like that – the victim was much more likely to end up in the ICU, with permanent brain-damage, to boot. Much more cruel. Like last night (this morning!) when her cohabitee had been clouted in the face, his upper lip splitting dramatically, and one of his front teeth being broken off at the root. Not good for his looks, or his pride, or the party, or Eileen, or anybody. Not good at all!

For the umpteenth time her mind dwelt on that incident as she drove into Oxford, parked her apple-jack-green Metro in the Staff Only park of the JR2, and walked down to the Basement Cloak Room to change her clothes. It would do her good to get back on the Ward, she knew that. She'd found it easy enough so far to steer clear of any emotional involvement with her patients, and for the moment all she wanted was to get a few hours of dutiful nursing behind her – to forget the previous night, when she'd drunk a little too freely, and flirted far too flagrantly with a man she'd never even met before ... No hangover – although she suddenly began to wonder if she *did* have a hangover after all: just didn't notice it amid her other mental agitations. Anyway, it was high time she forgot all her own troubles and involved herself with other people's.

She'd noticed Morse (and he her) as he'd walked along to the Day Room; watched him walk back, half an hour later and spend the rest of the afternoon reading. Bookish sort of fellow, he seemed. Nice, though – and she would go and have a word with him perhaps once he put his books down. Which he didn't.

She watched him again, at 7.40 p.m., as he sat against the pillows; and more particularly watched the woman who sat beside him, in a dark-blue dress, with glints of gold and auburn in her hair, the regular small-featured face leaning forward slightly as she spoke to him. To Eileen the pair of them seemed so eager to talk to each other – so different from the conversational drought which descended on so many hospital visitations. Twice, even as she watched, the woman, in the middle of some animated little passage of dialogue, placed the tips of her fingers against the sleeve of his gaudy pyjamas, fingers that were slim and sinewy, like those of an executant musician. Eileen knew all about *that* sort of gesture! And what about him, Morse? He, too, seemed to be doing his level, unctuous best to impress *her*, with a combination of that happily manufactured half-smile and eyes that focused intently upon hers. Oh yes! She could see what each of them was feeling – nauseating couple of bootlickers! But she knew she envied them; envied especially the woman – Waggie's clever-clogs of a daughter! From the few times she'd spoken to Morse, she knew that his conversation – and perhaps, she thought, his life, too – was so *interesting*. She'd met just a few other men like that – men who were full of fascinating knowledge about architecture, history, literature, music . . . all the things after which over these last few years she'd found herself yearning. How relieved she suddenly felt that most probably her swollen-lipped forty-year-old wouldn't be able to kiss her that evening!

A man (as she now realized) had been standing patiently at the desk.

'Can I help you?'

Sergeant Lewis nodded and looked down at her. 'Special instructions. I've got to report to the boss whenever I bring the Chief Inspector a bag of plastic explosive. You're the boss tonight, aren't you?'

'Don't be too hard on Sister Maclean!'

Lewis bent forward and spoke softly. 'It's not me – it's him! He says she's an argumentative, bitchy old . . . old something.'

Eileen smiled. 'She's not very tactful, sometimes.'

'He's, er – looks like he's got a visitor for the moment.'

'Yes.'

'Perhaps I'd better not interrupt, had I? He gets very cross sometimes.'

'Does he?'

'Especially if . . .'

Eileen nodded, and looked up into Lewis's kindly face, feeling that menfolk weren't quite so bad as she'd begun to think.

'What's he like – Inspector Morse?' she asked.

Christine Greenaway stood up to go, and Morse was suddenly conscious, as she stood so closely beside the bed, how small she was – in spite of the high-heeled shoes she habitually wore. Words came back to his mind, the words he'd read again so recently: '. . . petite and attractive figure, wearing an Oxford-blue dress . . .'

'How tall are you?' asked Morse, as she smoothed her dress down over her thighs.

'How *small* am I, don't you mean?' Her eyes flashed and seemed to mock him. 'In stockinged feet, I'm five feet, half an inch. And don't forget that half-inch: it may not be very important to you, but it is to me. I wear heels all the time – so I come up to about normal, usually. About five three.'

'What size shoes do you take?'

'Threes. You wouldn't be able to get your feet in them.'

'I've got very nice feet,' said Morse seriously.

'I think I ought to be more worried about my father than about your feet,' she whispered quietly, as she touched his arm once more, and as Morse in turn placed his own left hand so briefly, so lightly upon hers. It was a little moment of magic, for both of them.

'And you'll look up that—?'

'I won't forget.'

Then she was gone, and only the smell of some expensive perfume lingered around the bed.

'I just wonder,' said Morse, almost absently, as Lewis took Christine's place in the plastic chair, 'I just wonder what size shoes Joanna Franks took. I'm assuming, of course, they *had* shoe-sizes in those days. Not a modern invention, like women's tights, are they? – shoe-sizes? What do you think, Lewis?'

'Would you like me to show you exactly what size she *did* take, sir?'

CHAPTER TWENTY-FIVE

Those who are incapable of committing great crimes do not readily suspect them in others

(*La Rochefoucauld,* Maxims)

MORSE WAS INVARIABLY credited, by his police colleagues, with an alpha-plus intelligence, of a kind which surfaced rarely on the tides of human affairs, and which almost always gave him about six furlongs' start in any criminal investigation. Whatever the truth of this matter, Morse himself knew that one gift had never been bestowed on him – that of *reading* quickly. It was to be observed, therefore, that he seemed to spend a disproportionately long time that evening – Christine gone, Lewis gone, Horlicks drunk, pills swallowed, injection injected – in reading through the photocopied columns from *Jackson's Oxford Journal.* Christine had not mentioned to him that, dissatisfied with her hand-written notes, she had returned to the Central Library in the early afternoon and prevailed upon one of her vague acquaintances there to let her jump the queue and photocopy the original material directly from their bulky originals. Not that Morse, even had he known, would have exhibited any excessive gratitude. One of his weaknesses was his disposition to accept loyalty without ever really understanding, certainly not appreciating, the sacrifices that might be involved.

When, as a boy, he had been shepherded around various archaeological sites, Morse had been unable to share the passion of some fanatic drooling over a few (disintegrating) Roman bricks. Even then, it had been the written word, rather than the tangible artefact, which had pricked his curiosity, and promoted his subsequent delight in the ancient world. It was to be expected, therefore, that although Lewis's quite extraordinary discovery was to prove the single most dramatic break-through in the supposed 'case', the sight of a sad-looking pair of shrivelled shoes and an even sadder-looking pair of crumpled knickers was, for Morse, a little anti-climactic. At least, for the present. As for Christine's offerings, though, how wonderfully attractive and suggestive they were!

From the newspaper records, it was soon clear that the Colonel had omitted no details of any obvious importance. Yet, as in most criminal cases, it was the apparently innocuous, incidental, almost irrelevant, details that could change, in a flash, the interpretation of accepted facts. And there were quite a few details here (to Morse, hitherto unknown) which caused him more than a millimetric rise of the eyebrows.

First, reading between the somewhat smudged lines of the photocopied material, it seemed fairly clear that the charge of theft had probably been dropped at the first trial for the reason that the evidence (such as it was) had pointed predominantly to the youth, Wootton, therefore necessitating an individual prosecution – and that against a minor. If any of the other crewmen were involved, it was Towns (the man deported to Australia) who figured as the safest bet; and quite certainly no obvious evidence could be levelled against the two men eventually hanged for *murder*. What was it then that the young man's covetous eyes may have sought to steal from Joanna Franks's baggage? No answer emerged clearly from the evidence. But there was surely one thing, above all, that thieves went for, whether in 1859 or 1989: *money*.

Mmm.

Second, there was sufficient contemporary evidence to suggest that it was Joanna who was probably the sustaining partner in her second marriage. Whatever it was that had caused her to 'fall deeply in love with Charles Franks, an ostler from Liverpool', it was *Joanna* who had besought her new husband to keep up his spirits during the ill fortune which had beset the early months of their marriage. An extract from a letter to Charles Franks had indeed been read out in court, presumably (as Morse saw things) to substantiate the point that, quite contrary to the boatmen's claim of *Joanna* being demented, it was *Charles* who seemed the nearer to a mental breakdown: 'Sorry I am to read, my dear husband, your sadly wandering letter – do, my dear, strive against what I fear will await you should you not rest your tortured mind. The loss of reason is a terrible thing and will blight our hopes. Be strong and know we shall soon be together and well provided for.' A poignant and eloquent letter.

Were *both* of them a bit unbalanced?

Mmm.

Third, various depositions from both trials made it clear that although 'fly' boats worked best with a strict enforcement of a 'two on – two off' arrangement, it was quite usual, in practice, for the four members of such a crew to permutate their different duties in order to accommodate individual likings or requirements. Or *desires*, perhaps? For Morse now read, with considerable interest, the evidence adduced in court (Where were you, Colonel Deniston?) that Oldfield, captain of the *Barbara Bray*, had paid Walter Towns 6*d* to take over from him the arduous business of 'legging' the boat through the Barton tunnel. Morse nodded to himself: for his imagination had already travelled there.

Mmm.

Fourth, the evidence, taken as a whole, suggested strongly that for the first half of the journey Joanna had joined in quite happily with the boatmen at the various stops: staying in their company, eating at the same table, drinking with them, laughing with them at their jokes. Few jokes, though, on the latter half of the journey, when, as the prosecution had pressed home again and again, Joanna figured only as a helpless, hapless soul – crying out (at times, literally) for help, sympathy, protection, mercy. And one decisive and dramatic fact: as the crew themselves grew progressively inebriated, Joanna was becoming increasingly sober;

for the coroner's evidence, as reported at the trial, was incontestable: *no alcohol at all was found in her body.*

Mmm.

Morse proceeded to underline in blue Biro the various, and most curious, altercations which the law-writer of *Jackson's Oxford Journal* had deemed it worthy to record:

'Will you have anything of this?' (Oldfield) 'No, I have no inclination.' (Bloxham) '—'s already had his concerns with her tonight; and I will, or else I shall — her.' (Oldfield) 'D—n and blast the woman! If she has drowned herself, I cannot help it.' (Oldfield) 'She said she'd do it afore, and now she seems to 'a done it proper.' (Musson) 'I hope the b—y w—e is burning in hell!' (Oldfield) 'Blast the woman! What do we know about her? If she had a mind to drown herself, why should we be in all this trouble?' (Towns) 'If he is going to be a witness against us, it is for other things, not for the woman.' (Oldfield)

Mmm.

Randomly quoted, incoherent, unchronological as they were, these extracts from the trials served most strongly to reinforce Morse's earlier conviction that they were not the sort of comments one would expect from murderers. One might expect some measure of shame, remorse, fear – yes! – even, in a few cases, triumph and jubilation in the actual performance of the deed. But not – no! – not the fierce anger and loathing perpetuated by the boatman through the hours and the days after Joanna had met her death.

Finally, there was a further (significant?) passage of

evidence which the Colonel had *not* cited. It was, apparently, Oldfield's claim that, at about 4 a.m. on the fateful morning, the boatmen *had*, in fact, caught up with Joanna – the latter in a state of much mental confusion; both he and Musson had discovered her whereabouts only by the anguished cries in which she called upon the name of her husband: 'Franks! Franks! Franks!' Furthermore, Oldfield claimed, he had actually persuaded her to get back on the boat, although he agreed that she had fairly soon jumped off again (again!) to resume her walking along the tow-path. Then, according to Oldfield, two of them, he and Towns on this occasion, had once more gone ashore, where they met another potential witness (the Donald Favant mentioned in the Colonel's book). But the boatmen had not been believed. In particular this second meeting along the tow-path had come in for withering scorn from the prosecution: at best, the confused recollection of hopelessly drunken minds; at worst, the invention of 'these callous murderers'. Yes! That was exactly the sort of comment which throughout had disquieted Morse's passion for justice. As a policeman, he knew only the rudiments of English Law; but he was a fervent believer in the principle that a man should be presumed innocent until he was pronounced guilty: it was a fundamental principle, not only of substantive law, but of natural justice . . .

'You comfy?' asked Eileen, automatically pulling the folds of his sheets tidy.

'I thought you'd gone off duty.'

'Just going.'

'You're spoiling me.'

'You enjoy reading, don't you?'

Morse nodded: 'Sometimes.'

'You like reading best of all?'

'Well, music – music, I suppose, sometimes more.'

'So, if you're reading a book with the record-player going—'

'I can't enjoy them both together.'

'But they're the *best*?'

'Apart from a candle-lit evening-meal with someone like you.'

Eileen coloured, her pale cheeks suddenly as bright as those of the dying Colonel.

Before going to sleep that night, Morse's hand glided into the bedside cabinet and poured out a small measure; and as he sipped the Scotch, at his own pace, the world of a sudden was none too bad a place . . .

When he awoke (was awoken, rather) the following morning (Sunday) he marvelled that the blindingly obvious notion that now occurred to him had taken such an age to materialize. Usually, his cerebral analysis was as swift as the proverbial snap of a lizard's eyelid.

Or so he told himself.

Chapter Twenty-six

> Now, there is a law written in the darkest of the Books of Life, and it is this: If you look at a thing nine hundred and ninety-nine times, you are perfectly safe; if you look at it for the thousandth time, you are in frightful danger of seeing it for the first time
>
> (*G. K. Chesterton,* The Napoleon of Notting Hill)

Just the same with crossword puzzles, wasn't it? Sit and ponder more and more deeply over some abstruse clue – and get nowhere. Stand away, though – further back! – further back still! – and the answer will shout at you with a sort of mocking triumph. It was those shoes, of course . . . shoes at which he'd been staring so hard he hadn't really seen them.

Morse waited with keen anticipation until his morning ablutions were complete before re-re-reading the Colonel's work, lingering over things – as he'd always done as a boy when he'd carved his way meticulously around the egg-white until he was left only with the golden circle of the yolk, into which, finally, to dip the calculated balance of his chips.

What were the actual words of the trial report? Yes, Morse nodded to himself: when Charles Franks had looked at the body, he had recognized it, dreadfully disfigured as it was, by 'a small mark behind his wife's left ear, a mark of which only a parent or an intimate lover could have known'. *Or a scoundrel.* By all the gods, was *ever* identification so tenuously asserted and attested in the English Courts? Not only some tiny disfigurement in a place where no one else would have been aware of it, but a tiny disfigurement which existed *on* the head of Joanna Franks only because it existed *in* the head of her new husband! Oh, it must have been there all right! The doctor, the coroner, the inspector of police, those who'd undressed the dead woman, and redressed her for a proper Christian burial – so many witnesses who could, if need ever arose, corroborate the existence of such a blemish on what had once been such a pretty face. But who could, or did, corroborate the fact that the face had been *Joanna*'s? The husband? Yes, he'd had his say. But the only others who might have known, the parents – where were they? Apparently, they'd played no part at all in the boatmen's trial at Oxford. Why not? Was the mother too stricken with grief to give any coherent testimony? Was she *alive*, even, at the time of the trial? The father was alive, though, wasn't he? The insurance man . . .

Morse brought his mind back to the central point he was seeking to establish before his own imagined jury (little 'j'). No court would have accepted such unilateral identification without *something* to support it – and there *had* been something (again Morse looked back to the actual words): corroboration was afforded 'by the shoes, later found in the fore-cabin of the *Barbara Bray*, which matched in the minutest degrees the contours of the dead woman's feet'. So, the matter was clear: one, the shoes in the cabin belonged to Joanna Franks; two, the shoes had been worn by the drowned woman; therefore, three, the drowned woman was Joanna Franks – QED. Even Aristotle might have been satisfied with such a syllogism. Incontrovertible! All three statements as true as the Eternal Verities; and if so, the shoes *must* belong to the woman who was drowned. But . . . but what if the first statement was *not* true? What if the shoes had *not* belonged to Joanna? Then the inexorable conclusion must be that whatever was found floating face-downward at Duke's Cut in 1859, *it was not the body of Joanna Franks.*

Just one moment, Morse!! (The voice of the prosecution was deafening against his ear.) All right! The identification as it stood, as it stands, may perchance appear a trifle tenuous? But have you – *you* – any – *any* – reason for discrediting such identification? And the answering voice in Morse's brain – *Morse's* voice – was firm and confident. Indeed! And if it should please my learned friends I shall now proceed to tell you exactly what *did* happen between 3 a.m. and 5 a.m. on the morning of Wednesday, the 21st June, in 1859.

Gentlemen! We who are engaged in seeking to reconstruct the course as well as the causation of crime are often tormented by the same insistent thought: *something* must have happened, and happened *in a specific way.* All theory, all reconstruction, all probability, are as nothing compared with *the simple, physical truth of what actually happened at the time.* If only . . . if only, we say, we could see it all; see it all as it actually happened! Gentlemen, I am about to tell you—

Proceed! said the judge (little 'j').

Chapter Twenty-seven

> Imagination, that dost so abstract us
> That we are not aware, not even when
> A thousand trumpets sound about our ears!
>
> (*Dante*, Purgatorio)

STANDING BY THE door at the left of the fore-cabin, she could see them both. A reporter, perhaps, would have had them dribbling or vomiting; snoring 'stertorously', certainly. But Joanna was to notice, at that point, only the simple fact, the undramatic circumstance: asleep, the pair of them – Oldfield and Musson – only the slight rise and fall of the faded-maroon eiderdown that covered them both betraying their fitful breathing. Drunk? Yes, *very* drunk: but Joanna herself had seen to that. Little or no persuasion required – but the *timing* important . . . She smiled grimly to herself, and consulted the little silver time-piece she always kept so carefully about her person: the watch her father had given her on her twenty-second birthday (not her twenty-first) – when some fees had been forthcoming from the London Patent Office. And again, now, her hand closed around the precious watch as if it were a talisman for the success of the imminent enterprise.

Occasionally she spoke quietly – very quietly – to the shifty, silly, spotty-faced youth who stood beside her at the entrance to the cabin: his left hand upon the Z-shaped tiller, painted in alternate bands of red, green, yellow; his right hand (where she had placed it herself!) fondling the bosom of her dress. Twenty-five yards ahead, the horse (rather a good one!) was plodding along a little more slowly now, the wooden bobbins stretched taut along its flanks as it forged forward along the silent tow-path – with only the occasional flap of the waters heard as they slurped against the *Barbara Bray*, heading ever southwards into the night.

Joanna looked briefly behind her now, at the plaited basket-work that protected the narrow-boat's stern. 'Over a bit *more*, Tom!' she whispered, as the boat moved into the elbow-bend at Thrupp, just past the village of Hampton Gay. 'And don't forget our little bargain,' she added as she stepped up on to the side, whilst Wootton gently manoeuvred the boat ever closer in towards the right-hand bank.

Wootton would not be celebrating his fifteenth birthday until the February of 1860, but already, in several ways, he was a good deal older than his years. Not in *every* way, though. Never, before Joanna had come on board at Preston Brook, had he felt so besotted with a woman as he was with *her*. Exactly as, he knew, the rest of the crew had been. There was something sexually animated, and *compelling*, about Joanna Franks. Something about the way she flashed her eyes when she spoke; something about the way her tongue lightly licked the corners of her mouth after a plate of mutton chops and peas at some low-roofed tavern alongside the canal; something wickedly and calculatedly controlled about her, as she'd drunk her own full share of liquor – that happily awaited, worry-effacing liquor that all the boatmen (including Wootton) drank so regularly along their journeys. *And Oldfield had taken possession of her* – of that Wootton was quite sure! Taken her in one of the pitch-black transit-tunnels when he, Wootton, had gladly taken Oldfield's 6*d*, and 'legged' the *Barbara Bray* slowly towards that pin-point of light which had gradually grown ever larger as darkly he'd listened to the strangely exciting noises of the love-making taking place in the bunk below him. Towns, too, had taken Oldfield's 6*d* in a tunnel further south. And both Towns and Musson – the lanky, lecherous-eyed Musson! – knew only too well what was going on, soon wanting a share of things for themselves. No surprise, then, that nasty incident when Towns had gone for Musson – with a knife!

As agreed, Thomas Wootton provided her with the lantern. The night, though dark, was dry and still; and the flame nodded only spasmodically as she took it, and leaped lightly off the *Barbara Bray* – her bonnet around her head, her shoes on her feet – on to the tow-path bank where, very soon, she had disappeared from the youth who now kept looking straight ahead of him, a smile around his wide, lascivious mouth.

It was not unusual, of course, for women passengers to jump ashore at fairly regular intervals from a narrow-boat: female toiletry demanded a greater measure of decorum than did that for men. But Joanna might be gone a little longer than was usual that night . . . so she'd said.

She stood back in the undergrowth, watching the configuration of the boat melt deeper and deeper into the night. Then, gauging she was out of ear-shot of the crew, she called out the man's name – without at first receiving a reply: then again; then a third time – until she heard a rustling movement in the bushes beside her, against the stone wall of a large mansion house – and a suppressed, tense, 'Shsh!'

The night air was very still, and her voice had carried far too clearly down the canal, with both the youth at the helm, and the man with the stoical horse, turning round simultaneously to look into the dark. But they could see nothing; and *hearing* nothing further, neither of them was giving the matter much further thought.

But one of the men supposedly asleep had heard it, too!

Meanwhile Joanna and her accomplice had flitted stealthily along the row of small, grey-stoned, terraced cottages which lined the canal at Thrupp, keeping to the shadows; then, gliding unobserved past the darkened, silent windows of the Boat Inn, they moved, more freely now, along the short hedge-lined lane that led to the Oxford-Banbury highway.

For the *Barbara Bray*, the next three miles of the Oxford Canal would interpose the Roundham, Kidlington Green, and Shuttleworth's locks – the latter just north of the basin of water known as Duke's Cut.

Negotiation of these locks (so carefully calculated!) would afford appropriate opportunity. No real problem. Much more difficult had been the arrangements for meeting each other; and certainly Oldfield, more than once, had looked at Joanna suspiciously in the last twenty-four hours as she had taken (but of necessity!) her diurnal and nocturnal promenades. She knew, though, how to deal with Oldfield, the skipper of the *Barbara Bray* . . .

'Everything ready?'

He nodded, brusquely. 'Don't talk now!'

They walked across to a covered carrier's wagon which stood, a piebald horse between its shafts, tethered to a beech tree just beside the verge. The moon appeared fitfully from behind the slow-moving cloud; not a soul was in sight.

'Knife?' he asked.

'I sharpened it.'

He nodded with a cruel satisfaction.

She took off her cloak and handed it to him; taking, in return, the one he passed to her – similar to her own, though cheaper in both cloth and cut, and slightly longer.

'You didn't forget the handkerchief?'

Quickly she re-checked, drawing from the right-hand pocket of her former cloak the small, white square of linen, trimmed with lace, the initials J.F. worked neatly in pink silk in one corner.

Clever touch!

'She's – she's in there?' Joanna half-turned to the back of the wagon, for the first time her voice sounding nervous, though unexpectedly harsh.

He jerked his head, once, his eyes bright in the heavily bearded face.

'I don't really want to see her.'

'No need!' He had taken the lantern; and when the two of them had climbed up to the front of the wagon, he shone it on a hand-drawn map, his right forefinger pointing to a bridge over the canal, some four-hundred yards north of Shuttleworth's Lock. 'We go down to – here! You wait there, and catch up with them, all right? Then get on board again. Then after that – *after* you get through the lock – you . . .'

'What we agreed!'

'Yes. Jump in! You can stay in the water as long as you like. But be sure no one sees you getting out! The wagon'll be next to the bridge. You get in! And lie still! All right? I'll be there as soon as I've . . .'

Joanna took the knife from her skirt. 'Do you want *me* to do it?'

'No!' He took the knife quickly.

'No?'

'It's just,' he resumed, 'that her face, well – well, it's gone *black*!'

'I thought dead people usually went white,' whispered Joanna.

The man climbed on to the fore-board, and helped her up, before disappearing briefly into the darkness of the covered cart; where, holding the lantern well away from the face, he lifted the dead woman's skirts and with the skill of a surgeon made an incision of about five or six inches down the front of her calico knickers.

The man was handing Joanna two bottles of dark-looking 'Running Horse' ale, when he felt the firm grip of her hand on his shoulder, shaking, shaking, shaking . . . 'Some soup for you, Mr Morse?'

It was Violet.

(Not the soup.)

Chapter Twenty-eight

Mendacity is a system that we live in. Liquor is one way out and death's the other
(*Tennessee Williams,* Cat on a Hot Tin Roof)

THE 'REPORT' WAS a regular feature of all the wards in the JR2, comprising a meeting of hospital and medical staff at the change-over points between the Early, Late, and Night shifts. In several of the wards, the weekends offered the chance for some top consultants and other senior medical personnel to concentrate their attention on such sidelines as boating and BMWs. But in many of the semi-surgical wards, like Ward 7C, the Reports went on very much as at any other times; as they did on what was now the second Sunday of Morse's stay in hospital.

The 1 p.m. meeting that day was, in fact, well attended: the Senior Consultant, a junior houseman, Sister Maclean, Charge Nurse Stanton, and two student nurses. Crowded into Sister's small office, the group methodically appraised the patients in the ward, briefly discussing convalescences, relapses, prognoses, medications, and associated problems.

Morse, it appeared, was no longer much of a problem.

'Morse!' The hint of a smile could be observed on the Consultant's face as he was handed the relevant notes.

'He's making fairly good progress,' Sister asserted, slightly defensively, like some mother at a Parents' Evening hearing that her child was perhaps not working as hard as he should be.

'Some of us,' confided the Consultant (handing back the notes) 'would like to persuade these dedicated drinkers that water is a wonderful thing. I wouldn't try to persuade you, of course, Sister, but . . .'

For a minute or two Sister Maclean's pale cheeks were flooded with a bright-pink suffusion, and one of the student nurses could barely suppress a smile of delight at the Dragon's discomfiture. But oddly, the other of the two, the Fair Fiona, was suddenly aware of lineaments and colouring in Sister's face that could have made it almost beautiful.

'He doesn't seem to drink *that* much, does he?' suggested the young houseman, his eyes skimming the plentiful notes, several of which he had composed himself.

The Consultant snorted contemptuously: 'Nonsense!' He flicked his finger at the offending sheets. 'Bloody liar, isn't he? Drunkards and diabetics!' – he turned to the houseman – 'I've told you that before, I think?'

It was wholly forgivable that for a few seconds the suspicion of a smile hovered around the lips of Sister

Maclean, her cheeks now restored to their wonted pallidity.

'He's not diabetic—' began the houseman.

'Give him a couple of years!'

'He *is* on the mend, though.' The houseman (and rightly!) was determined to claim *some* small credit for the reasonably satisfactory transit of Chief Inspector Morse through the NHS.

'Bloody lucky! Even I was thinking about cutting half his innards away!'

'He must be a fundamentally strong sort of man,' admitted Sister, composure now fully recovered.

'I suppose so,' conceded the Consultant, 'apart from his stomach, his lungs, his kidneys, his liver – especially his liver. He might last till he's sixty if he does what we tell him – which I doubt.'

'Keep him another few days, you think?'

'No!' decided the Consultant, after a pause. 'No! Send him home! His wife'll probably do just as good a job as we can. Same medication – out-patients' in two weeks – to see *me*. OK?'

Eileen Stanton was about to correct the Consultant on his factual error when a nurse burst into the office. 'I'm sorry, Sister – but there's a cardiac arrest, I think – in one of the Amenity Beds.'

'Did he die?' asked Morse.

Eileen, who had come to sit on his bed, nodded sadly. It was mid-afternoon.

'How old was he?'

'Don't know exactly. Few years younger than you, I should think.' Her face was glum. 'Perhaps if . . .'

'You look as if you could do with a bit of tender loving care yourself,' said Morse, reading her thoughts.

'Yes!' She looked at him and smiled, determined to snap out of her mopishness. 'And you, my good sir, are not going to get very much more of our wonderful loving care – after today. We're kicking you out tomorrow – had quite enough of you!'

'I'm going out, you mean?' Morse wasn't sure if it was good news or bad news; but she told him.

'Good news, isn't it?'

'I shall miss you.'

'Yes, I shall . . .' But Morse could see the tears welling up in her eyes.

'Why don't you tell me what's wrong?' He spoke the words softly; and she told him. Told him about her wretched week; and how kind the hospital had been in letting her switch her normal nights; and how kind, especially, *Sister* had been . . . But the big tears were rolling down her cheeks and she turned away and held one hand to her face, searching with the other for her handkerchief. Morse put his own grubby handkerchief gently into her hand, and for a moment the two sat together in silence.

'I'll tell you one thing,' said Morse at last. 'It must be pretty flattering to have a couple of fellows fighting over you.'

'No! No, it *isn't*!' The tears were forming again in the large, sad eyes.

'No! You're right. But listen! It won't do you any

good at all – in fact' (Morse whispered) 'it'll make you feel far worse. But if *I'd* been at that party of yours – when they were fighting over you – I'd have taken on the *pair* of 'em! You'd have had *three* men squabbling over you – not just two.'

She smiled through her tears, and wiped her wet cheeks, already feeling much better. 'They're big men, both of them. One of them takes lessons in some of those Martial Arts.'

'All right – I'd've lost! Still have fought for you, though, wouldn't I? Remember the words of the poet? "Better to have fought and lost than . . . something . . . something . . ."' (Morse himself had apparently *forgotten* the words of the poet.)

She brought her face to within a few inches of his, and looked straight into his eyes: 'I wouldn't have minded a little bit if you *had* lost, providing you'd let me look after you.'

'You *have* been looking after me,' said Morse, 'and thank you!'

Getting to her feet, she said no more. And Morse, with a little wistfulness, watched her as she walked away. Perhaps he should have told her that she'd meant 'provided', not 'providing'? No! Such things, Morse knew, were no great worry to the majority of his fellow men and women.

But they were to him.

Chapter Twenty-nine

I think it frets the saints in heaven to see
  How many desolate creatures on the earth
  Have learnt the simple dues of fellowship
And social comfort, in a hospital
  (*Elizabeth Barrett Browning,* Aurora Leigh)

There is a sadness which invariably and mysteriously accompanies the conclusion of any journey, and the end of any sojourn. Whether or not such sadness is a presage of the last journey we all must take; whether or not it is, more simply, a series of last, protracted goodbyes – it is not of any import here to speculate. But for Morse, the news that he was forthwith to be discharged from the JR2 was simultaneously wonderful – and woeful. Music awaited him? Indeed! Soon he would be luxuriating again in Wotan's Farewell from the last act of *Die Walküre*; and turning up Pavarotti *fff* from one of the Puccinis – certainly in mid-morning, when his immediate neighbours were always out and about on their good works for Oxfam. Books, too. He trusted that the Neighbourhood Watch had done its duty in North Oxford, and that his first edition of *A*

Shropshire Lad (1896) was still in its place on his shelves, that slim, white volume that stood proudly amongst its fellows, carrying no extra insurance-cover, like a Royal Prince without a personal bodyguard. Yes, it would be good to get home again: to please himself about what he listened to, or read, or ate . . . or drank. Well, within reason. Yet, quite certainly, he would miss the hospital! Miss the nurses, miss the fellow-patients, miss the routine, miss the visitors – miss so much about the institution which, with its few faults and its many virtues, had admitted him in his sickness and was now discharging him in a comparative health.

But the departure from Ward 7C was not, for Morse, to be a memorable experience. When the message came – hardly a bugle call! – to join a group of people who were to be ambulanced up to North Oxford, he had little opportunity of saying farewell to anyone. One of his ward-mates ('Waggie') was performing his first post-operatively independent ablutions in the wash-room; another was very fast asleep; one had just been taken to the X-ray Department; the Ethiopian torch-bearer was sitting in his bed, with Do-Not-Disturb written all over him, reading *The Blue Ticket* (!); and the last was (and had been for hours) closeted behind his curtains, clearly destined little longer for this earthly life; perhaps, indeed, having already said his own farewells to everybody. As for the nurses, most were bustling purposively about their duties (one or two new faces, anyway), and Morse realized that he was just another patient, and one no longer requiring that special care of just one week ago. Eileen he had not expected to see again, now back to her normal Nights, as she'd told him. Nor was Sister herself anywhere to be seen as he was wheeled out of the ward by a cheerful young porter with a crew-cut and earrings. The Fair Fiona, though, he did see – sitting patiently in the next bay beside an ancient citizen, holding a sputum-pot in front of his dribbling lips. With her free hand she waved, and mouthed a 'Good luck!'. But Morse was no lip-reader and, uncomprehending, he was pushed on through the exit corridor where he and his attendant waited for the service-lift to arrive at Level 7.

CHAPTER THIRTY

Lente currite, noctis equi!
(Oh gallop slow, you horses of the night!)
(*Ovid,* Amores)

ALTHOUGH MRS GREEN had kept Morse's partial central-heating partially on, the flat seemed cold and unwelcoming. It would have been good for *anyone* to be there to welcome him: certainly (and especially) Christine – or Eileen, or Fiona; even, come to think of it, the dreaded Dragon of the Loch herself. But there was no one. Lewis had not been in to clear up the stuff stuck through the letter-box, and Morse picked up two white-enveloped Christmas cards (one from his insurance company, with the facsimiled signature of the managing director); and his two Sunday newspapers. Such newspapers, although there was an occasional permutation of titles, invariably reflected the conflict in Morse's mind between the Cultured and the Coarse – the choice between the front page of the present one, *Synod in Dispute over Disestablishment,* and *Sex Slave's Six-Week Ordeal in Silk-lined Coffin* of the other. If Morse chose the latter first (as, in fact, he did) at least he had the excuse that it was undoubtedly the finer headline. And this Sunday, as usual, he first flicked through the pages of full-breasted photographs and features on Hollywood intrigues and Soap infidelities. Then, he made himself a cup of instant coffee (which he much preferred to 'the real thing') before settling down to read about the most recent fluctuations on the world's stock-markets, and the bleak prospects for the diseased and starving millions of the world's unhappy continents.

At half-past five the phone rang, and Morse knew that if he had one wish only it would be for the caller to be Christine.

The caller was Christine.

Not only had she located the rare (and extraordinarily valuable) book of which Morse had enquired, but she had spent an hour or so that afternoon ('Don't tell anyone!') reading through the relevant pages, and discovering ('Don't be disappointed!') that only one short chapter was given over to the interview, between Samuel Carter and an ageing Walter Towns, concerning the trial of the boatmen.

'That's wonderful!' said Morse. 'Where are you ringing from?'

'From, er, from home.' (Why the hesitation?)

'Perhaps—'

'Look!' she interrupted. 'I've made a photocopy. Would you like me to send it through the post? Or I could—'

'Could you read it quickly over the phone? It's fairly short, you say?'

'I'm not a very good reader.'

'Put the phone down – and I'll ring you back! Then we can talk as long as we like.'

'I'm not as hard up as all *that*, you know.'

'All right – fire away!'

'Page 187, it begins – ready?'

'Ready, miss!'

'Of the persons encountered in Perth in these last months of 1884 was a man called Walter Towns. Although he was known as a local celebrity, I found it difficult to guess the quality which had avowedly brought such renown to the rather – nay, wholly! – miserable specimen to whom I soon was introduced. He was a small man, of only some five feet in stature, thin, and of a gaunt mien, with deeply furrowed creases down each of his cheeks from eye to mouth; furthermore, his exceedingly sallow complexion had remained untouched by the rays of a sun that is powerful in this region, and his hollow aspect was further enhanced by the complete absence of teeth in the upper jaw. Yet his eyes spoke a latent (if limited) intelligence; and also a certain dolefulness, as if he were remembering things done long ago and things done ill. In truth, the situation pertaining to this man was fully as melodramatic as my readers could have wished; for he had been reprieved from the gallows with minutes only to spare. It was with the utmost interest and curiosity, therefore, that I questioned him.

'A woman had been murdered near Oxford in

1860, on the local canal, and suspicion had centred on the crew of a narrowboat plying south towards London. The four members of the crew, including both Towns himself and a lad of some fourteen years, had duly been arrested and brought to Court. Whilst the youth had been acquitted, the three others had been convicted, and incarcerated in the gaol in the city of Oxford, awaiting public execution. It was here, two or three minutes following the final visit of the Court Chaplain to the prisoners in their condemned cells, that Towns had received the news of his reprieve. Few humans, certainly, can have experienced a peripeteia' (Christine here reverted to the spelling) 'so dramatic to their fortunes. Yet my conversation with Towns proved a matter of some considerable disappointment. Barely literate as the man was (though wholly understandably so) he was also barely comprehensible. His West Country dialect (as I straightway placed it) was to such an extent o'erlaid with the excesses of the Australian manner of speech that I could follow some of his statements only with great difficulty. In short, the man I now met seemed ill-equipped to cope with the rigours of life – certainly those demanded of a free man. And Towns *was* a "free" man, after serving his fifteen years' penal servitude in the Longbay Penitentiary. A broken, witless man; a man old before his time (he was but 47), a veteran convict (or "crawler") who had experienced the ineffable agonies of a man faced with execution on the morrow.

'Concerning the gruesome and macabre events

invariably associated with the final hours of such criminals, I could learn but little. Yet a few facts may be of interest to my readers. It is clear, for example, that the prisoners each breakfasted on roasted lamb, with vegetables, although it seems probable from Towns' hazy recollection that such or similar breakfasts had been available during the whole period following the fixing of the date for their execution. More distressing, from Towns' viewpoint, was being denied access to his fellow criminals; and if I understood the unfortunate man aright it was this "deprivation" which had been the hardest thing for him to bear. Whether he had slept little or not at all during the fateful night, Towns could not well remember; nor whether he had prayed for forgiveness and deliverance. But a miracle had occurred!

'Surprisingly, it had not been the hanging itself which had been the focal-point of Towns' tortured thoughts that night. Rather it had been the knowledge of the public interest aroused in the case – the notoriety, the infamy, the horror, the abomination, the grisly spectacle, *the fame*; a fame which might bring those hapless men to walk the last few, fatal yards with a degree of fortitude which even the most pitiless spectators could admire.

'Of the crime itself, Towns protested his complete innocence – a protestation not without precedent in criminal archives! But his recollection of the canal journey – and especially of the victim herself, Joanna Franks – was vivid and most poignant. The woman had been, in Towns' eyes, quite wondrously attractive, and it may cause no surprise that she became, almost immediately, the object of the men's craving, and the cause of open jealousies. Indeed, Towns recalled an occasion when two of the crew (the two who were eventually hanged) had come to blows over that provocative and desirable woman. And one of them with a knife! Even the young boy, Harold Wootton, had come under her spell, and the older woman had without much doubt taken advantage of his infatuation. At the same time, from what Towns asserted, and from the manner of his assertion, I am of the view that he himself did not have sexual dealings with the woman.

'There is one interesting addendum to be made. In the first indictment (as I have subsequently read) the charge of either rape or theft would possibly have been prosecuted with more success than that of murder. Yet it was to be the charge of murder that was brought in the second trial. In similar instances, we may observe that the minor charge will frequently be suppressed when the major charge appears the more likely to be sustained. Was this, then, the reason why Towns seemed comparatively loquacious about the suggestion of *theft*? I know not. But it was his belief, as recounted to me, that Wootton had rather more interest in theft than in rape. After all, the availability of sexual dealings in 1860 was hardly, as now, a rarity along the English canals.'

'Well, that's it! I'll put it in the post tonight, so you should—'

'Can't you call round, and bring it?'

'Life's, well, it's just a bit hectic at the minute,' she replied, after a little, awkward silence.

'All right!' Morse needed no further excuses. Having dipped the thermometer into the water, he'd found the reading a little too cold for any prospect of mixed bathing.

'You see,' said Christine, 'I – I'm living with someone—'

'And he doesn't think you should go spending all your time helping me.'

'I kept talking about you, too,' she said quietly.

Morse said nothing.

'Is your address the same as in the telephone directory? E. Morse?'

'That's me! That is I, if you prefer it.'

'What does the "E" stand for? I never knew what to call you.'

'They just call me "Morse".'

'You won't forget me?' she asked, after a little pause.

'I'll try to, I suppose.'

Morse thought of her for many minutes after he had cradled the phone. Then he recalled the testimony of Samuel Carter, and marvelled that a researcher of Carter's undoubted experience and integrity could make so many factual errors in the course of three or four pages: the date of the murder; Towns' accent; Towns' age; Wootton's Christian name; the dropping of the rape charge . . . Very interesting, though. Why, Morse had even guessed right about that dust-up with the knife! Well, almost right: he'd got the wrong man, but . . .

CHAPTER THIRTY-ONE

> The second coastline is turned towards Spain and the west, and off it lies the island of Hibernia, which according to estimates is only half the size of Britain
>
> (*Julius Caesar,* de Bello Gallico – *on the geography of Ireland*)

TEN MINUTES LATER the phone rang again, and Morse knew in his bones that it was Christine Greenaway.

It was Strange.

'You're out then, Morse – yes? That's good. You've had a bit of a rough ride, they tell me.'

'On the mend now, sir. Kind of you to ring.'

'No *great* rush, you know – about getting back, I mean. We're a bit understaffed at the minute, but give yourself a few days – to get over things. Delicate thing, the stomach, you know. Why don't you try to get away somewhere for a couple of days – new surroundings – four-star hotel? You can afford it, Morse.'

'Thank you, sir. By the way, they've signed me off for a fortnight – at the hospital.'

'Fortnight? A *fort*-night?'

'It's, er, a delicate thing, the stomach, sir.'

'Yes, well . . .'

'I'll be back as soon as I can, sir. And perhaps it wouldn't do me any harm to take your advice – about getting away for a little while.'

'Do you a world of good! The wife's brother' (Morse groaned inwardly) 'he's just back from a wonderful holiday. Ireland – Southern Ireland – took the car – Fishguard–Dun Laoghaire – then the west coast – you know, Cork, Kerry, Killarney, Connemara – marvellous, he said. Said you couldn't have spotted a terrorist with a telescope!'

It *had* been kind of Strange to ring; and as he sat in his armchair Morse reached idly for the World Atlas from his 'large-book' shelf, in which Ireland was a lozenge shape of green and yellow on page 10 – a country which Morse had never really contemplated before. Although spelling errors would invariably provoke his wrath, he confessed to himself that he could never have managed 'Dun Laoghaire', even with a score of attempts. And where was Kerry? Ah yes! Over there, west of Tralee – he was on the right bit of the map – and he moved his finger up the coast to Galway Bay. Then he saw it: Bertnaghboy Bay! And suddenly the thought of going over to Connemara seemed overwhelmingly attractive. By himself? Yes, it probably had to be by himself; and he didn't mind that, really. He was somewhat of a loner by temperament – because though never wholly happy when alone he was usually slightly more miserable when with other people. It would have been good to have taken Christine, but . . . and for a few minutes Morse's thoughts travelled back to Ward 7C. He would send a card to Eileen and Fiona; and one to 'Waggie' Greenaway, perhaps? Yes, that would be a nice gesture: Waggie had been out in the wash-room when Morse had left, and he'd been a pleasant old—

Suddenly Morse was conscious of the tingling excitement in the nape of his neck, and then in his shoulders. His eyes dilated and sparkled as if some inner current had been activated; and he sat back in the armchair and smiled slowly to himself.

What, he wondered, was the routine in the Irish Republic for *exhumation*?

Chapter Thirty-two

> Oh what a tangled web we weave
> When first we practise to deceive!
> (*Sir Walter Scott,* Marmion)

'YOU *WHAT*?' asked a flabbergasted Lewis, who had called round at 7.30 p.m. ('Not till *The Archers* has finished' had been his strict instruction.) He himself had made an interesting little discovery – well, the WPC in St Aldates' had made it, really – and he was hoping that it might amuse Morse in his wholly inconsequential game of 'Find Joanna Franks'. But to witness Morse galloping ahead of the Hunt, chasing (as Lewis was fairly certain) after some imaginary fox of his own, was, if not particularly unusual, just a little disconcerting.

'You see, Lewis' (Morse was straightway in full swing) 'this is one of the most beautiful little deceptions we've ever come across. The *problems* inherent in the case – almost all of them – are resolved immediately once we take one further step into imaginative improbability.'

'You've lost me already, sir,' protested Lewis.

'No, I haven't! Just take one more step *yourself.* You think you're in the *dark*? Right? But the dark is where we *all* are. The dark is where *I* was, until I took one more step into the dark. And then, when I'd taken it, I found myself in the *sunshine.*'

'I'm very glad to hear it,' mumbled Lewis.

'It's like this. Once I read that story, I was uneasy about it – doubtful, uncomfortable. It was the *identification* bit that worried me – and it would have worried any officer in the Force today, *you* know that! But, more significantly, if we consider the psychology of the whole—'

'Sir!' (It was almost unprecedented for Lewis to interrupt the Chief in such peremptory fashion.) 'Could we – could you – please forget all this psychological referencing? I just about get my fill of it all from some of these Social Services people. Could you just tell me, simply and—'

'I'm boring you – is that what you're saying?'

'*Exactly* what I'm saying, sir.'

Morse nodded to himself happily. 'Let's put it *simply*, then, all right? I read a story in hospital. I get interested. I think – *think* – the wrong people got arrested, and some of 'em hanged, for the murder of that little tart from Liverpool. As I say, I thought the identification of that lady was a bit questionable; and when I read the words the boatmen were alleged to have used about her – well, I knew there must be something fundamentally *wrong.* You see—'

'You said you'd get to the point, sir.'

'I thought that Joanna's father – No! Let's start again! Joanna's father gets a job as an insurance rep. Like most people in that position he gets a few of his own family, if they're daft enough, to take out a policy with him. He gets a bit of commission, and he's not selling a phoney product, anyway, is he? I think that both Joanna and her *first* husband, our conjurer friend, were soon enlisted in the ranks of the policy-holders. Then times get tough; and to crown all the misfortunes, Mr Donavan, the greatest man in all the world, goes and dies. And when Joanna's natural grief has abated – or evaporated, rather – she finds she's done very-nicely-thank-you out of the insurance taken on his life. She receives £100, with profits, on what had been a policy taken out only two or three years previously. Now, £100 plus in 1850-whenever was a very considerable sum of money; and Joanna perhaps began, at that point, to appreciate the potential for *malpractice* in the system. She began to see the insurance business not only as a potential *future* benefit, but as an actual, *present* source of profit. So, after Donavan's death, when she met and married Franks, one of the first things she insisted on was his taking out a policy – not on *his* life – but on *hers.* Her father could, and did, effect such a transaction without any trouble, although it was probably soon after this that the Notts and Midlands Friendly Society got a little suspicious about Joanna's father, Carrick – Daniel Carrick – and told him his services were no longer—'

'Sir!'

Morse held up his right hand. 'Joanna Franks was *never* murdered, Lewis! She was the mastermind – mistressmind – behind a deception that was going to rake in some considerable, and desperately needed, profit. It was *another* woman, roughly the same age and the same height, who was found in the Oxford Canal; a woman provided by Joanna's *second* husband, the ostler from the Edgware Road, who had already made his journey – not difficult for *him*! – with horse and carriage from London, to join his wife at Oxford. Or, to be more accurate, Lewis, at some few points *north* of Oxford. You remember in the Colonel's book?' (Morse turned to the passage he had in mind.) 'He – here it is! – "he explained how in consequence of some information he had come into Oxfordshire" – Bloody liar!'

Lewis, now interested despite himself, nodded a vague concurrence of thought. 'So what you're saying, sir, is that Joanna worked this insurance fiddle and probably made quite a nice little packet for herself and for her father as well?'

'Yes! But not only that. Listen! I may just be wrong, Lewis, but I think that not only was Joanna wrongly identified as the lawful wife of Charles Franks – by Charles Franks – but that Charles Franks was the *only* husband of the woman supposedly murdered on the *Barbara Bray*. In short, the "Charles Franks" who broke down in tears at the second trial was *none other than Donavan*.'

'Phew!'

'A man of many parts: he was an actor, he was a conjurer, he was an impersonator, he was a swindler, he was a cunning schemer, he was a callous murderer, he was a loving husband, he was a tearful witness, he was the first and *only* husband of Joanna Franks: F. T. Donavan! We all thought – you thought – even *I* thought – that there were three principal characters playing their roles in our little drama; and now I'm telling you, Lewis, that in all probability we've only got *two.* Joanna; and her husband – the greatest man in all the world; the man buried out on the west coast of Ireland, where the breakers come rolling in from the Atlantic . . . so they tell me . . .'

Chapter Thirty-three

Stet Difficilior Lectio
(Let the more difficult of the readings stand)
(*The principle applied commonly by editors faced with variant readings in ancient manuscripts*)

Lewis was silent. How else? He had a precious little piece of evidence in his pocket, but while Morse's mind was still coursing through the upper atmosphere, there was little point in interrupting again for the minute. He put the envelope containing the single photocopied sheet on the coffee-table – and listened further.

'In the account of Joanna's last few days, we've got some evidence that she could have been a bit deranged; and part of the evidence for such a possibility is the fact that at some point she kept calling out her husband's name – "Franks! Franks! Franks!" Agreed? But she *wasn't* calling out that at all – she was calling her *first* husband, Lewis! I was sitting here thinking of "Waggie" Greenaway—'

'And his daughter,' mumbled Lewis, inaudibly.

'—and I thought of "Hefty" Donavan. F. T. Donavan. And I'll put my next month's salary on that "F" standing for "Frank"! Huh! Who's ever heard of a wife calling her husband by his surname?'

'I have, sir.'

'Nonsense! Not these days.'

'But it's *not* these days. It was—'

'She was calling *Frank Donavan* – believe me!'

'But she *could* have been queer in the head, and if so—'

'Nonsense!'

'Well, we shan't ever know for sure, shall we, sir?'

'Nonsense!'

Morse sat back with the self-satisfied, authoritative air of a man who believes that what he has called 'nonsense' three times must, by the laws of the universe, be necessarily untrue. 'If *only* we knew how tall they were – Joanna and . . . and whoever the other woman was. But there *is* just a chance, isn't there? That cemetery, Lewis—'

'Which do you want first, sir? The good news or the bad news?'

Morse frowned at him. 'That's . . .?' pointing to the envelope.

'That's the good news.'

Morse slowly withdrew and studied the photocopied sheet.

Twenty five minutes past 7 o'clock.
Drowned body was in cut
of wtr licensed to D of M –
taken to Plough Inn at Wolv –
probable identity? unknown.
Prelim findings wd suggest
death by drowning – no obvious
injury was seen – 5 3¾ in –
well nour – c 35 yrs. Bruise
on mouth (rt side) – body warm
full clothes, <u>not</u> bonnet &
shoes – face discoloured, black.

'Not the Coroner's Report, sir, but the next best thing. This fellow must have seen her before the *post-mortem.* Interesting, isn't it?'

'*Very* interesting.'

The report was set out on an unruled sheet of paper, dated, and subscribed by what appeared as a 'Dr Willis', for the writing was not only fairly typical of the semi-legibility forever associated with the medical profession, but was also beset by a confusion with 'm's, 'w's, 'n's, and 'u's – all these letters appearing to be incised with a series of what looked like semi-circular fish-hooks.

Clearly the notes of an orderly-minded local doctor called upon to certify death and to take the necessary action – in this case, almost certainly, to pass the whole business over to some higher authority. Yet there were one or two real nuggets of gold here: the good Willis had made an exact measurement of height, and had written one or two most pertinent (and, apparently, correct) observations. Sad, however, from Morse's point of view, was the unequivocal assertion made here that *the body was still warm.* It must have been this document which had been incorporated into the subsequent *post-mortem* findings, thenceforth duly reiterated both in Court and in the Colonel's history. And it *was* a pity; for if Morse had been correct in believing that another body had been substituted for that of Joanna Franks, that woman must surely have been killed in the early hours of the morning, and could *not* therefore have been drowned some three or four hours later. *Far* too risky. It was odd, certainly, that the dead woman's face had turned black so very quickly; but there was no escaping the plain fact that the first medical man who had examined the corpse had found it still *warm.*

Is that what the report had said, though – 'still warm'? No! No, it hadn't! It just said 'warm' . . . Or *did* it?

Carefully Morse looked again at the report – and sensed the old familiar tingling around his shoulders. *Could* it be? Had everyone else read the report wrongly? In every case the various notes were separated from each other by some form of punctuation – either dashes (eight of them) or full stops (four) or question-marks (only one). All the notes *except* one, that is: the exception being that 'body warm/full clothes . . .' etc. There was neither a dash nor a stop between these two, clearly disparate, items – unless the photocopier had borne unfaithful witness. No! The solution was far simpler. There had been no break requiring any punctuation! Morse looked again at line 10 of the report,

on mouth (rt side) – body warm

and considered three further facts. Throughout, the 's's were written almost as straight vertical lines; of the fifteen or so 'i' dots, no fewer than six had remained un-dotted; and on this showing Willis seemed particularly fond of the word 'was'. So the line should perhaps – should certainly! – read as follows: 'on mouth (rt side) – body was in'. The body 'was in full clothes'! The body was *not* 'warm'; not in Morse's book. There, suddenly, the body was very, very cold.

Lewis, whilst fully accepting the probability of the alternative reading, did not appear to share the excitement which was now visibly affecting Morse; and it was time for the bad news.

'No chance of checking this out in the old Summertown graveyard, sir.'

'Why not? The gravestones are still there, some of them – it says so, doesn't it? – and I've seen them myself—'

'They were all removed, when they built the flats there.'

'Even those the Colonel mentioned?'

Lewis nodded.

Morse knew full well, of course, that any chance of getting an exhumation order to dig up a corner of the greenery in a retirement-home garden was extremely remote. Yet the thought that he might have clinched his theory . . . It was not a matter of supreme moment, though, he knew that; it wasn't even important in putting to rights a past and grievous injustice. It was of no great matter to anyone – except to himself. Ever since he had first come into contact with problems, from his early schooldays onwards – with the meanings of words, with algebra, with detective stories, with cryptic clues – he had always been desperately anxious to know the *answers*, whether those answers were wholly satisfactory or whether they were not. And now, whatever had been the motive leading to that far-off murder, he found himself irked in the extreme to realize that the woman – or *a* woman – he sought had until so very recently been lying in a marked grave in North Oxford. Had she been Joanna Franks, after all? No chance of knowing now – not for certain. But if the meticulous Dr Willis had been correct in his measurements, she *couldn't* have been Joanna, surely?

After Lewis had gone, Morse made a phone call.

'What was the average height of women in the nineteenth century?'

'Which end of the nineteenth century, Morse?'

'Let's say the middle.'

'Interesting question!'

'Well?'

'It varied, I suppose.'

'Come *on*!'

'Poor food, lack of protein – all that sort of stuff. Not very big, most of 'em. Certainly no bigger than the Ripper's victims in the 1880s: four foot nine, four foot ten, four foot eleven – that sort of height: well, that's about what *those* dear ladies were. Except one. Stride, wasn't her name? Yes, Liz Stride. They called her "Long Liz" – so much taller than all the other women in the work-houses. You follow that, Morse?'

'How tall was *she* – "Long Liz"?'

'Dunno.'

'Can you find out?'

'What, now?'

'And ring me back?'

'Bloody hell!'

'Thanks.'

Morse was three minutes into the love duet from Act One of *Die Walküre* when the phone rang.

'Morse? Five foot three.'

Morse whistled.

'Pardon?'

'Thanks, Max! By the way, are you at the lab all day tomorrow? Something I want to bring to show you.'

So the 'petite' little figure had measured three quarters of an inch *more* than 'Long Liz' Stride! And her shoes as Lewis had ascertained, were about size 5! Well, well, well! Virtually every fact now being unearthed (though that was probably not *le mot juste*) was bolstering Morse's bold hypothesis. But, infuriatingly, there was, as it seemed, no chance whatever of establishing the truth. Not, at any rate, the truth regarding Joanna Franks.

Chapter Thirty-four

Marauding louts have shot the moping owl:
  The tower is silent 'neath the wat'ry moon;
But Lady Porter, lately on the prowl
  Will sell the place for pennies very soon
(*E. O. Parrot,* The Spectator)

The communication from the Insurance Company had been a third and final demand for his previous month's premium; and the first thing Morse did the following morning was to write out a cheque, with a brief letter of apology. He understood very little about money, but a dozen or so years previously he had deemed it provident (as it transpired, Prudential) to pay a monthly premium of £55 against a lump sum of £12,000, with profits, at sixty – an age looming ever closer. He had never given a thought about what would happen if he pre-deceased his policy. No worry for him: for the present he had no financial worries, no dependants, a good salary, and a mortgage that would finish in two years' time. He knew it, yes! – compared with the vast majority of mankind he was extremely fortunate. Still, he ought perhaps to think of making a will . . .

Coincidentally, he had been talking to Lewis about insurances the day before and (he admitted it to himself) largely making it all up as he went along. But it was *far* from improbable, wasn't it – what he'd guessed? Those insurance fiddles? He looked out the first material that Christine had brought in to him at the JR2, and once again studied the facts and figures of the Nottinghamshire and Midlands Friendly Society for 1859:

PLAN OF THE ASSOCIATION. 7

The following Table (I.) exhibits the scale of Premiums for the assurance of £100 on the lives of Members; also the Net Premiums payable after seven years, allowing a reduction of 72 per cent., to which persons now assuring will then be entitled if the present rate of abatement be maintained.

Age next Birthday.	Annual Premium.			Reduction 72 per cent.			Net Premium.			Age next Birthday.	Annual Premium.			Reduction 72 per cent.			Net Premium.		
	£	s.	d.	£	s.	d.	£	s.	d.		£	s.	d.	£	s.	d	£	s.	d.
21	2	10	0	1	16	0	0	14	0	45	4	9	9	3	4	7	1	5	2
22	2	10	9	1	16	6	0	14	3	46	4	12	9	3	6	9	1	6	0
23	2	11	6	1	17	1	0	14	5	47	4	16	3	3	9	4	1	6	11
24	2	12	6	1	17	10	0	14	8	48	4	19	9	3	11	10	1	7	11
25	2	13	6	1	18	6	0	15	0	49	5	3	6	3	14	6	1	9	0
26	2	14	6	1	19	3	0	15	3	50	5	7	6	3	17	5	1	10	1
27	2	15	6	2	0	0	0	15	6	51	5	11	9	4	0	6	1	11	3
28	2	16	6	2	0	8	0	15	10	52	5	16	0	4	3	6	1	12	6
29	2	17	9	2	1	7	0	16	2	53	6	0	6	4	6	9	1	13	9
30	2	19	3	2	2	8	0	16	7	54	6	5	0	4	10	0	1	15	0
31	3	0	6	2	3	7	0	16	11	55	6	9	6	4	13	3	1	16	3
32	3	2	0	2	4	8	0	17	4	56	6	14	6	4	16	10	1	17	8
33	3	3	6	2	5	9	0	17	9	57	6	19	6	5	0	5	1	19	1
34	3	5	3	2	7	0	0	18	3	58	7	4	6	5	4	0	2	0	6
35	3	7	0	2	8	3	0	18	9	59	7	9	6	5	7	8	2	1	10
36	3	8	9	2	9	6	0	19	3	60	7	15	0	5	11	7	2	3	5
37	3	10	9	2	10	11	0	19	10	61	8	0	9	5	15	9	2	5	0
38	3	12	9	2	12	5	1	0	4	62	8	7	0	6	0	3	2	6	9
39	3	14	9	2	13	10	1	0	11	63	8	13	9	6	5	1	2	8	8
40	3	17	0	2	15	5	1	1	7	64	9	1	0	6	10	4	2	10	8
41	3	19	3	2	17	1	1	2	2	65	9	8	9	6	15	11	2	12	10
42	4	1	6	2	18	8	1	2	10	66	9	17	0	7	1	10	2	15	2
43	4	4	0	3	0	6	1	3	6	67	10	5	0	7	7	7	2	17	5
44	4	6	9	3	2	6	1	4	3										

Joanna had been born in 1821, so she was thirty-eight in 1859. If she'd taken out a policy a year, two years earlier, that would be – age next birthday thirty-six – an annual premium of £3. 8*s* 9*d.* Under £7, say, for a return of £100. Not bad at all. And if Donavan had already pocketed a similar packet . . .

Morse left his flat in mid-morning (the first excursion since his return) and posted his single letter. He met no one he knew as he turned right along the Banbury Road, and then right again into Squitchey Lane; where, taking the second turning on his left, just past the evangelical chapel (now converted into a little group of residences) he walked down Middle Way. It was a dark, dankish morning, and a scattering of rooks (mis-taking, perhaps, the hour) squawked away in the trees to his right. Past Bishop Kirk Middle School he went on, and straight along past the attractive terraced houses on either side with their mullioned bay-windows – and, on his left, *there it was*: Dudley Court, a block of flats built in cinnamon-coloured brick on the site of the old Summertown Parish Cemetery. A rectangle of lawn, some fifty by twenty-five yards, was set out behind a low containing wall, only about eighteen inches high, over which Morse stepped into the grassy plot planted with yew-trees and red-berried bushes. Immediately to his left, the area was bounded by the rear premises of a Social Club; and along this wall, beneath the straggly branches of winter jasmine, and covered with damp beech-leaves, he could make out the stumps of four or five old headstones, broken off at their roots like so many jagged teeth just protruding from their gums. Clearly, any deeper excavation to remove these stones in their entirety had been thwarted by the proximity of the wall; but all the rest had been removed, perhaps several years ago now – and duly recorded no doubt in some dusty box of papers on the shelves of the local Diocesan Offices. Well, at least Morse could face one simple fact: no burial evidence would be forthcoming from these fair lawns. None! Yet it would have been good to know where the stone had marked (as the Colonel had called it) the 'supra-corporal' site of Joanna Franks.

Or whoever.

He walked past Dudley Court itself where a Christmas tree, bedecked with red, green, and yellow bulbs, was already switched on; past the North Oxford Conservative Association premises, in which he had never (and would never) set foot; past the Spiritualist Church, in which he had never (as yet) set foot; past the low-roofed Women's Institute HQ, in which he had once spoken about the virtues of the Neighbourhood Watch Scheme; and finally, turning left, he came into South Parade, just opposite the Post Office – into which he ventured once a year and that to pay the Lancia's road-tax. But as he walked by the old familiar landmarks, his mind was far away, and the decision firmly taken. If he was to be cheated of finding one of his suspects, he would go and look for the other! He needed a break. He would *have* a break.

There was a travel agency immediately across the

street, and the girl who sat at the first desk to the right smiled brightly.

'Can I help you, sir?'

'Yes! I'd like' (Morse sat himself down) 'I'd like to book a holiday, with a car, in Ireland – the Republic, that is.'

Later that day, Morse called at the William Dunn School of Pathology in South Parks Road.

'Have a look at these for me, will you?'

Refraining from all cynical comment, Max looked dubiously across at Morse over his half-lenses.

'Max! All I want to know is—'

'—whether they come from M&S or Littlewoods?'

'The tear, Max – *the tear.*'

'Tear? *What* tear?' Max picked up the knickers with some distaste and examined them (as it seemed to Morse) in cursory fashion. 'No tear here, Morse. Not the faintest sign of any irregular distension of the fibre tissue – calico, by the way, isn't it?'

'I think so.'

'Well, we don't need a microscope to tell us it's a cut: neat, clean, straight-forward *cut,* all right?'

'With a knife?'

'What the hell else do you cut things with?'

'Cheese-slicer? Pair of—?'

'What a wonderful thing, Morse, is the human imagination!'

It was a wonderful thing, too, that Morse had received such an unequivocal answer to one of his questions; the very first such answer, in fact, in their long and reasonably amicable acquaintanceship.

Chapter Thirty-five

Heap not on this mound
Roses that she loved so well;
Why bewilder her with roses
That she cannot see or smell?
(*Edna St Vincent Millay,* Epitaph)

Inspector Mulvaney spotted him parking the car in the 'Visitor' space. When the little station had been converted ten years earlier from a single detached house into Kilkearnan's apology for a crime-prevention HQ, the Garda had deemed it appropriate that the four-man squad should be headed by an inspector. It seemed, perhaps, in retrospect, something of an over-reaction. With its thousand or so inhabitants, Kilkearnan regularly saw its ration of fisticuffs and affray outside one or more of the fourteen public-houses; but as yet the little community had steered clear of any involvement in international smuggling or industrial espionage. Here, even road accidents were a rarity – though this was attributable more to the comparative scarcity of cars than to the sobriety of their drivers. Tourists there were, of course – especially in the summer months;

but even they, with their Rovers and BMWs, were more often stopping to photograph the occasional donkey than causing any hazard to the occasional drunkard.

The man parking his Lancia in the single (apart from his own) parking-space, Mulvaney knew to be the English policeman who had rung through the previous day to ask for help in locating a cemetery (for, as yet, no stated purpose) and who thought it was probably the one overlooking Bertnaghboy Bay – that being the only burial ground marked on the local map. Mulvaney had been able to assure Chief Inspector Morse (such was he) that indeed it would be the cemetery which lay on the side of a hill to the west of the small town: the local dead were always likely to be buried there, as Mulvaney had maintained – there being no alternative accommodation.

From the lower window, Mulvaney watched Morse with some curiosity. It was not every day (or week, or month) that any contact was effected between the British Police and the Garda; and the man who was walking round to the main (only) entrance looked an interesting specimen: mid-fifties, losing his whitish hair, putting on just a little too much weight, and exhibiting perhaps, as was to be hoped, the tell-tale signs of liking his liquor more than a little. Nor was Mulvaney disappointed in the man who was shown into his main (only) office.

'Are you related to Kipling's Mulvaney?' queried Morse.

'No, sor! But that was a good question – and educashin, that's a good thing, too!'

Morse explained his unlikely, ridiculous, selfish mission, and Mulvaney warmed to him immediately. No chance whatsoever, of course, of any exhumation order being granted, but perhaps Morse might be interested in hearing about the business of grave digging in the Republic? A man could never *dig* a grave on a Monday, and that for perfectly valid reasons, which he had forgotten; and in any case it wasn't Monday, was it? And if a grave *was* dug, even on a Monday, it had always – *always*, sor! – to be in the morning, or at least the previous evening. That was an important thing, too, about all the forks and shovels: placed across the open grave, they had to be, in the form of the holy cross, for reasons which a man of Morse's educashin would need no explanation, to be sure. Last, it was always the custom for the chief mourner to supply a little quantity of Irish whiskey at the graveside for the other members of the saddened family; and for the grave-diggers, too, of course, who had shovelled up the clinging, cloggy soil. 'For sure, 'tis always a t'irsty business, sor, that working of the soil!'

So Morse, the chief mourner, walked out into the main (only) High Street, and purchased three bottles of Irish malt. An understanding had been arrived at, and Morse knew that whatever the problems posed by the Donavan-Franks equation, the left-hand side would be solved (if solved it *could* be) with the full sympathy and (unofficial) co-operation of the Irish Garda.

In his mind's eye, Morse had envisaged a bank of arc-lights, illuminating a well-marked grave, with barricades erected around the immediate area, a posse of constables to keep the public from prying, and press photographers training their telescopic lenses on the site. The time? That would be 5.30 a.m. – the usual exhumation hour. And excitement would be intense.

It was not to be.

Together, Morse and Mulvaney had fairly easily located the final habitation of the greatest man in all the world. In all, there must have been about three or four hundred graves within the walled area of the hillside cemetery. Half a dozen splendidly sculptured angels and madonnas kept watch here and there over a few former dignitaries, and several large Celtic crosses

marked other burial-plots. But the great majority of the dead lay unhonoured here beneath untended, meaner-looking memorials. Donavan's stone was one of the latter, a poor, mossed-and-lichened thing, with white and ochre blotches, and no more than two feet high, leaning back at an angle of about 20 degrees from the vertical. So effaced was the weathered stone that only the general outlines of the lettering could be followed – and that only on either side of a central disintegration:

'That's him,' said Morse triumphantly. It looked as if his name *had* been Frank.

'God rest his soul!' added Mulvaney. ' – that's if it's there, of course.'

Morse grinned, and wished he'd known Mulvaney long ago. 'How are you going to explain . . .?'

'We are digging yet another grave, sor. In the daylight – and just as normal.'

It was all quite quick. Mulvaney had bidden the two men appointed to the task to dig a clean rectangle to the east of the single stone; and after getting down only two or three feet, one of the spades struck what sounded like, and was soon revealed to be, a wooden coffin. Once all the dark-looking earth had been removed and piled on each side of the oblong pit, Morse and Mulvaney looked down to a plain coffin-top, with no plate of any sort screwed into it. The wood, one-inch elm-boarding, and grooved round the top, looked badly warped, but in a reasonable state. There seemed no reason to remove the complete coffin; and Morse, betraying once again his inveterate horror of corpses, quietly declined the honour of removing the lid.

It was Mulvaney himself, awkwardly straddling the hole, his shoes caked with mud, who bent down and pulled at the top of the coffin, which gave way easily, the metal screws clearly having disintegrated long ago. As the board slowly lifted, Mulvaney saw, as did Morse, that a whitish mould hung down from the inside of the coffin-lid; and in the coffin itself, covering the body, a shroud or covering of some sort was overspread with the same creeping white fungus.

Round the sides at the bottom of the coffin, plain for all to see, was a bed of brownish, dampish sawdust, looking as fresh as if the body which lay on it had been buried only yesterday. But *what* body?

''Tis wonderfully well preserved, is it not, sor? 'Tis the peat in the soil that's accountin' forrit.'

This from the first grave-digger, who appeared more deeply impressed by the wondrous preservation of the wood than by the absence of any body. *For the coffin contained no body at all.* What it did contain was a roll of carpet, of some greenish dye, about five feet in length, folded round what appeared to have been half a dozen spaded squares of peat. Of Donavan there was no trace whatsoever – not even a torn fragment from the last handbill of the greatest man in all the world.

Chapter Thirty-six

A man's learning dies with him; even his virtues fade out of remembrance; but the dividends on the stocks he bequeaths may serve to keep his memory green

(*Oliver Wendell Holmes,* The Professor at the Breakfast Table)

MORSE GREW SOMEWHAT fitter during the days following his return from Ireland; and very soon, in his own judgement at least, he had managed to regain that semblance of salubrity and strength which his GP interpreted as health. Morse asked no more.

He had recently bought himself the old Furtwängler recording of *The Ring*; and during the hours of Elysian enjoyment which that performance was giving him, the case of Joanna Franks, and the dubious circumstances of the Oxford Tow-path Mystery, assumed a slowly diminishing significance. The whole thing had brought him some recreative enjoyment, but now it was finished. Ninety-five per cent certain (as he was) that the wrong people had been hanged in 1860, there was apparently nothing further he could do to dispel that worrying little five per cent of doubt.

Christmas was coming up fast, and he was glad not to have that tiring traipsing round the shops – no stockings, no scent to buy. He himself received half a dozen cards; two invitations to Drinks Evenings; and a communication from the JR2:

XMAS PARTY

The Nursing Staff of the John Radcliffe Hospital
request the pleasure of your company
on the evening of Friday, 22nd December,
from 8 p.m. until midnight,
at the Nurses' Hostel, Headington Hill, Oxford.
Disco Dancing, Ravishing Refreshments, Fabulous fun!
Please Come! Dress informal. RSVP.

The printed card was signed, in blue biro, 'Ward 7C' – and followed by a single 'X'.

It was on Friday, 15th December, a week before the scheduled party, that Morse's eye caught the name in the *Oxford Times* 'Deaths' column:

> DENISTON, Margery – On December 10th, peacefully at her home in Woodstock, aged 78 years. She wished her body to be given to medical research. Donations gratefully received, in honour of the late

Colonel W. M. Deniston, by the British Legion Club, Lambourn.

Morse thought back to the only time he'd met the quaint old girl, so proud as she had been of her husband's work – a work which had brought Morse such disproportionate interest; a work which he'd not even had to pay for. He signed a cheque for £20, and stuck it in a cheap brown envelope. He had both first- and second-class stamps to hand, but he chose a second-class: it wasn't a matter of life and death, after all.

He would (he told himself) have attended a funeral service, if she'd been having one. But he was glad she wasn't: the stern and daunting sentences from the Burial Service, especially in the A.V., were ever assuming a nearer and more personal threat to his peace of mind; and for the present that was something he could well do without. He looked up the British Legion's Lambourn address in the telephone directory, and after doing so turned to 'Deniston, W. M.'. There it was: 46 Church Walk, Woodstock. Had there been any family? It hardly appeared so, from the obituary notice. So? So what happened to things, if there was no one to leave them to? As with Mrs Deniston, possibly? As with anyone childless or unmarried . . .

It was difficult parking the Lancia, and finally Morse took advantage of identifying himself to a sourpuss of a traffic warden who reluctantly sanctioned a temporary straddling of the double-yellows twenty or so yards from the grey-stoned terraced house in Church Walk. He knocked on the front door, and was admitted forthwith.

Two persons were in the house: a young man in his middle twenties who (as he explained) had been commissioned by Blackwells to catalogue the few semi-valuable books on the late Denistons' shelves; and a great-nephew of the old Colonel, the only surviving relative, who (as Morse interpreted matters) was in for a very pretty little inheritance indeed, if recent prices for Woodstock property were anything to judge by.

To the latter, Morse immediately and openly explained what his interest was: he was begging nothing – apart from the opportunity to discover whether the late Colonel had left behind any notes or documents relating to *Murder on the Oxford Canal*. And happily the answer was 'yes' – albeit a very limited 'yes'. In the study was a pile of manuscript, and typescript, and clipped to an early page of the manuscript was one short letter – a letter with no date, no sender's address, and no envelope:

Our dear Daniel,

We do both trust you are keeping well these past months. We shall be in Derby in early Sept. when we hope we shall be with you. Please say to Mary how the dress she did was very successfull and will she go on with the other one if she is feeling recovered.

Yours Truely and Afectionatly,
Matthew

That was all. Enough, though, for the Colonel to feel that it was worth preserving! There was only one 'Daniel' in the case, Daniel Carrick from Derby; and here was that one piece of primary-source material that linked the Colonel's narrative in a tangible, physical way to the whole sorry story. Agreed, Daniel Carrick had never figured all that prominently in Morse's thinking; but he *ought* to have done. He was surely just as damningly implicated as the other two in the deception – the twin deception – which had seen the Notts and Midlands Friendly Society having to fork out, first for the death of the great uncoffined Donavan, and then for the death of the enigmatic Joanna, the great undrowned.

Morse turned over the faded, deeply creased letter and saw, on the back, a few pencilled notes, pretty certainly in the Colonel's hand: 'No records from Ins. Co. – Mrs C. very poorly at this time? Not told of J.'s death? 12 Spring St. still occupied 12.4.76!'

There it was then – palpable paper and writing, and just a finger-tip of contact with one of the protagonists in that nineteenth-century drama. As for the two principal actors, the only evidence that could have been forthcoming about them was buried away with their bodies. And where Joanna was buried – or where the greatest man in all the world – who knew, or who could ever know?

CHAPTER THIRTY-SEVEN

> Modern dancers give a sinister portent about our times. The dancers don't even look at one another. They are just a lot of isolated individuals jiggling in a kind of self-hypnosis
>
> (*Agnes de Mille,* The New York Times)

THE PARTY-GOERS WERE fully aware that when the caretaker said midnight he meant 11.55 p.m.; but few had managed to arrive at the Nurses' Hostel before 9 p.m. In any case, the event was never destined to be of cosmic significance, and would have little to show for itself apart from a memory or two, a few ill-developed photographs, and a great deal of clearing up the following morning.

As soon as he took his first steps across the noisy, throbbing, flashing room – it was now 10.30 p.m. – Morse realized that he had made a tragic error in accepting the invitation. 'Never go back!' – that was the advice he should have heeded; yet he had been fool enough to recall the white sheets and the Fair Fiona and the Ethereal Eileen. Idiot! He sat down on a rickety, slatted chair, and sipped some warm insipid 'punch' that was handed out in white plastic cups to each new arrival. Constituted, if taste were anything to go by, of about 2% gin, 2% dry Martini, 10% orange juice, and 86% lemonade, it was going to take a considerable time, by Morse's reckoning, before such Ravishing Refreshments turned him on; and he had just decided that the best thing about it was the little cubes of apple floating on the top when Fiona detached her sickly-looking beau from the dance-floor and came up to him.

'Happy Christmas!' She bent down, and Morse could still feel the dryness of her lips against his cheek as she introduced the embarrassed youth, repeated her Christmas greeting, and then was gone – throwing herself once more into a series of jerky contortions like some epileptic puppet.

Morse's plastic cup was empty and he walked slowly past a long line of tables, where beneath the white coverings he glimpsed sugared mince-pies and skewered sausages.

'We'll be starting on them soon!' said a familiar voice behind him, and Morse turned to find Eileen, blessedly alone and, like only a few of the others, wearing her uniform.

'Hullo!' said Morse.

'Hullo!' she said softly.

'It's good to see you!'

She looked at him, and nodded, almost imperceptibly.

A tall man, looking as if he might have been involved in a fight recently, materialized from somewhere.

'This is Gordon,' said Eileen, looking up into the shaded planes of Gordon's skull-like face. And when Morse had shaken hands with the man, he once more found himself alone, wondering where to walk, where to put himself, how to make an inconspicuous exit, to cease upon the five-minutes-to-eleven with no pain.

He was only a few feet from the main door when she was suddenly standing in front of him.

'You're not trying to sneak away, I hope!'

Nessie!

'Hullo, Sister. No! I'm – I mustn't stay too long, of course, but—'

'I'm glad you came. I know you're a wee bit old for this sort of thing . . .' Her lilting Scottish accent seemed to be mocking him gently.

Morse nodded; it was difficult to argue the point, and he looked down to pick out the one remaining apple cube from his cup.

'Your sergeant did you rairther better – with the drink, I mean.'

Morse looked at her – suddenly – almost as if he had never looked at her before. Her skin in this stroboscopic light looked almost opaline, and the colour of her eyes was emerald. Her auburn hair was swept upward, emphasizing the contours of her face, and her mouth was thinly and delicately lipsticked. For a woman, she was quite tall, certainly as tall as he was; and if only (as Morse thought) she'd worn something other than that miserably dowdy, unflattering dress . . .

'Would you like to dance, Inspector?'

'I – no! It's not one of my, er, things, dancing, I'm afraid.'

'What—?'

But Morse was never to know what she was going to ask him. A young houseman – smiling, flushed, so happily at home here – grabbed her by the hand and was pulling her to the floor.

'Come on, Sheila! *Our* dance, remember?'

Sheila!

'You won't try to sneak away – ?' she was saying over her shoulder. But she was on the dance-floor now, where shortly all the other dancers were stopping and moving to the periphery as the pair of them, Sheila and her young partner, put on a dazzling display of dance-steps to the rhythmic clapping of the audience.

Morse felt a stab of jealousy as his eyes followed them, the young man's body pressed close to hers. He had fully intended to stay, as she had asked. But when the music had finished, the newly metamorphosed Nessie, pretending to collapse, had become the centre of enthusiastic admiration, and Morse placed his plastic cup on the table by the exit, and left.

At 9.30 the following morning, after a somewhat fitful sleep, he rang the JR2 and asked for Ward 7C.

'Can I speak to Sister, please?'

'Who shall I say is calling?'

'It's – it's a personal call.'

'We can't take personal calls, I'm afraid. If you'd like to leave your name—'

'Just tell her one of her old patients from the ward—'

'Is it Sister Maclean you wanted?'

'Yes.'

'She's left – she left officially last week. She's off to be Director of Nursing Services—'

'She's left Oxford?'

'She's leaving today. She stayed on for a party last night—'

'I see. I'm sorry to have bothered you. I seem to have got the wrong end of things, don't I?'

'Yes, you do.'

'Where is she going to?'

'Derby – Derby Royal Infirmary.'

Chapter Thirty-eight

> The very designation of the term 'slum' reflects a middle-class attitude to terrace-housing, where grand values are applied to humble situations
>
> (*James Curl*, The Erosion of Oxford)

SINCE FAST DRIVING was his only significant vice (apart from egg-and-chips) Lewis was delighted, albeit on one of his 'rest' days, to be invited to drive the Lancia. The car was a powerful performer, and the thought of the stretch of the M1 up to the A52 turn-off was, to Lewis, most pleasurable. Nor had Morse made the slightest secret of the fact that the main object of the mission was to find out if a thoroughfare called 'Spring Street' still stood – as it had stood until 1976 – on the northern outskirts of Derby.

'Just humour me, Lewis – that's all I ask!'

Lewis had needed little persuasion. It had been a momentous 'plus' in his life when Morse had intimated to his superiors that it was above all with him, Sergeant Lewis, that his brain functioned most fluently; and now – moving the Lancia across into the fast lane of the M1 at Weedon – Lewis felt wholly content with the way of life which had so happily presented itself to him those many years since. He knew, of course, that their present mission was a lost cause. But then Oxford was not unfamiliar with such things.

Spring Street proved difficult to locate, in spite of a city-map purchased from a corner-newsagent in the northern suburbs. Morse himself had become progressively tetchier as the pedestrians to whom Lewis wound down his window appeared either totally ignorant or mutually contradictory. Finally, however, the Lancia homed in on an area, marked off by hoardings, announcing itself as the 'Derby Development Complex', with two enormously tall, yellow cranes tracing and retracing their sweeping arcs above the demolition squads below.

'Could be too late, could we?' ventured Lewis.

'It doesn't *matter* – I've *told* you, Lewis.' Morse wound down his own window and spoke to a brick-dusted, white-helmeted workman.

'Have you flattened Spring Street yet?'

'Won't be long, mate,' the man replied, pointing vaguely towards the next-but-one block of terraced houses.

Morse, somewhat irked by the 'mate' familiarity, wound up his window, without a 'thank you', and pointed, equally vaguely, to Lewis, the latter soon pulling the Lancia in behind a builder's skip a couple of streets away. A young coloured woman pushing a utility pram assured Morse that, yes, this *was* Spring

Street, and the two men got out of the car and looked around them.

Perhaps, in some earlier decades, the area had seen some better times; yet, judging from its present aspect it seemed questionable whether any of the houses in this unlovely place had ever figured in the 'desirable' category of residences. Built, by the look of them, in the early 1800s, many were now semi-derelict, and several boarded-up completely. Clearly a few remained tenanted, for here and there smoke rose up into the grey air from the narrow, yellow chimney-pots; and white-lace curtains still framed the windows yet unbroken. With distaste, Morse eyed the squashed beer-cans and discarded fish-and-chip wrappings that littered the narrow pavement. Then he walked slowly along, before stopping before a front door painted in what fifty years earlier had been a Cambridge blue, and into which a number-plaque '20' was screwed. The house was in a terraced group of six; and walking further along, Morse came to the door of an abandoned property on which, judging from the outlines, the figures '16' had once been fixed. Here Morse stopped and beckoned to Lewis – the eyes of both now travelling to the two adjacent houses, boarded up against squatters or vandals. The first house must, without question, have once been Number 14 – and the second, Number 12.

The latter, the sorry-looking object of Morse's pilgrimage, stood on the corner, the sign 'Burton Road' still fastened to its side-wall, although no sign of Burton Road itself was any longer visible. Below the sign, a wooden gate, hanging forlornly from one of its rusted hinges, led to a small patch of back-yard, choked with litter and brownish weeds, and cluttered with a kiddy's ancient tricycle and a brand-new trolley from a supermarket. The dull-red bricks of the outer walls were flaking badly, and the single window-frame here had been completely torn away, leaving the inside of the mean little abode open to the elements. Morse poked his face through the empty frame, across the blackened sill, before turning away with a sickened disgust: in one corner of the erstwhile kitchen was what appeared to be a pile of excrement; and beside it, half a loaf of white bread, its slices curled and mildew green.

'Not a pretty sight, is it?' whispered Lewis, standing at Morse's shoulder.

'She was brought up here,' said Morse quietly. 'She lived here with her mother . . . and her father . . .'

'. . . and her brother,' added Lewis.

Yes! Morse had forgotten the brother, Joanna's younger brother, the boy named after his father – forgotten him altogether.

Reluctantly Morse left the small back-yard, and slowly walked round to the front again, where he stood in the middle of the deserted street and looked at the little terrace-house in which Joanna Carrick-Donavan-Franks had probably spent – what? – the first twenty or so years of her life. The Colonel hadn't mentioned exactly where she was born, but . . . Morse thought back to the dates: born in 1821, and married to the great man in 1842. How reassuring it would have been to find a date marked on one of the houses! But Morse could see no sign of one. If the house had been built by the 1820s, had she spent those twenty years in and around that pokey little kitchen, competing for space with the sink and the copper and the mangle and the cooking-range and her parents . . .? And her younger brother? He, Morse, had his own vivid recollections of a similarly tiny kitchen in a house which (as he had been told) had been demolished to make way for a carpet-store. But he'd never been back. It was always a mistake to go back, because life went on perfectly well without you, thank-you-very-much, and other people got along splendidly with their own jobs – even if they were confined to selling carpets. Yes, almost always a mistake: a mistake, for example, as it had been to go back to the hospital; a mistake as it would have been (as he'd intended) to go along to the Derby Royal and nonchalantly announce to Nessie that he just happened to be passing through the city, just wanted to congratulate her on becoming the Big White Chief . . .

Lewis had been talking whilst these and similar thoughts were crossing and recrossing Morse's mind, and he hadn't heard a word of what was said.

'Pardon, Lewis?'

'I just say that's what we used to do, that's all – over the top of the head, as I say, and put the date against it.'

Morse, unable to construe such manifest gobbledegook, nodded as if with full understanding, and led the way to the car. A large white-painted graffito caught his eye, sprayed along the lower wall of a house in the next terrace: HANDS OFF CHILE – although it was difficult to know who in this benighted locality was being exhorted to such activity – or, rather, inactivity. TRY GEO. LUMLEY's TEA 1s 2d, seemed a more pertinent notice, painted over the bricked-up first-floor window of the next corner house, the lettering originally worked in a blue paint over a yellow-ochre background, the latter now a faded battleship-grey; a notice (so old was it) that Joanna might well have seen it every day as she walked along this street to school, or play – a notice from the past which a demolition gang of hard-topped men would soon obliterate from the local-history records when they swung their giant skittle-balls and sent the side-wall crumbling in a shower of dust.

Just like the Oxford-City-Council Vandals when . . .

Forget it, Morse!

'Where to now, sir?'

It took a bit of saying, but he said it: 'Straight home, I think. Unless there's something else *you* want to see?'

Chapter Thirty-nine

And what you thought you came for
Is only a shell, a husk of meaning
From which the purpose breaks only when it is
fulfilled
If at all. Either you had no purpose
Or the purpose is beyond the end you figured
And is altered in fulfilment
(*T. S. Eliot,* Little Gidding)

Morse seldom engaged in any conversation in a car, and he was predictably silent as Lewis drove the few miles out towards the motorway. In its wonted manner, too, his brain was meshed into its complex mechanisms, where he was increasingly conscious of that one little irritant. It had always bothered him not to know, not to have heard – even the smallest things:

'What was it you were saying back there?'

'You mean when you weren't listening?'

'Just *tell* me, Lewis!'

'It was just when we were children, that's all. We used to measure how tall we were getting. Mum always used to do it – every birthday – against the kitchen wall.

I suppose that's what reminded me, really – looking in that kitchen. Not in the front room – that was the best wallpaper there; and, as I say, she used to put a ruler over the top of our heads, you know, and then put a line and a date . . .'

Again, Morse was not listening.

'Lewis! Turn round and go back!'

Lewis looked across at Morse with some puzzlement.

'I said just turn round,' continued Morse – quietly, for the moment. '*Gentle* as you like – when you get the *chance*, Lewis – no need to imperil the pedestrians or the local pets. But just *turn round*!'

Morse's finger on the kitchen switch produced only an empty 'click', in spite of what looked like a recent bulb in the fixture that hung, shadeless, from the disintegrating plaster-boards. The yellowish, and further yellowing, paper had been peeled away from several sections of the wall in irregular gashes, and in the damp top-corner above the sink it hung away in a great flap.

'Whereabouts did you use to measure things, Lewis?'

''Bout here, sir.' Lewis stood against the inner door of the kitchen, his back to the wall, where he placed his left palm horizontally across the top of his head, before turning round and assessing the point at which his fingertips had marked the height.

'Five-eleven, that is – unless I've shrunk a bit.'

The wallpaper at this point was grubby with a myriad fingerprints, appearing not to have been renovated for half a century or more; and around the non-functioning light-switch the plaster had been knocked out, exposing some of the bricks in the partition-wall. Morse tore a strip from the yellow paper, to reveal a surprisingly well-preserved, light-blue paper beneath. But marked memorials to Joanna, there were none; and the two men stood silent and still there, as the afternoon seemed to grow perceptibly colder and darker by the minute.

'It was a thought, though, wasn't it?' asked Morse.

'Good thought, sir!'

'Well, one thing's certain! We are *not* going to stand here all afternoon in the gathering gloom and strip all these walls of generations of wallpaper.'

'Wouldn't take all that long, would it?'

'What? All this bloody stuff—'

'We'd know where to look.'

'We would?'

'I mean, it's only a little house; and if we just looked along at some point, say, between four feet and five feet from the floor – downstairs only, I should think—'

'You're a genius – did you know that?'

'And you've got a good torch in the car.'

'No,' admitted Morse. 'I'm afraid—'

'Never mind, sir! We've got about half an hour before it gets too dark.'

It was twenty minutes to four when Lewis emitted a child-like squeak of excitement from the narrow hallway.

'Something here, sir! And I think, I *think*—'

'Careful! *Careful*!' muttered Morse, coming nervously

alongside, a triumphant look now blazing in his blue-grey eyes.

Gradually the paper was pulled away as the last streaks of that December day filtered through the filthy skylight above the heads of Morse and Lewis, each of them looking occasionally at the other with wholly disproportionate excitement. For there, inscribed on the original plaster of the wall, below three layers of subsequent papering – and still clearly visible – were two sets of black-pencilled lines: the one to the right marking a series of eight calibrations, from about 3′ 6″ of the lowest one to about 5′ of the top, with a full date shown for each; the one to the left with only two calibrations (though with four dates) – a diagonal of crumbled plaster quite definitely precluding further evidence below.

For several moments Morse stood there in the darkened hallway and gazed upon the wall as if upon some holy relic.

'Get a torch, Lewis! And a tape-measure!'

'Where—?'

'Anywhere. Everybody's got a torch, man.'

'Except you, sir!'

'Tell 'em you're from the Gas Board and there's a leak in Number 12.'

'The house isn't *on* gas.'

'Get *on* with it, Lewis!'

When Lewis returned, Morse was still considering his wall-marks – beaming as happily at the eight lines on the right as a pools-punter surveying a winning-line of score-draws on the Treble Chance; and, taking the torch, he played it joyously over the evidence. The new light (as it were) upon the situation quickly confirmed that any writing below the present extent of their findings was irredeemably lost; it also showed a letter in between the two sets of measurements, slightly towards the right, and therefore probably belonging with the second set.

The letter 'D'!

Daniel!

The lines on the right *must* mark the heights of Daniel Carrick; and, if that were so, then those to the left were those of *Joanna Franks*!

'Are you thinking what I'm thinking, Lewis?'

'I reckon so, sir.'

'Joanna married in 1841 or 1842' – Morse was talking to himself as much as to Lewis – 'and that fits well because the measurements end in 1841, finishing at the same height as she was in 1840. And her younger brother, Daniel, was gradually catching her up – about the same height in 1836, and quite a few inches taller in 1841.'

Lewis found himself agreeing. 'And you'd expect them that way round, sir, wouldn't you? Joanna first; and then her brother, to Joanna's right.'

'Ye-es.' Morse took the white tape-measure and let it roll out to the floor. 'Only five foot, this.'

'Don't think we're going to need a much longer one, sir.'

Lewis was right. As Morse held the 'nought-inches' end of the tape to the top of Joanna's putative measurements, Lewis shone the torch on the other end as he knelt on the dirty red tiles. No! A longer tape-measure was certainly not needed here, for the height measured only 4′ 9″, and as Lewis knew, the woman who had been pulled out of Duke's Cut had been 5′ 3¾″ – almost seven inches taller than Joanna had been after leaving Spring Street for her marriage! Was it possible – even wildly possible – that she had grown those seven inches between the ages of twenty-one and thirty-eight? He put his thoughts into words:

'I don't think, sir, that a woman could have—'

'No, Lewis – nor do I! If not impossible, at the very least unprecedented, surely.'

'So you were right, sir . . .'

'Beyond any reasonable doubt? Yes, I think so.'

'Beyond *all* doubt?' asked Lewis quietly.

'There'll always be that one per cent of doubt about most things, I suppose.'

'You'd be happier, though, if—'

Morse nodded: 'If we'd found just that *one* little thing extra, yes. Like a 'J' on the wall here or . . . I don't know.'

'There's nothing else to find, then, sir?'

'No, I'm sure there isn't,' said Morse, but only after hesitating for just a little while.

Chapter Forty

The world is round and the place which may seem like the end may also be only the beginning

(*Ivy Baker Priest,* Parade)

IT SOUNDED AN anti-climactic question: 'What do we do now, sir?'

Morse didn't know, and his mind was far away: 'It was done a long time ago, Lewis, and done ill,' he said slowly.

Which was doubtless a true sentiment, but it hardly answered the question. And Lewis pressed his point – with the result that together they sought out the site-foreman, to whom, producing his warranty-card, Morse dictated his wishes, making the whole thing sound as if the awesome authority of MI5 and MI6 alike lay behind his instructions regarding the property situated at Number 12 Spring Street, especially for a series of photographs to be taken as soon as possible of the pencil-marks on the wall in the entrance hall. And yes, the site-foreman thought he could see to it all without too much trouble; in fact, he was a bit of a dab hand with a camera himself, as he not so modestly admitted.

Then, after Lewis had returned torch and tape-measure to a slightly puzzled-looking householder, the afternoon events were over.

It was five minutes to six when Lewis finally tried once again to drive away from the environs of Derby (North) and to make for the A52 junction with the M1 (South). At 6 p.m., Morse leaned forward and turned on the car-radio for the news. One way or another it had been a bad year, beset with disease, hunger, air crashes, railway accidents, an oil-rig explosion, and sundry earthquakes. But no cosmic disaster had been reported since the earlier one o'clock bulletin, and Morse switched off – suddenly aware of the time.

'Do you realize it's gone opening time, Lewis?'

'No such thing these days, sir.'

'You know what I mean!'

'Bit early—'

'We've got something to celebrate, Lewis! Pull in at the next pub, and I'll buy you a pint.'

'You *will*?'

Morse was not renowned for his generosity in treating his subordinates – or his superiors – and Lewis smiled to himself as he surveyed the streets, looking for a pub-sign; it was an activity with which he was not unfamiliar. 'I'm driving, sir.'

'Quite right, Lewis. We don't want any trouble with the police.'

*

As he sat sipping his St Clements and listening to Morse conducting a lengthy conversation with the landlord about the wickedness of the lager-brewers, Lewis felt inexplicably content. It had been a good day; and Morse, after draining his third pint with his wonted rapidity, was apparently ready to depart.

'Gents?' asked Morse.

The landlord pointed the way.

'Is there a public telephone I could use?'

'Just outside the Gents.'

Lewis thought he could hear Morse talking over the phone – something to do with a hospital; but he was never a man to eavesdrop on the private business of others, and he walked outside and stood waiting by the car until Morse re-appeared.

'Lewis – I, er – I'd like you just to call round quickly to the hospital, if you will. The Derby Royal. Not too far out of our way, they tell me.'

'Bit of stomach trouble again, sir?'

'No!'

'I don't think you should have had all that beer, though—'

'Are you going to drive me there or not, Lewis?'

Morse, as Lewis knew, was becoming increasingly reluctant to walk even a hundred yards or so if he could ride the distance, and he now insisted that Lewis park the Lancia in the AMBULANCES ONLY area just outside the Hospital's main entrance.

'How long will you be, sir?'

'How long? Not sure, Lewis. It's my lucky day, though, isn't it? So I may be a little while.'

It was half an hour later that Morse emerged to find Lewis chatting happily to one of the ambulance-men about the road-holding qualities of the Lancia family.

'All right, then, sir?'

'Er – well. Er . . . Look, Lewis! I've decided to stay in Derby overnight.'

Lewis's eyebrows rose.

'Yes! I think – I think I'd like to be there when they take those photographs – you know, in, er . . .'

'*I* can't stay, sir! I'm on duty tomorrow morning.'

'I know. I'm not asking you to, am I? I'll get the train back – no problem – Derby, Birmingham, Banbury – easy!'

'You *sure*, sir?'

'*Quite* sure. You don't *mind* do you, Lewis?'

Lewis shook his head. 'Well, I suppose, I'd better—'

'Yes, you get off. And don't drive too fast!'

'Can I take you – to a hotel or something?'

'No need to bother, I'll – I'll find something.'

'You look as though you've already found something, sir.'

'Do I?'

As the Lancia accelerated along the approach road to the M1 (South) Lewis was still smiling quietly to himself, recalling the happy look on Morse's face as he had turned and walked once more towards the automatic doors.

Epilogue

The name of a man is a numbing blow from which he never recovers

(*Marshall McLuhan,* Understanding Media)

On the morning of Friday, 11th January (he had resumed duties on New Year's Day) Morse caught the early Cathedrals' Express to Paddington. He was programmed to speak on Inner City Crime at 11 a.m. at the Hendon Symposium. Tube to King's Cross, then out on the Northern Line. Easy. Plenty of time. He enjoyed trains, in any case; and when Radio Oxford had announced black ice on the M40, his decision was made for him; it would mean, too, of course, that he could possibly indulge a little more freely with any refreshments that might be available.

He bought *The Times* and the *Oxford Times* at the bookstall, got a seat at the rear of the train, and had solved *The Times* crossword by Didcot. Except for one clue. A quick look in his faithful Chambers would have settled the issue immediately; but he hadn't got it, and as ever he was vexed by his inability to put the finishing touch to anything. He quickly wrote in a couple of bogus letters (in case any of his fellow-passengers were waiting to be impressed) and then read the letters and the obituaries. At Reading he turned to the *Oxford Times* crossword. The setter was 'Quixote'; and Morse smiled to himself as he remembered 'Waggie' Greenaway finally solving the same setter's 'Bradman's famous duck (6)' and writing in DONALD at 1 across. Nothing *quite* so amusing here – but a very nice puzzle. Twelve minutes to complete. Not bad!

Morse caught a subliminal glimpse of 'Maidenhead' as the train sped through, and he took a sheaf of papers from his briefcase, first looking through the alphabetical list of those who would be attending the conference. Nobody he knew in the A-D range, but then he scanned the E-F:

Eagleston
Ellis
Emmett
Erskine
Farmer
Favant
Fielding

Tom Eagleston, yes; and Jack Farmer, yes; and . . .

Morse stopped, and looked again at the middle of the three delegates in the Fs. The name was vaguely familiar, wasn't it? Yet he couldn't remember where . . . Unusual name, though. Morse's eye continued down the list – and then he remembered. Yes! It was the name of the man who had been walking along the

Oxford Canal at the time when Joanna Franks was murdered – when Joanna Franks was *supposedly* murdered; the man, perhaps, who had been traced to the Nag's Head where he'd signed the register. A mystery man. Maybe not his real name at all, for the canal had been full of men who used an alias. In fact, as Morse recollected, two of the crew of the *Barbara Bray* itself had done so: Alfred Musson, alias Alfred Brotherton; Walter Towns, alias Walter Thorold. It might well be of some deep psychological significance that criminals sometimes seemed most unwilling to give up their names, even if this involved a greater risk of future identification: Morse had known it quite often. It was as if a man's name were almost an intrinsic part of him; as if he could never shed it *completely*; as if it were as much part of his personality as his skin. Musson had kept his name, hadn't he? So had Towns.

Morse spent the rest of the journey looking idly out of the window, his brain tidying up a few scattered thoughts, as the train drew into Paddington: Donald Bradman – Don Bradman, the name by which everyone recognized the greatest batsman ever born; and F. T. Donavan, the greatest man in all the world; and . . .

Ye Gods!!

The blood was running cold through Morse's limbs as he remembered the man who had identified the body of Joanna Franks; the man who had been physically incapable (as it seemed!) of raising his eyes to look into the faces of the prisoners; the man who had held his hands to his own face as he wept and turned his back on the men arraigned before the court. Why did he do these things, Morse? Because *the boatmen might just have recognized him.* For they had seen him, albeit fleetingly, in the dawn, as 'he had made to get further on his way with all speed'. Donald Favant! – or Don Favant, as he would certainly have seen himself.

Morse wrote out those letters D-O-N-F-A-V-A-N-T along the bottom margin of the *Oxford Times*; and then, below them, the name of which they were the staggering anagram: the name of F T DONAVAN – the greatest man in all the world.